THE GREEN-EYED MAN

THE DARK AMULET BOOK 2

JENNIFER EALEY

To all those men and women, who see each other as equal.

ACKNOWLEDGEMENT

I would like to thank my sister and editor, Wendy Ealey, my proofreader Neil Gardner, my narrator William Merryn Hill and his wife for eagerly awaiting the next instalments, giving me the impetus to keep writing.

PART I

S heldrake and Maud had been summoned to the palace to confer with the King.

A dour, solid woman in black ushered them into the same study that Jon and Sasha had entered. On this occasion she was not glaring. In fact, she smiled in welcome, but her eyes narrowed briefly in warning.

The King was not pleased.

"Thanks Josie," said Maud casually. "I've brought you a bunch of our lovely bottlebrushes. I'll give them to you after I've seen Gav... His Majesty."

Josie's smile broadened. "Lovely," she murmured as she withdrew.

Maud turned to the King and executed a low curtsey, lower than usual, while Sheldrake bowed, bending one knee. Gavin waited a moment before allowing them to rise, a sure sign of his displeasure. Once he had made his point, he waved them to armchairs and took up his favourite position, seated behind his desk. For a full minute, Gavin scrutinised them without speaking. They waited, knowing it was he who must speak first.

"So," Gavin said at last, picking up a gold pen and tapping it idly on the desktop. "Do I have your complete loyalty?" Then he held up a hand. "No. Don't answer that. Silly question. You're bound to say yes." He grimaced. "I know you finally told me about Jon and Sasha and that we have worked out their future living arrangements, but it preys on my mind that you did not do so straight away and that your loyalties may be compromised by your care for them. I have discovered for myself that they possess a vulnerable charm that is hard to resist. I need your objective reasoning and knowledge to help me decide what to do. Are you able to provide that? And can you explain your actions?"

Maud did not gush with reassuring words. In fact, she spoke with more reserve than usual. "I hope so, Your Majesty. As you say, Sasha and Jon are endearing, aren't they? We have become very fond of Sasha and were stunned, as you may imagine, when we discovered that our recently employed stable boy was actually a stable girl. Then Jon turned up and decided to trust us with the knowledge that Sasha was the rightful, but usurped, Queen of Kimora; a fact he had kept, even from her."

"And that you and he also decided to keep from me," interposed Gavin, with a clear note of censure.

"Ah. Yes." Maud looked uncomfortable

Sheldrake came to her rescue. "But not with the intention of deceiving you, Your Majesty."

"We will come back to that. Go on."

Sheldrake took up the thread. "By this stage, we had already begun to suspect that Sasha was someone out of the ordinary, Sire. People were looking for her, you see." He drew a breath. "And then, on top of all that, Jon told us that he was Sasha's elder brother."

Maud gave a tight smile. "Not something you'd guess,

really; with Jon blue-eyed, fair and blond and Sasha the complete antithesis; dark hair, eyes and complexion."

"And we learnt all of this in the space of two days, Sire," said Sheldrake. "It was a lot to take in." He took a deep breath. "Sasha and Jon's identities had far-reaching implications, Sire, for them, for you, for us, for our country and theirs." He sat forward to give his next words emphasis. "But from the moment we knew who Sasha was, we thought through the ramifications of harbouring her, in terms of our loyalty to you and to Carrador. Under no circumstances would we compromise either."

"I am pleased to hear it. I would, however, have preferred to be a party to the consideration of those ramifications." Gavin's voice was not sharp, but his face was still shuttered.

"We were concerned, Sire," countered Sheldrake, "that you would not want to appear complicit in supporting a pretender to a neighbouring throne. So we thought that if you didn't know about it, the issue could be avoided."

Now Gavin did sound annoyed. "Sheldrake, I am quite capable of appearing ignorant of information, if it is politic to do so. I do it all the time." He took a breath to rein himself in, then gave a faint smile. "You have not cornered the market on intrigue, you know."

"I beg your pardon, Sire," said Maud with true contrition, "I believe we have been remiss, but not through any desire to undermine you. You have our undivided loyalty."

Gavin leant back in his straight-backed chair and let out a long breath. "I am pleased to hear that, and I accept your apology. I would never say this in front of my other advisors, but I depend very heavily on you two; you, Sheldrake, for your wealth of knowledge and contacts, and you, Maud, for your wisdom and the way you find patterns in that information to guide me."

Maud smiled warmly at him, the need for formality past. "You are doing well, Gavin. You are a fine king; authoritative, but receptive and fair, or as fair as you can be. Regardless of our loyalty, it is in our own best interests, as citizens of Carrador, to keep you as our sovereign."

Gavin gave a short laugh. "Thanks. Thank you indeed. Coming from you, who rarely praises and never flatters… "

"Oh Gavin," protested Maud. "I'm not that bad, am I?"

"Yes," said Sheldrake baldly. When she looked shocked and perhaps a little hurt, he smiled and added, "But… you are also warm and joyful and a tower of strength in times of trouble."

This was said with such rarely expressed, deep emotion that an awkward silence ensued. It was broken by Gavin who said prosaically, "And she's clever."

Sheldrake let out a little breath of relief. "Naturally. I would not align myself with someone tedious."

Maud looked from one to the other, smiling. "When you two have quite finished…"

"So," said Gavin, bringing them back to business. "As you are aware, my father's younger brother, Alfred, married Crown Princess Corinna, with the intention that he become Prince Consort when she became Queen, thus allying our two nations. Needless to say, that plan died in its infancy when my uncle and Corinna were assassinated. Until recently, I had no idea that my cousins had survived or that Queen Toriana was behind the attack." He paused, tapping the gold pen on his desk, frowning. He looked up suddenly. "Are we sure the Queen is implicated? It wasn't just a random bandit attack, as has been widely believed until now?"

"That is a good question," returned Sheldrake. "Our only source of information about the actual attack is Jon, who was only twelve at the time. He did not say that the attackers were Toriana's men."

"However," continued Maud, "from what he says, the attackers were clearly bent on obtaining the amulet, which is the symbol of authority and source of shamanic power in Kimora. Only a usurper would want that, don't you think?"

"Not an evil, power-hungry shaman?" asked Gavin.

Maud and Sheldrake both looked sceptical.

With a slight smile, Sheldrake answered, "From the information I have gathered, Toriana fits that description pretty well. She has bound shamans to her will using shamanic powers, which has never been done by previous monarchs. She has misled her people into believing that she has the one true amulet. She threatens or imprisons families of shamans, while hunting down those who have not yet been forced into binding their will to hers."

"And she has infiltrated your kingdom to do it."

"I have tried to find witnesses to, or participants in, the attack on Corinna's family." Sheldrake shrugged. "Naturally, no one is talking. But interestingly, within months of Toriana ascending the throne, an elite band of the Queen's warriors was sent by boat along the Kempsey River to quell a disturbance in a western province. Apparently, their boat capsized and all were lost." The spy master leaned forward. "But even more interesting; apparently a freak wave rolled down the river and swept them away."

Gavin looked from one to the other. "So you're saying...?"

"Strong shamans can control the weather, currents and the flow of water," said Sheldrake flatly.

Maud stood up and began to pace around the room. "Gavin, we are dealing with a very evil woman here. We must proceed very, very carefully."

"I see." Gavin stood up and crossed to a small side table that held a forest of cut crystal decanters and an array of glasses. "Drink, anyone? I think I need one."

Gavin poured himself a fine old amber brandy and one for Maud. Then he looked enquiringly at Sheldrake who opted for port.

Once he had handed them their drinks, Gavin sat down, this time in an armchair, an indication that his suspicions of them had been allayed. He idly rolled his brandy around his glass, watching the light playing in the amber liquid. After a minute, he said, "It is uncomfortable for me not to acknowledge my cousins for who they are, but I think we are agreed that the risks are too high if we openly declare that we are hosting them. Sasha doesn't just rival her aunt's rule; the existence of Sasharia wearing the High Shamanic amulet actually invalidates Toriana's right to rule. Toriana needs that amulet and she must force Sasha to say the words of power to pass it on to her."

"The amulet protects Sasha," Sheldrake reminded him.

Gavin sipped his brandy before putting his glass down on a side table. "Perhaps so, though to what extent I think none of us is sure. But it does not protect those around Sasha. All Toriana would have to do is threaten to kill or maim Jon or Jayhan. Sasha would do anything to protect them. And once Toriana had been given the true amulet, she would kill Sasha. Don't you think?"

Maud felt her blood run cold. An involuntary shudder coursed down her backbone. "And already, a military force has made an incursion within your borders and nearly succeeded in abducting Sasha."

Sheldrake laid a reassuring hand on Maud's arm. "We think they were simply looking for unregistered shamans to take back and force into service with the Queen. They might suspect or hope or dread that Sasha survived the attack on her family but only a very few know for sure. And the only survivors of that attack are safely in your custody, Sire." He stood up and paced to the window, looking out at white cumulus clouds billowing on the horizon beyond the lake. After a few moments, he turned back to face the other two. The lines in his face seemed deeper than before. "The force we tangled with may have been small, but where there is one small force, there may well be more."

"I agree," said Gavin. "Even though we have already made it clear to Toriana, have we not, that her shaman hunters are not welcome within our borders?"

"Yes, Sire, we have," said Maud, tucking her legs up under her as she sipped her brandy, rather reminiscent of a cat. "And I am sure the message has had time to reach her."

The King ruminated while he swirled the brandy in his glass. When he looked up, he had clearly come to a decision. "So not only has she had my uncle killed, she is continuing to hunt people within our borders, despite a clear prohibition from me. Still, I do not want to push Kimora to war with us. It would hurt both of our countries and their people. She may not care about that, but I do. But I do want these incursions to stop. Sheldrake, our borders are already guarded but obviously not well enough. Where are our weaknesses?"

Sheldrake crossed to the large map of Carrador that hung on the study wall. Using it to demonstrate his points, he said, "Two main roads run between our nations, one through the Great Forest and one to the south of it through fields and farms. These both have secure checkpoints that can be placed on high alert. There is also a narrow, twisting, overgrown path in the south of the forest but few people know of it or can even navigate it. However, a skilful elite force is much more likely to cut across the fields or infiltrate through the forest. There we have a problem."

"Couldn't we enlist the aid of the farmers near the

borders?" asked Gavin, glancing at Maud for her opinion. "Perhaps offer rewards for information about strangers in the area or put them on a retainer?"

Maud nodded. "Good idea. I think rewards might be more motivating. I suppose you may get some who will try to falsify trails or give false evidence." She looked at Sheldrake "But I presume your spiders could sort the wheat from the chaff, couldn't they?"

Sheldrake looked pained, as she knew he would, at having his agents referred to as spiders, but everyone knew them as the King's Spiders, whether he liked it or not. He sighed. "Yes. Time would be wasted, of course, following up false leads, but overall I think the idea has merit." He shrugged. "It does not, however, solve the problem of incursions through the forest."

Gavin frowned. "No, it doesn't, and the border between our two countries winds through more than a hundred miles of forest." He stood up and walked over to study the map closely. "Most of it follows the Charville River but that is no deterrent. There are many places where the river can be easily crossed... and most of them are deep within the forest, out of view of checkpoints or farmers." The king straightened and looked at Sheldrake. "The stakes are high. We must secure our borders. I'll give you a fortnight to consult and come up with a plan to secure the border within the forest. Meanwhile, we will strengthen our checkpoints and instigate incentives for farmers to be our eyes and ears. Agreed?"

This was a rhetorical question, but Sheldrake and Maud both nodded dutifully and soon afterwards were sent on their way.

Just as Josie was about to close the door behind them, Gavin called them back. "By the way, as agreed, I've arranged for a master at arms to take up residence with you. Don't let his looks belie you. He's good, very good. He will protect and teach Sasha and Jayhan. His name's Stefan." He flashed a knowing smile at Sheldrake. "If you're wanting to do a background check on him, his men call him Stefan Longshanks."

2

S tefan arrived two days later.

He walked up to the front gate late in the morning and peered left and right along the low, white-painted picket fence that fronted Batian House. It looked innocuous, but he was not fool enough to enter a mage's house unannounced. He rang the big brass bell that hung on the right-hand side of the gate and waited.

A well-muscled man of above medium height arrived a couple of minutes later and stood looking down at him, studying him and the backpack slung over his shoulders. After a moment, the man said, "Good morning. May I help you?"

Stefan grinned. "I believe you are expecting me. My name's Stefan."

Leon's eyes widened in surprise although he quickly quelled his reaction. Stefan knew he would be wondering at his short, slight stature and gave a mental shrug. "We are indeed. Just a minute." Leon touched a series of points on the gate then lifted the latch and swung the small gate open.

As he stepped through, Stefan nodded his approval. "Magical ward, I'm assuming?"

"It is. I'm Leon, coachman, henchman, general factotum and recently, babysitter."

When Stefan raised his eyebrows in query, Leon gave a short laugh. "Sasha and Jayhan get up to all sorts of tricks and I try to keep an eye on them amongst my other duties."

Stefan nodded. "Pleased to meet you. Sounds like I'll be sharing some of your duties. Well, the babysitting at least."

"It's not onerous. They are friendly and polite, just a bit too adventurous."

Just as they reached the front door, it swung open and a tall, solid butler looked down his nose at him before glancing a query at Leon, who responded by saying, "Stefan, our new master at arms; Clive, our butler."

Clive returned his gaze to Stefan, staring at him poker-faced for a moment, clearly taking his measure. Suddenly he smiled. "I believe the King thinks very highly of you. Welcome to Batian House. Let me take your backpack and I will show you to the salon and inform Maud and Sheldrake of your arrival."

"Thank you. The rest of my equipment should be here later this afternoon."

Left alone in the salon, Stefan studied the portraits on the wall, the dark wood wainscot and the small antique chandelier that hung from the ceiling before walking lightly to the window to gaze out into their lovely cottage garden. A ginger cat was crouched under a grevillea, swivelling its hips as it readied itself to pounce on a lovely little grass parrot. Stefan tapped the window, distracting the cat and startling the parrot into flight. Giving himself a little satisfied grin, he turned back into the room to find himself being surveyed by the lady of the house.

Maud, a vision in her billowing deep green, swept across

the room, beaming and holding her hands out to take his. "How do you do? I see you just saved one of our little parrots. What a good beginning. I am Maud."

"How do you do, Ma'am?"

"No, please call me Maud." The door opened further and Sheldrake, dressed in his customary black coat and breeches over a white shirt, stepped neatly into the room. "And this is Sheldrake."

Stefan disengaged his hands from Maud's and gave a small bow. "How do you do? I have heard a great deal about you both. It is an honour to meet you."

"Your reputation also precedes you," said Sheldrake, smiling. "I believe the King put a lot of thought into your appointment. You are far and away their best marksman, I believe. So, welcome."

Stefan grinned. "You did some research, did you? I thought you might. That's why you two don't look shocked, as Clive and Leon did. You could have warned them." His green eyes twinkled up at them, the top of his light brown hair at the height of Sheldrake's shoulder.

Sheldrake gave a little chuckle. "I want you to spar with Leon before he has had time to take your measure. He is big and strong but lacks a certain subtlety in his approach. I am hoping you may have enough time to train with him too."

"Unarmed combat is my least favourite form of attack, but I will do my best."

His eyes strayed to the door as Clive entered, carrying the best silver teapot on a tray with cups, sugar and milk. As he set it down on a low polished table in the centre of the room, Sheldrake's eyes met his butler's and they shared a private smile. Stefan's brows twitched together, hoping he was not a source of amusement to them.

Maud noticed his disquiet and said, as she moved to pour

14

the tea, "Our best teapot. I see you have already earned Clive's approval."

"Have I? I don't know why. I've only just arrived." Stefan accepted a cup of tea and blew on it to cool it. "Thank you. This will be most welcome. It was a bit further than I expected from the King's palace."

"Good heavens! You didn't walk, did you? It's over twelve miles. Didn't they provide you with a carriage?" asked Sheldrake, shocked.

Stefan waved his hand at the view of the garden through the window. "It's a lovely day for a walk and I saw some beautiful gardens on the way here." He smiled. "I must say yours is one of the best. It will be a pleasure to stay here for a while."

While Sheldrake and Maud were digesting this unexpected side of their new arms master, the sounds of chatter and laughter preceded the precipitous entry of two children, who drew up short at the sight of an unknown visitor. One was clearly the son of the house, dressed in expensive but practical shirt, breeches and jerkin, while the other appeared to be a stable boy, dressed similarly but in rougher plainer clothes. Two pairs of eyes, one piercingly pale and the other meltingly dark brown, stared at him.

Then the children performed neat bows and straightened, smiling.

"How do you do," said Jayhan, on his best behaviour.

"I am well, thank you, young man," responded Stefan. "My name is Stefan."

A slight interrogatory lift on the end of Stefan's words prompted Jayhan to add, "Oops. Sorry. I am Jayhan and this is Sasha."

"Hello. Are you our new master at arms?" asked Sasha. When he nodded, she smiled, "Your eyes are a beautiful colour. I've never seen green eyes before."

15

Stefan blinked. His face scrunched in thought. "You know, now that you mention it, neither have I. I never thought about it before."

"Then you and Jayhan are both special," pronounced Sasha cheerfully. "His eye colour is unique too."

"When will we have our first training session?" asked Jayhan eagerly.

"Oh yes, we are dying to learn how to fight," added Sasha.

"I am not sure," interrupted Maud, "that badgering someone is the best way to begin an acquaintanceship."

Sasha coloured. "I beg your pardon, Madam. Um, perhaps I had better go. I need to check the poultice on Chester's hock anyway."

"No, Sasha, don't go." Maud's voice had softened as she held an arm out. "Come here." She wrapped her arm across Sasha's shoulders. "I am not cross. I just think Stefan might like a little time to get settled and find his bearings first." She smiled down at Sasha. "After lunch, perhaps you two would like to show Stefan around the farm and the stable and some of your favourite places in the bush?"

Sasha and Jayhan's faces lit up. Maud hoped that Stefan had not been planning on having a formal relationship with the children because she doubted he would be able to maintain it by the end of the afternoon. But from what she had seen of him, he did not seem very formal or stringent.

"Sasha, have your ponies saddled up and ready after lunch. Who do you think for Stefan?"

Stefan cut apologetically into her thoughts as Sasha was running her mind along the row of horses in the stable. "If you don't mind, something not too big and not too mettlesome. I like quiet, gentle horses."

Everyone looked at him in surprise, their view of an arms

master undergoing yet another revision. He just shrugged and gave an embarrassed smile.

Maud glanced at Sasha. "I think we'll give him Maisy."

Sasha's eyes widened. "Really?"

Maud sighed in exasperation at Sasha's lack of duplicity. "Yes. Really. She needs the exercise." Narrowing her eyes, she added dryly, "Apparently she is getting a little tubby."

"Oh, not tubby, madam. Just a little... hm... solid?" Sasha winced and looked beseechingly at Jayhan, who just chuckled and didn't help at all.

Stefan watched this interchange, feeling once more that he was missing something. He frowned. "Well, I hope this horse is not so broad that I won't be able to straddle her. I don't have very long legs, you know."

This sent Jayhan and Sasha off into gales of laughter. Maud frowned repressively at them before saying, "Don't worry. They're not laughing at you. They're laughing at the thought of Maisy being that fat. She's not at all, as you will see," she folded her arms and added firmly, "and she has a wonderful temperament."

Stefan was at a loss to see why this sent the two little miscreants off into renewed laughter. Sheldrake was unimpressed with their lack of manners and shooed them out with a flea in their ear, before apologizing on their behalf.

On the surface, Stefan accepted the apology but underneath, he was wondering whether he was about to endure yet another repetition of the teasing and bullying he had faced over the years because of his size. It was not a promising beginning.

3

After lunch, Maud excused herself, saying she wanted to check that the horses were ready. So Stefan was a little surprised when she wasn't there to see them off on their tour around the property.

"Hello," said Jayhan when he saw Stefan approaching. "I'm sorry we got the giggles. I promise it wasn't about you." He indicated a beautiful, quiet, grey pony. "This is my pony, Slug." He shrugged. "I called him Storm when I first got him but..."

Stefan grinned. "He sounds perfect for me."

Jayhan smiled back. "That's what *I* thought, but Mum wants you to ride Maisy." He nodded at a solid, dark brown mare that Sasha was just leading out of the stables. "She's not much bigger than Slug but she is definitely kinder. Slug's a pain. I have to turn myself inside out to make him trot and when he canters, he acts like I'm trying to kill him. He's a lazy little layabout. We're hoping Maisy might be able to sort him out."

Seeing Stefan's confusion, Sasha stepped in. "You know, like dogs affect each other's behaviour sometimes. If the other two horses keep up a good pace, maybe he won't want to be left behind."

Stefan looked dubiously at Maisy standing stolidly beside Sasha. "I hope she doesn't keep up too good a pace." He walked up to her and, just as Sasha was about to offer to give him a leg up, leapt lightly into the saddle. He took the reins from her and gathered them, holding them lightly but firmly.

Sasha frowned at him. "I thought you couldn't ride."

"I didn't say that. I just said I like placid horses."

"Huh." Sasha swung herself up with practised ease onto her wilful little pony. "This is Tosser," she said, as her pony promptly lived up to his name by tossing his head and trying to nip Slug.

They walked their horses down the gravel road between the fields, with Jayhan and Sasha pointing out particular trees with bird's nests in them, waving vaguely at the mob of sheep, introducing the farmhands, Jake and Thompson, to Stefan, and telling him about their tree house and the various adventures they had had together. Stefan's apprehension that he might have to deal with being the butt of their teasing lessened. He wasn't afraid of the possibility; it just wearied him.

As they neared the bushland behind the paddocks, Sasha asked, "Do you mind if we canter for a short while, just to the tree line so Mau... Maisy can try to sort out Slug?"

"Go on then," said Stefan. "Come on Maisy, a canter if you please." He pressed with his legs, increasing the pressure until the horse beneath him responded, changing straight from a walk to a canter. She had a rocking horse gait which Stefan found very comfortable. As he came up alongside Jayhan who was kicking Slug futilely, Maisy turned her head and nudged Slug sharply in his side behind the saddle. Slug kicked out a back leg then forced himself into a bone-shattering trot, but no more. Maisy cantered ahead then slewed into his path, forcing him to skid to a halt. Jayhan jerked forward in the saddle, nearly going over his stubborn little pony's head. On Maisy's back, Stefan sat firmly despite the sudden change in direction and made no move to direct her. Maisy tossed her head up and down, baring her teeth and even snapping a couple of times.

Slug backed up, the whites of his eyes showing. Maisy snorted, then swung around abruptly and bolted up the road towards the bushland. Sasha put her heels to her feisty little pony and bolted after her.

Even though he was being carried at a full gallop, Stefan looped the reins over the pommel of the saddle before letting go of them entirely. Then he looked back over his shoulder, completely unconcerned at the pace, to see Slug galloping after them, his tail flicking in irritation. He leaned forward and patted Maisy on the shoulder. "Well done. You got that naughty little bag-o-bones moving."

Then as the bushland loomed, he leaned even further forward and whispered into her ear, "And now I would like you to pull up." Her ear flicked back and forth. For a moment, he felt her muscles bunch as she actually increased her pace. Stefan chuckled. He leant over again. "Now please, or I will have to use the reins." Immediately, he felt the drumming lessen as her hooves hit the ground less forcefully and she gradually slowed to a stop. Stefan chuckled again. "I don't know exactly what is going on, but you are no ordinary horse. I thought you might understand me. Usually, I teach my horses to respond to my voice, but you already do so with no training of mine. Interesting."

Sasha and Jayhan caught up with them and pulled up their ponies. Tosser was, predictably, tossing his head with the excitement of a good run. Slug just stood there as placid and boring as ever, although Jayhan was a bit breathless. His face was glowing as he praised Slug and gave him a hearty pat on the shoulder.

"That was better," he said enthusiastically. "So do you want to come and see our creek? It's not too far."

They had stopped fifty yards short of the bushland and Stefan ran his eyes along the fence line to the left and right of him before asking, "Isn't there a magical ward at the rear of the property?"

Jayhan shrugged. "I don't know. Maybe. This isn't the end of our place though. We have two hundred acres of bush out the back here. Miles more land than we have with sheep on it."

"It makes a great playground," said Sasha, grinning. "Maud and Sheldrake wanted to save some of the bushland before all the houses from Highkington took over. The outskirts of the city aren't here yet. We are still quite a way out of town, but the city is growing."

"Huh. That's good." Stefan let his gaze travel across the canopy of eucalypts, their leaves glistening in the sunlight and then lowered his gaze to the grevilleas and wattle growing between them, little gold pompoms and red intricate flowers dotted amongst their foliage. He watched a little family of blue wrens darting across the grass near the bushes at the edge of the forest and nodded at the brown wrens. "You know the duller brown ones are called Jenny wrens? And only the males have that glorious blue? Sad for the ladies really, isn't it?"

"I suppose so," said Sasha dubiously.

Stefan stored away the knowledge that Sasha wasn't totally pleased about her future role as a lady of the court but didn't comment. Instead, he said, "I come from the forest myself, you know. I grew up among trees and bushes and birds and animals. I'm glad someone wants to look after them. Let's go and see your creek."

As they urged their horses into motion, Sasha asked,

"Which forest do you come from?" As soon as she asked, she realised she probably wouldn't know it anyway. But surprisingly, she did.

"The Great Forest, the forest between Carrador and Kimora. My parents own an inn deep in the forest called…"

"The Creeping Vine," chorused Jayhan and Sasha.

Stefan was surprised. "You know it?"

They nodded enthusiastically but then fell silent, glancing at each other.

For a few minutes they walked on in silence before Stefan reined up. He leaned forward and asked quietly in Maisy's ear, "Can you hear or smell anything untoward in our surroundings? Is this a safe place for me to talk to these two?" Maisy did not respond but her ears flicked back and forth. "If all is clear, stamp your front left hoof."

Maisy stamped her front left hoof and Stefan patted her shoulder in thanks.

"Excellent horse you have here," he said conversationally to the children. "Now, before we go any further, let's sort out our trust levels. You don't have to tell me about Maisy here, but I can see you're worried what you can and can't tell me. Given your situation, Your Highness," he said with a twinkle in his eyes and a slight bow to Sasha from the saddle, "I applaud your caution. I know who and what you are, Sasharia, and I know you, Jayhan, received a medal for saving her life. Not only that, I have also been told about the extraordinary power of your eyes, Jayhan, and the extraordinary power of your amulet, Sasha." He grinned at them. "I don't know everything, but I know enough that you can trust me with the rest when the time is right and it is relevant."

Both children let out a sigh of relief and smiled.

"So your inn, The Creeping Vine," began Sasha, "is where we all met before we went into the forest tò tell a small group of refugees that I... well, tell them who I am and that Jon is to be regent for me until I come of age."

"And that's where the attackers came and nearly hurt Sasha," added Jayhan. "In the forest, not at the inn, although they did stay at the inn before going into the forest." Catching an irritated frown from Sasha, he gave a lop-sided smile. "Okay. I'll shut up now."

"Aha!" said Stefan, ignoring the last little interchange. "Well fancy that! Then you probably met my father – he's the innkeeper – and one or two of my brothers."

Sasha thought back. "The innkeeper was nice; big and round and cheery. I think I saw one other man working there. Yes, he looked quite a lot like the innkeeper, now you mention it. Both had pale faces but black hair. I don't remember what colour their eyes were, but not green. I would have remembered if they were green." She hesitated then added, "They were a bit taller than you, I think."

"Yes. A lot taller than me, actually. A good six inches." Stefan gave a rueful grimace. "I'm the runt of the family, I'm afraid."

"Who else is in your family?" asked Jayhan. Maisy sidled and grunted, making him add hastily, "if you don't mind telling us."

"No, I don't mind telling you, but we might as well keep walking now that we've cleared the air a little bit." When the other two horses moved forward, Maisy fell into step beside them with no instruction from Stefan. He noted it but kept to the topic under discussion. "I have two older brothers and an older sister and I also have two younger brothers. They all look alike... well, similar, and none of them looks like me. Even my sister, Marjorie, is taller than me."

"Do you mind?" asked Sasha kindly.

Stefan smiled at her. "Thank you for asking. No, I don't

mind how I look or how I'm built, but I did get sick of being the brunt of the family's jokes and being bullied by my bigger, stronger brothers." He shrugged. "I guess that is part of the reason I became so good at fighting."

"What? For revenge?" asked Jayhan, a hint of eagerness in his voice.

"No, young sir." He reached over and ruffled Jayhan's hair. "Not for revenge. To protect myself."

"Oh." Jayhan thought about it for a minute. "Hmm. I can see that if you tried to take revenge on them, there'd be five against one coming back at you even worse."

"No, they didn't usually gang up on me. Usually just one or two poked fun at me or sometimes started to get physical. Sometimes the ones not involved would even tell them to lay off. Mostly they thought they were being funny. But if anyone outside the family picked on me..." Stefan gave a short laugh. "Well, you don't pick on the Vine family; that's all there is to it."

Jayhan considered him. "So would you protect your sister or brothers if they needed it, even after they treated you badly?"

"In a heartbeat," said Stefan.

———

4

Sasha, Jayhan and Stefan met at mid-morning the next day in the space behind the stables where Leon kept piles of gravel, soil and sand, stacks of firewood, scrap pieces of metal and wood and some of his tools. He had cleared a roughly circular sandy patch in the middle to use for fighting practice until they could set up an area in one of the paddocks and was now sitting on a pile of firewood watching to see what they would do.

Maud and Sheldrake also wandered over to watch and, rather to the mage's surprise, so did the rest of their household; Eloquin the governess, Clive the butler, Clive's wife Beth who was also the head groom, Rosie the maid, her little brother Edgar and even Hannah, the cook. At the last minute, even Jake and Thompson, the farmhands, came running to join them, wiping their hands on their breeches and looking a little sheepish.

Stefan stood in the middle of the sandy patch, hands on hips and gradually turned a full circle to observe his audience. Eventually he said, "You do know I am not an entertainer?"

This produced murmurs among his audience but failed to move any of them.

"Please, sir," said Rosie, "we'd like to see what you do. We're all very excited to have an arms master in our household. We promise we won't come every morning." She glanced at Sheldrake. "Anyway the master won't let us. We usually have lots to do, you know."

Stefan turned a puzzled frown to Sheldrake, who looked just as bemused as he did. "Huh. Very well. Well, I can't do this alone. So, who would like to shoot some arrows?" A forest of hands went up, making Stefan laugh. "You're an enthusiastic lot, I'll give you that. Leon and Beth, can we set up a hay bale as a target? I don't want to blunt my arrows by shooting into a tree or the side of the stables."

He reached down and rummaged in his big tote bag, which had arrived by coach several hours after him. He withdrew four bows and set about stringing them as he spoke, pausing occasionally for grunts of effort. "We will begin with each of you trying to draw back each bow so that the string is level with your right ear, unless you're left-handed, in which case it will be your left ear."

He demonstrated with the first strung bow before setting it down and moving on to stringing the second as he spoke. "The stronger the bow, the greater the distance you will be able to shoot. However, if the bow is too difficult for you, your accuracy is likely to be affected. So it is a balance. You can also increase your distance to some extent by angling your bow upwards, but that requires more practice and accuracy." He grinned. "Then of course, there is the wind to consider." He glanced around. "But there is little wind this morning and we are in a sheltered spot here, so that won't be a factor we have to worry about today."

When he had the bows all strung, he lined them up on the ground and asked, "Okay, who's first?"

Rather to his surprise, Sasha and Jayhan hung back and allowed the servants to have first shot. When Stefan looked enquiringly at them, Jayhan shrugged and said quietly, "We will be training with you often, whereas they will not have the same chance. So it is better to give them the most time today."

"Well said, young man. However, I do want you to try the bows today so that I can order one to suit you."

Jayhan's eyes widened. "My own bow?"

Stefan smiled. "Yes. On the King's orders. Once he decides to act, there are no half measures. You too, Sasha... and Leon."

Only Leon and Jake could draw back the full-sized bow, but Sheldrake, Thompson, Clive and Beth could draw the second largest to Stefan's satisfaction, while Hannah, Rosie and Maud could manage the third largest. Much to their disgust, Jayhan, Edgar and Sasha were only able to convincingly draw back the string on the smallest bow.

"Don't look so disappointed," chided Stefan. "These are not the smallest bows in existence; only the smallest bows I thought worth bringing with me." When this did not console them, he added, "Once you have mastered a bow of this size, you will naturally graduate to a larger one as you grow older and your arm strengthens. Anyway, small bows are much handier for carrying around. I often use a small bow even now, when I am travelling light."

With the bows chosen, he set up the targets and, using the small bow, gave a demonstration of how to hold and aim an arrow. Then everyone took turns in using the correct bow for their strength. Their lack of skill led to high hilarity as many of the arrows missed the hay bale altogether, skidding along the ground or sailing over the fence into long grass in the adjoining paddock. Stefan made a mental note to enlist the children in a treasure hunt for the arrows hidden in the grass, knowing they would not be easily found.

When they had tired of this, Hannah and Rosie enlisted Jake and Thompson. The four of them slipped away to the kitchen, returning shortly afterwards with trays of lemonade and sandwiches.

"Thank you, Hannah," said Sheldrake. "Do we have time for more? When do you need to start dinner?"

"If this counts for lunch, sir, I could spare another couple of hours." Hannah gave a warm smile. "It's like a holiday, isn't it, sir? A rare thing indeed."

Sheldrake gave a little shake of his head and smiled in return. "I don't know what's come over me. A new member of the household does not usually warrant such attention." He heaved a contented sigh. "But it is enjoyable for a change and I hope that every staff member can spend some time with Stefan learning at least the rudiments of self-defence."

Hannah glanced at him, worried. "Are you expecting trouble, sir?"

"I hope not. No, I don't think so, but I hope not anyway."

This did little to reassure his cook, who determined to speak further at a later date with Maud. After the archery came sword play, using wooden practice swords that Stefan drew from his apparently bottomless tote bag. He only had six of them, so he paired up people of similar strength and let the others watch as he took them through the rudiments of stance, grip, basic thrusts and parries. Then they swapped so that everyone had a turn.

In the middle of the afternoon, after another refreshment break, he introduced hand-to-hand fighting. He was so quick, lively and encouraging that no one grew weary of the lessons.

He began by standing with his arms loosely at his side and inviting Beth and Maud to lift him up. They did this with relative ease and lowered him back to the ground looking a little puzzled. Then he bent his knees slightly, held his arms crooked before him and focused hard. When he repeated the request to lift him, Maud and Beth stepped forward confidently but found it took everything they had to shift him even slightly. Lifting him into the air was out of the question. After a few minutes of strenuous effort, they stood back puffing and grinning.

"Are you using magic?" demanded Sheldrake.

Stefan laughed. "No. Not at all. You can all do it. Pair up and try it. On the second try, imagine yourself as a tree rooted into the ground, your weight low, heavy and connected to the earth. You'll see."

Once they had all tried this to their satisfaction, he asked Rosie and Hannah to step forward to demonstrate fighting techniques. He used them as models to explain low and high blocks and the use of fingers in the eyes and a kick to the crotch, all in slow motion and not connecting.

"These last two are fighting dirty," he explained cheerfully. "But if you ever find yourself in a position where you have to fight, don't pussyfoot around. Fight fiercely and fight dirty. For now, let's just practise the low and high blocks in pairs. One person, try to attack; the other, block. Three minutes, then swap. I don't want to hear any sounds of flesh connecting with flesh. This is just shadow fighting to get the hang of it. All right?"

When they had finished, Stefan gave them a flourishing bow and said firmly. "And that is it for today. You have all done remarkably well. You must be exhausted, but I hope you have learnt something and if you wish it, I can organise further training for you around your other duties."

A ragged round of applause greeted this pronouncement, but a couple of voices were raised in protest that they hadn't seen Stefan fight. Then Jake urged Stefan to challenge Leon while others urged Leon on. Sheldrake watched with his arms folded, a gleam of anticipation in his eye.

Leon stepped up to Stefan, whose head barely reached his shoulder. But instead of squaring off against him, he put his arm across the smaller man's shoulders and turned to the onlookers. "I may look big and bovine, but that doesn't make me totally stupid." He shot a speaking glance at Sheldrake as he said this. "Stefan didn't become a master-at-arms without being an accomplished fighter. I'm more of a street brawler myself, but I have nothing to prove and neither does Stefan. I have no doubt he'd wipe the floor with me, but I would rather he taught me how to do that, than have him do it to me now."

Although a couple of them were still disappointed, they knew an impasse when they saw one and the rest chuckled quietly and left, well satisfied with the day's activities. As the crowd dispersed, Stefan smiled up at him. "You know, it is a nice change, not having to prove myself."

Leon gave him a slow smile in return, clapping him on the shoulder and removing his arm. "Even if I could beat you, which maybe I can and maybe I can't, I wouldn't do it to a newcomer, just to satisfy this lot." He shrugged. "Besides, what's in it for me? If I win, I look like a bully; if I lose, I look like a fool."

Stefan raised his eyebrows. "You could do it to let me show off... "

Leon scratched his chin. "You know, I didn't think of that. Do you want to?"

A derisive snort of laughter was his answer.

5

J ust as the family were finishing their dinner, a knock
sounded on the dining room door and Clive popped his
head in to say that Stefan had asked to see Sheldrake.

Sheldrake wiped his mouth neatly with his napkin before
informing Clive that they would see him in the salon in fifteen
minutes. "And bring down the fine Montreyan port that
Argyve gave me the other week." He smiled at Maud. "Will
you be joining us, my dear?"

"I will. I don't want Stefan to get into the way of only
conferring with you, do I? Besides, I want some of that port."

They finished their coffee, bid Jayhan and Eloquin goodnight and made their way downstairs. They came upon Stefan
in the hallway, squatting down, intent on scratching a large
tortoiseshell cat under the chin. The cat was purring its appreciation and pressing itself up against his knees.

"You asked to see me?" asked Sheldrake dryly.

Stefan turned his head but did not immediately stand up.
"Oh, hello. You are wonderfully punctual. Good to know."

"That cat is George and he knows he should be in the

kitchen," said Maud, with an edge to her voice that George ignored.

Stefan gave him a final stroke and stood up. "He must have followed me in. Would you like me to take him back before we get started?"

"No," said Maud, sailing past Sheldrake who was holding the door open for her. "He'll wander back when he's ready."

Sheldrake and Maud arrayed themselves in armchairs before him and waved him to another. Stefan sat down neatly and attempted a smile. He was just about to speak when Clive arrived to deliver a tray bearing a cut glass decanter of a dark ruby port and three glasses. Stefan looked a bit startled. After all, he had eaten his dinner earlier with the servants in the kitchen.

"Don't worry," said Maud kindly, "we won't force port on you every time you want to see one or both of us. It is our custom to have a quiet drink after dinner and we thought you might like one after you did such an excellent job with the staff today."

"Besides," Sheldrake added shrewdly, "I suspect you have quite a bit you need to discuss with us, now that you've seen the place."

Stefan accepted a port from Clive and nodded his thanks. "I do." He waited until Clive left, then began, "Firstly, I need to know who among your staff knows Sasha's true identity. I'm feeling my way in the dark, not knowing who I can say what to."

"Oh, of course you are. So silly of us not to have thought of that." Maud rolled her port in her glass, enjoying the blood red light that shone through it. "Leon, Clive and Beth know. Eloquin also knows, since she dines with us, but she is not as involved as the other three. Hannah, Rosie and Edgar and the farmhands don't know."

"And why is that?" asked Stefan. "Are they untrustworthy? I thought your staff were particularly recruited for their discretion. Unlike other households, none of them is ever heard to gossip or let slip information about you or the household's affairs."

Sheldrake took a sip of his port, allowing the silence to linger. "You are correct. Sasha's revelations are relatively new to us and I suppose we are still feeling our way. Edgar only started with us a few weeks ago and Rose, his older sister, has always shown an antipathy towards Sasha, which concerns us."

"And we are not convinced of their acting skills, if we are trying to maintain Sasha's deception of being a boy when outsiders come to visit," added Maud. "We decided the fewer who knew the better..." Her tone indicated that it was open for discussion.

Stefan looked into his port, then took a little sip. His face lit up. "Oh, very nice." He did not seem to have an obsequious bone in his body. After a moment he asked, "What does Leon think?"

"We didn't ask him," replied Sheldrake.

"Ahuh. Or Clive or Beth?"

Sheldrake frowned. "No."

Stefan cocked his head to one side. "Is it worth me venturing an opinion? I don't want to waste your time... or mine, if it comes to that."

Maud and Sheldrake exchanged a glance.

"You are very cocksure, young man," said Sheldrake repressively.

Stefan just grinned. "No, I just like to be clear. If you don't want my opinion, I won't give it. After all, you haven't asked anyone else's."

"We are the master and mistress of this house, Stefan. It is our decision," said Maud firmly.

Stefan restrained himself from saying that was obvious and merely said, "Of course."

"Go on then," urged Sheldrake, leaning forward. "Tell us what you think."

Stefan leapt lightly to his feet and took up a position in front of the window before turning to address them. "I think you are both very clever, can command magical powers although I am not sure what they are yet, you have great influence at court and are kind to your staff and people you know."

"But?" asked Sheldrake dryly.

Stefan gave a grunt of laughter. "But... I think perhaps you underestimate people... in particular, your staff." Before they could respond, he waved his hand. "A simple example is Leon, who knows you think he's not clever... hence the remark about being big and bovine... but he took all of two seconds to overcome his surprise at my size when we first met. I was never going to catch him before he had my measure. His fighting technique may be unsubtle... I haven't seen it, I'm just going by what he said... but he knows his limitations, which is worth its weight in gold..." He paused. "Shall I go on?"

"Please do," said Sheldrake, in a tone that did not bode well for Stefan's future with them.

"From what I saw today, Hannah has remarkable hand-eye coordination, even though her girth means she mightn't be able to move very fast. Rose is very competitive and, given a chance, would strive to develop her fighting skills." Stefan nodded. "You're right, though. She does resent Sasha. Perhaps she is aware that he/she is getting special treatment and doesn't know why. You see? Competitive... and hierarchical. She firmly believes that indoor servants should be given precedence over outdoor servants."

He crossed to the table where he had left his port, picked it up and sipped it, taking a moment to savour it, before continuing, "Jake is enthusiastic but clumsy. He does what he thinks a bloke should do, without thinking it through. Now, he really *isn't* the sharpest tool in the shed and he was the one goading Leon to fight me. Luckily, he will follow Thompson if Thompson leads, and Thompson is sensible and quietly competent. He has trained with a bow at some time in the past and was better with the sword than anyone but Leon. Beth has excellent reflexes and anticipation; you could see that from the blocking exercises. Clive lacks confidence in himself but may be good if he trusts his instincts. Same with Edgar."

"My word," breathed Maud, "the amount you learnt in one morning."

Stefan gave a self-deprecating shrug. "That's my job, training people. If I don't know where they're starting from, how can I know what to teach them?"

"And what about Sasha and Jayhan?" asked Maud.

"Oh!" Stefan grinned. "They are full of energy and enthusiasm. Jayhan curbed his natural impetuousness to let your staff have first turn. Impressive in one so young. Made Rose a bit uncomfortable, though. They are both quick and agile but Jayhan has a tendency to get carried away and fall over his own feet, so to speak."

Sheldrake chuckled. "A masterful description of my son."

"And what about Sheldrake and me?" asked Maud.

Stefan shook his head. "I have no idea. You both masked your strengths."

After a considering silence, Sheldrake stood up and crossed to the tray where the decanter stood. With a wag of the decanter, he offered Stefan another, before pouring another for Maud and himself. Stefan took this as a hopeful sign that they weren't about to toss him out on his ear.

Sheldrake sat down, leaned back and crossed his legs, all aimed, Stefan suspected, at keeping him in suspense. "And what," asked Sheldrake, "is your opinion about informing all the staff about Sasha?"

Stefan hid his satisfaction at being asked and answered matter-of-factly, "I would consult with Beth, Clive and Leon before making a decision, because they know your staff better than I do. But from my short acquaintance with them, I think that if you include them and train them, you more than double the defences around Sasha. An hour, even half an hour, a day would improve their fighting skills immeasurably."

"But what about the risk of them spreading the word about Sasha, especially Edgar?" asked Maud.

"You're right," Stefan answered, skipping a few lines in the conversation, "I think Rose will change her attitude if she understands why. Edgar would be well-intentioned, but his little mouth might run away with him in the village or with his mother. Jake could also be a problem if he felt the need to brag after a few pints in the pub." He looked at Sheldrake, "Any suggestions, Master Mage?"

Sheldrake frowned at his casual tone, but bent his mind to it nevertheless. He sipped his port and gazed into it, then looked around the room and generally kept the other two waiting for a good five minutes. At last he said slowly, "If and only if they are willing, I could bind them from using particular words; for instance Queen, Kimora, amulet, shaman."

Instead of being impressed, Stefan gave it his consideration and then said dubiously, "But you could say those, hmm, concepts without saying the actual words, couldn't you? A female leader from a neighbouring country, for instance?"

Sheldrake stared at him icily. "I thought that by the time they came up with an alternative like that, they would have remembered to keep the secret."

"True. Good point," said Stefan, completely unfazed by

Sheldrake's obvious dislike of having his ideas vetted. "Any other ideas?"

Maud smothered a laugh as Sheldrake's eyes nearly bulged out of his head in outrage.

"You know," continued Stefan, aware of, but unmoved by, Sheldrake's reaction, "it's a bit tough for a little boy not to be able to talk to his mum. Who else is in their family? Could his mother be trusted to keep this secret?"

Maud thought for a minute, keeping a weather eye on Sheldrake. "I think there are a couple of younger children, too. Their father died a few years ago. I know nothing about the woman but I suppose we could find out easily enough. Sheldrake's network could tap into the village gossip."

"Hmm." Stefan thought for a moment before turning to the mage. "Sheldrake, if Edgar's mother passed the vetting process, is there a way for her to temporarily override, then re-instigate your spell? After all, we'd still want it in place while he's on his way home and when he went out to play with other village children, wouldn't we?"

Sheldrake's mouth quirked in a half smile. He was beginning to get used to Stefan's equal-to-equal approach. He nodded. "Yes, I think I can do that. It will be an interesting little exercise for me."

"The other thing to consider," continued Stefan, "is that Sasha's gender is going to become harder to conceal as she gets older, especially if the King expects her to dress for court before she leaves here. Your staff are bound to find out."

Maud sighed. "You are absolutely right. I hadn't really thought about it yet, but it would be ludicrous to think we could hoodwink our staff for long. Her first visit to court is next week and I have brought three dresses from town for her to try on. We will tell them tomorrow evening. We already have an important meeting scheduled for tomorrow morning. I would like you and Leon to attend both meetings, if you please."

Just as Stefan was about to take his leave, a discreet knock on the door was followed by the advent of Clive bearing a letter on a tray.

"I beg your pardon, sir, but this has just arrived from the King. Apparently, it is urgent."

"Thank you." Sheldrake tore open the envelope and scanned its contents. He glanced up at Stefan and Maud, also noticing in his periphery vision that Clive was trying to make himself inconspicuous by the door and had not left immediately as he normally would. "The shaman and two of the men who attacked us in the forest have escaped. The other six are still in custody."

Maud had paled with shock. "Oh, Sheldrake! If that man gets back to Toriana, she will know that Sasha still lives and of her association with us."

Sheldrake nodded grimly. "Send Leon to me," he ordered Clive, without even looking at him. "And with the heightened risk, I think we must tell the staff about Sasha first thing in the morning. I think we can squeeze it in before our meeting with Jon, Electra, Argyve and Yarrow."

6

A s soon as the light streamed in through his window, Jayhan jumped out of bed, dressed quickly and sped out the door, jumping down the stairs four at a time and nearly crashing into Clive who was carrying a tray of glassware along the downstairs corridor.

"Oops, sorry, Clive," he said cheerily as he dashed down the side corridor, through the kitchen, skilfully dodging Rose who was carrying a stack of plates to the sink clearing up after the servants' breakfast, and across to the stables. Hannah shook her head in fond exasperation in his wake.

Sasha was already working, filling the horses' feedbags before getting started on mucking out the stalls. Without a word, Jayhan grabbed an armful of hay and delivered it to Slug, then a cup of oats. "This much?" he asked, holding the tin cup up for inspection.

Sasha nodded.

"What bout Tosser? Same?"

"No. A bit less. Maybe two thirds."

Once they were in rhythm with their work, Jayhan asked casually, "When do you first have to dress up to go the palace?"

Sasha came out of stall and scowled at him. "I have to try on the dresses tomorrow morning so there is time to alter them before next week. Why?"

Jayhan grinned. "Because I want to see you in a dress."

Sasha put her hands on her hips and said primly, "King Gavin said to tell you that he orders you not to tease me."

This did not have the effect she wanted. Jayhan exploded with laughter as he grabbed an armful of hay for another horse further down the line.

"What is so funny?" demanded Sasha.

"Who's going to tell him? You? Mum? You can handle yourself perfectly well without getting help from him."

"I'll have to tell him if he asks."

"Depends how you tell him, doesn't it? You can make it sound mean or you can make it sound fun." Jayhan smiled broadly at her. "When have you ever known me to be mean, at least, mean on purpose?"

Sasha did not smile back. "Jayhan, I'm really worried about this. I'm going to feel like an idiot in a big swishing dress."

"Didn't you ever wear dresses in the orphanage?"

"No, I've been pretending to be a boy for most of my life."

Jayhan stood stock still as he tried to imagine what it would feel like to wear a dress. After a moment he shook his head. "Yep. Pretty tricky."

Beth interrupted his reverie as she entered the stables. "Sasha, the top paddock has recovered. Take Flurry, Tosser, Slug and I think, the two bays, up there to graze. You can go with her, Jayhan, but you'll have to go straight from there to breakfast or you'll be late. Sasha, you can finish feeding the others when you get back."

Inevitably, Jayhan turned up late for breakfast, cheeks

flushed from the cold morning air and emanating a faint odour of horse dung. His mother immediately ordered him from the table to wash and present himself to her for inspection before sitting down again.

They had barely finished their meals and Sheldrake was still drinking his tea when Clive entered and announced, "Unfortunately it is raining, sir, so the staff are assembled in the stables awaiting your arrival, rather than out in the courtyard."

Jayhan looked in surprise at Maud. "What's going on, Mum?"

"If you wipe away the egg from around your mouth, you may come with us and find out. You come too, Eloquin," Maud added.

As Maud and Sheldrake entered the stables, Jayhan ran ahead and joined Sasha and Edgar where they were standing off to one side so that they could see past the adults. He noticed Leon conferring with Stefan near the front of the group and wondered idly whether Stefan really could beat Leon in a fight. Then his eyes shifted to his father as he began to speak.

"Thank you all for making the time to meet this morning. I will be brief and answer any questions you may have afterwards." He raised his arm in Sasha's direction. "Sasha, come here please."

Sasha, with a feeling of foreboding, obeyed.

Sheldrake continued, "Some of you already know this but I have decided it is only fair that you all know. Firstly, Sasha is female, not a boy," he paused for the intakes of breath and asides to subside, "but more importantly, she is the rightful holder of the Kimoran throne."

Amidst exclamations of shock and astonishment, Sasha crept closer to Maud's side. Maud looked down and, realising the girl was trembling, put an arm around her shoulders. Jayhan saw Rose, white with shock, both hands held up to her mouth. He could tell she was reviewing her behaviour towards Sasha and finding it wanting. He gave a little snort of derision; it shouldn't take a revelation like this to make a person behave with consideration.

Sheldrake held up his hand and when the talking stopped, said, "The current ruler of Kimora is Sasha's aunt, but she is the younger sister. Sasha's mother was the legitimate heir. Ten years ago, Toriana attempted to wipe out her elder sister's entire family. She almost succeeded. But in a last desperate effort, Sasha's mother flung the symbol of power to Sasha, her last surviving daughter, and thrust onto her twelve-year-old son the task of escaping with her, while she held back the attackers and faced her death. Queen Toriana sits uneasily on the throne, unable to find the amulet to legitimize her rule and unsure whether Sasha, the true queen, has survived."

Maud gave Sasha a little prod and bent over to whisper, "Come on now, you're a queen. Look up and be proud." When this produced little more than a couple of quick glances, Maud added, "Look at Jayhan or Leon then, but keep your eyes up."

Reluctantly Sasha raised her head and stared fixedly at Leon, her face muscles taut. Leon gave her a big wink and smiled. Immediately she relaxed and smiled back, realising she had been needlessly working herself up.

"Hmm," Hannah stood with her hands crossed comfortably over her belly. "So would I be right in saying that Jon is her brother? And that Sasha has only recently discovered her identity?" She thought for a moment. "Let me see, I'd say it was when Yarrow was visiting and I sent up the champagne and lemonade and cakes a few weeks ago?"

Sasha nodded and grinned at her.

Further back, Edgar leaned over and whispered in Jayhan's ear, "So do I have to call her Ma'am or miss or something now?"

"No, 'course not. She'd hate it if you did that."

Edgar straightened up, reassured.

His sister, however, was tying herself in knots. Rose was wringing her hands and curtseying all at once. "I'm sorry, Your Highness, Your Grace... What do I call her?" she asked in a frantic aside to Hannah, who just glanced derisively at her and shrugged. "Anyway, Your... maybe it's Your Majesty... Yes, that's it... Your Majesty, I am truly sorry that I have not been treating you as befits your station. I didn't know, you see. No one told me. When I think of all those times I have been less respectful than I should... But I would never have behaved like that if I had *known*..."

Stefan shook his head and mouthed to Sheldrake, "See? Total snob."

If Sasha could have stumbled backwards and disappeared, she would have. Rose was making her feel so uncomfortable. She glanced up at Maud but one look at her face told her that she was being expected to manage this herself. She took a deep breath and held up her hand. "Rose. Stop." Startled, Rose froze mid-sentence. Sasha thought furiously and finally said, "Rose, my aunt is still looking for me. I have to stay in disguise to be safe. The best thing you can do to help me is to treat all of the outside staff, Beth, Leon, Edgar and me, the same way." She gave a slight smile at Leon and Beth. "Actually, Leon and Beth are senior to me so they should be treated with greater respect, but Edgar and I are the same." She saw Stefan raising his eyebrows at her and added hastily. "And Stefan, he's senior too."

To Sasha's relief, Maud took over and told them who else knew of Sasha's true identity and explained about Sasha's upcoming visits to the palace. "And to answer your question from yesterday, Hannah, if any of Toriana's agents gets wind of Sasha's presence here, Sasha and possibly all of us, could be in danger. As more people become aware of her identity, the risk increases... and we have just heard that three of the people who attacked Sasha and Jon in the forest two weeks ago have escaped from custody."

"They'll have to get though me first if they want to hurt my little Sasha," said Hannah, still standing with her hands held loosely over her round stomach, but suddenly looking like an immovable obstacle. She turned her gaze to Stefan. "You'd better come into my kitchen and teach us how we can use what we have to hand, to fight off intruders. There's no supposing we'll have time to nip out and grab one of your weapons."

Stefan smiled and gave her slight bow. "It would be my pleasure. And all of you are welcome to work with me to improve your fighting skills so that we are better able to defend ourselves. Sheldrake and Maud are happy to consider half an hour a day of arms training as part of your duties rather than expecting you to do it in your spare time. You can also do this in a block of one hour every second day, if that suits you better."

"What if we want to do more?" asked Jake.

"I am also happy to train you in your own time."

"Great. Thanks."

Sheldrake looked around the staff gathered there, all willing to share the risk without any objections. His plan to ask them to bind their words withered. Instead, he said, "I am proud to have such a loyal courageous staff and although it may be difficult to hold our secret when other people visit here or when you are out in the village, I have complete faith in your ability to do so. The more time you spend treating Sasha as you always have, even though you now know her identity, the easier it will be. If there are no further questions, you may return to your duties. Thank you."

7

The Kimoran ambassador's dashing red high-perch phaeton swept into the driveway of Batian House and was brought to a neat halt just outside the front door by its driver, Lady Electra.

"Well done, my lady," said Jon cheerily, as he hopped down from behind the driver's seat and opened the door for her. Jon, dressed in the blue and orange livery of a Kimoran footman, looked up at her with laughing eyes as he held out his hand for her to steady herself as she stepped down from the high phaeton.

Her eyes narrowed as she stepped primly past him to greet Maud who had just arrived in time to see her in. Maud smiled at Electra's fixed expression. "You may relax, Electra. All of our staff now know Jon and Sasha's identities. So you don't have to continue to pretend to be his mistress."

Electra sagged with relief. "It is difficult, you know, but I am happy to do whatever it takes to keep them both safe. Jon has already taken up his new identity as Lord Johnson, Minister for Transport, but we have kept up the pretence that he is still my footman for a few weeks so that his departure is not so abrupt that it might arouse suspicion. Our story is that he will be leaving me at the end of this week to live closer to his aging mother in the south of the country."

She entered the salon with Maud to find Yarrow, teacher of all things shamanic and Kimoran, Sheldrake and Lord Argyve, the Eskuzorian ambassador, already waiting for them. She seated herself neatly on the sofa, a short distance from Argyve.

Jon entered a few minutes later, having divested himself of his livery and now wearing a plain tan coat. "That's better," he said, grinning at her.

Two voices could be heard approaching down the corridor. As they drew closer, the voice with a gentle lilt was asking, "But how high does it extend? And how strong is it? Could another mage or a shaman overturn it?"

"And this, if I'm not mistaken," said Sheldrake dryly, holding out his hand in introduction as Stefan walked in the door, "is our new master at arms, Stefan." He almost added Longshanks then decided he did not yet know Stefan well enough to use his nickname. "And Leon, of course."

Stefan waved a cheery hand in greeting then stopped himself, said, "Oops," and gave a bow, from which he rose, grinning. He noticed a stocky gentleman sitting next to the curricle driver staring at him in puzzled surprise. Did he know him from somewhere else? Stefan didn't think so.

His attention was drawn back to Sheldrake who was shaking his head dolefully and saying, "And he seems to have no inherent sense of what is due one's status. He just tries to remember the niceties from time to time."

"Not surprising," muttered Argyve to himself, so quietly that no one was sure what they had heard.

"I beg your pardon?" asked Sheldrake.

Argyve blinked, as though pulling himself together. "Don't

worry." He took a breath and smiled formally. "How do you do? I'm Lord Argyve, Ambassador from Eskuzor."

Before Stefan could respond, he was distracted by Jon striding forward and giving a bow to Stefan in return. "Pleased to meet you. I've heard a lot about you from Stavros. I've only met him once so far, but he is going to be *my* master at arms when I move to the palace." He looked down at Stefan, his eyes twinkling. "He said to me that since I was so tall, it was surprising they hadn't assigned Stefan Longshanks to train me." He chuckled. "Cheeky bugger, isn't he? I don't know how you put up with him."

"You'd be surprised what I have to put up with." Stefan decided instantly that he liked this tall, blonde young man.

Jon gave him a friendly smile. "Well, you won't have to put up with it from me. I'm Jon, by the way, Johnson at court. Jondarian's my real name but everyone just calls me Jon." He went on to introduce Yarrow and Electra.

"And these are the people, Stefan," said Sheldrake, "who know Sasha's true identity and are working together to secure her future. Beth and Clive have both known as long as Maud and I have, but they prefer just to give her the friendship and support of co-workers and leave the shamanism and the politics to others." He indicated the lounge chairs and sofa. "Do be seated, everyone. Clive will be in shortly with tea."

Leon stationed himself inside the door, but the others, including Stefan, seated themselves as Sheldrake continued, "The King has tasked me with protecting our borders against these raiding parties from Kimora. I think we have the roads and farmlands reasonably well covered by the farmers being rewarded for any reported sightings, but the Great Forest presents us with a problem."

"You come from that area, don't you, Stefan?" asked Maud. "Doesn't your father own the Creeping Vine?"

Stefan's eyebrows flicked together briefly. "How did you know that? Oh, that's right. We were talking about it on the ride. Sasha must have told you." He glanced at Sheldrake. "Is that it, or was it a background check?"

Sheldrake smiled and said in a neutral tone that begged the question, "I gathered *my* knowledge from a background check."

"Hmm. Am I missing something here?" demanded Stefan, quickly on the defensive.

Suddenly Maud grinned at him. "Maisy and I have a strong connection."

"Maisy? The horse? Can you talk to horses?"

Maud shook her head. "No. I *am* the horse. I'm a shapeshifter, Stefan."

Then she blushed and he blushed and everyone else laughed.

Discomforted, Stefan bounced out of his chair and strode to the window, peering out into the morning's sunlight with his back to the room. As the laughter died, he turned on his heel to face them and put his hands on his hips. Taking a deep breath to overcome his chagrin, he said, "Well, you're a pretty good horse. That's all I can say."

Amid relieved laughter, Maud smiled at him. "Thank you. As you know, Sasha thinks I'm a bit solid."

His face cleared. "Oh, so that's why you all laughed when I said I was worried that Maisy might be too broad for me."

"And now that I know you better, I have told you about my shapeshifting, so that you are not at a disadvantage. Very few people know about it."

Stefan gave a little bow. "Then I am honoured." He sent a quick glance around the room and, with no further ado, returned to the question Maud had asked him. "Yes, I am from the Great Forest. My family have owned and run the Creeping Vine for generations."

"Your family owns an inn, do they?" asked Argyve, looking puzzled.

Stefan frowned at him. "Yes. That's what I just said." When Argyve lapsed into a thoughtful silence, he continued, "I'm not sure how keen my father would be on shopping his customers, though. Taverns work on the premise that anyone and everyone is welcome."

"He would allow one of our agents in there though, wouldn't he? Based on the same premise..." Sheldrake looked to the door, as Leon held it open for Clive to enter with a tray full of crockery and the large silver teapot. Once he had set it down on the low table in the middle of the room and begun to pour and hand out cups of tea, Sheldrake renewed his query with a lift of his eyebrows.

"Of course he would. He just lets his patrons get on with their own schemes and dreams, unless they become raucous or violent. Then he boots them out 'til they settle down." Stefan accepted a cup of tea with a nod of thanks and sat down again. "He would also talk to you about what he'd seen, if you asked him. He doesn't cover up for people but equally he won't come looking for you to tell you and he definitely wouldn't accept payment for information."

Sheldrake nodded. "We can work with that."

Stefan shrugged. "It still only covers people who emerge onto the road at the Inn. It won't help you intercept anyone who stays deep within the forest."

"Have you spent much time in the forest yourself?" asked Electra, aware that Argyve tensed at her question.

"I spent all my childhood there. I loved it; much more than my brothers and sister. If anyone wanted herbs, mushrooms or firewood, I would be the first to volunteer. Anything to get out into the trees and among the ferns and bushes." Stefan stopped talking to blow on his tea and take a sip. While he sipped, he glanced at Lord Argyve who couldn't seem to keep his eyes off him.

"So you know this forest pretty well, do you?" asked Jon. "Do you know all the trails through it?"

Stefan nearly choked on his tea. "Know all the trails?" he asked incredulously. "Have you any idea how vast the Great Forest is? Behind our inn, the forest stretches for seventy miles to the south. On the other side of Park Lane, it stretches over one hundred miles to the north into Eskuzor. Our inn is twenty miles from the farmlands that lead to Highkington and ninety miles from where the forest peters out inside Kimora." He gave a quirky smile. "Mind you, it is only thirty miles to Carrador's border from our inn. I know most of that pretty well, and I have explored several other trails, but the whole forest is over fifteen hundred square miles."

The room fell into a gloomy silence until suddenly Sheldrake set down his cup and sat forward. "We are looking at this wrongly. We don't have to cover fifteen hundred square miles. We just need to cover a thin strip where the border is, mainly along the Charville River."

"And just a thin strip one hundred and sixty miles long," said Argyve heavily, who was finally focused on something other than Stefan. "Probably a lot longer, if I know anything about rivers."

"We don't have to follow the exact path of the river," snapped Sheldrake testily.

"Still a long way," said Argyve.

Sheldrake ran a hand through his neat black hair, a testament to the stress he was feeling with having to come up with a solution in such a short timeframe.

"Now, now, dear," Maud crooned. "You know we will think of something in the end."

He shook his head. "It's not feasible. How far apart do guards stand?

Argyve did not rush with his answer. His brow furrowed as he thought about it.

"But doesn't it..?" began Stefan, but was stopped by Argyve's raised hand.

"Yes, young man, it does depend on the terrain. On a flat, treeless plain, you could space guards up to two hundred yards apart, possibly even further. In a dense forest, you might need guards every... hmm... hundred yards. At least every hundred yards, possibly even closer. What do you think, Stefan?" Finally Argyve seemed to have stopped staring at him as though he had two heads.

"I'd say fifty yards in the densest areas. Even then they would have to keep watch at ground level while, at the same time, look for movement in the trees above them. Still, some parts of the river would be uncrossable. So you wouldn't need guards stationed there." Stefan started counting off on his fingers. "Well, let's say, for argument's sake, that you need an average of one guard every hundred yards. That means about eighteen guards per mile. So for one hundred and ten miles you'd need about nineteen hundred and eighty, let's round it up to two thousand soldiers guarding the border through the forest in each shift. So at least six thousand men, I'd say, if they each stood guard for a total of eight hours a day, not in one shift of course. Then you'd need officers, mess staff...."

Sheldrake waved his hand. "All right, all right. Enough. That plan obviously requires far too many resources."

"A magical barrier?" suggested Yarrow. The mirrors on her dress twinkled as she leaned forward to put her cup down. "Like the one you have here?"

Sheldrake and Leon's eyes met, before Sheldrake gave an embarrassed shrug. "The barrier we have across the front of this property will alert me if someone tries to enter uninvited. It's a plain, straight fence line. We haven't actually got around to trying to erect a barrier through or around the land out the back. I'm not sure," he gave a self-conscious cough, "well, actually I *am* sure that I couldn't create one around or through the whole bushland out the back, let alone over so vast a distance as the border between Carrador and Kimora."

The room lapsed into another thoughtful silence.

Then Argyve harrumphed. "I might have an idea. It's a long shot, but it might help."

All eyes turned to him.

"In Eskuzor, we have vast forests in the middle of our country that run across the mountains then south across our borders with Carrador. A few years ago, wide lines of forest sprang up across the land so that if you wanted to, you could travel from one end of the country to the other without leaving the woodlands."

"Yes...?" prompted Maud, in a tone that implied she didn't see where this was going.

"Well, we have our Forest Guardian to thank for that. When I say *thank*, I'm not sure all the farmers were delighted to lose some of their pastures to forest, but the benefits are that our borders are almost inviolable." He looked around the room and gave a smile that carried a hint of pride. "You probably don't realise this, but visitors to our kingdom are welcome if they travel along the roads but if they try to enter through the forest, our soldiers are alerted to apprehend and question the intruders. Sometimes those trying to enter through the forests are allowed in and sometimes they are not, depending on their motives. High Lord Tarkyn, through his network, becomes quickly aware that there are interlopers in the forests. Maybe he could help us to set up a similar system between Carrador and Kimora."

Maud leant forward, clasping her hands tightly in her lap. "This sounds very promising, Argyve. Two questions, though: What do these corridors of forest have to do with protecting the borders? Secondly, why would High Lord Tarkyn help us – or, to be more exact, help Sasha?"

Argyve gave an embarrassed grimace. "I know the reason for the forest corridors but I'm afraid it's a state secret. As to the second, I'm not sure that he will help us. I can only ask. It is two days' ride to the border. From there, the message can be sent to him very quickly to wherever he is in Eskuzor. If he chooses to respond, he can be here within another day or the messenger can ride back with the message of refusal." He gave a private little smile. "But I think I may be able to persuade him."

PART II

8

A rgyve entered the library upstairs, intent on writing a letter for High Lord Tarkyn.

Jayhan looked up from his labours with multiplication and beamed at him. "Hello. What are you doing here?"

Argyve glanced apologetically at Eloquin, "I have come to write an important letter. I will try not to disturb you."

"Don't worry," said Eloquin, "Jayhan is already champing at the bit. He knows that when he has finished the ten questions I have given him, he can go."

Unfortunately, Jayhan immediately interpreted this to mean he could chat to Argyve as long as he liked, provided he did the ten questions before he left the room. "There's a little writing desk in the corner. It a special desk, called an escr... escritoire, with lots of little drawers full of pens and paper and things." He pulled his mouth down. "I don't get to use it much because Mum and Dad say I mess it up, but I expect they'd let you."

Argyve chuckled. "I expect they would."

He crossed to the escritoire, sat down on the cushion of a beautifully carved chair and extracted pen and paper. He picked up the pen, ready to begin his missive.

"Who are you writing to?" asked Jayhan, multiplication temporarily forgotten.

"Someone you don't know; High Lord Tarkyn."

"Oh." Jayhan managed not to make it a question while at the same time showing he was interested in knowing more.

Argyve began to write.

After a minute during which all that could be heard was Argyve's pen scratching across the paper, Jayhan's voice piped up again. "Lord Argyve, what is a High Lord? We only have lords, kings and queens, princes and princesses, don't we?"

Argyve put the pen down, accepting defeat. He smiled at Eloquin to include her. "This may be of interest to you, too. I was there when Prince Tarkyn's older twin brothers died. As far as we knew, Prince Tarkyn had suddenly become our king and was treated as such. However, the populace was unaware that Prince Tarkyn had a sister, who was older than he but younger than the twins. She had been exiled as a baby because her magic was rogue."

"Rogue?" asked Eloquin who, despite her duty to keep Jayhan focused, had become interested in the conversation.

"Uncontrolled and dangerous." When she had nodded, Argyve continued. "She had trained hard in exile and, as a young woman, was now not only in control of her magic but had developed to become a powerful wizard; what you would call a mage here."

Jayhan looked puzzled. "So why's he called a High Lord? Don't get it still."

Argyve held up his hand. "Patience, young man, I am coming to that... The Eskuzorian rule of succession is absolute primogenitor. In other words, the eldest child, regardless of gender, inherits the throne. Prince... King Tarkyn had only recently become aware of his sister's existence himself. But even though he had the backing of both the northern and southern armies and the whole population, he stepped aside and gave Navira the throne."

Jayhan's face scrunched up. "But that's right, isn't it? That was the right thing to do."

"Yes, but not everyone with power does the right thing. Anyway, in an agreement between them, Prince Tarkyn assumed the title of High Lord Tarkyn, Guardian of Eskuzor with powers to veto the monarchy's decision, in exchange for allowing Navira the throne."

Eloquin blinked. "But doesn't that effectively make him the ruler?"

"No. I suppose it could if he overused it, but High Lord Tarkyn is our watchdog, so to speak. By keeping himself aloof from court politics, he ensures that our monarchy is fair and informs Queen Navira and her Prince Consort Danton of issues arising around the kingdom. In many ways, his role is similar to that held by Maud and Sheldrake, except that he has the power to enforce his opinions if he chooses to."

"That is a most unusual set-up," said Eloquin, as she packed up a stack of papers. "I have not heard of its like in any other country."

"It is unusual, but I believe it is sound and will provide stability for our country for generations to come." Argyve hesitated, knowing he might release a barrage of questions and readying himself to stem it. "Since he is a true Guardian of the Forest, High Lord Tarkyn will live through the reigns of several monarchs." As Jayhan opened his mouth to ask another question, Argyve raised his hand. "And now, I must have this letter written before lunch. If you want to know more, you might like to research Forest Guardians as part of your studies."

As Argyve turned resolutely back to his letter, Eloquin raised an eyebrow at Jayhan who returned reluctantly to his arithmetic, determined to ask his father about Forest Guardians later.

9

A s he laboriously finished his last multiplication, Jayhan realised Eloquin was hovering anxiously at his elbow. He looked up. "May I go?"

"Just a minute. I'll have to check them first." She ran her eye quickly down the line of sums and gave a relieved smile. "Thank goodness! You got them all right. And now, I have to go." When Jayhan looked puzzled at her haste, she said, "Remember? Maud and I are helping Sasha to put on a gown for the first time."

"Can I come too?"

"No, Jayhan. You can see her when she's ready. We will bring her down to the salon, just before lunch. So you can see her then." She wagged her finger at him. "And I don't want any witticisms from you. She will be very nervous. Be the kind friend I know you are."

She left behind a very thoughtful-looking Jayhan. If she hadn't been so preoccupied, this might have worried her more, but as it was, she sped along the corridor to Maud's dressing room, where Maud and Rose had hung up the three dresses on hooks around the room and were already talking to Sasha about which one she would like to wear first. Sasha looked up at her arrival, a pleading, trapped expression on her face.

Eloquin smiled reassuringly at her. "Hello, Sasha. It's a big day for you, isn't it? These are beautiful gowns, aren't they? I wish I could afford gowns of this quality." She walked over to a soft green dress embroidered in blue silk and finished with white lace at the neckline and cuffs. "Look at these pretty blue birds," she said, running her hand over the embroidery.

"It would look good on you," said Sasha. "It would be wishy-washy on me." She coloured as she realised that what she said could be construed as an insult. "I don't mean you're wishy-washy. It's just I'm used to tan and black and brown; strong colours." She waved her hand in despair at the next gown, which was a white frothy creation. "I mean, look at this. Can you even imagine me in this?"

Eloquin glanced at Maud, who was looking harassed and Rose, who was trying not to appear flustered.

Sasha walked to the last of the three and waved her hand at it dramatically. "And this one? *Me?* It's pink with ribbons and revolting little white dogs with umbrellas on it. Honestly, whoever sent these dresses knows nothing about me. No one asked my opinion. No one cared what I thought." Her voice choked up. "Is this going to be my life from now on? People forcing me to be someone else?" Tears overcame her and she sank to the floor against the wall, pulling her knees up to her chest and wrapping her arms around her head and knees.

"Oh dear," said Maud, totally flustered. "Rose, you'd better bring her a cup of tea."

Rose fled thankfully. As she left, Jayhan slipped in the door.

"What are you doing to her?" he demanded.

Maud rolled her eyes. "Nothing, Jayhan. She just doesn't like the dresses."

Jayhan plopped himself on the floor next to Sasha and put his arm around her while he studied the dresses. A variety of expressions, mostly, but not all, of distaste, crossed his face as he considered each one. "So why has that made her sad?"

"She thinks she will be forced to be someone she's not."

"Oh. Well, that's silly. How can anyone make you, Sasha? They can't force you screaming and crying down the stairs in a dress you hate." He smiled at his mother. "Anyway, they wouldn't want to. Mum likes you a lot. She's not trying to be mean to you."

Eloquin and Maud looked at him with new respect.

"You know," he said into her ear, "these are just practice dresses, to get the hang of wearing them. You can tell, because they are all dull colours; you know, just like the scruffy saddle you use at home, not the beautiful new saddle you'd use for a show. I bet if you asked, they would try to find dresses you like for when you go out in *real* public."

Sasha sniffed and raised her head a little. "Do you think so?"

"Oh, definitely," he answered, winging it and raising his eyebrows at his mother for confirmation.

"Of course we will, Sasha," said Maud throwing a relieved glance at Eloquin. "What sort of colours do you like; besides black, brown and tan?"

"I love Lady Electra's dresses." Sasha sat up and wiped her nose on her sleeve, making Maud glad she had not yet donned one of the gowns. "She wears beautiful bright colours; oranges, yellows, reds. I like your dresses too. I really like tan, dark green, blue and brown. I *hate* pastel colours," she added with a venomous look at the gowns and received an admonitory dig in the ribs from Jayhan. She glared at him but turned her attention to Maud when she spoke.

"You see, Sasha, girls and young women generally wear paler colours. It just seems to be the fashion." As Sasha's face tightened, Maud hastened to add, "But I can see we may have to help you to start a new trend instead."

Rose arrived with a single large mug of tea and handed it to Sasha with a quick curtsey.

Sasha smiled at her from her tear-streaked face. "Thanks. Sorry to put you to the bother." She had had time to think about Jayhan's jab in the ribs. "And sorry I'm being a pain. I know you're just trying to help but... it's hard."

"I think the pale green one is the best," pronounced Jayhan suddenly. "Obviously the pink one is disgusting but the white one might look good against your dark skin, even if it is a bit frilly." Sasha looked at him in amazement. "Go on," he urged. "Pick one and try it on. Just think of it as an old saddle."

Rose, who had missed his earlier comments, looked scandalized.

Jayhan hopped to his feet. "By the way, I think Sasha might like the green one better if it had dark blue around the edges, instead of the white lace, though the white lace would look good against her skin. See you later, Sasha." He grinned and walked out, leaving four astonished women in his wake.

It was nearly an hour later that Sasha emerged warily and, under instruction from Maud, descended the stairs and entered the salon where the others were still chatting among themselves. They looked towards the door as it opened and beheld Sasha, head held high, but dark eyes anxious, as she walked carefully into view in the soft green gown, now trimmed with blue material that matched the embroidery, cut from one of Maud's favourite scarves. With her hair brushed and pinned into soft dark waves, she had been transformed into a young lady of fashion. Everyone clapped and smiled at her. She gave an uncertain smile in return and performed a stiff curtsey.

Jon came forward and held out his hand. "You look lovely, sister mine. You always look lovely, but especially today."

Sasha took his hand and felt her way into the room, carefully placing each foot so that she didn't trip on the skirts, even though they were only ankle length. When she was safely seated, she had time to relax a little and look around the room. "Where's Jayhan?" she asked, experiencing a pang of disappointment.

Sheldrake looked around. "He was here. I don't know where he has shot off to. I'm sure he'll be back. He'll be sorry to have missed your entrance."

Suddenly they heard through the door a series of thumps, a smothered oath, then a louder thump followed by a ringing clang. Sheldrake strode to the door and opened it. Clive was picking himself up and retrieving a silver tray that had landed somewhere further down the corridor. A white heap lay at his feet and seemed to be emitting groans of pain. It moved and resolved itself into Jayhan surrounded by layers of white lace. He dragged himself to his feet, grimacing as he took his weight on his left leg. "Ow." He looked up at everyone then straightened and grinned sheepishly. "Well, that wasn't quite the entrance I planned. I was going to help Sasha get used to old saddles, you see," he explained, to the mystification of everyone but Maud and Eloquin.

"Jayhan, you are wearing a dress, not a saddle. A very frilly dress, I might add." Sheldrake shook his head. "I would have thought you could play dress-ups when we did not have a house full of visitors."

Clive put an arm under Jayhan's elbow and guided him through the crowd into the salon. "Here, young one, sit down a minute. You took quite a tumble there." As Jayhan tripped again, Clive said calmly, "I believe you trip less if you lift your skirts. That is possibly how you fell down the stairs in the first place."

"Ow. Thanks, Clive. It's a bit long for me, actually. I keep stepping on it."

Sasha walked over and surveyed him critically. "White is a little bright for you but I'm glad you didn't wear the pink." Then she giggled. "You're an idiot, Jayhan. But the nicest idiot I've ever known."

He grinned back at her. "Thanks. I think."

Ignoring his sore leg, Jayahn pulled himself out of his chair and, for the next few minutes, Jayhan and Sasha joyously paraded in their dresses, sashaying back and forth, tripping and striking poses, both laughing uproariously as they thought of new ways to pretend to be ladies of fashion. Maud and Electra, who both *were* ladies of fashion, applauded and provided suggestions and laughed with the rest of them.

By the time they had safely negotiated their way up the stairs and sat down to lunch, Sasha had forgotten her stiffness and was chatting and laughing quite unselfconsciously.

Maud leaned in and whispered to Sheldrake, "You realise your son is a genius, don't you?"

Sheldrake raised his eyebrows, watched the two children for a minute, then smiled.

10

As the road curved to the left, the setting sun shone directly into the face of a tired, lanky young man dressed in the blue and red of Eskuzor. He squinted against the light and slowed his pace, knowing the road would return to its northerly bearing in another mile. He might as well take the opportunity to rest his horse, since to ride breakneck, blinded by the sunlight, was idiocy. He knew riders who did it, but he wasn't one of them.

He leaned forward in the saddle and patted the roan horse's neck. He didn't know her very well, although he had ridden her a few times in the past. He vaguely remembered that her name was Patsy. She was one of the many horses who lived in the posthouses on the highway route from Highkington to Montreya.

Jackson had been riding since lunchtime yesterday. He had ridden for six hours yesterday, staying the night at the waystation in the tiny village of Creekside. At dawn, he had been in the saddle and on his way again. An hour ago, he had passed the left-hand turn that would have taken him to the small kingdom of Farenz that ran along the coast in the northwest corner of Carrador, just south of Eskuzor. It meant he was getting close to Eskuzor's border.

The horse he was currently riding was his eighth for the day. She was reasonably fresh; he was close to exhaustion. As she walked quietly down the road, he unstoppered his drinking flask and took a long draught before waving to a traveller driving an old cart laden with firewood in the other direction. Then he rummaged in the hessian bag slung over his shoulder and pulled out a wad of dried beef and an apple, which he munched as the corner in the road drew closer. By the time the road swung back to the north, he felt revived enough to push through the final miles to the border.

When he finally reached the border post, twenty miles south of the Eskuzorian city of Montreya, Jackson nodded in greeting to the Carradorian guards before riding over the border to stop at the Eskuzorian guard station. Here he dismounted and tied his horse to the hitching rail. One of the border guards, a casual fellow with dirty blonde hair that had evaded all of its owner's half-hearted attempts to tame it, walked over to talk to him.

Seeing Jackson's sweat-streaked face, he asked, "Urgent?"

The messenger nodded. "And for High Lord Tarkyn's personal attention."

"Really? We have a specific protocol for that. Come inside and have a coffee. I'll send Markos into the woods with it."

Jackson smiled with relief and handed the guard a slightly bulging envelope. "Thanks, Sandy. Lord Agyve said you had a system for sending urgent messages to the High Lord. Saves me the extra ride. Usually I just keep going until it is delivered into the recipient's hand. This is all new for me."

Sandy looked at the envelope in his hand and shook his

head. "Funny how their messages are always flat and ours are rolled into canisters."

Jackson shrugged. "As long as they fit in my jacket or bag, I don't mind which way they pack them."

He followed Sandy into the little guardhouse and watched as he handed the envelope to an older man who was not in uniform. Jackson frowned a query at Sandy.

"This is Markos. He is a retired teacher. When an urgent letter arrives, he walks out into the woodlands, down that path," Sandy indicated the path out the window, "until he reaches the old oak. A large brass bell is strapped to the trunk of the tree, but the tongue is fastened so that the bell is silent when the wind blows. When he wants to send an urgent message to High Lord Taykyn, he unfastens the tongue and rings the bell three times. Then he waits. After forty minutes, he reads the letter out loud word for word, pausing after each sentence."

Markos did not wait to hear the end of an explanation he already knew, but gave a curt wave before heading out into the gloom of the forest.

Sandy poured coffee into a battered tin cup from a pot on an iron stove and handed it to Jackson. "Sugar?" When Jackson shook his head, he continued, "If the matter is not urgent, Markos simply leaves the letter in the wooden box at the base of the oak. By the next morning, it is gone. The replies come to us by carrier pigeon. We have cotes here that the pigeons fly back to. From time to time, we send a crate of our pigeons to various places around the kingdom so that when they need to send us a message, they can use a pigeon to carry it."

Jackson frowned. "Why don't you just use pigeons yourself to contact Lord Tarkyn?"

"We do use pigeons for messages to Montreya that they can then relay further afield. But no one can be sure where the

High Lord will be, so that doesn't work for him. But somehow, the messages left or read at the old oak always find him."

An hour later, Markos returned. "Done," he said shortly.

"Thanks. Aren't you worried walking through the woods on your own at night? What about wolves and mountain lions and bandits?" asked Jackson, as the older man walked through the door and sloughed off his coat.

Markos shook his head. "No. Lord Tarkyn has placed some sort of protection on the area around the old oak and the path between here and there. Never have any trouble." He gave a throaty chuckle. "I once saw a wolf. It saw me too but it just paused, blinked at me then went on its way."

"Huh." Jackson crossed to the stove and scooped some stew from a big saucepan into a bowl and handed it to the old man. "Here. It's good. Your Sandy's a good cook," he grinned, "much to my surprise!" and scooted out of the way laughing, as Sandy swung his booted foot at him.

11

S andy was just about to go out and let the other guard, Warren, come in for some dinner, when they heard a thump on the ground behind the guardhouse on the forest's edge. The three of them rushed out and found a pale young man sprawled on the ground beside a lavender bush, his long black hair half covering his face. The man groaned and dragged himself into a sitting position, wrapping his arms around his knees. His nondescript soft brown shirt and leggings did not seem any the worse for wear, although not warm enough to stop him from shivering against the misty cold that was seeping through the trees. When he had regained a little strength, he dragged his huge wolfskin cloak around his shoulders.

"High Lord Tarkyn!" exclaimed Markos, bowing deeply.

The man in question raised his head and Jackson found bright amber eyes glaring at him through the rays of light from the guardhouse window. "I have you to thank for this, do I?" he croaked.

"Sorry?" Jackson had no idea what he had done. "I beg your pardon," he said hastily, bowing as the older man had done.

Prince Tarkyn, High Lord of Eskuzor, moved his focus to Sandy who bowed, then said, "Just a minute," and raced back indoors, leaving Jackson gaping in astonishment.

Sandy reappeared less than a minute later with a cup of water, which he proffered.

"Thank you." Tarkyn reached out and grasped the cup, downing its contents in one draught. He breathed out and wiped his hand across his mouth. "Ah. That's better."

As Tarkyn hoisted himself to his feet, Jackson's gaze travelled from near ground level to well above his own height. This man was tall.

"So Markos, where is this envelope?" asked Tarkyn, "Did you bring it back with you or leave it at the foot of the oak?"

"I left the letter and brought back the envelope and its other contents, my lord." Markos reached into his pocket, withdrew the envelope and handed it to the High Lord.

"Good man." Tarkyn opened it and peered inside. "Hmm. A gumnut." Unexpectedly, he smiled at Jackson. "Let's hope they know what they're doing."

Jackson was so totally confused by now that he just blinked.

Tarkyn chuckled. "When I translocate, I focus on an object, which returns me to the place where the object was created. To come here, I focused on a piece of lavender that originated on that bush in the guardhouse garden."

Jackson glanced at the lavender bush then frowned. "And are you going to use a gumnut to translocate again? Isn't it a bit dangerous to land high up in a eucalyptus tree? They are very tall. Even more dangerous, if it makes you feel sick."

"Yes, very. So I am hoping that this gumnut comes from a low branch. I think Lord Argyve knows the story of when I translocated into the high branches of an oak tree and plummeted twenty feet to the ground. I hope so." He grimaced. "I must admit I would feel more confident with a grevillea flower or leaf."

"Very prickly, landing in most grevilleas, Sire, I would think," offered Jackson.

Tarkyn gave a grunt of laughter. "Good point... What is your name? I know the other two, but you are new to me."

"I am Jackson, Sire, the messenger who brought the envelope and its contents from Highkington."

"And when did you leave?"

"Two hours after noon yesterday, Sire. I rode until dusk, then have ridden since first light this morning."

"Oh, my word! And here I am keeping you standing out here in the dark. You must be near to dropping."

Jackson smiled. "A bit tired, Sire." His smile broadened. "But my interest in your novel mode of travel is managing to battle off my weariness. I have not seen a translocation before."

"You have an unusual turn of phrase, Jackson," said Tarkyn as he made his way into the guardhouse, ducking his head to get through the doorway.

"My mother is a librarian," replied Jackson, by way of explanation. As he followed him in, he hesitated then asked, "Would you like some stew or are you still feeling a bit crook?"

"Crook?"

Jackson grinned. "A word I picked up in Carrador."

Tarkyn raised his eyebrows. "Hm. Well, I was feeling very *crook* but I'm nearly back to normal now. However, I won't have any stew, thank you."

While Tarkyn sat down at the table and sipped his water, Jackson muttered to Sandy, "Do we have anything better to offer His Highness?"

"I heard that," interrupted Tarkyn. "Now, don't be rude to Sandy. He makes excellent stews."

Jackson's face coloured. "Oh, but I thought..."

"I am happy to eat any well-prepared food," the High Lord smiled, "as long as I don't have to prepare it myself. I am not eating because I intend to translocate again very shortly, and I don't want to vomit Sandy's stew up all over Lord Sheldrake's front lawn."

"Oh, good decision in that case... Sire."

Tarkyn noted the hesitation. "Independent sort of a character, aren't you?"

Jackson grimaced. "I don't mean to be, Sire, but I spend a lot of my time on my own between one place and another. I'm pretty good at protocol when I'm picking up or delivering messages, but that's about as far as it goes. The rest of the time I don't have to answer to anyone."

The High Lord considered him; the messenger's neat brown hair held back firmly in a queue with only a few wisps around his face after hours of riding, his clothes and boots well cared for under the patina of dust that covered them and his loose-limbed frame that moved with the grace of a born athlete. Tarkyn drummed his fingers on the table. "What are your current plans?"

Jackson looked surprised. "Mine? I was going to stay the night here, then head back to Lord Argyve tomorrow, carrying the dispatches that have been waiting here for delivery. On my return, he wanted me to confirm that I had delivered his message and that it had been passed on," he grinned, "but I guess your appearance will confirm it, long before I get back."

"Would you like to come with me? I could give you a lift back, so to speak." Jackson's eyes widened. It seemed to be with excitement but, when he did not respond straightaway, Tarkyn thought perhaps he had been mistaken and it was fear that he was seeing, so he added, "It can be uncomfortable for a few minutes, nauseating, but it passes as you have just seen. You don't have to come, though. It was not a command."

"No, I would love to come, Sire. It would be an honour. No, I was just thinking through my responsibilities before I replied." Jackson looked over at Sandy. "Could you mind the horse? I was going to ride her back tomorrow but the next post rider through can take her back to her stables, if that's all right with you."

Sandy grinned at him. "I would be a surly bugger to stand in the way of a chance like this. Of course I'll mind the horse."

Tarkyn smiled at them. "Translocating is not an experience I hanker after. I do it as rarely as possible. Oh, and just so that you know, Jackson, this particular ability of mine is close to being a state secret. Only a few trusted people know, so please don't broadcast it."

Jackson considered for a moment then nodded.

Tarkyn frowned. "Were you deciding whether to accede to my request?"

"No, of course not. You're the High Lord. I was just thinking through the reasons for it, the tactical advantages of having such a skill up your sleeve, instead of out in the open."

"Hmm. I think I will ask Lord Argyve to re-assign you to be my aide-de-camp while I am in Carrador. Would you be happy with that?"

"It's not up to me, but since you are asking," he paused while he thought about it, "I think it would be a very interesting experience. Much as I like the long stretches of solitary riding, I think I will enjoy being in your company."

Rather to Jackson's surprise, the High Lord coloured a little. "Thank you. Likewise. That, among other reasons, is why I asked."

"Huh." Jackson smiled and bowed. "I am honoured, Sire."

Tarkyn stood up, crossed to the water barrel and refilled his glass. Once he had finished drinking, he turned to Jackson. "Right. Shall we go?"

"Just a minute. I need to get my kit."

"No kit, I'm afraid. You can probably bring a small satchel slung over your shoulder with the dispatches and a few other things. We'll have to procure you spare uniforms in Highkington."

"Uh-huh."

Tarkyn smiled as he watched the now familiar sight of Jackson thinking something through.

"Right," said Jackson. "Back in a minute."

When he returned, he had washed the grime off his hands and face, brushed the dust from his boots and uniform and retied his hair so that the flyaway wisps had been recaptured. He had a small canvas bag slung across his shoulders. He bowed. "Ready, Sire."

Tarkyn raised his eyebrows. "Impressive transformation in so short a time."

"Thank you, Sire. If I am to be your offsider, I have to do you as proud as I can."

High Lord Tarkyn walked over and clapped his arm across Jackson's shoulders. "You are a gem among men. I am glad our paths have crossed. Let's go outside for this."

Sandy and Markos trooped out behind them as they returned to the spot next to the lavender bush where Tarkyn had first appeared.

"Do you have to be in the same place for the next translocation that you arrived in from the last?" asked Jackson.

"No. We just have more room to manoeuvre out here. Now Jackson, I will have to hold onto you very firmly to pull you through with me. The last time I did this, I was rescuing someone who was injured so he wasn't conscious enough to object to me putting my arms around him." Tarkyn grinned. "You are. So I hope you can manage a little indignity."

"I'll cope."

"Now I think about it, it would be much easier for me if you hold onto me too, then I won't have to hold on so hard. Last time, it nearly dragged my arms out of their sockets."

Jackson frowned. "Are you sure you want to do this, Sire?"

Tarkyn waved his hand airily. "Oh yes. Definitely. A bit of pain and discomfort never hurt anyone." Seeing three bemused faces around him, he added, "I did say 'a bit'. Never mind." He pulled the gumnut out of his pocket and held it firmly in one hand. "So Jackson, stand in front of me, wrap your arms around me and link your hands behind me. I will link mine over the top of yours because I must be able to see this little gumnut."

They manoeuvred into position, which felt uncomfortably intimate. Tarkyn peered over Jackson's shoulder at the gumnut held in his linked hands. "Goodbye, you two," he said to Sandy and Markos, then intoned, *"Maya Mureva Araya! Ka Mureva Araya!"* and the two of them faded from sight.

12

Jackson felt as though he were being sucked through a warp in space. He seemed to fold him in on himself until he was almost gone, then expand suddenly to land with a jolt, tangled in Prince Tarkyn's arms. A rush of nausea welled inside him and he flailed to disentangle himself, pushing Tarkyn away unceremoniously, just in time to turn his head and vomit on the lawn.

"Aaah. Now I'm the one vomiting on Lord Argyve's front lawn. I feel horrible."

When he looked, he saw Tarkyn lying on his back, propped on his elbows with his head back. After a minute, Tarkyn shuddered and lifted his head. "You do know it is a capital offence to assault me?" he said, with an edge to his voice.

Jackson's stomach lurched, from fear not nausea this time. This new assignment might be harder than he thought or worse still, very short-lived. "I did my best," he replied levelly. "It was the lesser of two assaults, in my opinion. Better to be pushed than to be spewed on."

Tarkyn's eyes twinkled in response, his irritation dissipating. "How true. For future reference, I give you permission to lay hands on me, provided you are not genuinely planning to harm me."

Jackson breathed a sigh of relief. "You really scared me. I'm not used to dealing with royalty. You'd better let me know what else might get me into strife."

Tarkyn sat up, the laughter gone from his eyes. "I will, but we have at least established the most important ground rule... and very few people have been given that permission." He stood up. "I think we are both a little tetchy from the translocation. Being nauseated makes one a little short-tempered, I find."

He put his hand out for Jackson to pull himself up, a clear gesture of reconciliation.

Jackson's mouth quirked into a smile as he accepted the proffered hand. "Thank you. And thank you for your trust."

Now that they had recovered, they took time to look around themselves. They were standing next to a young gumtree, only a few feet high, clearly the source of the gumnut. Much larger eucalypts stood close by, towering into the night sky. The light from inside the house spilled across the cultivated lawn beneath their feet and partly lit the towering gums and the garden beds of shrubs behind them that lined the front wall of the stables.

They spun around at the sound of scrabbling and saw two legs appear high up in one of the gum trees. Moments later, the rest of a small person appeared, climbing down a wooden ladder. Then another appeared, to follow the first. Soon Tarkyn and Jackson were looking down at two children, both dressed in leggings and jerkins. The boy whose clothes were of better quality, had unnervingly pale eyes while the other's eyes were liquid brown.

The boy with the pale eyes bowed. "Hello. You must be Prince... High Lord Tarkyn. I am Jayhan Batian and this is

Sasha." He grinned. "We've been watching out for you, although we weren't sure you'd arrive today or even come at all."

"But it gave us a great excuse to be in our cubby in the dark." Sasha glanced at Jayhan, then bowed too. "Oops."

Tarkyn gestured to his companion. "This is Jackson, the messenger who rode all the way to the border to contact me."

"Hello," said Sasha. "You must like horses if you do all that riding. So do I. I'm the stable... boy, you know."

Tarkyn raised his eyebrows. "Are you indeed?"

In the face of his sceptical tone, Jayhan rushed into the breech. "You two looked very funny all tangled up on the lawn. Just as well you didn't land in the salon. You'd have knocked everything over."

"Which is no doubt why Lord Argyve chose the lawn for our arrival," replied Tarkyn.

A certain dryness in this remark made Jayhan squint anxiously up at him. "I didn't mean to be rude. Sorry if I was. Would you like to come inside? My parents are dying to meet you."

Tarkyn couldn't help smiling, although he was by no means relaxed. "Thank you. Lead the way."

As they walked across the lawn to the house, carefully avoiding the little pile of regurgitated stew, Jayhan said, "Just a minute," and disappeared ahead of them. Tarkyn looked enquiringly at Sasha who shrugged her lack of answer. For a couple of minutes, they stood irresolutely outside the front door, waiting for Jayhan to return.

Losing patience, Tarkyn said, "I think we will knock," just as the front door swung open to reveal Clive, with Jayhan hopping from one leg to the other and smiling in satisfaction in the background.

Clive gave a deep bow. "This way, if you please, Your Highness. Would you like me to take your cloak?"

"Thank you, but I will keep it until I am warmer."

"Have you eaten, Sire? Dinner is ready to be served, pending your arrival."

Tarkyn raised his eyebrows. "Really? And what if I had chosen not to come?"

"Lord Sheldrake and Lady Maud would have become increasingly hungry until later this evening. I suspect they would have requested the occasional refreshment, Sire." Clive gave a slight smile. "The same would apply if you had already eaten."

The High Lord laughed. "For their sakes, I am pleased to say that I would indeed like to dine with them, although not straight away. My stomach needs time to settle."

Clive raised his eyebrows very delicately in Jackson's direction.

"My aide-de-camp, Jackson, will of course be joining us... and I suspect his stomach needs even more time to settle."

"Very good, Sire." Clive opened the door to the salon and entered first, announcing, "His Royal Highness, Prince Tarkyn, High Lord of Eskuzor, and Jackson, aide-de-camp to His Highness." Once Tarkyn had entered, Clive introduced Sheldrake and Maud to him.

Sheldrake was rooted to the spot with astonishment. "Good Lord! You actually came. Lord Argyve was right. He said he'd written something that might interest you enough to come. And here you are!" He suddenly remembered his manners and gave a deep bow. When he straightened, he said, "Very pleased to meet you, Your Highness."

In contrast, Maud surged forward and performed an elegant curtsey. As she rose, she said, "Oh, you poor man. You're freezing. Come to the fire."

In the face of such effusion, mistaking warmth for sycophantry, Tarkyn took an involuntary step backwards, made obvious by the fact that his wolfskin cloak swayed forwards. He nearly cannoned into Jackson who had entered the room behind him.

"You too," she added to Jackson. "What would you like to drink?"

"Water," they chorused.

"Oh." Maud motioned to Clive, who withdrew. "Anything else?"

"Tea for me," said Tarkyn.

"A brandy?" Jackson glanced uncertainly at Tarkyn, unsure whether he should drink on duty.

Tarkyn smiled. "If that's what your stomach feels like, by all means."

"I am sorry I missed your arrival. I would dearly love to see a translocation," said Sheldrake. "I wandered out onto the lawn from time to time but really, I don't have the patience required to wait around for hours on the off-chance that you'd decide to come."

"No. Neither do I. If it makes you feel any better, I don't think you missed much," Tarkyn replied, accepting a glass of water from Clive and pausing to down it. "I believe I just appear out of nowhere from the bystander's point of view."

"Really? This is most interesting. And how do you experience it?"

"Now Sheldrake," protested Maud. "Leave Lord Tarkyn alone. He hasn't even had time to take in his surroundings and you are already badgering him about magic. Have some compassion." Maud turned to Tarkyn. "He's a mage, you see. I believe you call them wizards. Anyway, he can be a little obsessive about magic."

Sheldrake frowned. "Not at all. I am an enthusiastic,

passionate scholar." Suddenly, his austere face relaxed into a grin. "Your pardon, Your Highness. Maud is right, of course. Do not feel obliged to answer my question."

Tarkyn raised his eyebrows, tacitly reminding them that he had no obligation to them whatsoever. Once he had made his point, he replied to the original question. "From *my* point of view, I must relinquish my existence for a few seconds then come back to myself somewhere else. It is a sickening experience both mentally and physically. Before I say the incantation, I must focus on an object that originates from the place I wish to go. You must be very specific with the origin of the object. Someone once gave me an acorn they had found on the forest floor but it had originated from high in the oak tree. Disastrous."

Clive arrived with the tea for Tarkyn. As he set it down, he asked, "When would you like to dine, Your Highness? Hannah needs time to prepare."

Tarkyn was not yet feeling particularly hungry, but one glance at the dark shadows beneath his new aide-de-camp's eyes told him that Jackson needed to retire soon. "Does half an hour seem reasonable?"

"Perfectly, Sire."

Tarkyn held up a hand. "Before you go, what happened to the children? They did not follow us in here."

"They were under strict instructions to show you in, then to make themselves scarce, Sire."

"I see. For future reference, I am very fond of children. I have a niece, an adopted ten-year-old son and now, my own daughter who is just two years old. So do not feel you have to shield me from them unless, of course, we are discussing state matters."

Standing in front of the fire, towering above them in his long wolfskin cloak, the High Lord did not seem at all the sort of person to enjoy the company of children, but Clive bowed and with a glance at Maud, suggested, "Perhaps you would like to see them before they go to bed?"

"No, tomorrow will be soon enough." Tarkyn's gaze travelled from Maud to Sheldrake then settled back on Maud, rather to Sheldrake's chagrin. "I must see King Gavin tomorrow, Lady Maud. It would be discourteous to be in his kingdom without making myself known. From what I hear, I believe you can arrange that." Sheldrake was a little mollified when Tarkyn then turned to him. "And I believe you and I hold similar roles, Lord Sheldrake, at least in terms of being the centre of our country's intelligence network. Your role, of course, is not so widely known as my own. Lady Maud, as I understand it, decides what the King needs to know and the King makes the final decisions under advisement from her... and you. Is that about right?"

"It is," said Sheldrake shortly, not liking a foreigner being so clear about Carrador's secret power structure.

Tarkyn smiled. "Whereas I perform both your roles and leave the decision-making to my sister, Queen Navira and her Prince Consort Danton, who happens to be my best friend."

"But you have the power to overturn their decisions if you feel the need to. Correct?" asked Sheldrake.

Now it was Tarkyn's turn to frown. "Yes, I do, but I am hoping the need will never arise. If, through my network, I discover some aspect of Eskuzor's functioning that worries me, I make them aware of it and its implications. We discuss it and then I leave them to work out what they want to do about it. If it remains unresolved, I repeat the process. Our current monarch is both clever and well-intentioned. So, I do not anticipate the need to pull rank." Suddenly he grinned. "But it is a great comfort to me that I have the option."

A chuckle, quickly suppressed, came from Jackson standing beside him at the fire.

Tarkyn looked around at him quizzically. "I'm glad you find me amusing, Jackson."

Jackson was not sure whether this was sarcastic or not. "Sorry, Sire. It's just... most people are comforted by a hot toddy or a grandson who visits them, not by the power of veto over a queen. Just a bit different, Sire, that's all."

Tarkyn raised his eyebrows then, to his aide-de-camp's relief, laughed. "Yes. It is a bit, isn't it?"

"And can I just say, Sire, that I understand exactly why you think it's a comfort? You had to work so hard with so few people behind you to prevent the war between your brothers. It is also a comfort to us that you will be there through the next several generations to protect us. The whole nation regards you in the highest esteem, almost reverence, for what you did to stabilise our country." He smiled warmly at his liege. "As do I."

Much to Maud and Sheldrake's amusement, Tarkyn turned a delicate shade of pink and harrumphed. "Thank you, Jackson."

Partly to rescue Tarkyn from his embarrassment, Sheldrake frowned and asked, "Through several generations?"

Tarkyn nodded, relieved to move the conversation on. "I'm afraid so. Were you aware that I am a guardian of the forest, once known as the Guardian of Eskuzor in the time when forests covered the whole country? It means, among other things, that I will live for three or four hundred years, over-seeing the monarchy and wellbeing of Eskuzor." He gave a grimace. "Not actually something I am looking forward to; seeing all my friends and family die around me while I live on."

"How old are you now?" asked Maud.

"Twenty-three."

She frowned with worry. "Hmm. That is tough. People yearn for longevity but... Hmm."

Luckily Clive arrived, carrying a tray which bore the best silver tea set, a brandy decanter and a couple of glasses.

"Ah, good," said Tarkyn, dispelling the morose silence. "You can take my cloak while you are here. I am well and truly warm now."

"Ah, good," said Maud at the same time. "I think Lord Tarkyn needs a cup of tea." She smiled warmly at Tarkyn. "And when you are ready, we will explain our particular need for border security."

13

The next morning, while Sheldrake and Maud slept on, the High Lord broke with his usual practice and rose with the dawn. He dressed quickly, then wrote a note which he slipped under the door of his aide-de-camp before making his way downstairs and across to the practice yard behind the stables.

Stefan came out of the shed bearing an armful of wooden swords in preparation for the morning's practice. He stopped in surprise as he saw a tall stranger leaning with his elbows on the top rail of the newly constructed post and rail fence that surrounded their little arena. The stranger was watching him intently.

"Hello," said Stefan cheerily. "You're new. I haven't seen you before." He put down the wooden swords in a pile just outside the arena, but when he straightened, he was frowning. "Now, just a minute. Are you this High Lord that Argyve said he might be able to recruit?"

Tarkyn suppressed a grin at the man's casual disregard of rank and merely nodded. "I am."

"Uh. Hmm." Stefan produced a low bow but was already talking as he straightened. "How do you do? You got here quickly. You're an early riser, aren't you? Unusual in a nobleman. Were you wanting to join in with our practice?"

Tarkyn smiled. "I am a prince of the royal house of Tamadil, not simply a nobleman, but you are right; I am not by nature an early riser. Today I made the effort, so that I could see you before leaving to meet your king this morning."

"Well, I'm sure I should feel honoured by your more than noble effort," responded Stefan with a cheeky chuckle, "except that I have no idea why you would want to see me. I have won many tournaments, but I doubt my reputation has passed the borders of Carrador."

Tarkyn chuckled. "I, too, am a tournament champion and I agree. I doubt my reputation has passed the borders of Carrador, at least not in that capacity."

Stefan's interest quickened. "Really? What's your favourite event? Mine is archery. Not too keen on wrestling."

"I'm afraid mine is the magical event: shafts and shields of power."

"Oh, I see. Fascinating! You might be able to spar or train with Sheldrake then."

"Perhaps, but that is not why I am here." Tarkyn shifted his weight. "I understand that your family owns an inn deep in the Great Forest. I would like to stay at this inn with my new aide-de-camp, Jackson, and you. I need to investigate some aspects of the forest, partly in pursuit of your king's wish to better secure your borders, but also for reasons of my own. I believe you know the forest like few others."

"Stars above! You get straight to the point, don't you?" Stefan began to sort through the swords, leaning them against the middle railing in order of size. Once he had lined them up, he looked up. "I would be happy to accompany you, but I have been assigned to Lord Sheldrake's household, specifically to protect and equip them against possible attack."

"If I particularly requested you, the King could provide a stand-in for the time you are gone, couldn't he?"

Stefan scratched his head. "Yes, I suppose so, although I don't want my new position here jeopardized. I really like it here and the work is important. Just a minute." Stefan disappeared into the shed and returned with an armful of bows, which he dumped at a spot fifty yards from a target painted on the wall of the barn.

Tarkyn watched while he sorted them by size before saying, "I can make sure your position is secure. I am, after all, conferring a favour on your king by assisting him."

"There are other arms men with knowledge of the forests," said Stefan slowly. He straightened to look the High Lord in the eye, "but somehow I don't think you want them, do you?" Before Tarkyn could reply, he continued, "Lord Argyve told you about me in his letter, didn't he?" He shook his head. "Something odd is going on here. Lord Argyve couldn't take his eyes off me when we first met. He settled down after a while, but now he's written about me to someone from another land. This doesn't feel right."

"He was surprised to see someone with green eyes," said Tarkyn.

Stefan put his hands on his hips and cocked his head. "Really? And did he mention Jayhan's even more astonishing eye colour?"

Tarkyn stared at him for a long minute, his amber eyes gleaming in the first rays of the sun as it rose between the trees. Finally, he lifted his weight off his elbows and straightened up, letting out a long sigh. "No, he didn't. Of course, he has known Jayhan for some time, so his eyes are not novel to him whereas yours are, but..." Tarkyn shrugged. "I am hopeless at prevaricating, so I won't lie to you. You present a conundrum to Lord Argyve and to me, but until I know more, I can't tell you why. However," he added with a lop-sided smile, "I will tell you that, more than anything else, it was concern for your welfare that made me accede to Argyve's request for me to come to Carrador... So, will you come?"

Stefan puffed out his cheeks and blew out a long breath. "Well, now I really do feel honoured, even if I don't understand what is going on. The fact that you have put in so much effort on my behalf demands respect. I will come with you."

14

To Tarkyn's irritation but not surprise, King Gavin insisted on a formal welcome the following day, followed by a long, tedious luncheon peopled by every person of power and influence who could be mustered on such short notice. Jackson had proved himself to be an invaluable aide-de-camp by procuring formal attire in deep blue for the High Lord, which he presented with a proud smile, halfway through the morning.

"Thank you, Jackson," said Tarkyn, "you are a wonder."

"Lady Maud is the wonder. I just enlisted her help." Jackson gave a worried frown. "I don't know much about these things, but aren't you supposed to wear a sash and a star-shaped brooch to show your rank, if it's formal?"

Tarkyn reached into his pocket and casually produced a rather crumpled deep blue sash bordered with a thin line of red from his pocket. He rummaged around deeper in the pocket until he withdrew a small black velvet bag. From this, he produced a diamond-studded silver star as big as Jackson's palm. An indigo sapphire nestled in its centre. Jackson just stared, his mouth hanging open.

"Get this ironed for me, would you?" said Tarkyn, smiling at his reaction. "This is the sash and Order of Tamadil. I keep them with me always, but rarely wear them. They really wouldn't look right on my light brown forest garb."

Jackson recovered himself enough to produce a weak chuckle. "No, Sire, I'm sure they wouldn't. Not to mention the fact that the star is likely to get snagged in the undergrowth."

"Exactly." Tarkyn grinned and motioned him away.

A transformed Tarkyn, wearing the deep blue frock coat and breeches in the style currently favoured by Carradorian nobility, with the sash and Order of Tamadil worn across his white shirt proclaiming his royal status, his long black hair confined by an ebony clip at the base of his neck, exited the carriage and trod up the steps of the palace to be greeted by King Gavin, who was wearing the red and gold uniform of Commander of the Carradorian armed forces.

Tarkyn stopped one step below Gavin where he could meet the monarch eye to eye. Tarkyn held out his right arm and they grasped each other's arms in greeting, making it clear that they held equal status. A formal round of introductions and the luncheon followed, so that it was not until mid-afternoon that Tarkyn found himself alone with the King in his study over-looking the rear gardens of the palace.

Gavin threw himself into an armchair and gestured to Tarkyn to do likewise. "Thank goodness that is all over. I'm sorry I put you through it, but too many noses would have been out of joint if people found out you'd been here without invitations being issued. Thank you for coming to assist us." He took a deep breath and smiled before continuing more slowly. "So, now perhaps you can tell me how and why you plan to help us secure our borders within the forests."

"Firstly, because your problem is also our problem. Many of these Kimoran refugees are cutting through your forests and travelling further into Eskuzor." The High Lord leaned forward as he spoke. "Now, we are willing to accept refugees, but we are not willing to allow in members of the Kimoran specialist forces who are acting without our official sanction. In fact, even if they sought it, I doubt we would give it. Once refugees cross into Eskuzor, it is up to our authorities to judge their right to stay. If Kimora is seeking a particular criminal, their courts have to file an extradition request, which we will consider on its merits."

"I agree entirely," said Gavin. "I consider the presence of Kimoran armed forces within my borders as tantamount to a declaration of war, especially when I have already made my objections known to the Kimoran queen." He shrugged. "But I do not want a war. I value my people more than that. But I must find a way to stop the infiltration of these foreign troops."

Tarkyn leaned back and smiled. "My brothers were willing to throw lives away for their own ends, but I have never seen Eskuzor's people as tools to use to resolve conflict. I am very glad you feel the same way."

Gavin stood up and offered Tarkyn a drink. When he had poured a brandy for himself and a white wine for Tarkyn, he resumed his seat. "I understand from Maud that Lord Argyve has said you have a way of stopping these people infiltrating your kingdom through your forests. Is that so?"

Tarkyn nodded. "Absolutely. We seek out and deport or imprison any Kimoran military personnel who cross our borders."

"How?"

"Ah. Now this is where it becomes tricky. Very tricky." Tarkyn took a sip of wine, mainly to give Gavin time to prepare himself to face a possible issue. "I can give you two choices.

Either I attempt to implement measures to keep you notified of infiltrators passing through your forests, but don't tell you how..."

"Or..."

"Or you must swear an oath of secrecy and non-intervention. If you do this, I will tell you all."

Gavin's eyes narrowed.

"Either way," said Tarkyn, "I will try to help you if you let me."

"What is your other reason for offering your assistance? You did say, 'Firstly.'"

Tarkyn smiled. "So I did. Unfortunately, the second reason requires your oath before I can divulge it. However, I can give you *my* oath that it is not to your nation's detriment."

Gavin sprang to his feet and began to pace. "I have no problem with swearing secrecy. After all, my position is fraught with state secrets. But swearing not to intervene in something within my borders..." He shook his head. "How can I swear that, when I might need to intervene to support people or save lives?"

Tarkyn looked at him and scratched his ear as he tried to find a way through. "My father, King Markazon, was generally a good king. He tried to be just, he never led our people to war and he did not tax them excessively. But he was autocratic, and unswerving in his belief that all his subjects owed him unquestioning loyalty and obedience."

"Yes? I hope that I, too, fit that description," said Gavin, a note of hauteur entering his voice.

Tarkyn smiled up at him. "You do, I suppose, but you are not fearsome like my father was. Your people are relaxed around you in a way my father's people never were. And all credit to you." He raised his glass in acknowledgement before taking a sip of his wine. "Anyway, there was one group of independent but innocuous people to whom my father did something very wrong. He forced their allegiance by making them swear an oath, bound by sorcery to the wellbeing of their... home area. If any of them were disloyal or disobedient, the homes and livelihood of all of them would be destroyed."

Gavin raised his eyebrows and let out a whistle. "That was excessive. Why was he so harsh in that instance?"

"Because they had been dwelling within his kingdom without his knowledge and without having given their allegiance."

"Still harsh, I think." Gavin sat down again and picked up his glass. "Surely that would have made them feel resentful, not loyal."

Tarkyn chuckled. "Yes, very resentful. I had to bear the brunt of it."

"So, in your convoluted way, are you saying that I have a group of people living in my kingdom who have not acknowledged my sovereignty?" The Carradorian King was no fool. "And," he added, thinking back to the beginning of their conversation, "you don't want me to interfere with them or demand their fealty."

Tarkyn gave a relieved smile "Yes. And to never let others know of their existence, if indeed they do exist."

Gavin blinked. "*If* they exist?"

"Yes. They exist in Eskuzor but I don't know about Carrador, except for one small, compelling piece of evidence that they do. Before I tell you any more, will you at least swear to keep their existence secret, in both our countries?"

Gavin nodded decisively. "I give you my oath to keep these people's existence secret and I can also assure you that I will not force sorcery on them."

Tarkyn let out a long breath, "They are known as the wood-folk and live deep within the forests of Eskuzor. It is they who give us early warning of infiltration by undesirables from Kimora. Until sixteen years ago, no one of non-woodfolk blood knew of their existence. Even now, very few sorcerers know of their existence, even though they relay messages throughout the kingdom and guard our forested borders."

"How extraordinary. And you say they are innocuous? Does that mean they are weak, or unwarlike?"

Tarkyn shook his head. "Oh, they are by no means weak. It was they who helped me to stymie a small army without killing anyone and eventually to prevent civil war. They are quick, deadly, virtually invisible and skilled far beyond your own troops." Tarkyn laughed. "Don't look so worried! Given a choice, they will melt away rather than hurt anyone."

The little frown of worry on Gavin's forehead did not dissipate. "So what was your second reason?"

"I care very deeply for the woodfolk. I have been made an honorary member of their nation and, after a rough beginning, they have accepted me as their liege lord." Tarkyn smiled warmly. "I am married to a feisty woodwoman. When I say feisty, I mean she hunts, is rostered onto guard duty, uses a bow and arrow and slingshot as well as any woodman, as do all woodwomen."

"Hmm. There go my matrimonial plans for my younger sister," said Gavin regretfully, but with a twinkle in his grey eyes.

Tarkyn grinned. "I'm afraid so. Few people know I am married because of the secrecy surrounding the woodfolk."

"Ah. Of course."

"My two-year-old daughter is half woodfolk and so is my ten-year-old ward. But that is beside the point. What is to the point is the fact that all woodfolk are generally a little shorter than us, have green eyes and light brown hair. No other people that I know of have green eyes."

Gavin's eyes widened. "Stefan! Lord Argyve wrote to you of Stefan."

"You are very quick. It is a pleasure talking to you."

"Does Stefan know?"

Tarkyn shook his head. "I can't say for sure because Carradorian woodfolk, if they exist, may behave quite differently from those in Eskuzor. However, since you clearly know of only one person with green eyes, I would say they also maintain the secrecy of their existence and so presumably he has no idea who he is."

"Huh! No wonder you were intrigued enough to come here. Stefan's presence amongst men and sorcerers sounds like a complete anomaly." Gavin gave a little smile. "You know, of course, that he is by far the best archer we have ever had."

"He did mention he had won several tournaments. It just provides more evidence that he is indeed a woodman."

"So, your plan?"

"Hazy at best. Somehow, I have to make contact with a nation of woodfolk who do not wish to be known and then enlist their aid on your behalf." Tarkyn hesitated. "I have asked several of my woodfolk to meet me in your Great Forest. I hope you don't mind. But I will need all the help I can get."

"They are welcome. In fact, I would like to meet them at some stage, if that is at all possible."

"And of course, I will need Stefan. Could you replace him temporarily, but only temporarily? He is worried about losing his new position."

"Anything else?" asked the king, his tone becoming dry.

Tarkyn laughed disarmingly. "Not at the moment, thank you. The woodfolk are forever berating me for being too autocratic, so I will not take it in bad part if you do the same."

15

The day after Tarkyn's meeting with the King, the gate to Batian House opened again and the family coach, driven by Leon, rolled out, headed for the Royal Palace in Highkington. It was accompanied by a small company of the King's Guard which had been provided to ensure Sasha's safety in the absence of her parents and the arms master.

Inside, Sasha, wearing a teal blue gown trimmed in pale orange, sat opposite Jayhan, who was wearing his best breeches and jacket. Neither of them looked at ease.

Sasha pushed back an unruly stand of hair and sighed. "I know I need to go to the palace and learn all this etiquette stuff, but I really don't want to."

"Huh! You reckon you've got problems. Everyone's going to stare at my eyes."

Sasha laughed, not unkindly. "No, they're not. You and your eyes are famous now, after you received that award."

"Exactly."

She leant over and dug him in the ribs. "Stop being a grumpy-boots. The King did the best he could to make everyone admire your eyes instead of being spooked by them. They'll get used to them." She gave a discontented huff. "At least you know how to act at court. You've been going there all your life."

"Not often. Mostly Mum and Dad leave me at home when they go." He shrugged. "But I guess I know it better than you."

"I'm glad Maud finally let you come too. It will be much better with you there."

"And we'll see Jon and maybe Electra."

Sasha nodded. "And I bet the Royal Stables are worth a visit."

Suddenly Jayhan's bad humour dissipated and he grinned. "If you're allowed near them in your fancy dresses."

"Just watch me." Sasha leaned forward so she could watch the Royal Guards riding beside them. After a few minutes, she gave a gusty sigh. "I wish I could be a Royal Guard. Look at those beautiful saddlecloths! All hand-stitched. And the saddles. Look at the quality of the leather."

"Not to mention the horses," said Jayhan dryly.

"Of course, the horses." She crossed her arms, straight away on the defensive. "Not as good as our horses, obviously."

Jayhan chuckled.

Suddenly, Sasha's attention was caught by a scruffy man who looked somehow familiar, skulking on the far side of the road. She craned her neck for a better look, but her view was blocked by the guards' horses. She turned to Jayhan. "I saw someone watching us."

Jayhan was not impressed. "Of course you did. Lots of people will be watching us go past with all these Guards around us. I'd be watching if I were out there."

"Hmm. No. Not the same. This man ducked into an alley as we came closer."

Jayhan chewed on his lip for a moment as he thought.

"Ducked? Didn't just happen to be going that way?" When Sasha looked ready to hit him, he threw up his hands. "Okay. Okay. Just checking." He glanced up at the ceiling of the carriage. "Dad taps the ceiling with his cane if he thinks someone is following." He grimaced. "But I don't really want to make a fuss in front of all these guards. Do you think the person was following us? We're going slowly enough for someone to follow on foot if they run a bit."

Sasha shook her head. "I have no idea. I only caught a glimpse of him."

"Probably nothing."

"Probably."

Neither of them sounded convinced.

After a minute Jayhan suggested, "We'll tell Leon when we get there, just in case."

Sasha nodded. "Yeah, good idea."

But as the journey progressed, many people and houses of interest caught their interest and by the time they drew up at the steps of the palace, they were so preoccupied with preparing themselves to face the stares and expectations that they had forgotten all about it.

They looked out to see two rows of liveried servants lining the steps up to the great doors at the top. Sasha's heart thumped hard. She had not received this treatment last time when she had visited the king with her brother. Clearly, they were being given a formal welcome.

To their relief, Jon came running down the stairs to greet them, just as the door to the carriage was opened by a poker-faced, liveried footman. Sasha politely inclined her head, smiled her thanks and stepped forward primly into the waiting arms of her brother who grabbed her and twirled her around, lifting her feet off the ground and bringing a reluctant grin to her face.

"Jon!" she said repressively, as she was returned to earth. "I am supposed to be learning to be dignified."

Seeing Jayhan standing to one side, trying not to look envious, Jon ignored her and took hold of him, twirling him around in the air until he shrieked with laughter.

"Come on," said Jon, holding out a hand to each of them.

"What will all these servants think of us?" whispered Sasha, as they proceeded up the stairs between the two rows of expressionless servants.

"If they are kind," said Jon in a voice loud enough to be heard by the staff, "they will be pleased that you have been given a warm welcome. If they are judgemental, they are not worth worrying about. They are people, just like us." He smiled. "Remember? I have been a footman for years. I know what I am talking about."

Jayhan, who was not as overwhelmed as Sasha, noticed barely suppressed smiles on the faces of several people they passed.

At the top of the stairs, however, stood the King's stern steward, dressed in black bombazine, her hands linked on her stomach. She was not smiling.

Although the children quailed inwardly, she had no effect on Jon, who smiled sunnily at her. "Good afternoon, Josie. You have met Lady Natasha before, I believe," he said, carefully using Sasha's new pseudonym, "but have you met Lord Jayhan? He has been here several times with his parents and, of course, for the presentation of his Star of Courage, but I'm not sure whether your paths have crossed."

Josie bosom heaved. "Lord Johnson," she began, "You know my views on unruly children."

Jon raised his eyebrows. "Actually, I don't, but I can imagine." He shrugged. "However, I struggle to see their relevance at the moment." Josie pursed her lips and her face darkened but before she could say anything further, Jon asked, "So, are you here to usher the children to their rooms or to see Gavin? He will be delighted to hear how welcoming you have been to his little cousin and her friend."

Josie glared at him for several long seconds. "You are very cheeky, young man. We clearly have different views on what constitutes a welcome. I have spent most of the morning making sure the children's rooms are warm, comfortable and, I hope, welcoming for their arrival. And what have you done?"

Jon grinned. "Nothing at all. Just run down the steps and hugged them."

"Good," she said tartly. "So between us, we have covered everything."

Jon gave a slight bow. "I stand corrected, ma'am."

Josie quirked an eyebrow at him, the faintest hint of a smile on her lips, before whirling and beckoning with her finger for them to follow. "This way, children."

Jayhan's room opened off the lounge room of his parents' apartment and was much as he had last seen it, although there were biscuits and a mug of lemonade waiting for him in the dining room and a cheery fire in his bedroom. Once he had had a cursory look around and fiddled with a few of his toys, they continued on to inspect Sasha's new room.

Sasha approached with trepidation. All the way to the palace, she had been envisaging swathes of pink and white lace, which would make her feel ill at ease and nauseous. Instead, as she walked past Josie through the doorway, she found herself in a room painted oyster grey with stained wood trim, hung with paintings of horses. Her bed covers were in soft but warm autumn colours. The room was large; larger than the kitchen at Batian House and, besides the three-quarter-sized bed, contained a dressing table, a small bookcase, two armchairs and a round table with four chairs. A doorway that Sasha had not yet noticed, led to a walk-in wardrobe and a private bathroom.

Sasha gasped in wonder and turned to Josie, a great smile blooming on her face. "Oh, thank you so much. This is..." Tears sprang to her eyes. "Oh, it's just what I always... so much more than I've ever wanted. It's wonderful."

She scanned the books, noting that they ranged from stories to heavy tomes of heraldry, history and court etiquette. Aware that Jon and Jayhan were waiting for her, she dragged her eyes away, then noticed the huge bunch of wildflowers in a large vase on the dressing table and a tray loaded with milk and cookies that waited for her on the table. In a daze, she crossed to the window and found herself looking out over the lake in the back garden.

For a minute she stood there trying to fight the tears that were threatening to overwhelm her. With a supreme effort, she swallowed and managed to say thickly, "Look, Jayhan. Come here. You can see the swan's nest from up here."

Jayhan, who was no fool, walked up next to her and casually put his arm around her waist. She gave a watery giggle and murmured, "I thought you weren't huggy."

"I'm not usually," he said gruffly. "Just sometimes."

In the doorway, Jon smiled down at Josie, who was watching them with an air of satisfaction. "Well done, Josie. Well done."

16

Two days later, Tarkyn, Jackson, Stefan and Sheldrake rode out early from Batian House towards the Great Forest. Maud had insisted they wait long enough to ensure that no panic-stricken messages were being sent home from the palace.

Jackson rode a strong but well-mannered chestnut gelding who had been named Bosco for reasons no one could remember. Stefan was riding Slinky, a tall, narrow-backed mare whose ebony coat gleamed in the sunlight, while Tarkyn had been mounted on the frisky young Clydesdale, Flurry. Even though her main work would be as a plough horse, Beth thought Flurry was best suited to Tarkyn's weight and wanted her to get used to being ridden. She had been training her as a saddle horse around the farm, with Jon in mind as her rider, but this was Flurry's first foray further afield. Beth had insisted that Tarkyn spend an hour with her while she watched him critically to check that he was up to the task of riding her.

To Stefan's private amusement, Sheldrake was mounted on Maisy.

The morning was crisp and clear, and dew still glittered on the roadside grasses. Few travellers were out and about this early, but a steady trickle of carts laden for market passed them from the opposite direction, heading towards Highkington. As the road narrowed over a one-lane bridge, they found their way blocked by an old woman trying to persuade her mule to step onto the rickety boards of the bridge on the far side of the stream.

Realising she was holding up a prestigious group of riders, the old lady became flustered and consequently more aggressive with her mule, which in turn became frightened, confused and even more stubborn.

While the others waited, Tarkyn dismounted and led his huge draught horse onto the bridge. As he approached the old woman, she seemed to calm down, as did the mule. He left Flurry in the middle of the bridge, where she stood quietly, waiting for him. Then he approached the mule, stroked its neck reassuringly and led it, unresisting, onto the rickety bridge. Once the mule and cart were both moving across the bridge, Tarkyn walked ahead of them to Flurry, mounted and wheeled her, riding back to wait with the others, while the old woman completed her crossing.

Sheldrake nodded his appreciation. "Beth will be very impressed to hear how well Flurry behaved. You certainly have a way with her."

"Thanks." Tarkyn smiled. "But I am a forest guardian, after all."

Because he was concentrating on making sure that Maisy found her way safely across the loose boards, Sheldrake didn't really take in what Tarkyn had said and so did not pursue it.

Once across the bridge, Tarkyn rode beside Sheldrake, exchanging desultory comments on the scenery they passed, and listening while Sheldrake explained the route they were taking and the breadth and direction of the border within the great Forest.

Eventually Tarkyn held up his hand. "Much as I would like to gain an appreciation of the area, I have absolutely no sense of direction so you will need to make sure Jackson understands everything we need to know as well, so he can haul me back if we head off in the wrong direction."

Sheldrake chuckled. "Right. I'll remember that."

Houses soon gave way to fields and the quality of the road deteriorated as they drew further away from the city. Gravel, sharp stones and runnels across the road made the horses pick their way more slowly.

"I don't remember the road being so bad when we came through here a few weeks ago," muttered Sheldrake.

"I think heavy rain last week washed away the surface, sir," suggested Stefan.

Sheldrake smiled. "We'll have to let Jon know. He's the new Minister for Transport. Happily, it is no longer my problem."

Suddenly, Tarkyn jerked upright as though he had been hit. Even as he drew Flurry up, his hands not touching the reins, Sheldrake had thrown a translucent lilac dome of protection over all four horses and riders.

"Thanks," said Tarkyn. "But I was not reacting to danger. As far as I know, there is none." He swung down from the saddle. "Keep your horse still, Jackson," he ordered, walking over to him.

"What's wrong?" Jackson glanced around, checking for possible hazards.

"Nothing drastic," Tarkyn assured him, "I just need to check your horse's hooves. He hurt his hind right hoof on a sharp stone back there and I think it may have become lodged. Stay mounted. I'll just check."

Watched by a rather bemused Jackson, Tarkyn walked behind Bosco and lifted his hoof. Sure enough, a sharp stone was jammed between the frog and the shoe, digging into the sole of the hoof. Tarkyn pulled out his knife and flicked away the offending rock. The sole below was red and, to Tarkyn's forest guardian senses, radiating pain.

"Just sit still a minute," he instructed Jackson. "I need to heal him."

Tarkyn focused inside himself, drew forth his *esse* and sent his power into the horse. After a long minute, he let go of the hoof and straightened. He gave the gelding a pat on the rump and returned to his own horse.

As he mounted, Sheldrake's eyes were alight with curiosity. "What just happened? What did you do?"

Tarkyn smiled. "I told you before, I'm a forest guardian. I pick up the feelings of people and animals, also the mental images of horses, other animals and some people. So when Jackson's gelding hit that stone, I felt his wave of pain. I sent him a query; no words, I'm afraid, just images and impressions. He showed me that his hoof was hurt." He shrugged. "So then I healed it straight away before it could get any worse and send the horse lame."

"Is that how you handled that mule on the bridge?"

"It is. I sent out waves of calm and reassurance to the woman and the mule. Then I rode Flurry onto the bridge to show the mule that it would hold his weight. Once the mule was calm, I could send it images of the cart and itself safely crossing the bridge." Tarkyn grinned. "By the way, Flurry tells me that Maisy is your wife... using images, of course."

Sheldrake and Stefan both laughed, while Jackson frowned in confusion. "Really? What? Maisy is really Lady Maud?"

Maisy sashayed sideways then did a little buck,

"She's embarrassed," explained Tarkyn kindly. "Yes, this

lovely little mare is Lady Maud... but you mustn't tell other people, Jackson. Closely kept secret apparently."

Soon after the road entered the forest, Sheldrake swapped places with Stefan so that he could re-explain the geography and terrain of the Great Forest to Jackson, leaving Stefan to ride beside Tarkyn.

For a time they rode in silence; the only sounds the creaking of their saddles, the occasional chirruping of birds hidden in the bushes along verge of the road and the indecipherable voices of Sheldrake and Jackson behind them.

Stefan caught Tarkyn glancing sideways at him a couple of times. On the third time he demanded, "What?"

Tarkyn gave a sheepish grin. "I was wondering whether you might be able to receive my mind-images. Only a few people can, and you may be one of them."

Stefan's eyes narrowed as he thought about it. Eventually he asked, "Why me? Why not Lord Sheldrake? He's a trained mage, after all."

"It is not to do with magical power. No sorcerer I know of, other than me, has the ability to send and receive mind messages."

"Aha. This has something to do with that conundrum I apparently present to you and Lord Argyve, doesn't it?"

Tarkyn nodded. "I could try to push into your thoughts without your permission but firstly that would be bad manners and secondly, it might confuse or even frighten you if you didn't know what was happening. So I won't do that." He looked hopefully at Stefan. "But would you like to try?"

Stefan chuckled. "How could I resist such an entreaty? Besides, it will help to pass the time and may be interesting. Go on then."

"Maybe I'll tell you a bit about it first." As he spoke, Tarkyn was scanning the sky and trees for a bird he might be able to connect with. "If you have this ability, you can receive and send mental images of memories, ideas, what you are currently seeing and mental images from a third party."

"What do you mean, from a third party?"

For a moment, Tarkyn was a little distracted as he had just spotted a large white parrot perched high in a gum tree ahead of them on their left. "Hmm? Oh, I mean that I could connect with another person or a bird or animal then share their images with you." He pointed up into the tree. "What is that bird? We don't have them in Eskuzor."

Stefan squinted up into the tree. "That? That is a sulphured-crested cockatoo. Wait 'til it squawks. They have the most raucous cries. They are cheeky and very smart. I love them."

"Do you?" Tarkyn smiled. "Perhaps we could start with it then. I will connect with the bird, then try to connect you to its images. What do you think?"

"Yeah. Great. That would be wonderful if you could do it." Stefan grinned with the excitement of a little child. "Though I only half know what you're talking about."

"Hold onto your pommel... and it might help if you focus on the bird. I'm not sure."

"I can ride, you know," said Stefan defensively. "I don't need to hold onto the pommel if the horse becomes skittish."

"Of course you don't. It's to make sure you don't fall off while the horse is walking quietly." Tarkyn shrugged. "Up to you. But if you fall off, don't say I didn't warn you."

Stefan frowned but on balance, decided to follow Tarkyn's advice. Once he had overcome his pride enough to take a firm grip on the pommel, he focused his attention on the sulphur-crested cockatoo, aware at the same time of Tarkyn riding beside him, outwardly appearing to do nothing.

The first sign of anything unusual was the cockatoo shrieking, raising its crest and bobbing its head up and down. It pranced up and down the branch, bobbing its head and spreading its wings. Beside Stefan, Tarkyn laughed. "I can see why you like them. This one is a real character, isn't she?" For a minute he said nothing, then, "Right. Now I am going to try to connect to you."

One moment, Stefan was watching the cockatoo in the tree, with his peripheral vision on the road and Tarkyn. The next moment, he was looking down at four horsemen far below him on the road. With a sickening lurch, he travelled with the bird as she took off and began to swerve and sway her way down until she landed on a short, stunted tree fifty yards in front of the horsemen, studying them with intense curiosity. He felt her raise her crest and shriek in greeting, bobbing along the small branch, clearly excited by the connection she felt with the tall man on the huge horse. After a little dance, she took off once more and came swooping in, to land on Tarkyn's head. There she bobbed up and down a couple more times, shrieking and flapping her wings, blithely digging her claws into Tarkyn's scalp.

"Enough!" said Tarkyn firmly, breaking the connection to Stefan while at the same time reaching up to stroke the over-excited cocky. He sent out waves of calm and gratitude to the cocky, who hopped onto his hand and rode it down as he brought it to rest on the saddle before him. She raised her crest a few more times but refrained from shrieking or bobbing, just making little comfortable grinding sounds with her beak.

Tarkyn turned to find Stefan looking dazed and a little green, his knuckles white from his hands clenching the pommel. "Looks like you can receive mind images then," he said, then peered at him in concern. "Are you all right? It is a shock for people who are familiar with mind images when they first look through the eyes of a bird, now I think about it.

Hmm. Perhaps I should have started with something stationary."

"Maybe," croaked Stefan. He prised his fingers from the pommel, attempted a grin which went sadly crooked, and blinked. He wiped his hand across his face and took a deep breath. "That was absolutely amazing but very disconcerting... but amazing. Phew. I'm glad I held onto the pommel. No way could I have kept my balance otherwise."

Tarkyn chuckled. "I remember showing something similar to a group of people without warning them; half of them fell over."

Just then Sheldrake and Jackson came trotting up and stopped either side of them.

"What's going on?" asked Sheldrake, frowning. "You asked that cockatoo to come down, didn't you, with your forest guardian skills? And why is Stefan looking like a stunned mullet?"

"Careful," murmured Tarkyn, gently stroking the cocky's head. "You'll frighten our little friend here. She has been very brave to come down amongst us, as it is."

Jackson grinned. "She has, hasn't she? What a cutie." He manoeuvred his horse around behind Tarkyn's, bringing Bosco up beside Stefan. He leaned across to Stefan, handing him his waterbag. "Here. Drink this. You look like you've seen a ghost."

Stefan shot him a grateful glance as he accepted the waterbag. He didn't feel he had the coordination at the moment to reach his own waterbag, tied behind him with his saddlebags. After a long draft, he wiped his mouth, re-corked the waterbag and handed it back. "Thanks."

Jackson just nodded, not pressing Stefan to answer any questions, and retied his waterbag to his saddle.

When he was sure the cockatoo was happy where she was, Tarkyn answered Sheldrake's question. "I shared images with this bird and then connected with Stefan to see whether he could receive mind images. It turns out he can. He is looking sickly because his mind followed the cocky on her zig-zaggy course down," he chuckled, "and he's not used to flying."

"Really?" Sheldrake was agog with interest. "Do you think I could do it too?" A restive stamp from Maisy beneath him reminded him of his obligation to his staff member, making him add, "How are you, Stefan? Should we rest for a while, do you think?"

Stefan had recovered enough to appreciate the interaction between Sheldrake and Maud. He smiled and shook his head. "No. I am happy to sit quietly on Slinky for a while. I don't mind whether we're stationary or moving."

Tarkyn gave the cockatoo a final stroke and sent her on her way before saying, "I can try. Do you want to try too, Jackson?"

Jackson shrugged, trying to look nonchalant. "It could be interesting."

"Right. I will try to connect with your minds." Tarkyn glanced at Stefan and raised his eyebrows slightly in a conspiratorial sign that he thought this would be a waste of time. "If I do, I will replay the cockatoo's mind-images of her flight down into that little tree over there. Just close your eyes and think about joining your thoughts to mine."

After several minutes of effort, neither Sheldrake nor Jackson received any mind images. Eventually, Tarkyn gave up. "No. I'm sorry. I did try but I can't connect with either of you. I didn't really think I would be able to, but I did try." He smiled ruefully. "I'm afraid there is a good chance you will pick up on some of my emotions whether I want you to or not, but not images, apparently." He gathered his reins and urged Flurry forward. "Let's move on, shall we?" Seeing Sheldrake's crest-fallen expression, he added, "It is a very rare gift. If you like, I will try again later once we have arrived at the inn, but it is unlikely to work."

Sheldrake brought Maisy alongside Flurry as they resumed their journey. "But you were fairly certain, weren't you, that Stefan would have that gift?"

Tarkyn glanced at him briefly. "Yes."

"But you won't tell me why?"

"Not yet. Not until I tell him why first and I'm not ready to do that yet, either."

Sheldrake gave a grimace of frustration.

Tarkyn laughed. "And I will annoy you further by telling you that I can share images with your wife... at least I can while she is a horse. I haven't tried when she is her human self." He smiled. "I didn't share the bird's images with her in case she fell over and took you with her. Probably would be all right on four legs, but you never know."

To Tarkyn's surprise, this had the effect of engaging Sheldrake's natural curiosity, distracting him from his disappointment. "That's interesting. We'll have to experiment, won't we?"

As they rode further from Highkington, the stream of travellers coming from the Great Forest dwindled and for the rest of the journey, nothing untoward happened. They arrived at the Creeping Vine Inn by mid-afternoon. The inn was a sturdy, two-storey cottage-style building, white-washed under a thatched roof. At the sound of their arrival, a broad-shouldered man a few years older than the younger three travellers walked out of the inn to greet them. His pale skin contrasted with his thick black hair and pale blue eyes. He ran his eyes over them and smiled broadly when he saw Stefan among them.

"Stefan, my man! What a great surprise to see you." He strode up to Stefan's pony, grabbed him bodily and whirled him out of the saddle to stand him on the ground before him. "Dad will be pleased as punch! Who are your friends?"

Stefan, whose head barely cleared his shoulder, slapped him on the back, obviously used to this boisterous treatment. "Hello, you big bear. It's great to see you too." He turned to make the introductions, waving his hand to indicate each of his companions, "This is Prince Tarkyn, High Lord of Eskuzor, Lord Sheldrake whom I believe you have already met, and Jackson, aide-de-camp for Lord Tarkyn." Then he indicated his brother. "And this is Anton, my eldest brother."

"Excellent company you're keeping." Anton put his fingers to his mouth and let forth a loud whistle that brought two younger versions of himself running from the stables. Stefan grinned and hugged each of them in turn before turning to introduce them too. "And this is Javier and this is Marin."

"Pleased to meet you all," said Sheldrake, smiling. "We didn't get a welcome like this last time we came."

Stefan laughed. "You didn't have me with you."

As the other three dismounted, Anton said to his brothers, "Right you two, take their horses, give them a good rub down, feed and water. You can come in and see Stefan as soon as you've finished."

Tarkyn frowned a query at Sheldrake, who gave a conspiratorial little smile and said to the boys, "Maisy loves oats, but if you don't mind, don't tie any of our horses up. They are well behaved and happy to stand calmly in the stalls." He gave a Maisy a cheery pat on the rump before turning to walk inside.

"Fair enough." Marin grinned and took Maisy's and Slinky's reins, clicking his tongue to encourage the horses to follow him, while Javier led the other two.

Tarkyn nodded at Jackson. "Go with them please, unload the horses, take our bags up to our room and meet us in the bar."

Jackson who, like Tarkyn, was concerned for Maud in her horse's guise, obeyed with alacrity.

The travellers entered the inn in order of precedence. As protocol demanded, the lords entered first while Stefan's brother, as host, entered last with his arm firmly around Stefan's shoulders. As soon as they were inside, Anton bellowed, "Hey, Da, look what the cat dragged in."

The rotund innkeeper gave a perfunctory bow to the two lords before surging past them to envelope Stefan in a huge bear hug. The small arms master was almost lost to sight. Shortly, a couple of smothered squawks signalled Stefan's need for air so, with a solid slap to his back, his father let him go and held him out at arms' length to look him over. "Stefan, my son, you haven't grown any, but you're looking fine, very fine."

"Hi, Da. You're looking pretty good yourself. Haven't got any thinner though."

His father roared with laughter. "Cheeky boy! Ah, your mother will be pleased to see you. We haven't seen you these many months, busy as you are in the big city." He gave Stefan a push in the direction of the kitchen and turned to the others of his party.

Stefan gave an embarrassed smile and shrugged at his companions as he made his way through a door behind the bar, but the quickness of his gait belied his apparent reluctance.

The Innkeeper beamed. "Welcome, gents. Any friend of my son's is a friend of mine. Come in, come in and sit down. What can I get you?"

Tarkyn ordered tankards of ale for Sheldrake, Jackson and himself. Jackson re-joined them soon after and once the three of them were settled with the ale in front of them, the innkeeper, whose name turned out to be Ivan, chatted to them for nearly twenty minutes before the demands of other customers called him away. A group of merchants from Kimora, five women and three men, had entered, and they were hungry and thirsty after their long trip while at the bar, a few local foresters had drained their glasses and were waiting patiently for Ivan's return.

Sheldrake swept his eyes across the bar's inhabitants, noting a scruffy young couple who appeared to be celebrating something, various other workers, both male and female, and an unobtrusive woman in the corner, knitting while she sipped her ale. He made no comment but turned instead to Tarkyn. "So here we are, my lord. What is our next move?"

Tarkyn looked pensive. "Hmm. Stefan is well loved by his family, I think. I will need to speak privately with Stefan's parents. It will have to be after the inn has shut for the evening. Can you organise that please, Jackson? Meanwhile, let us have a good dinner and settle into our rooms." Suddenly he grinned. "Sheldrake, I believe your wife is about to join us."

Sheldrake was unperturbed. "I was expecting her sooner or later."

Sure enough, five minutes later, the front door opened and Maud surged in, dressed in her favourite green gown. Jackson jumped up to pull out a chair for her. She smiled graciously and sat down. "I'll have a large tankard of ale too, if you please. I have earned it, I think."

"I'll say," said Jackson appreciatively. "I couldn't walk that far in one day, let alone carrying someone."

Maud laughed. "I couldn't either, in human form."

Jackson signalled and a tall, big-boned woman with dark hair pulled back into a bushy ponytail walked straight over to them and smiled a welcome. "Hello. I'm Marjorie. You're Stefan's friends, aren't you? Welcome. What can I get you?"

"An ale for Maud here, please," replied Tarkyn, smiling in return. "You're Stefan's sister, I take it. You have the same look as Anton, Javier and Marin."

Marjorie frowned. "Big and strong, you mean. Now, don't you go picking on Stefan. He can't help it if he's a bit smaller than the rest of us. He's the deadliest shot this side of the border."

Tarkyn raised his eyebrows in surprise and held his hands up in a placating gesture. "I was casting no aspersions at all. Stefan is clearly a force to be reckoned with."

Marjorie beamed at him. "Yes, he is, isn't he? Sorry. It's just we have been defending him since he was a little 'un, as in *very* little 'un, from the slurs of customers. Kind of comes naturally to jump to his defence."

"But it's all right for you to take a little dig at him."

She waved her hand. "O' course. He's family."

"U-huh. And do you think we'll ever get to see him again?" asked Tarkyn.

Marjorie laughed. "Not unless you really need him. The boys came in from the stables to see him but then that Kimoran lot arrived, so they had to go back out again. And Karl is coming in with supplies on his way through to his own cot. He should be here in half an hour or so. He lives a bit away from us now that he's married. He's set up his own business, you know, selling herbs and plants from the forest. Doing well. And o' course Ma hasn't stopped fussing over Stefan since he got here. We haven't seen him for more than a half a year, you know."

"Right. Thanks. In that case, I think we'll order more ale and dinner, if you please." Tarkyn settled back, preparing for a long but pleasant evening and the strong possibility that he would not get the chance to see Stefan's parents until the following day. In fact, as soon as Marjorie left, he leaned over to Jackson and said, "Don't worry about organising that meeting. I think today is too soon. Some things should not be rushed."

PART III

17

S tefan had remembered himself enough to present himself to Lord Sheldrake, late in the evening and notably worse for wear, to enquire when he might be needed. Sheldrake kindly suggested that lunchtime tomorrow would be soon enough and that he could spend the intervening time with his family.

When Tarkyn arose the next morning for a late breakfast, he found Sheldrake and Jackson waiting for him in the deserted bar of the tavern, drinking coffee. Other customers had already left, either going home the previous night or heading off earlier that morning for their destinations.

"Have you two eaten yet?"

"About two hours ago," responded Sheldrake dryly. "I have been out for a short walk but since we don't know why we are here, we have resorted to drinking coffee until you arrived."

Tarkyn smiled, quite unrepentant. "And where is Maud?"

Sheldrake's eyes shifted. "Oh, around somewhere."

"By which I gather she is currently reconnoitring for you. A very handy asset for your information-gathering toolbox, as long," a slight edge developed in Tarkyn's voice, "as it is not used to gather information about me." Tarkyn said nothing more as he sat down and poured himself a coffee from the pot in the middle of the table. He let his mind wander up the stairs to the corridor where his room was situated. A fluffy, grey cat was running along next to the wall in short bursts, stopping now and then to peer around and sniff the air. Tarkyn's mind nudged the cat's and connected. Not only did he become aware of the cat's view of the corridor, he also recognised the mind as Maud's, intent on finding a way into his room.

In that moment of recognition, two things happened simultaneously.

The fluffy grey cat's back arched, her hair standing on end, as she hissed at the image of Tarkyn in her mind, while downstairs, Sheldrake and Jackson clutched at the table, as the ground beneath the Creeping Vine Inn shuddered. Bottles rocked on shelves behind the bar and one picture fell off the wall. Ivan nearly lost his balance and grabbed at the bar to save himself.

Sheldrake's eyes widened. "What was that?"

"Earthquake," muttered Jackson, his body tense as he waited to see whether it would settle or get worse.

Tarkyn rose from the table and stood staring down at Sheldrake, his mouth thinned with anger. After a moment he took a breath and said, "That was not an earthquake. That was my outrage. Just be glad that I have learnt to control my feelings, at least to some extent."

Leaving behind him two shaken men, he turned and strode out of the inn.

Once outside, he stood for several minutes until his rational mind gradually overcame his initial reaction. As an information-gatherer himself, Tarkyn could understand that Sheldrake wanted to know more about him, a powerful mage from another country who was not being open about all of his motives for being in Carrador. He could not expect them to trust him implicitly after so short an acquaintance. He remembered wryly when Danton, his lifelong friend and now his brother-in-law, had said that integrity tended to shine most strongly out of the most accomplished con artists.

He gave a grunt of laughter at himself. He was no con artist, witnessed by the fact that he hadn't kept quiet about his ulterior motive. Mentally forgiving Sheldrake and resolving to apologize both to him and the innkeeper, he walked down the side of the inn and into the forest behind it.

He let his senses range, trying to discover whether any of his Eskuzorian woodfolk had arrived. Tarkyn himself had used translocation to travel almost instantaneously to the border then to Sheldrake's, while his woodfolk friends would have had to walk the whole way. Using Sheldrake and Jackson's knowledge, he had sent mental images of the Creeping Vine's location so that they could cut through forest directly from Eskuzor to reach here, but his geographical skills were suspect, to say the least, so he hoped he had not misdirected them.

Suddenly a raucous cry split the air as a great mountain eagle came into view above the trees. Her huge black and gold wings beat the air as she glided overhead and disappeared slowly out of sight above the canopy. Tarkyn almost jumped up and down with excitement. He sent her a mental wave of greeting and waited until she reappeared above the forest road and, with harsh cry, glided down and around, heading at speed towards Tarkyn to land on his shoulder, her powerful talons gripping the leather shoulder pads on his shirt. Despite all his past experience, Tarkyn still staggered under her weight. She shuffled around, her tail brushing across his face and filling his mouth with down and feathers as she turned to face forward.

"Blasted bird!" protested Tarkyn. "Why don't you turn the

other way?" The eagle just cocked her head at his tone then gently ran her wickedly sharp beak along strands of his long black hair. Tarkyn lifted his hand up to stroke her. "Yes. All right. I'm glad to see you too, even if you do a weigh a ton." He gave the eagle an image of his woodfolk bloodbrother, Waterstone, accompanied by a sense of query.

In return he received an image of five adult woodfolk and three youngsters threading their way through dense forest. He queried how far away and was given an image of the sun setting, then directly above him.

"A day and a half away, I think." Tarkyn turned and headed back inside, the great eagle bouncing gently on his shoulder with every stride. "I had better speak to Stefan's parents."

As he entered the inn, he saw Maud, back in human form, with Sheldrake and Jackson seated around the remains of their rolls and tea, in the middle of a heated discussion. A look of relief passed over Jackson's face when he saw Tarkyn. Then his eyes widened in amazement as he spotted the eagle riding Tarkyn's shoulder. A murmur ran though the patrons in the bar.

Tarkyn walked over to the table and sat down. The three at the table could not take their eyes off the eagle.

"What a beauty. Is that why you have leather pads on your shirt?" asked Jackson.

Tarkyn gave a rueful nod. "Yes. She lands on me, whether I want her or not, and she leaves deep gouges in my shoulder if I don't wear the leather pads." He transferred his attention to Sheldrake. "I apologize for the miniquake. I did not intend it. I understand your suspicion but can only reiterate that I intend no harm. If I did, I would not have announced my presence to you, when I first arrived."

Sheldrake and Maud glanced at each other, clearly embarrassed. Sheldrake cleared his throat. "I don't know what to say."

Tarkyn gave a short laugh. "I know what you want to say; that you're sorry you were caught but not really sorry that you were investigating me. It is, after all, your job. At least you have spared me an empty apology."

Sheldrake frowned and took refuge in sipping his tea.

"It is, of course, a diplomatic disaster to offend a visiting head of state." Tarkyn let that little pearl hang in the air for a few moments before reaching into his pocket and slapping a key on the table. "Here. If you want to search my room, be my guest. I have been outside, so I have not had the opportunity to remove any incriminating evidence. So help yourselves." Without waiting for a response, he turned to Jackson. "Have you asked Stefan's parents to make time to see me?"

Jackson nodded, glad to move on to a new topic. "Once the breakfasts have been served and cleared away, they can meet with you for a short time before they have to start preparing for lunch. Mornings are usually slow in the bar, I gather. Anyway, I think their kids can cover for them if need be."

"Thank you. I believe there is a private parlour we could meet in.'

Jackson nodded again. "I have already booked it."

Tarkyn smiled. "Well done. I can see your talents have been wasted as a messenger."

There was a pause before Jackson said slowly, "Not wasted, Sire. Just in abeyance, while I used a different set of talents for a different important role."

Aware of the censure in the remark, Sheldrake watched the High Lord for his reaction. Tarkyn stared at Jackson for a long moment, then stood and with a nod at the other two, walked out, the huge eagle bobbing gently on his shoulder.

"You're pushing the boundaries, young man," said Sheldrake. "That was an ungracious way to receive a compliment, even if you do, presumably, have strong views about messengers being undervalued."

Jackson coloured a little but when he started to protest, Maud added, "No matter how valuable messengers are, and I agree, we couldn't do without them, you did not pick your time well to ram that down Lord Tarkyn's throat. If he has to monitor everything he says to you, you will find yourself with a very aloof liege, which would be a shame. He seems to like you and always treats you with respect and courtesy. But don't forget; despite his power, he is still a stranger in a land strange to him. Your role is to support him, not just practically."

"Thank you for your advice." Jackson stood up and gave a small ironic bow. "It is also a shame that you two have shown yourselves to be neither trusting nor trustworthy."

As he walked out, Maud said, so quietly that he didn't hear her, "That's better, young man."

Word of the eagle had spread quickly, and Jackson walked out to find Tarkyn surrounded by a small crowd, two of Stefan's brothers among them, eagerly seeking a closer look at the eagle on his shoulder.

The eagle was not happy. She squawked from time to time, spreading and flapping her wings, each time hitting Tarkyn on his head and digging her talons into his shoulder. People were pressing so close that it would be hard for him to raise a shield. Amidst his efforts to keep his eagle calm, Tarkyn had thought of using a spell to immobilize the crowd but was vaguely concerned that it could be construed as a hostile act. So, he was currently contemplating levitating the eagle and himself above the crowd, even though he was loath to provide even more entertainment.

Jackson knew none of this but could see that Tarkyn was feeling harassed. Without hesitation and admittedly, with no thought for the eagle's reaction, Jackson put his fingers to his mouth and let forth a piercing whistle, which the eagle answered with an ear-splitting shriek but other than that, seemed to calm down a little.

"Move back please," ordered Jackson firmly. "You are upsetting His Highness and the eagle. You do realise that touching High Lord Tarkyn constitutes a capital offence." He had no idea whether the same applied to Carradorians as to Eskuzorians but he guessed no one in the crowd knew either. "And mountain eagles are known for their ferocity. I'm amazed she has attacked no one so far and can only assume His Highness has been battling with her to protect you all."

The crowd backed away and even from a distance, Jackson could see Tarkyn heave a sigh of relief. He met Jackson's eyes and gave a nod of thanks before addressing the crowd. "Bird is a wild eagle. She will only let one other person and me, touch her. Jackson is right. She will go for you if you come too close. It was taking everything I had to keep her from attacking those closest to me. I'm surprised she stayed so long. I would have expected her to fly away. Perhaps she thought she was protecting me."

As though in answer, Bird launched off Tarkyn, driving herself upwards with slow beats of her wings. Once she had gained enough height, she swooped down and glided over the crowd, a mere foot above their heads, making them duck in panic. Then she let out a satisfied shriek and returned to Tarkyn's shoulder. Jackson, standing a little further away, chuckled in appreciation.

Gradually, as the novelty wore off and nothing new happened, the crowd dispersed. Tarkyn gave Bird a reassuring stroke before walking towards the west side of the inn, away from the people and the stables. Without a word, Jackson fell in beside him.

As they neared the huge gum tree at the rear of the inn where Jayhan had hidden, Tarkyn said, a new note of formality in his voice. "Thank you for your intercedence." He turned his attention to the eagle and said in a more friendly tone, "Go on, Bird. Go up in the tree for a while. My shoulder is getting tired."

The eagle responded by preening his hair for a few seconds just to make sure he knew she was the one making the choice, then launched herself up into the tree.

Jackson glanced at him and could see that he was, as Maud had predicted, less relaxed with him. "I'm sorry, Sire," he said in a rush. "I'm sorry I sniped at you before." He ran a hand over his forehead. "I suppose... It's just that I had been sitting with Maud and Sheldrake who were feeling... hmm... anxious, quite deservedly, I might say, about how you would behave towards them when you returned. It was very tense and I guess I was on edge and snapped at you, the last person who deserved it. So, I'm sorry."

Tarkyn turned and looked at him, keeping him waiting while he decided on his response. Finally, he smiled. "That was a very handsome apology, which I accept. Can we enter the private parlour via this side door? Then I can avoid Sheldrake and Maud for a while." He gave a slight smile. "I have forgiven them too, but I'll let them sweat a bit longer."

Jackson grinned in relief. "Yes, we can. Come this way."

18

He led them through the door along the corridor and into the kitchen, where Vera, Stefan's mother, looked up from a large slab of dough she was kneading. A look of surprise crossed her face when she registered that it was not one of her children entering. She stopped what she was doing and dropped a curtsey.

"Good morning, my lord. Are you waiting for me? I'll just finish this, if you don't mind, and be along in a few minutes. I need to get it into the oven, ready for lunch."

Marjorie and Marin smiled at them from the other side of the kitchen where they were cutting up a bunch of carrots.

"Keep her as long as you like," said Marjorie. "She could do with a morning off. Shall I bring you some tea or coffee while you're waiting?"

Tarkyn nodded. "Yes please. Enough for the four of us."

Jackson led him out of the internal kitchen door into a short passageway on the lefthand side of the bar. A door in the oak panelling on their left opened into a good-sized private parlour, decorated with whitewashed walls and dark panelling in a similar fashion to the public bar, but with more comfortable lounge chairs placed around a polished, unscratched table in the middle and a few armchairs around the walls. The window looked out at the gum tree so that Tarkyn could see Bird perched patiently in one of the higher branches.

Not long after they had seated themselves, Ivan and Vera arrived, Ivan bearing a tray full of pots, cups, plates and freshly baked scones filled with jam and cream.

"Oh, well done. This looks excellent," said Tarkyn. He gestured to the other chairs. "Do take a seat."

Jackson suddenly realised that, for some reason, Tarkyn was nervous.

Once everyone was settled, Ivan opened the proceedings by saying, "You asked to see us, my lord."

Tarkyn gave a slight cough. "Uh yes. It is about your son, Stefan."

Ivan frowned. "What about him? He's not in any sort of trouble, is he?"

Tarkyn waved his hand. "No. Nothing like that. From everything I have seen, he is very well respected."

"So, what then?"

"Well, this is very awkward, but I was wondering whether Stefan is really your son?"

Ivan scowled. "Now, don't you go picking on him because he's smaller. He's worth his weight in gold, he is."

"I know he is. I've just said that he's well respected. No. It is not just his size. It is also his eye and hair colouring." Tarkyn leaned forward. "Is he your biological son? I ask because I have several particular friends who look just like him."

Ivan and Vera exchanged looks. Jackson saw them clasp hands. Ivan squeezed Vera's hand and very slightly raised his eyebrows at her. When she squeezed his hand back, Ivan turned resolutely towards Tarkyn. "Stefan is as much our son as any of the others but you're right; he is not our biological son."

"There was a terrible flood, you see," said Vera in a rush, as though anxious to explain themselves. "Anton was out walking in the forest down by the river, looking to see what the river had swept up onto its shores and to see how much damage it had done. We warned him to be careful, but the flood waters had mostly subsided by then." She waved her hand in the air. "Anyway, he thought he heard a cat or a kitten mewling but when he looked for the source of the sound, he found a baby, maybe two months old, wrapped in a shoulder sling that had caught on the branches of a sunken log. The current must have pushed the child past the log, then the sling had snagged on the branches and held him firm while the water subsided. It was a miracle he survived. We looked all along the banks of the river for any sign of the mother, but there was nothing." She shrugged. "As fate would have it, I'd just lost a newborn child so recently that I was still producing milk." Her eyes shone with the tears of an old grief. "So we brought him home."

"And he's been our son ever since." Ivan scowled again. "And he always will be, no matter what."

"Thank you for telling us his story." Tarkyn studied Vera's strained face and asked, unknowingly echoing Maud, "Would you like some tea?"

When she nodded, he reached for the teapot but was forestalled by Ivan who growled, "I'll do it."

Once she had taken a few sips and settled down a little, Tarkyn asked, "Does Stefan know? Who, other than Anton, knows? Or was he too young to remember?"

"Anton, Karl and Marjorie knew, but I think we all more or less forgot." Ivan sighed. "We never spoke of it. We just accepted him as part of the family."

"So does Stefan know?" pressed Tarkyn, as gently as he could.

Ivan frowned and shook his head uncertainly. "Not as far as I know. I suppose one of the older ones could have told him when they were teasing him, but I think he would have come to us, if they did."

"They'd tease him about his size and push him around a bit but they all did that to each other, including Marjorie at one time or another," said Vera. "They never *really* hurt each other, I don't think."

Tarkyn thought about his own biological brothers who had conspired to imprison or hang him. Then he thought of his woodfolk blood brothers who might tease or disagree with him but would support him to the ends of the earth. He smiled. "I am glad Stefan has grown up in such a warm, kind, if somewhat boisterous family."

Ivan chuckled. "That he has." He took a ruminative sip of his tea. "But he's given us back full measure, you know. He's great with the horses, the chooks, the cow. He's the best of them at finding mushrooms and herbs in the woods. He's the most accurate of us when we go hunting. And now he's making a name for himself in the big city." He shook his head. "He used to be the worst at rough and rumble but he worked at it, and now I wouldn't take him on in a fight, if I didn't have to." Suddenly Ivan's scowl re-emerged. "So what do you want with him? I'm not a fool. This hasn't been idle curiosity. You're up to something."

"Yes and no. I can probably manage without Stefan's help in my endeavours on Carrador's behalf. My main motivation is Stefan's welfare." Tarkyn glanced at Vera before meeting Ivan's eyes. "But before we go any further, I must ask you to take an oath to keep a secret." He half-turned to Jackson. "You too."

"We are not going to keep secrets from our family, especially when we don't know what they are," said Vera firmly.

"No, I wouldn't expect you to." Tarkyn gave a wry smile. "Your family is far too close for that to work, although the choice is yours whether you tell them of it. They, too, including Stefan, will have to be sworn to secrecy. If it helps, it is about his heritage."

Vera and Ivan looked at each other, then Ivan asked, his scowl firmly fixed on his face. "Why? Is there something disgraceful about his heritage?"

Tarkyn looked startled. "No. Not at all. It is a heritage to be proud of, but I cannot say more without your oath."

"Give us a minute," grumbled Ivan, turning to his wife. "What do you think?"

"Stefan's heritage has never been anything we discussed with outsiders or patrons, except to defend him as a family member."

"So we'd only talk within the family about it, anyway, wouldn't we? Hmm. But what if this heritage posed a threat of some kind? We might want to warn people of it." Ivan turned to Tarkyn. "Well?"

"I know more of Stefan's heritage than any man or sorcerer alive, and I do not believe that there is, or will be, any threat."

Ivan's eyes narrowed as he surveyed Tarkyn, clearly assessing the value of his word, an impertinence the High Lord endured in silence. "And what about Karl's spouse and children when he has them?" he demanded at last.

Tarkyn grimaced, waving his hand in a helpless gesture. "I don't know. I suppose his spouse would have to know but perhaps it will be old, irrelevant history, just as the truth of Stefan's birth is now, by the time the children are old enough to listen in on conversations."

Vera placed her hand on her husband's arm. "Ivan, I would

like to know where Stefan came from. I am willing to take the chance."

Ivan grunted. "Very well. But," he said belligerently to Tarkyn, "I am not necessarily going to allow you to tell Stefan."

Tarkyn eyes glinted dangerously. "I do not need your permission. Stefan is a grown man. I could have gone straight to him but I have come to you first, to make sure that my surmises were facts and to discuss with you the wisdom of telling him of his true heritage. Do not push me too far, Ivan. I do not take orders from anyone, either in Carrador or in Eskuzor."

Vera squeezed Ivan's arm in warning, but the landlord shook her off. "Get off me. I will protect my family, no matter what the cost."

"The cost," said Tarkyn evenly, "is being civil to me. That, at least, will give you a say in what I do."

The two men glared at each other, while Vera and Jackson watched in trepidation. Outside, the mountain eagle screeched her disquiet to the surrounding trees. The sound pulled Tarkyn out of his anger. Suddenly he smiled. "Now look what you've done. You've upset Bird. If you're not careful, you'll have every raptor for miles around circling your inn and swooping down on your customers."

Ivan frowned, confused by the sudden change in atmosphere. "Is that a threat?" he asked uncertainly.

Tarkyn laughed. "Not at all. I don't control the raptors... but they do look after me. Even when Bird is off somewhere hunting, if you look, you will always see at least one hawk, or eagle or owl, or some other raptor, watching me from a nearby tree."

Ivan stared at him, perplexed. "I am dealing with things beyond my ken. I will take your oath, but can I ask you, please, to be kind to my Stefan? We love him dearly and do not want him distressed."

"Neither do I," said Tarkyn. "That is why I came to you first."

Once all three were sworn to secrecy, Tarkyn told them about the woodfolk, just as he had told the king.

"So," concluded Tarkyn, "I do not know if woodfolk inhabit your woodlands, but Stefan's existence implies that they do. A small group of Eskuzorian woodfolk, my family included, are even now on their way to rendezvous with me here... well, out in the forest somewhere near here. I can introduce Stefan to them, but..." He leaned forward and spoke earnestly. "I think it is important for any man to know his antecedences. For Stefan, it would make his stature, colouring and skills make sense. My woodfolk could teach him a whole new set of skills that the rest of us could not accomplish. I know he is sensitive about his size. I have seen him become defensive about chance remarks, not even directed at him. Now, he could understand the reason for it and maybe be proud of it." He leaned back again. "But he would also lose. He would lose the certainty of being a member of your family." He held a hand up to forestall their protests. "I know you will not reject him, but how will he feel when all his assumptions come tumbling down?"

Vera wrung her hands. "Oh dear! Maybe we should have told him. We never dreamt his true mother or family or whatever might turn up. Silly, really. It was always a possibility, when you think about it."

"Are you giving us the choice whether to tell him?" growled Ivan.

"Honestly, I don't know. I am talking it through with you so that we can decide together. At the very least, I want to know your views." Tarkyn threw his hands up. "You do not know these people as I do. To become an honorary woodman was the greatest honour of my life... and I have had many honours, being the son of a king. It would be a terrible shame for someone to live his life, ignorant of the wonderful people he belonged to."

Ivan heaved a great sigh. "I hope we don't lose him. He will be more like them than us, from what you're saying. And he will be angry at us for not telling him." Tears sprang to his eyes. "I love that boy. I don't want to lose him."

"Are you saying we should tell him?" asked Tarkyn.

Ivan nodded miserably. "How can I say I love him if I don't let him be who he really is?"

"Who he really is, and has always been, is part of our family," said Vera, threading her arm under his and around his back, to pull him close. "Even if he forgets that for a while, he will come back to it."

Tarkyn put his elbows on the table and ran his hands through his hair. "Whew. I knew this would be hard. I'm glad you have agreed."

Unasked, Jackson filled his teacup, added milk and handed it to him. Tarkyn took a long swallow and let the tension leech from him.

"So now what? Who tells him?" asked Jackson, voicing the question they all were thinking.

With Vera's arm still across his back, Ivan put his arm across her shoulders, presenting a solid front. "We will tell him. He is our son. It is our responsibility. We will tell him."

"I applaud your courage," said Tarkyn. "When will you tell him? It is entirely up to you. I only ask to make sure I don't say anything before you do."

"We will tell him now, before the midday rush," said Ivan heavily. He waved his free hand at them. "You go. Tell Stefan to come here. We will talk to him now."

Tarkyn stood and gave them a slight bow, as a gesture of respect for what they were about to do and left the room.

19

As they stood in the corridor outside, Jackson raised his eyebrows in query and Tarkyn gave a slight nod before continuing into the public bar.

Maud and Sheldrake were the only patrons still in the bar. Those who had stayed the night had moved on and the lunchtime crowd had not yet arrived. They watched Tarkyn as he approached, cautious of his grave expression.

He gave them a slight smile, which Maud thought looked strained. "I am sorry for keeping you waiting," he said. "It is a beautiful morning outside. Would you like to come for a walk with me, perhaps along the road in the direction of Kimora?" After a tiny pause, he couldn't help adding, "If you have finished with my room, of course," and grinned.

"Yes to both," said Maud with great aplomb, as she rose from the table to join him.

Sheldrake frowned at her, as he, too, rose from the table. "Maud. You know we didn't..."

Maud laughed. "So does he."

"I could be bluffing," suggested Tarkyn, as they walked through the door into the morning sunshine.

Maud shook her head, squinting against the light. "No. I doubt that you could. Too honest and from the earthquake we all felt, I suspect your feelings would give you away if you tried." She held out her hand. "Here is your key."

They walked along the front of the inn but as they approached the stables, a thought struck Tarkyn, making him turn to Maud. "How do you explain to the stableboys the disappearance of the brown mare Sheldrake rode in on?"

Maud smiled. "We don't. We just take them into our confidence. There are a few hostelries up and down the country that we frequent for one reason or another. They all know."

Sheldrake gave a tight smile. "We tried at first to make up cover stories, but even if we could get away with it once, it pushes people's credulity too far for me to lose my horse every time I come to a particular inn." He shrugged. "So Maud's secret is only a secret in certain circles."

As they passed the stables, Javier gave them a nod and a smile from where he was pitching fresh straw into a wheelbarrow ready to take inside to freshen up the stalls.

Once they were past and had forest on either side of the road, Tarkyn finally swore them to secrecy and filled them in on the overall plan.

"I wasn't going to tell you until I had spoken to Stefan but I've talked to his parents and they are speaking to him instead." He told them what was happening, even now, back in the private parlour of the inn and grimaced. "And I think he may need support from all of us over the coming days."

"Oh, the poor boy." Maud's face creased with concern. "Do they have a dog?"

Tarkyn frowned in confusion. "Sorry?"

Sheldrake gave a dry chuckle. "Maud wants to comfort him, give him something to pat."

Tarkyn's face cleared. "Oh, I see. Might be a good idea. I'd like someone to keep an eye on him afterwards. He'll probably work out it's you, though."

Maud gave him her warm smile. "Even if he does, it might be good for him to have someone outside the family to talk to or be with."

"Now Maud," said Sheldrake, "Don't go rushing in. See how he goes."

"Yes, dear."

Tarkyn smiled, understanding full well that Maud would do as she saw fit.

20

Stefan entered the private parlour, cheerful and unsuspecting. "Hallo. This is nice; having a bit of time to catch up without the others around. How have you been? You both look well. I've missed you, you know. No one to tell me off if I forget to comb my hair. No one giving me big bear hugs. It's great to be home, even if it's just for a few days."

"Sit down, son," said Ivan heavily, at the same time as Vera said with forced cheerfulness, "It is lovely to see you again, too."

Stefan sat down slowly, looking from one to the other. "What's up?"

Ivan leaned forward and spread his hands on the table. "First of all, Stefan, son, let me say that we both love you with all our hearts and," he hesitated, "you are and always will be a loved, valued member of this family."

"Dad, what's wrong? You're scaring me now."

Ivan glanced at Vera, a plea in his eyes, to which Vera responded.

"Um, Stefan. Thirty-four years ago, there was a big flood."

Stefan nodded. "Yes, I know. You can still see the high-water mark. There hasn't been as big a flood since." He frowned. "So?"

"Well, you know how Anton likes to go rummaging around looking for things? Well, that's what he did after the flood."

Stefan gave a cautious smile. "I bet he did. He would have loved the junk that was chucked up by a flood."

Ivan grimaced. "Unfortunate choice of words," he said. "Junk can sometimes turn out to be very precious."

Stefan shrugged. "I suppose so. Everyone looks for that rare, overlooked treasure."

There was a short awkward silence.

Then Vera began again. "Well Stefan, you were that rare, overlooked treasure."

Stefan's eyebrows came together in a ferocious frown. "What! What are you saying?"

"Anton found you. After the flood. Caught in the branches of a log." Vera wrung her hands, fearful of his reaction. "And he brought you home and you have been our son ever since." She quailed before his thunderstruck expression. "And we love you. We always have and always will. We'd almost forgotten where..."

She trailed off as she realised that Stefan wasn't listening anymore. His eyes had glazed over with shock. Ivan and Vera looked at each other. Then she rose and moved around the table to hug Stefan. She was prevented by his raised hand. She returned to her chair and subsided into it.

They waited in silence for several long minutes before Stefan's vision cleared. "Kind of you to look after me for all those years," he said cuttingly.

"No, Stefan," rumbled Ivan. "It wasn't like that. We truly think of you as our son."

"So why tell me then?" Before they could answer, he rolled

his eyes. "Wait on. It's that bloody High Lord, isn't it? I don't know what's going on, but he and that ambassador have been taking an inordinate interest in me. Did he make you tell me?" He looked ready to go out and throttle Tarkyn.

"Not exactly. No," said Vera carefully. "But he made us realise that we were depriving you of your heritage. We never knew anything about it 'til he came. Never cared, really."

"And is it worth losing my family for?" stormed Stefan.

Ivan's face creased with worry. He looked like he might cry. "You haven't lost your family, lad. We're all still here and still love you."

Stefan stared at him. "No. You haven't lost *your* family. I have. I'm an outsider among you." Suddenly he threw back his chair, toppling it onto the ground, and pushed past them out of the room.

The words, "No, son!" rang in his ears as he slammed the door behind him.

Ivan and Vera sat in shattered silence then sought the refuge of each other's arms.

Stefan strode blindly through the kitchen, not even noticing Marjorie and Javier, his mind overwhelmed. He blundered outside and ran until he made the cover of the trees. Then he slowed, walking fast along a narrow path overhung with swaying lemon-scented eucalypts. Although he didn't consciously notice the bush around him, its shadows and soft greens salved his soul. He walked until the path he had chosen narrowed into a climb over tumbled rocks that he scrambled up until he reached a sheltered spot on the top of the hill, hidden among the granite boulders, a scraggly old she-oak giving it shade.

He threw himself down on the grass against a boulder. His chest was heaving with exertion and emotion, but he was so confused he didn't know whether he was angry or sad. He put his elbows on his knees and wrapped his arms around his head, trying to hide from the world. An hour ago, it had been a beautiful morning. He had been bouncing with joy at being home. Now, he didn't know where to put himself.

All those times he had played with his siblings. Had they known? They never said anything. All those times he had struggled to keep up with them, trying to be like them, when all the time he looked different. All those years waiting to grow taller as they did, realising in the end that it wasn't going to happen.

As time went on, he uncurled enough to sit up straight against the rock, but his arms were still folded across his knees. When he had thought and thought through the past, the questions started: Who was he? Where did he come from? Why did it matter to a foreign prince?

An hour, two hours passed; he didn't know. He was dragged out of his inward turmoil by the sound of boots on stone coming up the side of the hill. A minute later, Anton's head appeared above the rocks.

Stefan scowled at him, but Anton just smiled. "Hello, little brother. I thought I'd find you here."

Stefan wanted to say that he wasn't his brother but knew it would sound petulant. Instead he just grunted.

Anton swung himself over the last boulder and sat down next to him. "So you must be feeling pretty shitty then. I keep trying to imagine what it must feel like to suddenly find out I'm not who I thought I was." He shook his head. "I tried but I can't. My mind baulks at the thought. So I guess you're feeling crap."

Stefan tried to say, "U-huh," but his breath caught in his throat and after a shallow cough, he just managed, "Yep."

"We older ones, me, Karl and Marjorie, we always knew," he shrugged, "but we just forgot. Once Mum held you in her arms, the past was gone. You were just the new baby." His eyes slid sideways to study Stefan's set face. After a minute, he tried again. "Anyway, think of it this way. You'll always have us. You know that: I'm your brother, you're mine. Nothing will ever change that. But now you might have a lot of new people, as well as us, to belong to." He gave a lop-sided smile. "But I hope they're not too nice, whoever they are, because no matter what, they have to come second. You belong to us."

Finally Stefan looked up and met his brother's eyes. Tears sprang to his eyes and as Anton grabbed him and pulled him against his chest, the sobs came.

21

Not surprisingly, Stefan missed his appointment with Sheldrake at lunchtime. Dinner that evening was fraught as Tarkyn sat with Sheldrake, Maud and Jackson, watching the door from the kitchen for any sign of the arms master.

Marjorie served their food in severe silence, clearly blaming Tarkyn for Stefan's distress. As she came to clear the dishes away, Tarkyn said to her, "If Stefan wants to know more about where he came from, I am available any time to talk to him and some people he might like to meet are arriving here around midday tomorrow."

"He's not meeting anyone, without one of us with him."

Tarkyn nodded mildly. "As long as you are sworn to secrecy, any of you is welcome to accompany him."

"And where is Stefan now?" asked Maud.

Marjorie transferred her glare to Maud. "In his room. Not talking to anyone. Not even Anton. So, well done. I hope you're pleased."

Tarkyn went to stand up. "Perhaps I will..."

"No, you bloody won't. You leave him alone. You've done enough damage."

After she had flounced off, bearing their dirty dishes, Sheldrake blew out a long breath. "We are truly personae non gratae, aren't we?"

Tarkyn grimaced. "I'm sorry I dragged you into this."

"No need to apologize," replied Sheldrake. "You are, after all, trying to solve a problem for Carrador."

"Yes, but... I didn't actually have to involve Stefan in my efforts to contact Carradorian woodfolk. Although he is suffering now, it is for his sake that I came... well, and curiosity; to find out why a woodman was living among men and sorcerers." Tarkyn ran his hand through his hair. "But it's harrowing, isn't it?" He let his eyes roam around the bar, thinking how Stefan's sense of belonging here had been shaken.

Sheldrake leaned in closer and murmured, "See that couple over there in the corner? They are young local farmers. Just starting out in the world. Need a bit of extra cash. So they keep an eye on things for me." He moved his gaze to watch a group of three older men at the bar, so that no one noticed his particular interest in the couple in the corner. "They don't know who I am, of course. We keep in contact through notes and letters, sent with traders and passing messengers to my agent on the outskirts of Highkington. If something really urgent came up, I would expect one of them to get on a horse and ride like the wind to deliver the message."

"Huh." Tarkyn turned to smile at him. "Apology accepted."

The startled look on Sheldrake's face made Jackson chuckle. "Maybe you do trust him after all."

It was about then that they noticed Maud was no longer with them.

Outside, a fluffy grey cat was running along next to the wall, looking for a bedroom with lamplight shining through its window. At this hour, darkness had drawn in, but everyone was downstairs either eating or working. Only Stefan would be in his room. But would he have lit his lantern?

Along the western wall, all the windows were dark. Maud's heart sank. How could she find him? None of the family were going to tell her. She scurried past the entrance to the kitchen to the end of the wall and turned the corner. She gave a happy little 'prow' as she spotted a single shaft of lamplight coming from a window halfway along the back wall.

Now, how to climb up?

She surveyed the back wall. A drainpipe ran down the corner of the wall and guttering ran along the top. A straggly passionfruit vine clung to parts of the wall but not up as high as the first floor and it finished closer to the window next to Stefan's.

That will have to do, she decided.

Without waiting for thoughts to undermine her courage, she leapt onto the vine and clawed her way up to the top of it. Then, gathering her hind legs beneath her, she leapt the extra height onto the windowsill of the next-door window. The sill was narrow, and she was facing the wrong way. She had to arch her back until she was short enough to turn. Then she measured the distance, took three running steps and threw herself at the distant windowsill. She just managed to grab the edge of it with her front claws. It looked easy when she watched other cats but in actual fact, her arms were screaming with the strain of holding her whole body weight while her back legs scrabbled futilely in the air for purchase. With an almighty contraction of her front legs, she heaved herself up until her hind legs could latch onto the edge of the sill. She pulled herself up onto the ledge using all four legs, and lay there gasping for breath, shocked with how close she had come to disaster. Funny. She never saw other cats lying gasping for breath after a manoeuvre like that. They just carried on without giving such an astonishing feat of strength and agility a second thought.

When Maud had recovered enough to stand and investigate the windowsill, she realised that the window was shut. Blast! She should have checked that. She rubbed herself along the windowpane and produced a piteous miaow. Then she sat down and miaowed again. Nothing. She scratched at the window, sticking out her claws for maximum effect. Still nothing. She scratched a few more times then sat down and produced a really heart-rending yowl.

The window slammed upwards and Stefan shoved his head out, nearly knocking her off the sill.

She dug in with her claws then pushed towards his head and rubbed against his cheek. "Prowww?"

Stefan frowned. "Hello. What are you doing up here? You're a clever puss. You're new since I last came. Do you think I have something for you to eat?" He picked her up and brought her inside, stroking her as he walked. "Come on, come in here out of the cold. It's too dangerous for little cats to be so high up. Yes, I know you're a good climber. You must be, to have made it up here but it's pretty tricky out there." He held her against him as he reached over and pulled down the window. "There. You see? No more going outside on windowsills. Too dangerous for a little puss."

In truth, Maud had to agree. As he stroked her, she started to purr, encouraging him to hold her and stroke her more. In the corner of the room lay a plate containing his half-eaten dinner. He took her over to it and put her down in front of it.

"Look," he said gently, "here's a bit of chicken you might like. And here's a bit of cheese on the vegetables. See? You can have the chicken while I pull some of the cheese off the vegetables for you." Luckily Maud was not at all squeamish about eating someone else's leftovers. "There's a good puss. You were just hungry, weren't you?"

Not at all, thought Maud, *but this chicken is very tasty.* Once she had eaten her fill, she sat and cleaned herself meticulously. While she held her hind leg at a ridiculous angle, Stefan retreated to his bed and sat watching her for a while before lying down, lacing his hands behind his head.

When she had finished her ablutions, she jumped lightly on top of him and started kneading his chest. He reached one hand down to stroke her and after a minute, began to talk, "The world's gone mad, you know, little cat. Everything I knew is gone; blown away like a dandelion in the wind. I have to start all over again. Learn my life again from the beginning, from my first memories." He kept stroking her as he talked. "I have to be methodical, start at the beginning and work up through my ages. But it's hard, little cat. It's hard. All sorts of later memories keep intruding, shoving their way into my mind when I'm not up to them yet. I have to push them aside. They have to wait until I've worked through the years before them." He sat up, holding her to his chest as he changed position. When he let her go, she curled up in his lap, purring loudly. He smiled. "Life's so simple for you. You just eat, sleep, play and sleep some more."

Little do you know, thought Maud.

His smile faded. "But life is hard, little cat. Oh, suddenly so hard." He drifted off into a reverie, so she batted his hand until he started stroking her again.

After a while he said, "Anton's always been a rock for me. So have Mum and Dad but that was their job, if you know what I mean. Maybe it's because he found me, not just because he's the eldest." He gave a humourless laugh. "See, cat, what I mean? Every little thing has to be re-examined from a new perspective. Oh, my brain is so tired. I've done nothing but think all day. I'm nearly there, little cat. I'm up to when I left home when I was twenty. Trouble is, younger memories that I forgot to consider are intruding now, so I guess I won't be able to cover everything. But if I get most of it in order, I think I'll be able to face them tomorrow." He sighed. "But I'm too tired now. I have to sleep."

With an effort, he got himself off the bed and crossed to the door, where he stood uncertainly. "What am I going to do with you? I like having you in here, but you'll probably piss on the floor before morning. I don't want to leave the door open because I'm not ready to see anyone yet. No. I think you'll have to go," he said regretfully and, after listening a minute, opened the door and tossed her gently into the corridor. "Goodnight little one."

22

Next morning, breakfast came and went with no sign of Stefan. By mid-morning, even Anton, who thought he understood why Stefan needed time alone, was becoming anxious. Maud was unable to reassure anyone in the family without giving away what she had done and on balance, she thought that would be counterproductive.

Finally, an hour before noon, Stefan shoved up his window and yelled down at Javier, who was crossing the back yard. "Send Mum and Dad up, will you?"

Javier shot into the inn with a big smile on his face. "Mum, Dad, quick! Upstairs now! He wants to see you."

With no thought of standing on their pride or objecting to being ordered about, Vera and Ivan wiped their hands on their respective aprons and rushed up the stairs. Stefan was waiting for them at the door of his room and dragged them inside. He threw his arms around them both and for some time they just stood in each other's embrace.

Eventually he pulled back and said, "I've been through every single memory that I can think of. You have always treated me the same as the others," he gave a little chuckle, "except that I escaped the hand-me-downs, 'cause they were always too big. I love you and I know you love me." He gave a wry smile that was underpinned with sadness. "I feel like a spinning coin. One side of me feels safe and knows I'm a loved member of the family. The other side is on the verge of panic, alone, not knowing who I am." He took a deep breath. "But the safe side is keeping the other side together...just."

"Oh, I hope we've done the right thing, telling you," said Vera. "I hope, in the end, it is worth what you, and we, are going through now."

Ivan frowned anxiously at him. "Are you ready to come down now, son? Don't worry if you're not. We won't let anyone rush you."

"Yeah, I'm ready." They walked along the corridor with Stefan in the middle, his arms around both of them. "You know Anton came and found me yesterday?"

His father nodded. "Yes, we know. He's a good lad, isn't he? I think we all knew where you'd gone, but I knew he'd be the best one to go after you."

As they reached the top of the stairs, they let each other go as there was not room to walk three abreast down the stairs. Stefan went first, with his father's heavy hand on his shoulder to steady him. His siblings were clustered around the base of the stairs waiting for him, to drag him into a suffocating bear hug the second his feet touched the floor of the bar.

When they finally released their grip, Stefan was laughing. "Get off me, you great galoots. Can't you see I'm smaller than you?"

This led to joyous shouts, with Stefan being hoisted into the air and carried around the bar, much to the entertainment of those patrons who had already drifted in.

"Oh, my word," said Sheldrake dryly, watching from the side. "They really are a very demonstrative family, aren't they?"

"Yes. Delightful, I think," said his wife, smiling warmly in appreciation.

Sheldrake frowned at her. "Do you really think so?"

"Absolutely, dear."

Like a plague of locusts, the noisy family, including Vera and Ivan, processed their way out into the kitchen, still with Stefan on high, leaving those in the suddenly quiet bar to fend for themselves. No one took advantage of the situation, but just helped themselves to what they needed and left the money on the counter.

Tarkyn, who was feeling bad about the whole situation, had removed himself from the bar room and was standing near the tree line at the back of the inn, gazing into the forest. His eagle, sensing he was upset, was sitting on his shoulder, preening his hair. Tarkyn was absently stroking the long feathers of her wings, as he waited, both for news of Stefan and the arrival of his woodfolk.

Raucous laughter split the air behind him as the whole Vine family erupted out of the back door, Stefan in their midst. Tarkyn turned swiftly at the noise, nearly unseating Bird. His relieved pleasure at seeing Stefan once more connected with his family washed across the yard, but in the mayhem, no one but Stefan noticed it. He frowned then looked over at Tarkyn and cocked his head. Tarkyn smiled and nodded. Stefan stared at him a moment longer before pointedly turning his back on him and returning his attention to his family.

Not forgiven yet then, thought Tarkyn, repressing a flash of anger. *It is hard being in a foreign land. I would never accept that level of discourtesy in Eskuzor.*

Jackson, who had been sitting on a bench outside the kitchen door to keep a weather eye on his liege, had been nearly swamped by joyous Vines. He noticed the interchange and, skirting around the family, strolled over to talk to Tarkyn.

"Give him time, Sire. He is not naturally a discourteous man."

Tarkyn grunted. "No, at least he hasn't been until now. Perhaps this will change him. I almost wish I hadn't interfered. He seemed quite happy as he was."

"He seems happy now."

"No, he's not. You watch him." After a few minutes, Tarkyn pointed out, "See? Now and then his face stiffens and sometimes his eyes glisten with unshed tears. Then he pulls himself out of it. I don't know whether his family are noticing, but if so, they are pretending not to."

Gradually the family settled and various members drifted off to return to their duties, until only Marjorie and Anton remained standing with Stefan. They talked among themselves for several minutes until, in a concerted move, they turned and walked over to Tarkyn.

"All right then," said Anton, an edge in his voice. "Time for you to justify what you have done."

Bird ruffled her feathers and snaked her wicked beak towards him at his tone. Tarkyn placed a calming hand on her back but glared at Anton for a moment, unimpressed with his attitude even though he understood its reason. "I will." He raised his index finger. "But first, you need to realise to whom you are speaking. Your King Gavin and I are equals and I am here with his blessing. I have not demanded obeisance every time you approached me, but I cannot abide belligerence towards me."

Marjorie smiled slightly. "I'll translate for you, brother. He's saying, 'Back off.'"

Tarkyn gave a surprised frown and turned to Jackson. "Is my speech usually too florid?"

"No, Sire. And I think you were saying a little more than that."

Marjorie hesitated then dropped a shallow curtsey. "I beg your pardon, Your Highness. I did not intend to be disrespectful."

"No, you were not. It was your brother who erred. But enough of this. I do not want to labour the point any further. I came to Carrador to assist your king, but also to help Stefan." He grimaced. "So far, I have only hurt him, for which I am truly sorry. I do hope that when you meet his kindred, if you choose to, you will agree that it was worth it."

"Tell us about them," asked Anton, his tone no longer abrasive, "please."

"It would be my pleasure." Tarkyn took a breath then gave a quirky smile. "I suppose the first thing I should tell you is that I admire these people so much, I have married one of them. Her name is Lapping Water and she has the same colouring as you, Stefan, although her hair is straight and glossy and falls down her back almost to her waist. I have two blood brothers, Waterstone and Ancient Oak, and a thirteen-year-old niece called Sparrow." Suddenly his aloofness had vanished and he was grinning. "They too share your colouring. These people, collectively, are known as woodfolk. I know nothing about them in Carrador, except for your existence, Stefan. But in Eskuzor, they live within the forest, unknown to the general population... hence the oaths of secrecy I insisted on... and I am their liege lord and protector."

His whole face was alive. After a moment he chuckled. "Mind you, they don't really need my protection and they would take issue with me, if I said they did."

Stefan was standing with his arms crossed, trying to remain unaffected by Tarkyn's enthusiasm. "Uh-huh. So are these some sort of tribal people who live among the trees? Do they wear clothes? What are their houses like?"

Tarkyn frowned. "They are not tribal. They have different communities but people are free to swap between them at will. They wear the same clothes as I," he said, brushing his hand down the light brown of his shirt, "designed to blend into the forest. Except for the Forestals and Mountainfolk, woodfolk tend to be itinerant and live in shelters that can be quickly built and hidden. My family belongs to the Wanderers."

Seeing Stefan's continued resistance, Tarkyn added, "Perhaps it would be better if you just met some of them and formed your own opinions. I can tell you of their special talents that you share with them and I can describe why I like them. But against a closed mind, nothing will work. If anything, trying to persuade you will just stiffen your resistance."

"They don't sound too bad, Stefan," offered Marjorie. "Might be worth giving them a go. We'll come with you, then we can all see what we think."

"Yeah Stefan," drawled Anton. "Anyway, after all this, how could you live, not knowing where you really come from? Speaking for myself, I'm dying of curiosity."

Stefan swung out his arm and thumped Anton backhand across the chest, making him grin. "All right," he said. "I will agree to meet them. But that's all."

Tarkyn spread his hands placatingly. "There *is* nothing else, Stefan. I don't expect you to rush off and live with them. My greatest hope is that you learn more of who you are and maybe learn some of their skills. You already have a rich, successful life outside the forest. Why would you want to leave it?"

"Hmph. You destroy my peace of mind just for this?" he demanded.

Tarkyn put his head on one side as he considered the arms

master. "You are a strong competitor. Don't you want to be the best you can be, even if it is hard and takes work?" When Stefan re-folded his arms and thinned his lips, Tarkyn threw his arms up. "Oh, stars! What am I doing? I just said I wouldn't badger you, and I won't. It is close to noon. I'm off into the forest to be ready to meet them when they arrive. Do as you choose, Stefan."

As the High Lord swivelled on his heel and headed for the trees, Jackson asked, "May I come?"

"Certainly." Tarkyn glanced over his shoulder as though he might say more but after some thought he just repeated, "Certainly."

They walked out of the noon sunlight into the dappled shadows of the trees. A soft breeze brushed through the branches above them, lazily waving the leaves.

Suddenly Tarkyn smiled at Jackson. "Waterstone just sent me an image. They've arrived." He tapped Bird on the shoulder. "Go on. Up you go and find them. Then come back and show me the way."

The three Vines, hot on their heels, watched with interest as the eagle took to the skies, screeching as she disappeared towards the north above the trees. A few minutes later they heard her screeching to the west. For a moment, Tarkyn's eyes went out of focus before he turned to Stefan. "May I share this image with you? You will know better where we need to go."

Stefan glanced at Marjorie and Anton, scrunching his face in embarrassment.

Anton's eyes grew round. "Can you send mind messages? Wowee. You lucky thing." He nodded. "Go on then. Help the High Lord."

"Just put your arm on my shoulder to steady me, Anton. Last time I nearly fell off my horse."

"Ooh. Interesting."

Stefan rolled his eyes then looked at Tarkyn. "Go on then."

Instantly, an image of trees sweeping past below him appeared in Stefan's mind. If not for Anton's hand on his shoulder, he would have pitched forward. A small clearing appeared in the dense canopy and Stefan could see several figures waving up at the eagle. They were too far below the eagle to see details, but he could make out their light brown hair. With another shriek, the eagle wheeled down lower before thrusting upwards with her great wings and swinging in an arc. The next thing Stefan knew, she was swooping in from behind Tarkyn, aiming to land on his shoulder.

"Watch out," yelled Stefan involuntarily. "Here she comes."

Tarkyn glanced over his shoulder and braced himself just in time to save himself from being catapulted forward by the force of her landing.

"Thanks," said Tarkyn, chuckling. "You forgot that you were seeing that image through me. But thanks." He reached up and stroked Bird. "And you, young lady, are a menace." Once she was settled, he returned his attention to Stefan. "So, do you know where they are?"

"Yes. Don't you?"

Tarkyn shook his head. "Not really. Maybe over that way somewhere," he said, waving his hand vaguely.

Stefan smothered a laugh. "Follow me." He looked at Marjorie and Anton. "They're up near the grand old gum, close to the creek."

Stefan led them out onto the road and headed left towards Highkington for several hundred yards, before cutting back into scrub on the south side of the road along a very narrow path that wound tightly through thickets of tea tree and wattle. Ten minutes later, they came to a clearing beside a huge, gnarled old gum tree.

The clearing was deserted.

Stefan turned to Tarkyn, a look of confusion on his face. "I'm sure this is where I saw them."

Tarkyn smiled. "Don't worry. They're here." He gestured to his companions and introduced them to apparently thin air. "I would like you to meet Anton and Marjorie Vine, whose family runs an inn just down the road. Stefan here, who you can see is a woodman, has been a family member at the inn since he was born. And this is Jackson, my new aide-de-camp. He is Eskuzorian, so no doubt he has some sorcerous powers, but we haven't discussed what they are."

Anton, Marjorie and Stefan all turned their heads to look in astonishment at Jackson.

"Are you a sorcerer?" asked Marjorie, awe-struck.

"Yes," replied Jackson casually. "It's no big deal. Everyone in Eskuzor is." He nodded at Tarkyn. "But no one comes near the power of His Highness, except maybe his sister."

"Excuse me," interrupted Tarkyn, "I am in the middle of introductions. So, as I was about to say, these four and the other members of Stefan's family have been sworn to keep your existence secret, as have a couple of others, but I'll talk to you about them later."

A sound like driving rain on damp earth on their right resolved into a cocky voice. "That's all right then." A young green-eyed man with shoulder-length, light brown hair stood there, hands on hips, grinning at Tarkyn. "Hello. That was a long trip and no mistake. We've never before come further south than the swamps south of the mountains." He nodded at the others. "Hello, Tarkyn's friends. I'm Rainstorm."

Anton frowned. "Where did you come from?"

Rainstorm pointed. "Over behind that tree."

As he pointed to a tree behind him, a woodwoman holding a small child by the hand appeared next to Tarkyn. "Hello everyone," she said in a mellow voice, "I am Lapping Water." She indicated the little girl, "and this is Gurgling Brook." She gave a soft laugh. "She probably won't always sound like a gurgling brook, but she does now when she laughs."

"Dada," burbled the little girl with a wide grin, pulling away from Lapping Water and reaching up with small hands. Tarkyn grinned and in one fluid motion, scooped her into his arms. She turned and waved her hand. "Look, new peoples."

Stefan studied Rainstorm and Lapping Water with a sinking heart. Until now, some part of him had hoped that it was all a big mistake, just some sort of aberration amongst the Vine genes as he'd always thought. But one look at these two woodfolk was enough to show him his true origins. Despite himself, he felt an instant kinship, which he immediately quelled.

Hugging his daughter, Tarkyn looked around. "And where are Waterstone, Sparrow and Autumn Leaves?"

Lapping Water gave a warm smile. "Waterstone, Sparrow and Autumn Leaves currently have arrows trained on you until they are sure we are safe with you. They'll be down in a minute, I expect." Even as she finished speaking, two woodmen and a teenaged woodwoman appeared beside Lapping Water. "Here they are now."

When they had introduced themselves, Waterstone eyed Stefan curiously. "So you're a woodman, are you? You certainly look like one. But what are you doing living out in the open? For us in Eskuzor, we are exiled if we reveal our presence or the existence of our kin."

"I don't know if I'm a woodman." Stefan folded his arms defensively. "Only Lord Tarkyn says I am and only because of my green eyes."

"I checked," put in Tarkyn. "He can receive my mind images."

Waterstone's green eyes twinkled, and clear words formed in Stefan's mind. *"You're not happy about this, are you?"* He nodded at Marjorie and Anton without saying anything out loud and new words formed in the arms master's mind. *"So are these your blood sister and blood brother?"*

"I grew up with them. Anton found me after a flood. I only found out yesterday that they are not my true family." Unbidden, tears sprang to Stefan's eyes. Suddenly he realised that he was mindtalking.

"Ah, you poor old bugger. That must be dreadfully hard."

Anton frowned. "What's going on? Why has everyone gone quiet?"

Waterstone indicated Anton and spoke out loud. "They still seem to want to look after you. So that's good." His smile broadened and he spoke to Anton, "Just mindtalking with your brother. For your information, your Stefan can converse with us using words or images. Tarkyn can only use images but he can use them with animals as well."

Suddenly Tarkyn frowned. "Where's Midnight?"

In answer, leaves rustled above them. "Uh-oh," said Tarkyn and thrust Gurgling Brook into Lapping Water's arms just in time as Midnight leapt down, confident that Tarkyn would catch him. Tarkyn staggered back under the significant weight of a ten-year-old boy. Bird screeched and thrust herself upward in high dudgeon. Gurgling Brook squealed with laughter.

"Midnight," scolded Tarkyn. "You're too big now. Be kind to me."

In answer, the boy, whose hair was a darker brown and eyes were a deeper green, beamed up at him and threw his hands around Tarkyn's neck. Tarkyn hugged him back before sliding him to the ground. "And this," he said to his companions, "is Midnight. He's deaf, so can't introduce himself but he can share images, Stefan."

"Cup of tea?" asked Autumn Leaves urbanely. "Just a jiffy and we'll get a fire going. Rainstorm, where's the kettle?"

"I'll get wood," said Lapping Water. "You mind little madam, Tarkyn. I love her, but I have had her undiluted for over a week now."

"Delighted," said Tarkyn, holding his arms wide for the little girl to run into.

Twenty minutes later, they were all seated on the ground around a small but efficient fire. There were not enough cups, so they shared one cup between two.

"Stefan is a very good archer, you know," said Tarkyn, in an effort to start a conversation.

"Are you?" Rainstorm smiled. "Well, our very best archer is Thunder Storm, but he's not here. Lapping Water is probably next best. Maybe you'd like to compete with her sometime? What about slingshots? How are you with them?"

Stefan raised his eyebrows. "Slingshots? Haven't used them since I was a kid." He turned to Lapping Water. "Are you really the best archer here?"

She shrugged. "Probably."

"Okay. Let's set up some targets," said Stefan eagerly.

"I'll do it," said Rainstorm, springing to his feet. He peered around the clearing then walked through a narrow gap in the trees. After one hundred and twenty yards, he stopped at a thin tree and picked up a bit of clay. *"Will this do?"* he asked silently.

"Good Start," replied Lapping Water.

Rainstorm drew three sets of concentric circles down the trunk of the tree. The widest circle was only six inches in diameter. He stepped lightly back to the firesite, his feet leaving no trail. "Okay. Who's in?"

After a noisy discussion, everyone but Tarkyn and Gurgling Brook decided to have a go. When Anton asked why he refused, Tarkyn held up his hand. "I only use magic. Can't be bothered learning to use physical weapons when I have them inbuilt."

Anton raised his eyebrows. "Right. Fair enough."

"Everybody ready? Rules are: Three arrows. State which targets you're going for before firing." Rainstorm looked around. "Are you happy enough with our bows, Stefan? I gather you're a bit of an expert in arms."

"Your bows and your arrows are of excellent quality."

"Thanks." Rainstorm gave a broad smile. "I made the bow you've chosen myself." He gave a self-deprecating shrug. "My family are Forestals, specialize in craftwork. My dad still isn't sure whether I'm much of a craftsman."

Stefan was beginning to thaw. "Well, I'm impressed."

It soon became apparent that only Stefan was a match for any of the woodfolk. Anton's accuracy deteriorated under the strain of shooting so far; one arrow missed entirely, one scraped the edge of the tree and one didn't quite make the distance. Sparrow hit targets with two arrows and missed the tree completely with the third. Although only thirteen years old, she was clearly disappointed with her performance. Marjorie was a fair shot but knew she couldn't make the distance so stood thirty yards closer to the target so she could at least demonstrate that she could aim. Jackson was outright terrible, much to everyone's enjoyment, but Lapping Water trumped the field by hitting dead centre of each of the three bullseyes so fast that the first arrow had not stopped quivering before the third had hit its target.

Stefan's eyes widened in appreciation. "And you say this Thunder Storm is even better. I can't see how he could be."

Lapping Water smiled, completely unmoved by her performance. "Because it is much harder to use slingshots so accurately that you can knock out a man and know you haven't killed him. You need finesse as well as accuracy for that. Much harder."

"Thunder Storm can hit eight stones set up on a log so that they all rock gently at the same time, but none of them falls," said Rainstorm proudly.

"We all aspire towards that feat." Lapping Water's soft green eyes twinkled at Stefan. "We try not to kill people, you see, and the stones from slingshots leave no trace that we have been there, whereas arrows are a dead giveaway."

Just as Stefan and his family were digesting this information, they were interrupted by the sound of footsteps tramping through undergrowth on the path leading from the road. In the blink of an eye, the woodfolk were gone. Stefan, Marjorie, Anton and Jackson looked around, bewildered. Tarkyn smiled and showed them Gurgling Brook still seated on his lap. "She can't do it yet without her mother's help and I can't do it at all."

"Do what?" asked Stefan.

"Hmm. I call it flicking. I don't know that it has a name. Anyway, they just think themselves somewhere else, somewhere in sight... and they're there."

While they were digesting this, Javier and Marin pushed their way into the clearing.

"Hello, all. Couldn't get away 'til now," said Marin. "Had to help with lunch." This was said with no rancour at all at the three who could have been helping too.

"Yes. Followed your tracks and here we are. What's happening?"

A chuckle formed in Stefan's mind and he recognized Rainstorm's voice. "*My goodness! You are the odd one out. They're all as like as peas in a pod.*"

Stefan was starting to get used to this. "*They've both taken the oath too.*"

"*Oh good.*" Rainstorm appeared beside Stefan, grinning,

making Javier and Marin jump back in surprise. "Hello. I'm Rainstorm."

They stared and Javier said, "You must be Stefan's real brother. You look just like him."

Rainstorm turned and studied Stefan. "No, I don't. I don't look anything like him at all."

Tarkyn laughed. "No, he doesn't, but it takes a while to notice the differences."

The rest of the woodfolk appeared around them, alarming Javier and Marin so much that they found themselves instinctively standing back to back.

Waterstone waved his hands disarmingly. "Settle down. No one's going to hurt you." He introduced himself and the others, adding, "As far as we know, none of us is related to Stefan here. We're all from Eskuzor." He looked around into the surrounding trees. "But I wouldn't mind betting that some woodfolk in these forests are related to him."

23

By the end of the second day, Sasha was beginning to settle into palace life, secure in the knowledge that it was only temporary. She was introduced to Lady Teresa, daughter of the Queen Mother's Lady-in-Waiting, Lady Charlotte. At first, both Jayhan and she found Teresa insipid and too compliant but as Teresa got to know them and trust that they wouldn't go rushing off to report on her, she revealed a quietly irreverent sense of humour.

Teresa was kind and patient as Sasha was given intensive lessons in court etiquette and particularly in dining: using the proper utensils at the proper times, knowing to whom she could speak at the dinner table and learning which topics were acceptable for conversation. Sasha tried her best and brought her fearsome memory to bear so that she quickly mastered most of the requirements. However, she baulked at the expected treatment of servants who poured her drinks and served her food. It was impressed upon her that she could only acknowledge them if she were not engaged in conversation. Apparently, it was important to ignore servants while she was conversing with another diner. Otherwise she would be indicating that she placed the worth of the servant above the worth of her fellow diner, to whom she should be giving her undivided attention. Sasha thought this was complete nonsense and refused point blank to comply with it. All the arguments in the world would not convince her.

Josie and Charlotte were relieved that Gavin was elsewhere in the kingdom for the next few weeks and would not see Sasha until next time she came, as it gave them time to polish her manners without having to apply too much pressure. They did not meet her head-on. Instead, they organised a dinner and invited Lord Argyve, Lady Electra, Jon, and Bert, their head horse trainer.

Bert was laconic, had a healthy disrespect for everyone not directly involved with horses and did not suffer fools gladly. Knowing Sasha's love of horses, they had seated Bert next to her and then watched as a constant stream of servants offered a selection of entrees, drinks, platters of meat, several types of vegetables each offered by a different servant, gravy and sauces. Time and again, Sasha had to break off her conversation with Bert to acknowledge each servant. Eventually, annoyed by the constant interruptions, Bert lapsed into silence and addressed himself exclusively to his food.

Feeling flustered and disappointed that she had not had a chance to talk more with Bert, Sasha retired as soon as good manners would allow, retreating to her room to think.

The next morning, she rose with the dawn, donned a jerkin and breeches and trotted downstairs to the kitchens where, as she expected, she found the servants having their breakfast before preparing to serve those of their masters and mistresses.

Conversations ceased as she entered the room. This did not rattle her as she knew how things worked in the servants' domain.

"Good morning, my lady," said the butler, Stevenson, who was seated at the head of the table. "Can we be of assistance?"

Sasha smiled. "Yes. I hope so." She indicated the huge teapot in the middle of the table. "Would you mind if I sat down and joined you for a cup of tea? You don't have to stand on ceremony, you know. I have been working as a stable boy for the Batians and am used to eating with their servants in the kitchen." She grimaced. "It's quite hard, actually, waiting for the later breakfast time. I'm usually starving and it's such a waste of the morning." She squeezed onto the bench between a maid and a footman and accepted a cup of tea. "Thanks. Still, I suppose I can just do more things before breakfast, can't I?"

"And to what do we owe this visit, Ma'am?" persisted the butler. "We do have to get on shortly."

"Sorry. Um, well, I have this problem, you see. At these dinners they have, I'm not supposed to thank you when you give me drinks and food and stuff. Well, I insisted that I should be able to and that's what I want to do, but last night..." she shrugged, "with all those different courses and different choices, it was a nightmare. And I ended up annoying Bert whom I would have loved to talk to, and it all went wrong, really. Any ideas? I really don't want to be rude to you and ignore you."

This gave rise to some animated responses and quite a few poorly suppressed laughs. Sasha could feel her face going hot. Perhaps this had been a bad idea. When the butler held up his hand to silence them, Sasha said sharply, "I don't think it's funny that I want to be respectful to you. If you're laughing because you think I should treat you with disdain, you need to look at your values."

"Lady Natasha," said Stevenson, "I thank you for your concern. In some cases, you are right; the people we serve ignore us, take us for granted and never thank us. However, in some circumstances, we are trying to be as inconspicuous as possible. If we attract too much attention to ourselves, we have failed to do our job well. So, in situations like last night, you are helping us to perform our duties well if you let us blend in, so to speak. You are welcome to thank us beforehand or later if you choose but during the meal, it may be ... hmm... counterproductive for both you and us."

Sasha frowned furiously while she thought about it. Then she gave a cheery smile. "So, it's all right if I don't thank you all the time? You won't feel hurt or resentful or think I'm being mean or haughty?"

This time the laughter around the table was friendlier.

"No," said a portly fellow with a pencil-thin moustache. "Think of it as a play where we're all actors with roles we have to perform." He smiled around the table. "And we all know how you feel now... and speaking for myself, I'm glad you didn't just come into the palace and follow all those rules without thinking about them."

Sasha smiled. "Thanks. And if any of you ever need help, just let me know and I'll see what I can do." She extricated herself from her squashed position on the bench and headed out towards the stables, unaware that she had just won the hearts of the palace staff.

She walked until she found the cottage she was looking for in a small fenced-off garden a hundred metres from the back of the stables. She glanced at the green wooden door with its arched top and the darkened leadlight windows and wondered if perhaps Bert was not yet up. She knew he lived here alone and did not breakfast with the others, being of a higher status. His loss, she thought. After some hesitation, Sasha took a breath and knocked firmly on the door.

Almost immediately the door opened and Bert, dressed and ready to emerge, appeared in the doorway. His eyebrows rose in surprise as he surveyed her in her jerkin and breeches. "Good morning, young lady. And what can I do for you? Unusual wear for horse riding. Don't you have a riding habit?"

"Hello. I wasn't planning on going riding just now. I came to talk to you but I thought you might be busy so I thought I could help so you'd have time to talk."

"Help with what?"

"Mucking out the stables?"

Bert laughed. "I don't muck out the stables. I have stable-boys for that. And the grooms prepare the horses for riding or carriage work. I just train them."

"Oh. I see." She frowned at him. "Is that enough to do?"

"How many horses do you have in Lord Batian's stables? Twenty?"

"Not quite."

"I have over two hundred horses to train up. I train all the horses for the King's Guard as well as the riding and carriage horses for all the nobility who stay here, the horses for our own carts and the king's own horses, of course. There's a constant turnover."

Sasha's eyes widened. "Wow. What a wonderful job."

"It is." He raised an eyebrow, still not thawing. "Now, what did you want to talk to me about?"

Sasha looked down and scuffed her foot. "I wanted to say sorry for last night. I really wanted to talk to you but never found the time. It was very complicated with all those dishes. There didn't seem to be time for anything else. But while I was trying to be kind to the servants, I think I may have been rude to you. So, I'm sorry." She took a breath and looked up, meeting his eyes.

To her relief, he was smiling. "Apology accepted. You're a good girl to come and talk to me about it. I was a bit fed up by the end of the night, to tell you the truth." He closed the door behind him and began to walk towards the stables. "I hear you and your brother have quite a way with horses. You should come down sometime, meet some of the staff and the horses and watch me training... if you'd like to."

Sasha grinned. "I'd love to. Maybe not for a few days. I have to spend most of my time in dresses at the moment, to get used to it. Jayhan and I are allowed to play in the lake garden in the afternoons, but I still have to wear a dress." She rolled her eyes. "Makes tree-climbing difficult, I can tell you."

Bert chuckled. "I expect... I hope... you'll get used to it." He nodded in the direction from which she had come. "You'd better get back up to the palace and into harness, before they notice you wearing your breeches again."

"Yes, I suppose so." Sasha sighed. "It's not much fun, you know. I miss being with horses."

As it turned out, she wouldn't get much time to get used to her dresses.

24

E ach afternoon, Jayhan and Sasha ventured further and further afield in their exploration of the gardens, although always within the walls of the palace. Teresa had spent most of her life indoors, painting or embroidering or playing her flute, but after a couple of days of intense cajoling, she tentatively joined them.

Teresa clearly felt out of her element and while they pushed through the reeds to see the swan's nest, she would hang back standing uncertainly on the lawn, waiting for them to return and tell her what they had found. Jayhan and Sasha didn't mind. In fact they liked telling her all their adventures and discoveries. Twice they had slipped into the muddy mire at the edge of the lake while they were trying to sneak closer through the reeds to spy on the swans. Teresa delighted them by squealing in horror at the state of their clothing, the mud and reeds clinging to their shoes, the hem of Sasha's dress and the lower half of Jayhan's breeches.

After the second time that Sasha trooped back inside wearing ruined court slippers, Josie had compromised and allowed her to wear sturdy boots under her gown. Her gown could be washed but the fine satin of the slippers became stained beyond repair.

Around the other side of the lake, Jayhan and Sasha, with Teresa in tow, discovered a large gardening shed, piles of soil and gravel and a variety of interesting tools, all screened by a dense stand of wattle trees and grevilleas. None of these fascinations could be seen from the palace, which gave Jayhan and Sasha the great delight of having discovered a secret place. Of course, it was not an exciting secret place to the gardeners, who based all of their operations from there. It was, however, the gardeners' safe haven and they were not pleased by the intrusion of 'high-born folk from the palace.'

Feeling their antipathy, Teresa hung back, standing uncertainly at the edge of the bushes, her hands clasped over her delicate, perfectly clean, pale grey gown. She watched, half in admiration and half in trepidation, as Sasha and Jayhan trotted confidently up to a surly older woman who was seated on a sawn-off stump, smoking a pipe. The woman eyed them as they approached but offered no greeting.

Unperturbed, Sasha beamed at her. "Hello. Isn't the swan's nest marvellous? And there's a nest in the bottle brush at the edge of the lake near the entrance to the king's study. Are there any eggs in it? It's too high for me to see. Any other nests you know of?"

The woman scowled at her, then reluctantly removed her pipe from her mouth. After a noticeable pause, she growled, "Now don't you go disturbing those nests. This garden gives the birds a safe place to rear their young and we don't need the likes of you disturbing them."

Rather to Jayhan's surprise, Sasha drew herself up and answered, "Firstly, Jayhan and I love watching birds and would never hurt them. Secondly, what exactly do you mean by 'the likes of you'?"

For a moment, the woman looked startled before arranging her features back into a scowl. "I mean young visiting nobles with a care for nothing but their own entertainment." She put her pipe back into her mouth and drew on it with an air of finality.

Sasha glanced at Jayhan, who could see a myriad of responses flitting through her head and wondered what she would say. He thought she would point out that she had been, or was, a stable boy, but she didn't. "Fair enough," she said. "I can see we must seem that way to you. So, what can we do to help?"

The woman took her pipe out of her mouth and tapped the bowl against the side of the stump, sending a dark wad of tobacco to join a little pile at the bottom of the stump. "Ooh, there's plenty you could do, but if you go getting yourself dirty on my account, Josie will have my guts for garters."

"No, she won't," said Sasha confidently. "She's used to us getting dirty in the afternoons."

"Huh. Is that right?" The woman brushed a dirt-ingrained hand through her grey curly hair while she thought. Her fingers found a leaf trapped in the curls and she pulled it out, inspected it then flicked it away, frowning in irritation. She focused on Sasha and Jayhan again. "Well, as it happens, young Dave has been off sick for the last couple of days and I'm behind with planting these little seedlings. A new bloke started this morning but we're still way behind. He and the others are off trimming hedges and weeding at the moment." She pointed the stem of her pipe at a cluster of small potted plants. "Look at these poor seedlings. They're already too big for their pots." Her gaze travelled to Teresa standing hesitantly at the gap in the screen of shrubbery. "What about her? Does she want to join you?"

"I don't know," said Jayhan. "I'll go and ask her." A minute later, he was back. "No. She could see you didn't want us here. She worries a lot about etiquette and things, you know."

"Huh." The woman gave her pipe another thump, cleaned out the bowl with her little finger then stood up and stomped over to Teresa. Jayhan and Sasha watched her give a nod of respect to Lady Teresa that she had not given to them. Then they talked for a while before the gardener returned to them, Teresa walking by her side.

"Hello," said Sasha brightly, smiling a welcome. "We're going to learn how to plant little plants. Are you going to do it too?"

Teresa glanced down at her soft, manicured, white hands then back up at Sasha. She gave gentle smile. "No. But I'll watch."

"We do have gloves you can use," suggested the gardener.

"No thank you, Kate," Teresa's voice was gentle but firm.

Jayhan stared at her a moment longer, then shrugged. "Right. Let's go."

Kate disappeared into the shed and returned with a kitchen chair that she placed near her stump. "Here you are, Your Ladyship." She studied the chair, frowning at the smears of dirt on it. "Just a moment," she said, disappearing into the shed and returning with a rag that she used to wipe the seat. She shrugged. "Best we can do, I'm afraid."

"Thank you." Teresa sat down primly and folded her hands in her lap. An unexpected twinkle in her eyes made the other two children realise that she knew what they were thinking but didn't mind.

Kate showed them where she wanted the seedlings planted, how to dig the holes with the trowels she provided them and how much fertilizer to put in each hole. Then she gave them each a big bucket filled with water and showed them how to soak each plant and fill each hole with water before taking the seedling from its pot, placing it carefully in its new home and pressing the soil in around it.

"There's a mound of compost around the side of the shed. Take that wheelbarrow and fill it, then come back here for the plants and the buckets of water." She sat down on her stump and drew out her pipe again. "Off you go. See you shortly."

She pulled out a small pouch of tobacco from the pocket of her breeches, untangled a few strands, rolled them between her fingers into a rough sphere then pressed the little ball of tobacco into the bowl of her pipe.

"My father has a pipe," offered Teresa. "It has pretty carvings on it, birds mostly."

Kate nodded and continued to poke and prod with her fingers in the bowl of the pipe until she was satisfied that it was pressed in firmly enough to burn slowly, but not so firmly that it wouldn't light. "Does he now? Do you like the smell of the tobacco?"

Teresa scrunched up her nose in thought. "I think so. It just smells like my father and I like him, so I suppose I like the smell." As Kate's pipe caught alight and a tendril of smoke snaked towards her, she added, "His pipe smells more... hmm... sweet? Or scented."

"His tobacco has probably been soaked in some special liqueur." She drew on her pipe. "Costs more, of course."

They lapsed into silence and time passed. Still no sign of Jayhan and Sasha. After another five minutes, Kate took a last draw on her pipe and stood up. "Blast those children. What tricks are they getting up to? It does not take this long to fill a wheelbarrow, even for children."

Teresa watched her stomp around the corner of the shed,

glad that Kate was bent on confronting her friends rather than her. A minute later she heard Kate roar, "Jayhan! Natasha! Come out this instant. My nursery is not your playground for playing hide and seek. You haven't even started filling the wheelbarrow." Teresa heard an unladylike snort. "Huh! And to think I wasted my time teaching you how to plant seedlings. You won't be back around this side of the lake again in a hurry."

As Teresa listened, a frown gathered on her face. Her new friends were adventurous and lively, but she had not seen them being deliberately rude. It seemed out of character for them to leave Kate waiting for them. With her usual grace and lack of haste, she stood up and walked around the corner to join the irate gardener. "Excuse me, Kate."

Kate turned her angry glare on her. "Now what? Your two friends have snuck off. Looks like they didn't like the idea of a bit of hard work, after all."

Teresa shook her head, an anxious ball forming in the pit of her stomach. "No. That's just it. I don't think they'd run off on you. They're not like that. Lady Natasha works in a stable when she is not here in the palace and by everything I hear, she loves the hard work and strives hard to please the head groom."

Kate looked thunderstruck. "Good heavens! Does she?" She glanced around, seeing the empty wheelbarrow, still with the shovels lying in it. She frowned and took a closer look. The shovels, which were kept pristine, had damp bits of compost clinging to them. Her gaze travelled to the compost heap where darker moist hollows gave evidence that it had been recently disturbed. Enough to fill at least two wheelbarrows had been removed since the last shower of rain. Struggling to interpret what had happened or was happening, she broadened her gaze to take in the castle walls that towered several hundred yards away and the dirt paths leading from the stables, her gardening area and the kitchens that provided egress for supplies and removal of waste. The three paths converged into a single lane that led through the rear gate of the castle, past the palace guards and out into the working area of Highkington.

Even as she watched, a wooden cart piled high with rubbish, old straw and dirt trundled past the guards and out into the world beyond.

A jolt of shock ran through her. "Guards!" she yelled, but she was far from the nearest guard station. She turned to Teresa. "Run! Run to that gatehouse and alert the guards. You'll be faster than me. Gammy leg. I'll be right behind you."

Teresa didn't hesitate. She picked up her skirts and raced down the dirt path, in a display of athleticism that would have surprised her new friends. As she neared the guards standing on either side of the gates, she shouted, "Help! We need help. Get your captain!"

The guards glanced at each other but before they could respond, Kate roared from further away. "You heard her! Do what she says. This is an emergency. We need someone to get after that cart that just went through here."

The righthand guard fled indoors to send a message through. Moments later, he reappeared and took up his position again at the gate. "We can't leave our posts, but others are coming."

As she limped up, Kate muttered to Teresa, "You'd better be right about your friends."

"I agree," said Teresa. She glanced at Kate and gave a tense smile. "But it would actually be better if I were wrong."

The Captain of the Guard arrived, hastily buttoning the top button of his jacket. He nodded at Kate. "Explain."

"Two children have disappeared from around the side of my shed. Lady Teresa assures me they would not have run off. A cart bearing rubbish has just passed through these gates. I have enough compost missing to cover them both in that cart."

"And," added Teresa, "Lady Natasha is the king's cousin."

Kate paled. "Oh lord. Is she?"

Captain Bryant didn't debate. He turned and delivered a string of orders. The guards were questioned briefly but they had not been watching the path taken by the cart. Guards patrolling the tops of the walls were also questioned and one reported seeing the cart turn to the left at the second intersecting road.

Within minutes, twenty guardsmen had run through the gates, splitting into smaller groups that headed in different directions once they had reached the left-hand turn taken by the cart. Fifteen minutes later, a squad of twenty riders clattered through the gates to join and widen the search. Several guards prowled around Kate's shed, in case the children were hiding or were being held somewhere within the grounds.

Ten minutes later, Josie came puffing up, a train of servants in her wake. She demanded a report then sent servants off to inform the king, Sheldrake, Lord Jon and Lady Electra. She turned to the captain, "My staff are at your disposal to assist you in whatever way we can."

The guards on the gate were replaced, so they could be questioned more closely. They were both tense at having allowed an abduction to occur right under their noses, but anxious to help.

Samar, an older man who was looking forward to retirement in the spring, sat stiffly in a small room inside the gatehouse, helmet in hand, facing his captain. "We know the blokes who drive the carts in and out. We've been watching them for years. We even know the carts. That cart's left wheel has a lump in the metal rim that thumps each time it touches the ground. The bloke who drives it, his name is Rob." He glanced at his fellow guard. "We call him Rob Rubbish amongst ourselves, though he brings in clean hay, gardening supplies like gravel and such. We often inspect his cart to make sure it's clean when it comes back in. We don't look so hard when he's on his way out." A faint flush coloured the man's cheeks and he moved uncomfortably.

"And was the driver today Rob... Rubbish?" asked the captain, betraying no annoyance at their confessed error.

"Yeah. Same bloke as always."

"Did he speak to you?"

Samar shook his head. "No. Never does, unless he has to. Just drove on through, same as always."

The Captain thought for a moment. "Was anything about him different?"

The guards thought for a few moments. Then Samar scratched his beard and said slowly. "Well, he had his scarf wrapped around his face. But he gave a throaty cough and we, *I*, just assumed he had a cold. Not the first time. He's not the fittest character I know."

"Was the cart stacked high? Could someone having been hiding behind him, threatening him in some way?"

Garth, the younger guard, chimed in. "Yeah, maybe. He didn't seem tense though. It was pretty loaded up. There was a lot of old carpet and rubbish from one of the rooms they had redecorated, plus old straw and a pile of dirt."

"What colour was the dirt?" asked the captain.

Garth frowned at the unexpected question. "What?"

Samar responded before the captain could become impatient. "It was dark brown, sir, full of little bits, you know, bits of leaves, twigs, stuff like that."

The captain's blood chilled in his veins.

The abandoned cart was found an hour later.

PART IV

25

F ive pairs of green eyes lit in horror at Anton's invitation for the woodfolk to return with them to the Creeping Vine for dinner. The afternoon sun was sending slanted shafts of light through the trees of the Great Forest, which had reminded the four Vines that they would soon be needed at the inn for the evening rush and prompted the invitation.

"Sorry," said Waterstone, seeing him stiffen. "Your inn looks very nice... um, solid, from what Tarkyn has shown us and from the very little we know of inns. But none of us has ever been inside a building." He shrugged. "Besides, we are sworn to protect the secrecy of our kin, just as you now are. We would be exiled, condemned to a solitary existence, if we betrayed the existence of woodfolk by appearing in public."

Anton's eyes narrowed. "And what would happen to us if we betrayed your secret?"

Waterstone stared at him, hesitant to jeopardise their new relationship.

"We'd kill you," said Rainstorm matter-of-factly from the side, then grinned at their shocked faces.

Marjorie's eyes were wide. "Really?" When Rainstorm shrugged and nodded, she grew angry. "That is not funny. It's frightening."

Rainstorm spread his hands. "Why? I presume you are all trustworthy or Tarkyn would never have told you. So the issue will never arise."

"But what if some people who had visited the inn started talking as though we had told them when we really hadn't?" she asked. "What happens if you mistakenly think we have told someone?"

"Fair question," said Autumn Leaves, as he refilled the kettle and set it on the fire. When he was sure it was balanced, he looked over his shoulder at them. "If we didn't see or hear you directly telling someone, we would give you the chance to explain."

Stefan snorted. "Well, obviously we might lie to you if we had told someone and our life was on the line. So how could you believe we were telling the truth?"

Waterstone glanced at Tarkyn before saying, "If Tarkyn allowed it and you were willing, we could use our mindpower to overcome your will. Then if we asked for the truth, you would be unable to lie to us."

Anton rolled his eyes at Stefan. "These people of yours are a nightmare. Kill us or subvert our will without a second thought, just for talking about them."

"They are not my people," Stefan said in a hard voice. "I would never act like that." He turned to glare at Tarkyn. "What have you forced us into?"

Before Tarkyn could reply, Lapping Water rounded on Stefan. "Don't judge until you know what you are talking about. Imagine living in a land filled with sorcerers who are bigger, more powerful and more aggressive than you. Would you want your existence paraded around if you could keep safe by staying separate from them?"

Tarkyn and Jackson both frowned and chorused from opposite sides of the clearing, "We're not all bad."

Lapping Water's anger melted, and she grinned at Tarkyn. "Of course you're not. I married you... without coercion," she added hastily. She walked over to him and wrapped her arm around his waist. He re-adjusted Gurgling Brook's position in his arms so that he could put his arm around his wife's shoulders and gave her a wry smile.

"Oh yes. I can vouch for that," said Rainstorm cheerily. "Ancient Oak... that's Waterstone's brother... and I spent weeks trying to get Tarkyn and Lapping Water together."

The Vines watched this interchange in some bemusement.

"If you're trying to reassure us, it isn't working," objected Marjorie after a moment. "You're saying that sorcerers are even worse than you. That is no comfort at all. And you say you keep secret and separate from them and yet you have married one. Pardon me if I'm confused."

Waterstone's calm voice made itself heard. "I will explain." Everyone fell silent and listened. "We have a tradition of secrecy that stretches back for hundreds of years. Fifteen years ago, our existence was discovered by Tarkyn's father, King Markazon of Eskuzor. He forced us to swear allegiance to him and for that allegiance to transfer to Tarkyn after his death." Seeing them frown and cast considering glances at Tarkyn, he added hastily, "It was never Tarkyn's fault. If you want to know more, I will tell you over the days to come, but for now, I will remain brief. Before King Markazon, we had never encountered another sorcerer. Then, four years ago, Tarkyn was exiled by his brothers, unjustly I might add, and ended up in the forest living among us. Because we were oathbound, we had to accept him as our liege.

At first, we resented his presence among us," he glanced at Tarkyn, giving him a rueful smile, "... a lot. We have never had leaders even amongst ourselves, let alone accepting an outsider as our ruler. But slowly, a few of us came to know him better."

At this point Gurgling Brook began to grizzle, tired of being held immobile in Tarkyn's arms for so long. Tarkyn let her down and glanced at Midnight as he sent him a mind message. Midnight looked up from where he was squatted drawing the Vine family members in the dust of the clearing and gave a shrug and a smile before trotting over to take Gurgling Brook's hand and lead her to his drawing. He gave her a stick which she proceeded to smack the ground with, rather than draw, entertaining herself by hitting a variety of leaves, pebbles and the earth and listening to the different sounds. The point of this was, of course, lost on Midnight, who couldn't hear any of the wondrous noises she was creating, but he left her to it and went back to his drawing.

Once Tarkyn was sure she was settled, he continued Waterstone's story. "And because of their association with me, these woodfolk met my friend Danton, who came to look for me in exile and various other sorcerers who became entangled in my, *our*, cause to prevent civil war between my brothers."

"So," concluded Waterstone, "since Tarkyn's arrival among us, we have accepted," here he paused and counted on his fingers, "I'd say nearly twenty sorcerers knowing about us."

"Plus those from the Lost Forest," added Tarkyn. "There must be a couple of hundred of them."

"Yes, but they don't count because if they ever broke the oath of secrecy, everyone would think they're talking about fictitious people in the mythical Lost Forest," said Rainfall promptly.

"Even now," interposed Lapping Water, "although we work with the Royal Family to carry information the length and breadth of the kingdom, our existence is a state secret. Very few sorcerers know of us, and, as far as I know, neither do any of the people in Carrador who aren't sorcerers or woodfolk." A little frown appeared between her eyes. "What *do* you call your people?"

"People," answered Anton dryly.

"Oh." Suddenly Lapping Water grinned, easing some of the tension, since her grin was not cocky as Rainstorm's had been and reflected genuine amusement.

"They are not here to kill you," said Tarkyn, letting his authority enter his voice. "In fact, they are bestowing a great honour on you by allowing you to learn of their existence and to meet some of them."

Autumn Leaves was checking the kettle, but when he realised it was not yet simmering, he straightened to look at the Vines. "You don't understand the significance of this meeting. Our whole Eskuzorian woodfolk nation held widespread discussions before deciding that we could make ourselves known to you and we have walked over a hundred miles to reach you." He nodded at the arms master. "And it was mainly for your sake, Stefan, that we did."

Stefan's face reddened and he dropped his gaze to the ground, scuffing his foot until he had left a small furrow in the soft orange dirt. Everyone watched but said nothing. Then he heaved a breath and lifted his head. "I apologize for my harsh words earlier. You were right, Lapping Water. I did judge too hastily." But he looked on the edge of panic.

"*Steady, my friend,*" came Waterstone's voice in his head. "*We may have taken great pains to come to this point, but we have no expectations of you. We also wanted to know, for our own sakes, why a woodman was living among outsiders and what this means for us.*"

"*If you walk away, we will understand,*" Lapping Water

gave a warm smile. *"But we would love to..."* She shook her head and spoke aloud. "You have had enough for today. Go home to your family and your inn. Perhaps, if you wish it, we will see you tomorrow."

Anton glanced at his siblings before striding forward to wrap a sure arm around his brother's shoulders. Studying Stefan's face, he said, "You're overwhelmed, aren't you? All this care and attention from these people and from us, your family." The emphasis on the last words conveyed a distinct message.

He lifted his head to stare a challenge at the woodfolk but found himself looking at an empty clearing. Other than the Vines, only Tarkyn remained. As he watched, Tarkyn crossed to the fire and lifted the kettle out of the flames.

"Kettle's boiled," said Tarkyn, as he turned and headed out of the clearing in the direction of the road. "I'll be back later."

Feeling a little wrong-footed, the Vines followed.

H idden within the trees, the woodfolk watched the Vines depart then listened until their footsteps along the path had faded. In the distance they could hear the faint sounds of a carriage's wheels crunching along the gravel of the road.

"Right," said Waterstone. "Let's move deeper into the forest. This firesite is too close to that road for my taste."

"I agree." Autumn Leaves swung down out of the trees and set about making cups of tea. "Might as well drink this first, now that the kettle is boiled. Then we'll head off."

Autumn Leaves realised that Midnight was standing next to him looking forlornly along the way Tarkyn had gone, tears in his bright green eyes. The solid woodman crouched down next to the little boy and tried to reassure him, using images, that Tarkyn would be back for him soon.

"Poor little fella," said Rainstorm sympathetically, "He's been so brave being away from Tarkyn for so long." He had stayed where he was, standing on a thin branch twelve feet above the ground. "Tarkyn's eagle has followed him back to the inn, so we've lost our temporary lookout. I'll keep watch until we leave."

"Thanks, Rainstorm. I'll send Midnight up with a cup of tea for you. Maybe having something to do will cheer him up."

"I'm not surprised he's upset," said Rainstorm. "It wasn't a very friendly meeting, one way and another."

"I think you could have been a bit more tactful, rather than just blatantly telling them we'd kill them," said Waterstone, as he accepted a cup of tea from Autumn Leaves.

"It shouldn't have come as a shock to them," objected Rainstorm. "What did they think the oath 'I vow not to reveal the presence of woodfolk on pain of death,' meant?" After a moment, Rainstorm gave a wry smile. "All right. I take your point, though it had to be said somehow, once they'd asked the question."

"True."

Half an hour later, they left the clearing and walked quietly south, leaving no sign of their passing. They were all on edge. This bushland with its swaying gums and yellow-studded wattles was sparser than the oaks, elms and beeches of their native forests. A black-tailed wallaby startled them as it broke cover and hopped off between the trees. Overhead, three pink and grey galahs chirruped at each other from the boughs of a large eucalyptus tree and a pair of green, purple and orange rainbow lorikeets raced through the trees, twisting and zigzagging between branches at breakneck speed, tweeting loudly as they passed, before coming to land neatly on a branch a little way ahead of them, next to a hollow in the tree's trunk.

As the woodfolk drew deeper into the forest, the vegetation changed again to myrtle and mahogany, with curling tree ferns clustered in the valleys and long vines swinging between trees. It was breathtakingly beautiful but totally alien for the woodfolk from Eskuzor. More than that, Stefan's existence implied that another nation of woodfolk lived within these woods and they had no idea how these people would react to unknown intruders in their traditional forests. As evening approached, the birds settled and fell silent, adding to their sense of unease.

Sparrow pointed to a thick cluster of tree ferns that shaded a running creek and stood close to a space beneath a grand old mahogany. "Camp here?" she suggested. "It's getting dark. We don't want to be too far from Tarkyn. We've hardly had a chance to talk to him." She grimaced. "And he'll never be able to find us, even if we send him images."

"True." Lapping Water studied the area. "Yes, this looks good." She glanced up at the dense canopy above her and realized that his eagle would not be able to see them from above. She gave a rueful smile. "I think Tarkyn needed those people to help him find the last firesite, even when Bird had shown him where it was. He really is a navigational nightmare."

Sparrow was about to let her pack slide from her shoulders, indicating to Midnight that they were stopping, when suddenly, Waterstone stilled. He sent a sharp warning to the others. They all stopped moving and listened. Slowly, they crept together into a defensive circle around Gurgling Brook, facing outwards, bows in hand, arrows nocked.

"*I wish there were more of us,*" murmured Lapping Water in mind speech.

Waterstone scanned the surrounding trees. "*There could never be more of us than a whole nation of woodfolk, unless we were mounting a war, which we are not and never have. Let's just hope that our small number shows that we're not a threat.*"

"*PUT DOWN YOUR WEAPONS AND WE WILL REVEAL OURSELVES.*"

"Stars above!" breathed Rainstorm out aloud. "Who on earth yells in mind talking?"

"I don't know," muttered Waterstone, "but we'd better do as requested."

"We could flick out of sight," suggested Sparrow, keeping her message strictly to her companions.

"It would be tricky," replied Autumn Leaves, *"if they're woodfolk like us."* He grimaced. *"We'll keep it as a last resort. Let's see how this goes."*

Slowly, the little group of Eskuzorian woodfolk lowered their bows and placed them carefully on the ground. They made no move to remove their knives or slingshots from their belts, hoping to keep themselves at least minimally armed.

Suddenly, more than twenty woodfolk appeared in front of them. They were not holding weapons at the ready, but Waterstone had no doubt that archers would have arrows trained on them from the trees around them.

Waterstone and his companions studied the Carradorian woodfolk. They too had green eyes but their hair was a few shades darker, something they had not noticed about Stefan, and their clothes were a deeper brown tinged with green. Waterstone considered their surroundings, deep within the rainforest, and decided that the differences in their appearance reflected the differences in their environments.

"How do you do?" said Waterstone politely. "We are pleased to meet you. I am Waterstone."

"Well, we are not pleased to meet you," returned a thickset woodwoman with a severe face and eyes glittering with anger.

"I suppose it is understandable," said Lapping Water mildly. "After all, we would be concerned if completely new woodfolk appeared in our own forests. I am Lapping Water," there was a pause, "... and you are?"

It was customary for all woodfolk to introduce themselves the first time they spoke. Not to do so was the height of rudeness. But perhaps customs were different here.

For a moment, the tight-faced woman glared at her, not pleased to be prompted. Then she said grandly, "I am Red Gum."

"What sound does Red Gum make?" asked Sparrow, puzzled. She waved her hand to indicate her companions. "We are all named for sounds of the forest."

"We are named for things found in the forest, not for their sounds," she replied, her tone of voice implying that she thought being named for sounds was ridiculous.

A mousy little woman next to her said diffidently. "Red Gum is named after a huge, strong, river red gum." She gave a timorous smile. "I am Grevillea."

"Grevillea?" asked Lapping Water. "What is Grevillea?"

"You may have seen them a few miles back. They are small bushes sprinkled with complicated red or yellow flowers. Their flowers are very beautiful."

"That is enough, Grevillea," interrupted Red Gum. "We are displeased with these people. We have seen them conversing with outsiders."

The Eskuzorian woodfolk exchanged glances, knowing this was going to be difficult.

"Yes, indeed we have. You have clearly flouted wood-folk law," said a wizened old man at the rear of them, whose long, bright white beard looked like it would make camouflage difficult. He sounded almost apologetic. "So, poor welcome though it is, you will have to begin your acquaintance with us by standing trial for betraying our presence to outsiders." Although his words were harsh, his tone was not and he added courteously, "I am Sphagnum Moss."

"Surely they should be given a chance to explain, grandfather?" demanded a young woodwoman, standing beside Sphagnum Moss. "I am Tree Fern."

Red Gum glared at her and then huffed impatiently. "That is why we hold a trial, dear."

"I agree. I am Spinifex," said a stern, stringy man in his fifties. He waved his hand, "Secure them."

In a concerted agreement of thought and a blur of movement, Waterstone and his companions grabbed their weapons and flicked into hiding. Lapping Water and Autumn Leaves found themselves beside two of the hidden archers, but before the archers could react, Lapping Water and Autumn Leaves flicked again to trees further away, then up into the higher boughs.

Midnight, a forest guardian just as Tarkyn was, reached out with his mind into the surrounding area, alerting every bird within a four-hundred-yard radius that he and his woodfolk companions were in trouble. In answer, out of every nest and from every perch, parrots, bowerbirds, birds of prey and tiny scrub wrens and songbirds swooped down into the clearing they had just left.

Brightly coloured parrots, irritable because they had been disturbed just as they were settling for the night, zoomed between and around the Carradorian woodfolk, shrieking. Owls and hawks circled overhead or perched in overhanging boughs, glaring down. Five sulphur-crested cockatoos swept into the lower branches of a myrtle, shrieking and strutting back and forth along the branches, bobbing their heads and raising their crests in outrage.

The archers in the trees were beset by little birds buzzing around their heads and landing on their heads, shoulders or arms. There was no way they could take aim and fire. And while the woodfolk on the ground were occupied with using their hands to alternately block out the excessive noise and/or to fend off the swarming birds, the Eskuzorian woodfolk flicked and flicked until they were far from these woodfolk and their threats of imprisonment and exile.

They mentally coordinated their mad dash, keeping their communication strictly between themselves. Autumn Leaves stayed close to Lapping Water, keeping an eye on Gurgling Brook and making sure Lapping Water was able to keep up, since she was flicking for two. Waterstone made sure Midnight was close to him, giving him a congratulatory pat on the back between flicks. Without conscious intention, they soon found themselves in the eucalypts near the rear of the Vine Inn.

After a short conference, they sent out an urgent mind message to Tarkyn.

S tefan was seated near the end of the bar, away from the other drinkers, working his way stolidly through tankards of ale and talking in a low voice to his father when he was not otherwise engaged in serving customers. He was also keeping a weather eye on the little table of two sorcerers, a mage and a shapeshifter.

"When can we meet them?" Sheldrake was asking, sipping from his fourth glass of wine. He leaned forward, his eyes lit with alcohol and enthusiasm. "They sound fascinating. I can't wait to meet them."

Stefan frowned but Maud, oblivious to his gaze, just smiled and shook her head. "Please excuse my husband, Lord Tarkyn. He doesn't mean to make them sound like scientific specimens. Believe me, he uses all of us, even my son and me, to further his knowledge of magic."

Sheldrake took Maud's hint, realising he was becoming too intense. He leaned back in his chair, making a conscious effort to relax. Stefan saw him glance around the inn's dining room, relieved to see that no one was watching them. Until his eyes met Stefan's.

Stefan rose a little unsteadily from the bar and dragged a chair over with one hand while holding his tankard in the other, then plonked himself down at their table.

Maud raised her eyebrows at Sheldrake as though to say, *Now see what you've done.*

Jackson shifted along to make room for him and smiled warily at him. "Hello. How are you doing?"

Stefan thumped his tankard on the table with rather more force than he intended and gave a jerk of surprise at the sound it made. "I'm fine. Never better," he added sarcastically. He leaned forward and stared owlishly at Sheldrake. Then he spoke in a low, intense voice. "Now you'd better watch yourself, my lord. You're just lucky it was only me that heard you. That oath you took? Pain of death. You hear me? Pain of death." He shook his head. "They're not kidding, either. They're trained killers. Kill you, quick as look at you, if you put a foot out of line."

"They're not like that," protested Tarkyn.

"Oh yes, they are," insisted Stefan. He knew he was a bit drunk, but he also knew he was right. He vaguely wondered if one was causing the other. "And deadly? You think I'm good? Well, they're better. Specially that woodwoman. What's her name?"

Tarkyn glanced around to make sure they could not be overheard. "That woodwoman," he said quietly, his voice taut with anger, "is my wife, Lapping Water."

Stefan stared at him. "Sorry. Didn't mean to be rude. Just forgot her name, that's all. She's the best marks... person I've ever seen and she's beautiful and self-assured but in a quiet, not in-your-face way. No wonder you love her. She's impressive."

Tarkyn couldn't help smiling and Stefan breathed a little

sigh of relief. This man was not one to be crossed unnecessarily.

"She is, isn't she?" said Tarkyn. "I was raised knowing that I was supposed to marry a foreign princess for the good of the kingdom. Your King Gavin was hoping I'd marry his younger sister." He grinned. "But I threw those expectations to the wind by marrying Lapping Water instead." He gave a quirky grimace. "No one outside a very select group knows, of course. So the general public will gradually decide that I am a confirmed bachelor."

The other three chuckled quietly. Stefan smiled along with the rest but suspected they were all revisiting their knowledge that the man with whom they were sharing their table far outranked them. A less comfortable silence followed, during which Stefan contemplated the High Lord, realizing how generous Tarkyn had been with his time in his care for his woodfolk, for the people of Carrador to whom he owed no allegiance, and for Stefan himself.

"I understand why they're so deadly about being secret," Stefan conceded, "at least in Eskuzor. I mean, sorcerers are a force to be reckoned with and imagine a whole country of them! I'd be keeping myself well clear of them too." He shrugged. "Not so sure about the need in Carrador. Not many mages here, and the rest of us... of *them* are pretty ordinary." He heaved a deep sigh and glanced quickly at Tarkyn then away. He leaned his cheek on his hand, looking miserable. "I don't belong anywhere anymore."

Everyone around the table quelled their need to rush in and reassure him, realising he would know all the arguments. But after a minute, Sheldrake couldn't help himself. "You know, Stefan, you belong in more places than most people. Firstly, you belong with us, as our arms master to protect that little girl, Sasha. Just that, on its own, is important. You belong to the King's armed forces. You belong in this tavern and to the Vine family and lastly, you belong to an amazing, mystical group of people with exceptional powers."

Without taking his head off his hand, he swivelled his eyes to look at Sheldrake. His mouth quirked in the beginnings of a smile. "Hmph."

"If you're looking for someone who really didn't belong anywhere, look at Jon when he first came to Carrador," continued Sheldrake. "His whole family had been killed and he brought Sasha into Carrador and had to leave her in an orphanage because at twelve, he was too young to look after her but too old to stay in the orphanage. So he lived alone on the streets of Highkington for years."

"Sheldrake," said Maud reprovingly. "It does not help people to know that someone is worse off than themselves. Stefan has every reason to feel dislocated at the moment."

Jackson gave Stefan a pat on the back. "You belong in too many places, don't you? Not too few. Pretty confusing, I expect."

Stefan pulled himself upright and crossed his arms instead, still defensive but thawing. "Yep."

Suddenly he saw Tarkyn sit up and frown. When Sheldrake began to ask what was wrong, Tarkyn held up a hand to forestall him. After a minute of silence, his frown did not lessen but he became aware again of the people seated at the table with him. "My woodfolk are in trouble. So much so, that they have come close to the rear of the inn and want me to join them straight away." He took a deep breath, forcing himself to appear relaxed and to move slowly as he stood and said in a carrying voice. "Would anyone care to join me for an evening stroll?"

"That would be quite delightful," said Maud at her societal best.

Sheldrake sent him one penetrating glance and stood up. "I too would enjoy some fresh air before turning in."

"Jackson, meet us outside with our cloaks if you wouldn't mind," said Tarkyn, giving his aide de camp a reason to accompany them. "And Stefan, would you come with us so that we don't get lost? None of us knows the area very well..." Just as Stefan was thinking that he didn't want to see the woodfolk again so soon, the High Lord added, "if you wouldn't mind, that is. I am sure we can manage if you have other calls on your time."

And that concession was enough to make Stefan change his mind. Despite himself, Stefan smiled. "Thank you for your consideration but I think I can spare the time." He stood up, took a few breaths and became more focused than he had been. He realised that they would draw less attention to themselves if they did not all troop out past the bar, through the kitchen and directly to the back of the inn so he indicated the front door. "This way, if you please."

As Tarkyn nodded his thanks and preceded him through the front door, Stefan took the opportunity to catch his father's eye and indicate that he was going out for a while. Once outside, he found Tarkyn waiting impatiently, hopping from one foot to the other until Jackson joined them.

"Right. Let's go." Tarkyn turned to the arms master. "Once we get around the back, I will transmit the images of where they are, so that you can work out where to direct us to."

But when he was given the images, Stefan shook his head. "I don't recognise it in the dark. It could be one of several locations and I presume we don't have time for trial and error."

"No, we don't." Tarkyn turned to Maud. "What about you? Any ideas?"

"An owl could scan the forest and find them, but I'd need

some idea of direction. A bloodhound could follow their scent, but they didn't start from here."

"Hmm. Don't worry," said Tarkyn after a bit of thought. "I'll ask Midnight to send an animal."

"You'll what?" asked Sheldrake.

Tarkyn held up his hand. "Just a minute." After a noticeable pause, he smiled. "Midnight is a forest guardian, just as I am. But, unlike me, he is half woodman, half sorcerer. He has located an animal and has directed it to come towards the light of the inn. He will be able to see through its eyes. When it sees us, he will ask it to stop and we will be able to follow it back to my woodfolk."

Sheldrake raised his eyebrows. "Impressive. And these are woodfolk skills, I take it?"

"No. Not at all. Woodfolk cannot direct animals they don't know any better than sorcerers or outsiders can. No. It is a forest guardian ability. Far more rare. As far as I know, Midnight and I are the only forest guardians alive today."

Minutes later, a rat-like creature about a foot long, with small ears, an extremely pointy nose, and a long, skinny tail, hopped like a rabbit into the shadows at the edge of the light that was being shed by the inn's windows and sat on its haunches, quivering with fright. Now and then, it would let out a worried chuff-chuff noise.

"Our guide has arrived," said Tarkyn. He peered closer. "What on earth is it?"

Maud smiled. "It's a bandicoot. Cute, isn't it?"

"Really? A bandicoot? Surely you're making that up. That's the funniest name I've ever heard."

"Perhaps we should just follow the brave little creature and stop casting aspersions on its name," suggested Maud acerbically.

"Oh. I beg your pardon," said Tarkyn stiffly. Stefan smiled, seeing that Tarkyn had suddenly remembered that he was a guest in a foreign land. Without another word, the High Lord walked carefully towards the bandicoot and squatted down in front of it, sending it waves of reassurance. He gave it an image of Midnight with a request to go to him. Immediately, the bandicoot shot off with such incredible speed that it was impossible to keep track of it, especially in the gloom. Tarkyn had to ask it to wait for them. With an impatient whuff-whuff, it sat back on its haunches until the five of them came up closer to it. Then it hopped off at a more moderate rate, occasionally darting sideways to grab a spider, worm or insect it spotted as it passed.

Ten minutes later, the bandicoot led them to Midnight, who was standing by himself in front of a huge, spreading gum tree. As soon as he saw Tarkyn, his face split into a grin and he ran forward to meet him. Tarkyn was shocked by how close his woodfolk had chosen to come to the dwelling of an outsider.

"It's all right," called Tarkyn quietly, sending a matching mental image of Sheldrake and Maud standing, hand on heart. "These two have taken the oath too." He sent a message of thanks to the bandicoot who scuttled off into the undergrowth.

While the other three woodfolk climbed down out of the great eucalyptus tree, less nimbly than usual, Lapping Water, holding Gurgling Brook's hand, flickered rather than flicked to stand beside him and flung her other arm around him, almost sobbing with relief. "Oh, am I glad to see you!"

"We all are," said Waterstone tensely. "Please, put up your shield. Now."

Stefan watched a wave of annoyance cross Tarkyn's face at Waterstone's peremptory tone. Quelling it, Tarkyn immediately waved his hand, encompassing all eleven of them in a translucent dome, demanding as he did so, "What's happened? What's wrong?"

"The local woodfolk saw us associating with outsiders. They're not happy. We had to get away from them before they constrained us and put us on trial. "

"And even though we haven't left tracks," added Autumn Leaves tightly, "it won't be long before they find us."

"No, of course not. It's their home territory, after all." Tarkyn hesitated. "Do you want light or should you stay hidden?" he asked.

Waterstone shrugged, "Now we're protected, it doesn't matter much. They'll find us sooner or later."

Tarkyn nodded and created an orb of light in the palm of his hand, which he threw gently into the air, leaving it hanging above them.

Stefan was impressed with his magical facility and caught Sheldrake raising his eyebrows at Maud in a silent exchange of admiration at a feat that Tarkyn clearly took for granted. He watched Sheldrake examining the bronze sheen of the dome that surrounded them. Then he saw the mage turn his attention to these people, slight of stature and green-eyed who, even with the variation in shades and styles of their light brown hair, were so like himself. He wondered what Sheldrake thought of them and was surprised to find himself ready to spring to their defence as he saw Sheldrake frowning at them. Then he followed Sheldrake's gaze and saw what the mage was seeing; the woodfolk were close to exhaustion. In fact, as he looked closer, they seemed almost transparent.

"Are you all right?" asked Sheldrake in some concern. Remembering what Tarkyn told him of woodfolk customs, he added hurriedly, "I am Sheldrake."

"How do you do? Sorry. I should have introduced myself. I am Waterstone, Tarkyn's brother."

Sheldrake gave a slight smile. "I believe you had, and

presumably still have, more urgent matters on your mind. I repeat, 'Are you well?'"

"Not really," replied Lapping Water, giving her name. "We have travelled constantly since you last saw us, and for the last hour, we have flicked as fast as we know how, in a zig-zag, trying desperately to throw off pursuit." She sagged against Tarkyn's side.

"We have never flicked so fast so often. Usually we only do it once, to get out of sight," said Autumn Leaves. "But it's easy to evade outsiders. Far harder to evade other woodfolk. We are in serious trouble. I am Autumn Leaves."

Listening to the tiredness and underlying panic in their voices, Stefan revised his opinion of their invincibility. Little did he know it, but Tarkyn was also concerned by their sudden vulnerability.

"I'm sorry we took so long," said Tarkyn. "We had to make an unhurried exit from the inn to allay suspicion. Otherwise, twenty people might have followed us to see what was happening." He studied their drawn faces. "Have you eaten?" When they shook their heads, he turned to Jackson. "Can you hold a shield for long enough to get to the inn and back?"

Jackson nodded.

"Excuse me," Stefan interrupted. "I can understand you're concerned for these woodfolk, my lord, but what about my family? These woodfolk may come after my family because they know about woodfolk. Isn't that right?"

After an uncomfortable silence, Rainstorm answered, "Yes, it is." He shrugged. "I doubt they will go too close to your inn, but they could shoot from within the tree line, possibly."

"Yes, you will certainly have to warn them, Jackson," said Waterstone calmly, "but there are actually several precautions they can take. I doubt these woodfolk would try to kill them where other people could see it or discover it. If they did, it would trigger a manhunt into the forest and that is the last thing they'd want. Also, they will not enter your buildings."

"So, if they stay with other people or keep clear of windows when no one is around, they should be safe enough," added Rainstorm. He shrugged. "It's not ideal but with any luck, we'll soon be able to sort this out with your local woodfolk." He caught Stefan considering him and gave him a crooked smile. "Sorry we got you all into this. Our little group is used to sorcerers and outsiders. Other woodfolk are not, not even most of the Eskuzorian woodfolk. If it is any comfort to you, we seem to be in as much danger as you are."

"No, it's not. I don't want you hurt either, especially since you were just trying to befriend me."

Rainstorm wasn't sure how to take this. He was glad that Stefan at least liked them enough not to want them hurt, but on the other hand, he had said 'trying to befriend', as though they had not succeeded. He glanced away, feeling a little hurt, and focused instead on Jackson.

"So," he said cheerily to cover his uncertainty, "will you stay at the inn or return to us once you have warned them?"

"Or bring them back with you?" asked Tarkyn.

Stefan shook his head. "No, my lord. The inn won't run itself and we have three other overnight guests to cater for, besides you four. I think Rainstorm has outlined enough precautions for my family to remain safely at the inn for the time being. They might need you to shield them, Jackson, to go outside and bring in supplies of wood and water though."

"Jackson," asked Tarkyn, "Can you make your shield large enough for two?"

Jackson smiled. "Shielding is my strength, sire. I can make very large shields for long periods of time."

Tarkyn smiled in return. "Excellent. A very useful skill." He thought for a moment then turned to Stefan.

Even as Tarkyn drew breath to speak again, Stefan knew what was coming and pre-empted him. "Yes, I'll go with him and help him to bring back food, drink and other supplies." Unlike the woodfolk, Stefan was used to taking orders and took no exception to Tarkyn's unspoken request. Instead, rising to the occasion as host, he asked Waterstone, "Anything you'd like in particular?"

Waterstone gave a tired smile. "I'd kill for a good glass of wine at the moment." He frowned at his poor choice of words. "Not literally, of course."

Stefan actually grinned. "Of course not." He looked around at the others. "Anyone else?" but no one else had particular requests.

"Thanks, Stefan... and Jackson," said Tarkyn. "While you get supplies, I'll be helping my friends to recover."

Tarkyn lifted the edge of his shield in one corner and they slipped out to head back towards the inn. Even as they walked away, Tarkyn positioned himself against the eucalypt and began to draw on its strength to transmit into each of the exhausted woodfolk.

"Right," Stefan heard him say to the woodfolk, "Tell me all about it."

Jackson did not have the same facility with producing luminescence so, as they drew away from the woodfolk's firesite, they had to make their way by the light of a three-quarter moon that kept drifting behind clouds. To those still watching them from within Tarkyn's shield, the two of them disappeared into the gloom even before they turned the first bend in the path, with Jackson's dark burgundy shield barely visible in the moonlight.

Still, the path was well worn, and Stefan was very familiar with it. As they rounded the bend, their eyes became adjusted to the low light and Stefan was able to warn Jackson of protruding roots and soggy puddles.

Suddenly, something clattered against the outside of Jackson's shield. Instinctively they ducked then froze, waiting for a further attack. Hearts pounding, they peered into the darkness. After a few moments, they straightened slowly.

Jackson grinned sheepishly. "They can't hurt us through this shield, you know. I don't know why I ducked."

"Instinct," said Stefan, the arms master. "Very wise, even if unnecessary."

The two of them retraced their steps for a few paces and searched the ground for a missile but could find nothing.

"Keep walking, I think," suggested Jackson uncertainly.

Even as he finished speaking, four more objects clattered on the outside of his shield. They stiffened but this time did not duck. Stefan's keen eyes followed the trajectory of an object as it hit the shield and bounced off, but when they moved to where he indicated it had landed, they could see nothing untoward on the dirt of the path.

Stefan frowned and squatted to pick up a few stones "They must be using slingshots. That missile could be any one of these."

By unconscious agreement, they broke into a run, but before long, Jackson tripped on a raised root in the middle of the path and for a moment, his shield wavered as he recovered his balance.

He pulled up, taking a deep breath. "Wait. It's better for me to go more slowly and focus on keeping my shield in place. We will only be a few minutes later in warning your family, but at least we'll make sure we get there."

Stefan nodded in the dark, realised his nod couldn't be seen and said briefly. "I agree."

A few more missiles hit the outside of the shield as they

walked, but their frequency tapered off as Stefan and Jackson came into sight of the inn.

As they stepped into the light shining forth from the windows of the inn, Jackson let out a long breath. "Waterstone wasn't overreacting, asking for Lord Tarkyn's shield. The danger from these people is real."

28

Through the kitchen windows of the inn, the darkness outside seemed to loom with hidden danger. The whole Vine family sat around the kitchen table with Jackson, drinking tea, each of them taking a turn to go through and look after the bar. Initially, they had been dismayed when the situation had been explained to them and were inclined to cast blame on Tarkyn for meddling.

"Maybe he should have left well alone," said Ivan heavily, "but it's done now and I think Vera and I should come and meet these woodfolk of yours, Stefan."

"They're not my woodfolk," said Stefan tightly. Unable to sit still, he carried cups to the sink and began to wash them.

Anton walked over and put his arm around Stefan's shoulder. "Don't worry. I think we're safe enough. It doesn't sound as though the local woodfolk are going to storm in here, especially with other people around. Just as your friend, Waterstone, said..."

"He's not my friend," countered Stefan belligerently.

"Oh, put a sock in it, Stefan," Marjorie retorted.

Stefan scowled but before he could say anything further, Anton continued as though he hadn't interrupted. "...these local woodfolk wouldn't want to provoke a manhunt."

"No, but they will be a continuing threat until this is resolved," said Javier, joining Stefan at the sink to wipe the cleaned cups, "so you're going to have to help High Lord Tarkyn and his woodfolk negotiate with these local woodfolk, Stefan, since the whole issue pivots around you."

Stefan exploded. "No, it doesn't! I didn't ask them to come."

"No, you didn't," replied Marjorie, in a patient tone that conversely indicated she was losing patience with him, "but regardless of that, it does pivot around you. I don't know whether the local woodfolk are just about to discover your existence or whether they have been turning a blind eye all these years." She threw another cup to him. "Here! But when the Eskuzorian woodfolk go home, you'll still be here and so will we... and so will the local woodfolk who, at the moment, apparently want to kill us. You have to be part of the solution."

Just then Marin, the wiriest of the Vine brothers but still far bulkier than Stefan, walked into the kitchen and gestured with his thumb over his shoulder. "Tom the Baker has just accused Jack the Smith of, and I quote, 'blowing his bellows in other people's forges.'"

Jackson chuckled, Marjorie mouthed, "Ooh dear," and Anton glanced at Ivan who said, "You can do it, son. Vera and I are off out with Jackson and Stefan. Marjorie, you can come with us too, if you'd like to."

Anton grinned. "Right. Thanks, Dad. I'd better get out there." He clapped Stefan on the back before heading to the door to the bar. "Good luck. See you whenever you get back," and left before Stefan could reply.

Stefan straightened and swivelled to lean back against the

sink. He crossed his arms and glowered at them all. Then suddenly he let out a gusty breath. "I'm being a pain, aren't I?"

"Yep," said Marjorie without a second's hesitation.

"Hmph. Sorry." He gave a lop-sided smile. "Well, we'd better get organized and get going then."

Marjorie, Jackson and Stefan brought in several loads of wood until it was stacked high in the corner of the kitchen and filled the water butt and a couple of extra buckets, while Ivan and Vera gathered supplies for the woodfolk and themselves.

"What about the horses?" asked Javier suddenly. "I need to check on them before bed and feed them first thing in the morning."

"I'll help," said Stefan.

"I'll take you over there now before we go," offered Jackson, "and I'll come back early tomorrow, if we're not back by then anyway." Grimacing inwardly, he asked, "How early?"

Javier gave him a knowing grin. "Before dawn." He laughed. "No. Not really. The travellers we have staying here aren't planning to leave before midmorning. So maybe an hour after cockcrow would do."

"Fine. I'll be here."

"Thanks."

As he forked hay down out of the loft, Stefan's mind began to reflect on his belligerence. He knew he had a tendency to become tetchy if people assumed things about him. All his life, people had sniped at his lack of height and assumed a corresponding lack of fighting ability. Now his family were assuming that just because he looked like these woodfolk, he would feel close to them. Well, he didn't. He wanted nothing to do with them.

He thought about that a bit longer, in light of his sister's unequivocal reaction to his behaviour. *Maybe I'm not being fair to these woodfolk. It's not their fault I look like them and am probably one of them, any more than it is mine. They are deadly fighters, but no one has been aggressive to me or my family. And after all, I too am a fighter to be reckoned with.*

Stefan climbed down the ladder and started forking hay into the stalls that had already been cleaned by Jackson and Javier.

Rainstorm was unnervingly honest about the consequences for breaking their blasted oath of concealment, but not with any malice, he thought. *In fact, the woodman had assumed the consequences were irrelevant because he trusted our honour.*

He felt himself beginning to thaw.

And from the beginning, Waterstone understood my reticence and was sympathetic and gently amused by it... but not at me, with me. And Lapping Water, seeing that I was feeling overwhelmed, orchestrated the immediate disappearance of the woodfolk to give me breathing space.

He gave a grunt of censure at himself.

Jackson looked around from the next stall along. "What's up?"

"Nothing." Jackson didn't press but Stefan saw his shoulder lift in a shrug. After a minute, Stefan asked, "What do you think of these woodfolk?"

Jackson straightened and leaned on his broom. "If I say I like them, you'll bite my head off, thinking I'm trying to talk you into liking them. If I say I don't like them, it will worry you because, let's face it, whether you like it or not, you're definitely a woodman, at least by birth."

Stefan let out a low whistle. "You don't beat around the bush, do you?" He frowned. "Sorry I'm being so difficult. It's a lot to come to terms with. But I've been giving it some thought so I would really like to know your opinion, since you have the least emotional investment of all of us."

"Huh." Jackson did one of his long pauses while he decided

whether or not to risk Stefan's reaction. Finally, he said, "Ok, I'll tell you, but just remember you asked for it." He took a breath. "From what I have seen, they are close-knit, just as your family is. They are kind, clever, and seem to have a dry sense of humour, which I like. They are magically talented with their mind talking and their flicking, and very skilled at woodcraft and weaponry. But, saying that, they live very differently from us. In fact, I'm amazed the High Lord can live almost permanently with them." He gave a couple of sweeps with the broom before stopping again. "I'm sorry that their past has taught them to avoid sorcerers. I can understand, but I think they underestimate themselves, and overestimate us." He took a breath, but Stefan made no move to interrupt. "I have a strong sense of identity as a sorcerer and I would not wish to be a woodman and live purely within the woodlands, virtually camping all the time." He waited and when Stefan still did not respond he added, almost defiantly, "There! I have told you what I think. I like them, a great deal actually, but I wouldn't want to be one of them."

Jackson held his breath, waiting for the reaction. When no response came, he picked up his broom and swept out the last of the old straw from the stall he was working on.

"Huh," said Stefan's voice from behind him. He sounded quite cheery, if a little bemused. "Huh." He started forking straw into the newly cleaned stall. "Well, I do like camping. Maybe not all the time but a lot. Interesting. Thank you for being honest. You have given me a lot to think about."

29

Twenty minutes later, Jackson, Stefan, Marjorie and his parents made their farewells and headed out into the night beneath Jackson's burgundy shield, all bearing baskets of food and drink, and a bag full of blankets for those who chose to stay the night out there.

They walked beneath high branches, which hung over the track and partly obscured the moon and starlight. A soft wind wafted through the leaves, making the shadows dance on the trail in front of them, obscuring obstacles and forcing them to place their feet carefully. From time to time, Ivan and Vera murmured to each other, but mostly they were silent, listening for any sound of their attackers.

Once or twice, stones clattered against the outside of Jackson' shield but it was a half-hearted attack and Stefan suspected the woodfolk had figured out that stones could not penetrate the shield and so had desisted.

Sure enough, a few minutes later, four arrows struck hard against the shield. Those within its burgundy dome cowered instinctively but the arrows fell, ineffective, to the ground.

Gradually those within the shield straightened and Vera moved closer to Ivan, who put his arm around her. She drew in a breath and lifted her head high. "Come on then. Let's keep going."

Marjorie glanced at Jackson, but seeing that he didn't look concerned, folded her arms around herself and kept walking.

They rounded the last bend with no further attacks and saw the translucent bronze dome of Tarkyn's shield, twenty feet in diameter, lit up from within.

As they drew close, Jackson waved his hand, actually more of a wiggle of his fingers since he was carrying a big wicker hamper, and his burgundy shield blinked out. Immediately, Tarkyn expanded his own to include the newcomers.

Ivan looked around the inside of this new dome. "Well, that's interesting," he said. "I've never been inside a sorcerer's shield before and now, look at this! Two in one night. And they're different colours. Amazing!" He grinned, obviously enjoying himself. He quickly surveyed the woodfolk who were looking less tired but still ill at ease, and his grin broadened further. "Well, will you look at that? All of you, just like our Stefan here. That's marvellous." He placed a huge basket on the ground. "Look. We've brought you everything we would have given you, if you'd come to our inn for dinner... and more besides." Feeling a dig in his ribs, he added hastily, "Hello, I'm Ivan, Stefan's dad."

Stefan felt a rush of warmth for his kind, outgoing father who welcomed these kin of his without hesitation.

"Hello," said Vera a little shyly. "We brought more cups for tea, and more tea. We have flagons of wine, and the makings of a beef stew." She gave a shrug. "I've already got a good stew hanging over the fire in the kitchen, but it was too hot and awkward to bring and besides, we really need it for the customers tonight." At the end of all this, she bobbed a curtsy. "Hello, I'm Vera and I'm very pleased to meet you."

"No need for that," said Waterstone, standing up to greet her. "Hello, Stefan's mother and Marjorie. It's a pleasure to meet the people who have brought up one of our own, however extraordinary that may be. I am Waterstone." He caught the beginning of a scowl on Stefan's face. "*Sorry. Didn't mean to be provocative. I know you're not too pleased at having a bunch of primitive forest dwellers as relatives.*" He grinned, as Stefan, who had been taking a drink of water from Jackson's waterbag, choked and spluttered a spray of water over those nearby. In the general uproar from the people who had been sprayed, Waterstone added wickedly, "*And you think we're uncivilized!*"

"Sorry," gasped Stefan, adding mentally, "*I don't think that,*" and sending a searing glare at Waterstone, who merely smiled in return.

Ivan frowned at Stefan, not best pleased with his manners and having no inkling of the silent exchange that was going on between Waterstone and him. Stefan sighed as his father turned his attention to everyone else, a tacit demonstration of his displeasure, and took control, just as though they were in the bar room of his inn. "Well now, let's get this food and drink sorted out, then you can tell us what's been happening. Nothing good, I gather."

Waterstone and Rainstorm helped Vera cut up the meat and vegetables for the stew, while Sparrow and Marjorie went for a short walk with Jackson, carefully shielded, to collect wood for a fire. Once a big pot of stew was simmering over a newly lit fire, Ivan passed around wine, bread and cheeses.

Waterstone took a sip of the white wine and raised his eyebrows in surprise. "Oh, lovely. Where did you get this?"

Ivan thought for a moment. "I have a few travellers come

through with wines, ales and food that we purchase. Now, this particular wine came through about a year ago." He clicked his fingers. "I know. It was that old bloke, strange name, but always has good wares at reasonable prices. Always saying his wares have the Royal Eskuzorian seal of approval, whatever that's supposed to mean. He's a theatrical sort of chap."

"That strange name wouldn't have been Stormaway Treemaster, would it?" asked Watertone, his eyes twinkling.

"That's him. Do you know him?"

"He's... a friend of ours," said Tarkyn, clearly not wanting to provide too much detail. "And he does indeed provide wares to the Royal House of Eskuzor, both to my sister and to me."

"And the wine we are drinking comes from woodfolk vintners, the Mountainfolk, who live on the northern side of the mountain range that we've just crossed," said Waterstone. He raised his goblet. "And I thank you very much for it because it is of excellent quality and, I suspect, quite expensive."

Ivan went pink with pleasure. "You are welcome, sir. This is, after all, a momentous occasion." His face fell a little. "It is a shame that your visit to our country has been marred by such unpleasantness that you feel the need to be shielded. Even with a bar full of hooligans, I have never felt that need."

"You have never encountered the woodfolk of your forests," said Autumn Leaves bleakly and went on to describe what had happened for those who had not heard the first time. "In their eyes, all of us have transgressed, you as much as us."

"They didn't give us a chance to explain and we didn't want to risk the verdict of a formal trial." The strain had returned to Rainstorm's voice. "If they had taken us into custody, we could never have escaped from so many and you may never have been able to find us." He shook his head. "We don't work like that in Eskuzor. We don't put strangers on trial the second we meet them."

"Of course you don't," said Stefan spuriously. *"You just kill them out of hand, if they mess up."*

Rainstorm promptly rose to the bait and smiled sweetly. *"No. Not woodfolk. Woodfolk, we banish. Only outsiders, we kill.*

Ivan's brows drew together. "What's going on? Young man, why are you smiling like that? I hope it is not at our expense."

The smile was immediately wiped from Rainstorm's face. "Oh, not at all. If you must know, I was just teasing Stefan."

"Well, don't," said Ivan firmly. "The poor man has been teased all his life for looking different. I would hope that people who look like him might have no reason to tease him."

"Thanks Dad, but I think I can look after myself," muttered Stefan, embarrassed.

Rainstorm, distracted for the moment from his fears, gave a jaunty grin. "Plenty of other reasons to tease, I'm afraid. But if it makes you feel any better, Ivan, I only tease people I like."

Tarkyn, who had been overseeing a game between Midnight and Gurgling Brook while listening in, raised his head at that and gave Ivan a reassuring smile. "Don't worry. Rainstorm can be devastatingly straightforward, but he is never cruel. In fact, he is kind, quick-witted and frequently sails into awkward situations to repair them, while everyone else is just sitting around wondering what to do."

Rainstorm rubbed his face with his hands. "Oh, my word," he grumbled. "Tarkyn, you are every bit as embarrassing as Ivan is."

Stefan laughed, happy that the focus had been taken off him.

Once the stew had been cooked and served, Waterstone broached the question on everyone's minds. "So what are we going to do?"

"We will have to find a way to contact them, I suppose,"

said Autumn Leaves. He took a spoonful of beef and gravy. "Hmm. Very good. Well done, chefs. We don't usually get the chance to eat beef."

"Not easy to contact woodfolk, unless they want you to." Lapping Water ate a spoonful and expressed her appreciation, but the strain was back on her face. "And there is nowhere we can hide except out of the forest and we can't do that." She bent her head over her stew to hide panicked tears that sprang unbidden to her eyes.

Tarkyn saw that she was upset, but also saw that she was trying to hide it in front of people she didn't know, so he did not put down his dinner and go to her, as he wanted to. Instead he said firmly, "You woodfolk can't send a mind message through a sorcerer's shield to see whether they would respond, but I can send images. Failing that, I will find another way to contact them. I can use birds or animals to help, if I need to. Above all, we will protect you with our shields until we have come to some resolution with these local woodfolk."

"It would be our honour to assist you." Jackson gave a courtly nod and a smile from where he was sitting. "We can take it in shifts. Holding a shield is something I do well. I can last for several hours."

Sheldrake nodded his agreement. "And I, too, would be pleased to provide my shield. After all, you are here because of my country's need to protect its borders within the forests, so I feel partly responsible for your predicament."

"And he loves any excuse to use magic," added Maud, in an effort to make the woodfolk feel less beholden. Suddenly, she realised that no one was listening to her.

30

A stream of people was emerging from the forest to the left of the path that led to the inn. Their stature, which was all that could be seen in the half-light, suggested they were woodfolk.

Tarkyn's woodfolk ranged themselves around the arc of the dome of his shield, facing the oncoming woodfolk. Tarkyn stood behind them. The other non-woodfolk people seated themselves around the fire in the middle of the dome but Stefan was unsure where he should place himself.

After a moment, he mindmessaged Waterstone. *"Where do you want me?"*

"Back with your parents for now. We'll call you forward when the time is right."

The number of woodfolk outside the dome was already larger than the group that Tarkyn's woodfolk had previously encountered and still more were flowing out of the forest to join them. Upward of forty faces glared in through the bronze-tinted translucent shield.

"Flood and fire!" exclaimed Autumn Leaves in horror. "I have never been on the receiving end of so much animosity."

"They can't hurt you," said Sheldrake, thinking he was reassuring them.

Autumn Leaves glanced at him. "It is the intent, not the danger, that worries me. I'm glad Tarkyn reached us before they did."

Even as he spoke, several arrows flew from different directions to ping against the shield and fall harmlessly to the ground outside.

Waterstone's eyes narrowed as he considered the trajectory of the arrows. He took a breath and let it out. "Well. That's something, I suppose. None of those arrows would have hit any of us, had the shield not been there. They were just testing the shield."

"Those ones may have missed us," said Stefan trenchantly, "but the ones that hit Jackson's shield on the way to and from the inn were aimed directly at us. Most definitely."

Waterstone raised his eyebrows. "Uh-huh. So perhaps their intentions have changed? No. I think not. No doubt those who fired at you earlier reported it to the others. So perhaps they are now trying to work out a way to deal with sorcerers and outsiders so that they can exile or eliminate all of us who have, in their eyes, transgressed."

Maud stood up from where she was seated near the fire, gathered her voluminous green skirts and walked over to join them against the inside of Tarkyn's shield. "Clearly, we need to negotiate with them."

"Can you mindtalk through the shield?" asked Sheldrake.

Waterstone shook his head. "No. We can mindtalk among ourselves, however."

"Let's not do that." said Tarkyn "We don't want to antagonize them further. Besides, we are all in this together. So, I think woodfolk and outsiders alike should be included in our discussions. I can send images through my shield to those woodfolk outside, if any of you wish it. I am at your disposal."

"Send an image of us and them sitting around a fire with cups of tea," suggested Rainstorm promptly. "Please."

The others nodded assent.

Moments later, Tarkyn said, "I have sent that image, and tried to convey feelings of warmth and friendship. I have received no response."

Sheldrake was impressed to notice that Tarkyn seemed to be spending almost none of his attention on maintaining his shield. He determined to ask him about this later but, as he thought about it, he realized that Tarkyn was showing signs of strain

"Would you like me to take over making light?" he offered.

Tarkyn nodded and as soon as Sheldrake put words into action, some of the tension leeched out of him. "Thanks."

"At least they have come forward to confront us," said Lapping Water suddenly. She smiled at their surprised faces. "It may be unnerving, but it is actually a good thing. The alternative is that they gradually pick us off from within the shelter of the trees over the next days and weeks."

"I see," said Maud thoughtfully. "Then we had better make this opportunity count." Before anyone could object, she turned to the woodfolk outside the shield and smiled warmly at them. "Thank you so much for gracing us with your presence. I understand you have never met people from outside your forest before. So, it must have taken great courage for you to venture out to meet us. Oh, I almost forgot. My name is Maud." She waited but when no one responded, she continued. "Perhaps I should explain that all the outsiders you see before you have sworn an oath, on pain of death, never to reveal the existence of woodfolk."

"But someone must have told you about us in the first place," said Red Gum, her voice determined but sharpened by an undercurrent of panic. She folded her arms across her chest, blustering her way through her fear of strangers. Almost huffily, she added, "I am Red Gum."

"That would be me, I'm afraid," said Tarkyn disarmingly. "But I did insist on their oaths before I revealed anything. I am Tarkyn, Prince and High Lord Guardian of Eskuzor, none of which titles will mean anything to you."

Red Gum looked Tarkyn up and down, taking in his bright amber eyes, his long black hair and the long wolfskin cloak hanging from his shoulders. Tarkyn smiled to himself. He suspected she wouldn't be half so bold if she knew that, for him, the shield was one way. He could attack her, if he chose to, but she couldn't attack him.

"But," continued Tarkyn, "I am also a forest guardian, which may mean something to you." He turned around and gestured to Midnight to join him, adding, "And this is Midnight. He too is a forest guardian, perhaps the youngest ever known."

A ripple of amazement flowed through the local woodfolk.

"I beg your pardon," said the white-bearded man the Eskuzorian woodfolk had met before. "Did you just say that you're a forest guardian? Oh. How do you do? I am Sphagnum Moss."

Tarkyn nodded.

"Oh my word! This changes everything. How very interesting. We have not seen a forest guardian for generations. But now, *two* forest guardians." Sphagnum Moss turned to Redgum and his companions and a protracted silence of mindtalking ensued.

"He sounds just like Sheldrake," murmured Maud while they waited.

Eventually, the old woodman turned back and asked,

"Now Tarkyn, as a forest guardian, you can communicate with animals, can't you? So, was it you who sent those birds to interfere with our pursuit of these woodfolk?"

Tarkyn smiled and turned to Midnight, translating Sphagnum Moss's words into images. "Did you do that?" When Midnight nodded, his smile broadened. "You're a clever one, aren't you? And you did that in the middle of running away, did you? Well done."

Midnight beamed.

Tarkyn returned his attention to the old woodman. "No. Midnight did it."

Spinifex wound his way through the crowd to the front. "If you're a forest guardian, what made you betray the presence of woodfolk? Surely you understand the importance of keeping our existence secret?"

"I do, although being a forest guardian does not come with built-in omniscience."

"Being a forest guardian means," butted in Rainstorm, Tarkyn's self-appointed champion, "that he can communicate with animals, heal and make things grow. But more than anything, it means that he uses his enormous power to protect the forests and those who dwell in them."

"But," said Autumn Leaves, "we had to teach him woodfolk lore." He shrugged. "Most of it he accepts and lives by. Some of it, he can't or chooses not to. He is a sorcerer, after all," he chuckled, "and a prince."

Tarkyn spread his hands. "And here we are again; people talking about me as though I were not here."

Rainstorm and Autumn Leaves just grinned at him.

Another mind conference ensued. Then Banksia, a dumpy, comfortable woodwoman, spoke on behalf of her companions, "I'm being honest, here. We are in a quandary. We see before us, a flagrant flouting of woodfolk lore. No Carradorian woodfolk has ever spoken to outsiders before. Not to one, let alone... how many of you are there?... eight of you." She turned to Waterstone. "You should know this is forbidden. Yet not only have you revealed yourself to them, you are hiding behind their protection against us, your kindred."

"There are not eight outsiders here," replied Lapping Water, "There are only seven. We have travelled from Eskuzor exactly because of one of *your* Carradorian woodfolk has been permitted by *you* to live among outsiders." She stepped to one side indicating Stefan behind her. "This man, Stefan, is a woodman. He is no kin of ours, so he must be kin of yours. And yet you have allowed him to be brought up by outsiders, right in front of your eyes at the Creeping Vine Inn, within your forests, without lifting a finger to rescue him and bring him back into the woodfolk community." She paused. "We can explain our actions if you are willing to listen, but can you explain yours? I am Lapping Water."

Come forward, Stefan, requested Waterstone silently.

Spinifex frowned at Stefan. After a moment, he shook his head. "No. You're mistaken. He's not a woodman. This is the son of Ivan the innkeeper. He has lived there all his life. He is just shorter than the rest of his family and happens to have green eyes."

Before anyone could stop him, Ivan surged to his feet and stomped forward. "You're right. He is my son and always will be." He put his arm around Stefan before saying, "But Stefan was not born into our family. He was found near the river after the great flood." He smiled at his son and gave him a squeeze before continuing, "I have worked at the inn for nearly fifty years, ever since I was a lad. In that time, I have seen hundreds, possibly thousands of people pass through our inn but no one... no one other than Stefan, has had green eyes." A little crease appeared between his eyebrows. "Actually, I'd never really realized that before. Hmm. I am Ivan, by the way."

"And take it from me, as a forest guardian," said Tarkyn, pressing home their point, "no one but woodfolk can mindtalk.

I can exchange mental images with humans and animals, but not words. No other sorcerer or outsider can even do that." He hesitated. "If I remove my shield, will you undertake not to harm or take captive any of us, at least until we have reached an agreement? Then Stefan can demonstrate his ability."

After a brief mental consultation, Sphagnum Moss nodded. "We agree."

Tarkyn swept away his shield. Suddenly, everything felt more open and people from both sides breathed an unconscious sigh of relief. "Say something, Stefan."

Stefan was looking a little dazed. "What?' he asked out loud.

Rainstorm laughed. "You poor bugger. Tell them what you think of Tarkyn for turning your world upside down."

"Thanks, Rainstorm," said Tarkyn dryly.

Stefan took a deep breath to steady himself and began to mindspeak. *At first, I was resentful that Tarkyn had destroyed my whole view of my life but then, as I came to know Rainstorm and the other Eskuzorian woodfolk, I thought it might be all right to actually be someone other than who I thought I was. And after Lord Tarkyn's displays of power last night, I felt privileged that he had spent the time on me.*

Rainstorm rolled his eyes. *That's not very interesting. Everyone thinks he's great... well, arrogant and great... but basically great. I thought you'd be mad at him.*

Stefan laughed. *I was, at first. Very.*

And how long have you been able to mindtalk? asked Banksia.

"About four days." Stefan replied out loud. He shrugged. "Well, probably all my life, but no one was there to tell me I could, before Tarkyn came along." After hearing Lapping Water's diatribe, he was not feeling very friendly towards these people who had let him grow up unaware of his abilities. He was not going to let them indulge in a private conversation with him in front of his friends.

Banksia, Sphagnum Moss and Spinifex looked stricken, as did those around them. Grevillea had tears in her eyes and Red Gum looked shamefaced. Many of the woodfolk clustered closer to Stefan, studying him.

After a moment, Banksia held up a hand. "Could you give us a few minutes, please?" When she came back into focus, she gave a sad smile. "You have really caused a furore with this information. We are truly shocked. The forests are ringing with contrition, and renewed grief for those lost in the great flood... But a query has arisen." She addressed Vera, who was still seated in the background beside the fire. "We don't actually spend our lives spying on your family. It is more that we notice various aspects of your life over time as we pass by. But... I hope I am not rude in asking this, but weren't you swollen with child before Stefan appeared?"

Vera nodded. "Yes." Even in the dim light, her eyes seemed to be shining over-brightly. "But I lost the babe. It is the only child I lost, from six pregnancies. When we, or rather Anton, found Stefan and brought him home, the loss was so recent that I was still producing milk." She cleared her throat uncertainly. "Hello. I am Vera."

"Oh. That explains it," said Banksia thoughtfully. "You see, while we were in turmoil following the flood, we missed the event of Anton finding the baby. We don't see everything that happens in the woodlands, you know. Far from it. And when we saw a new member of your family, we just assumed it was your child." Her face crumpled. "Oh dear. That poor little boy." She drew a handkerchief out of a pocket and buried her face in it.

Amidst the grief, Sphagnum Moss braved the proximity of outsiders to walk over to Stefan, and take his hand, clasping it between both of his. "I am so sorry that we have neglected you. It is our fault, not yours, that this has happened. We will do everything we can to repair it." He, too, was, holding back tears. "It will take time. We don't know what to do."

Tree Fern threw a defiant glare at the outsiders as she, too, moved forward. But she had no interest in Stefan. Instead she placed a supportive, slightly protective, arm around her grandfather. Sphagnum Moss looked more annoyed by this than grateful.

"Leave me alone, girlie," he said tetchily. "Can't you see they're not planning to hurt us?"

Tree Fern's arm dropped to her side and for a moment she looked a little forlorn. Then she crossed her arms across her chest, attempting to reassert her belligerence to cover her uncertainty.

"*It is confusing, isn't it?*" said Waterstone into her mind. "*Don't worry. Your grandfather is safe among us.*"

Sphagnum Moss half turned and took one of his hands from Stefan's to place it on her arm, but she shrugged it off. He gave a little sigh of resignation and said silently to Stefan, "*She is all flame and no coals. It's nice that she's worried about me, but I can look after myself... I shouldn't have snapped at her. I suppose she's just frightened and upset. We all are.*"

In the midst of the maelstrom of emotion, Tarkyn had retreated to the fire and wrapped his arms around himself, his face pinched with suffering.

Lapping Water noticed him go. "What is it?" she asked gently.

Tarkyn looked down at himself, realized what he was doing and with a grimace, let his arms fall. "I can feel their sorrow. The forest is full of regret, and guilt and self-retribution." He shook his head. "It is as though all the trees are wailing."

"Gather yourself, Tarkyn," she said softly, coming to put her arm around him. "Help them."

Tarkyn, forest guardian, took a deep breath and nodded, looking across at Stefan, who stood among his true people with his foster father's arm around his shoulders and his hand held by the old woodman. He studied Stefan's firm mouth and the eyes that lit with humour, the arms and hands that handled weapons so well and thought about Stefan's perceptiveness that made him such a good teacher. He smiled at the way Stefan met everyone eye to eye, a legacy of his woodfolk heritage, he was sure. He remembered the flashes of resentment that showed through when Stefan thought he was being teased, which were allayed by his rock-solid belief in himself, instilled by Vera, Ivan and Stefan's four siblings with their fierce devotion to each other and to Stefan... And Tarkyn sent out emotion-charged images that showed to the grieving woodfolk the reality of Stefan.

Gradually Tarkyn straightened as the emotions flowing through the trees changed slowly from grief and guilt to the realisation that one of their number whom they had thought lost, had survived the flood and, despite his alien upbringing, had flourished. Then wonder and a sense of rejoicing washed like a wave through the hundreds of woodfolk throughout the forest.

All around the clearing, even more woodfolk, young and old, simply appeared between the trees and in the branches above them. Vera and Jackson, still seated at the fire, watched, knowing the something momentous was happening.

"Open your mind, Stefan," said Autumn Leaves quietly. "Come and join him, Vera. And Marjorie."

Slowly, the woodfolk converged on Stefan, now flanked by Vera, Ivan and Marjorie. As they drew closer, they encompassed both Stefan and his family members in their arms from all sides; layers upon layers of arms interlaced over each other. Jackson, who had seen little of woodfolk, looked on, his eyes bright with tears.

Stefan's mind was swamped with messages of welcome, not just from the thirty touching him now, but also from the hundreds of woodfolk elsewhere in the forest.

From somewhere inside the huddle, Banksia spoke out loud, "Vera and Ivan, we have seen over the years – although we didn't realise what we were seeing – and the forest guardian has shown us today, how well you and your children have cared for our kin, who is also your kin. Since Stefan is our kin, then so too are you, and we welcome you and your family."

Luckily Ivan, Vera, Marjorie and Stefan were used to an effusive, demonstrative family, which saved them from feeling completely overwhelmed by the flood of emotion that flowed to them from all sides. Gradually the woodfolk pulled back, many of them smiling shyly.

A small girl grinned up at Marjorie. "You're the first outsider I have ever come near. I am Lorikeet."

Marjorie smiled down at her and tousled her light brown hair. "Then I expect you have just been very brave."

The girl nodded solemnly. "Yes, I have." She waved her hand around to indicate her fellow woodfolk. "We all were." She glanced at Tarkyn and Jackson and took a little breath. "We still are."

At that, Jackson walked over slowly and crouched down in front of her. "Hello. My name's Jackson. I hope you don't stay scared of me. I am just the same as you, but just a bit less clever. I can't flick into hiding or mindtalk... but I can make a magical shield. That's about all the magic I can do. Other than that, I walk, talk, run, climb a bit, not much, and ride horses a lot." He grinned at her. "I have a mum and dad, just like you, although at the moment they are far away... and I have two sisters."

The little girl studied him. "Hmm. I suppose you are the same mostly. Just longer and ... leggy. And your eyes are a bit different, but brown eyes are good for hiding, just like green ones are." She looked across at Tarkyn and leaned forward to murmur quietly to Jackson. "His eyes are too bright, though. They're almost orange and you'd see all that black hair a mile away unless he was deep in the shadows."

Tarkyn rolled his eyes. "Have I mentioned how much I love being talked about?"

"That's lucky, isn't it?" said Jackson to the girl. "Because I bet people talk about him all the time."

As Lorikeet giggled, Jackson grinned at her and stood up.

"Hello, young lady." Sheldrake walked over and sketched a small bow that made Lorikeet giggle even harder, a puzzled frown appearing on her face.

Rainstorm laughed. "Don't worry. It is just a gesture that means something like, 'Hello' or 'Happy to be of service.'" His laughter faded away as he and all other woodfolk received a report from the lookouts that an unknown outsider was approaching their firesite. He sent an image of a dusty, travel-weary man to Tarkyn, who indicated that he did not know him.

Instantly, all the woodfolk disappeared.

PART V

3 2

Jayhan slowly became aware that he was being jostled as he lay in the dark. His first thought was that he was late getting up and someone was shaking him awake. His mind galvanised into action, in his fear that he might get into trouble for sleeping in too long. But as he tried to heave himself upward, he realised he had it all wrong. The jostling was not someone waking him, his limbs were restricted and could not respond to his wish to move ... and it was as dark as midnight. He didn't persist in struggling to rise. He dropped back and lay in the dark, trying to make sense of his situation.

He could feel a tight pressure around his hands and ankles and realised they were bound. He could smell a damp, earthy, leaf mouldy odour around him but he could see no light through a cloth covering his face. A surge of panic welled up, but he clamped down on it before it overwhelmed him. Suddenly another surge of panic hit him.

"Sasha?" It came out as a croak and he realised his mouth was dry.

A grunt sounded behind him.

"Sasha?" he whispered again. He swivelled a little and his arm connected with someone else's arm behind him in the darkness. A small someone else. He swung his arm up and down, using his elbow to feel the ropes on the wrists and the softness of the arm muscle. Definitely, probably, almost certainly, Sasha. He pushed his elbow down a little harder on the arm. "Sasha? Is that you? Are you all right?"

"Of course it's me, you idiot," came a hiss. "Who'd you think it would be?"

Jayhan subsided, feeling hurt.

After a minute, he felt a soft jab in his back from Sasha's bound hands. "Sorry," she whispered. "I feel sick and my head is all muzzy and I'm scared."

At that, Jayhan wriggled until he had turned over and was facing her, even if he couldn't see her. Bits of damp leaves and twigs trickled down the neck of his shirt, as he moved. He felt around until he found her hands and clasped them. "At least they haven't killed you... us."

"It's those escaped prisoners, isn't it?" she whispered. "We never did tell anyone about that person I saw on the way to the palace."

"Idiots!" replied Jayhan vehemently. After a pause, he asked, "How long do you think it'll be before they notice we're gone?"

"Dunno. That grumpy old gardener, Kate, will just think we've run off."

"Huh. Probably not 'til teatime then."

"That's *hours* away."

"I know," replied Sasha gloomily. "We could be anywhere by then."

Suddenly the jostling stopped and they could hear the sound of feet on cobblestones close by. Then each of them was grabbed and dragged upward, pulling their hands away from each other, cascades of compost falling from them as they rose. Both of them began to wail, hoping someone would hear but a hand was clamped over each of their mouths. Sasha bit the one holding her mouth and her kidnapper let out a yelp and the hand whipped away.

"Don't you dare!" commanded a harsh voice.

"She bit me! She deserves a thump." The man sounded aggrieved.

"Leave her alone. Use a rag around your hand so she can't bite. Shut her up but don't hit her."

"Blood and thunder! This is the namby-pambiest abduction I've ever been involved in."

"This is the most important abduction you've ever been involved. So get it right!"

If Sasha and Jayhan had harboured any hope that this might be a random abduction, they didn't now. The men began to feed them into sacks, feet first. They wriggled and tried to make it difficult, but their captors were too strong. As soon as the men let go of their mouths to tie the sacks, the children both began to shout but Jayhan received a savage kick and let out a gasp of pain.

"Jayhan," cried out Sasha.

"That's right, young lady. We won't hurt you, but if you cause us trouble, we *will* hurt him. Do you understand?"

Sasha thinned her mouth and refused to answer. Another cry of pain issued from Jayhan and she forced out, "Yes."

They heard the sound of metal scraping on cobblestones and were carried downwards. After a brief descent, they felt themselves bumping on the men's backs as they were carried forward. They could hear the sound of water trickling and the smell that now permeated the air was disgusting. Both of them struggled not to gag.

As time passed, the sound of the water changed from a

trickle to lapping and gurgling, then to a distant roar. Just when they feared they might be caught in a torrent, they felt themselves bumping as the men climbed upwards. They heard the scraping of metal above them and after a few more bumps, they breathed in fresh air.

"Right. Carry them into the trees over there. Then we'll let them out."

A few minutes later, they were swung off the shoulders of the two men and deposited on the ground. Jayhan did not feel the thump of landing that he had anticipated. Maybe the men were only unkind when they felt it was necessary. He hoped so. His thigh still hurt where he had been kicked.

The men hauled them out of the sacks and unknotted the ropes binding their legs, the ropes being carefully coiled and put away in a rucksack for later use. They pulled the coarse hessian hood from Sasha's head but left Jayhan's in place. Sasha nearly protested but didn't want to risk them hurting Jayhan again. Besides, she recognised two of the three men as members of the assault party who had tried to capture her and kill other shamans in the woods a few months ago. She would never forget how Jayhan's horror had transmitted itself through great beams of white light from his eyes to freeze his opponents with dread. Clearly they had not forgotten, either and were taking no chances with him this time. Poor Jayhan. He didn't even know how he'd done it, but she didn't expect they'd believe her or risk it happening again.

She risked a question. "Why have you abducted us?"

"Because you have something our queen wants and only you can give it to her."

Sasha raised her chin. "It is mine by right."

"Don't care." The man shrugged. "I work for Queen Toriana and she wants it."

Sasha glared at him. "I will not say the words of transfer and if I don't, she cannot take it from me."

"You will," said the man calmly. "Because you don't want your friend here to suffer, do you?"

The men tied a loose rope between the bound wrists of the two children, then led them in single file deeper into the woods. One man placed his hand under Jayhan's elbow to steady him, whenever he tripped or became unsteady. Each time Jayhan tripped, the bruise on his thigh hurt where he had been kicked. So he worked at lifting his feet a little higher and landing each foot a little flatter so that he could adjust for bumps and hollows underfoot.

Jayhan didn't like having a hood over his head but he liked the smell of the hessian. Now that he wasn't covered in compost or upside down in a sack in dark tunnels, he found he could see light and shade from within his hessian hood and could make out vague shapes. In fact, as they walked, his vision became clearer and clearer until he seemed to be looking straight through the hessian, as though it were no longer there. *Huh,* thought Jayhan, *that might be useful,* and proceeded to trip artistically every now and then, to maintain the illusion that he couldn't see.

At one point, the men hoisted the children onto their shoulders as they forded a swiftly running creek. The men simply waded through the water, putting up with wearing their wet boots until they dried. Jayhan did not enjoy hanging upside down and completely lost his sense of direction. When he was put down, they were well within the forest again and it crossed his mind that they could be heading back the way they had come, for all he knew. So, for the next little while he watched the shadows, seeing they were mostly facing ahead of him, which meant the west was behind them and they were still travelling east.

Gradually the light dimmed until he felt the patter of rain drops on his hood. He groaned inwardly. Now they were going to get wet and cold, on top of being frightened and tired. He heard the men muttering among themselves, followed by someone flinging a cloak around his shoulders as they walked. He bit back his thanks but couldn't repress a grunt of acknowledgement. He hunched his shoulders in disgust at himself and kept on tramping.

The shower passed and Jayhan felt the sun on his back. A shudder went down his back as its warmth began to thaw him.

The man guiding him noticed his reaction and said, "Count yourself lucky. We just caught the edge of that storm. I bet it's teeming closer to Highkington."

"Good," came a voice from further up the line. "Rain might wash away our tracks and make the going slower if anyone works out where we've gone."

Jayhan's spirits sank further. His legs were so sore and tired that it was all he could do to keep going. He was genuinely tripping more now, as his legs refused to work properly. There seemed to be more roots and small branches in their path now and he often had to dodge branches that swung back into his face as Sasha pushed through. Since her hands were tied, she couldn't do much about it, other than call a warning to him. As another thin branch thwacked him in the face, he decided there were benefits to wearing the hessian hood.

The man guiding him said gruffly, "Shay. Take a rest. The kids need a break. Otherwise we'll have to carry them. This one's nearly done in."

"It's only another half hour, Bart."

"Don't care. We need to rest now."

Shay reluctantly called a halt, but only allowed them ten minutes before they were ordered back onto their feet and on their way again.

The long summer day was drawing in by the time they turned off the track to approach a shabby hut, almost hidden by the overhanging branches of a stand of huge myrtle trees. The walls and roof were made from long thick strips of bark overlaying each other. One upright of the verandah had rotted through, so that its roof sagged alarmingly at one end. Accumulated leaves and twigs threatened to cascade down at any moment. Jayhan could see so well that he spotted a small skink scurrying up a verandah post to disappear into the bark of the roof. Luckily, his natural instinct to blurt out this piece of fascination to Sasha was dulled by his tiredness. Instead, it was all he could do to put one foot in front of the other.

They were ushered inside to a single room that was lined on three sides with built-in wooden benches. A fire burnt cheerily in a fireplace in the fourth wall where the mantelpiece and shelves were dotted with filled jars, bags and various utensils. A big pot hung over the fire, emanating the tantalising smell of stew. Jayhan suddenly realised he hadn't eaten for hours. A large kettle sat on the side of the coals, steam wafting from its spout. The only furniture was a farm table and six wooden chairs. The entire hut seemed to be just a large kitchen.

A tall woman was leaning over the fire stirring the contents of the pot, but she straightened as they entered.

It was the shaman who had been among those who had attacked them at the meeting of the refugees in the forest near the Creeping Vine.

At the time, Sasha's amulet had caused this woman to falter and lose consciousness but unlike Lady Electra, who had immediately switched allegiances, this woman was here working with kidnappers for Queen Toriana against Sasha.

The woman walked over to Sasha, leaned forward and pulled up the chain that hung around the girl's neck until her black amulet came into view. Immediately, a responding pale light from the woman's own amulet beamed though the material of her bodice.

For a long moment, dark eyes stared into Sasha's. Then she said roughly to the men, "Lock the door. Sit them at the table, untie their wrists. Shay, how is that child going to eat with a hood on him?"

"It can't come off, Ruby," growled the man who seemed to be the leader of the three men. "His eyes are too dangerous."

"Then put a blindfold on him," she snapped.

The man who had been leading Jayhan rummaged in his pocket and produced a red and white spotted scarf. He handed it to Shay, who raised his eyebrows in surprise, his lips twitching with the beginnings of a grin. "Lovely, Bart. Where did you get this?"

"Oh, just from a friend of mine." Bart said airily but his heightened colour betrayed him. "She gave it to me for good luck when we left Kimora." He scowled. "So look after it."

Shay smiled. "I will, Bart, I will. Now, turn the boy towards the wall so he can't see us when we take the hood off."

Jayhan, now blindfolded by the polka dot scarf, was guided to a seat beside Sasha at the table where the others were already seated, waiting while Ruby dished out bowls of stew. Sasha patted Jayhan's knee in sympathy a couple of times before withdrawing her hand.

The scarf had been folded so that several layers lay over his eyes. At first he couldn't see anything. But gradually, his eyes adjusted and he could see through it, although shade and dark were interfered with by variations of colour on the scarf. He was so busy dealing with being blindfolded and working out how to act so that he seemed blind that he'd almost forgotten to care for Sasha. As the thought struck him, he turned instinctively to look at her, then hoped his head movement hadn't given away that fact that he could see. Her face was drawn and her eyes were big with fear. He gave her comforting squeeze on the leg in return.

Ruby claimed his attention by saying, "Your stew is in front of you, young man. The spoon's sitting in the bowl."

Jayhan didn't want to answer her but he couldn't overcome his training and muttered a reluctant, "Thank you."

Sasha took his hand and guided it to the spoon. He pretended to grope for the spoon awkwardly until he had his fingers around the handle.

"I'd lean over, if I were you," murmured Sasha. "Otherwise you're going to get it all down your front while you're finding your mouth."

"I know where my mouth is," he grumped. "It's the bowl I'll have trouble with."

"Keep your other hand on it," Sasha suggested.

"Hmph." Jayhan decided he would eat with his eyes shut for a while so he could work out how to act. He soon found that he couldn't quite estimate where the end of the spoon was relative to his hand and he did, in fact, often slightly miss his mouth and spill some of the stew.

"Hold your bowl under your chin," whispered Sasha, "You know, to catch the bits."

"I can't. The bowl's too hot to hold." He threw down the spoon in disgust.

"Then keep trying as you are, I'm sure you'll get better at it."

"Or I can feed you," said Ruby dryly, "or you can go without."

Jayhan heaved a sigh, felt around for the spoon and pulled the bowl closer to the edge of the table so he could lean over it. Suddenly, he could barely repress a grin at the thought that they were all playing along in his game while he was the only one who knew he could actually see if he wanted to. Then the gravity of the situation bore in on him and he remembered the kicks to his leg. Suddenly, his near laughter converted to a rush of fear. His breath hitched on a sob.

"It's all right, Jayhan. Take your time. You'll get the hang of it," crooned Sasha.

"It's not all right." Despite his best efforts, the tears welled up. Between sobs, he mumbled, "They're going to make you hand over your amulet to that bad queen, then hundreds more people will die. So you know you can't do that. But it's going to hurt me and I'm scared."

Sasha put her arm around his shoulders. "Oh Jayhan." She wanted to reassure him, but escape seemed the only thing that could save him and she couldn't mention that possibility, even unlikely as it was, in front of their captors.

"What have you done to this boy?" demanded Ruby, glowering at the three men.

Bart shrugged. "Nothing much. Just gave him a couple of kicks to go on with, to shut the two of them up."

"And threatened to slit his throat," interrupted Sasha indignantly, "until I let them put a handkerchief to my mouth back in the palace garden."

"Bart didn't hurt him too badly," said Shay. "The kid's just scared about what'll happen when we get to... But if the girl cooperates, he won't have anything to fear."

Sasha saw a glance pass between Shay and Bart and knew with absolute certainty that once they had forced her to transfer the amulet to Queen Toriana, they planned to kill them. After all, she and Jayhan would pose an ongoing threat of exposure to the queen. Why would they keep them alive?

Despite their fear, Jayhan and Sasha felt a resurgence of strength rise in them as they ate. Perhaps they had just been too hungry. Once their meal was finished, the two men retied the children's hands and directed them to sleep on adjoining benches, flinging cloaks over them for warmth. Two of the men and the woman also settled down to sleep, just as the first drops of rain fell outside. The third man stayed sitting near the dying fire, keeping watch and listening to the steadily increasing drumming of rain on the roof.

Jayhan manoeuvred himself around so that his head was close to Sasha's.

"Are you awake?" he whispered.

"Yes." She wriggled closer. "That man, Shay, has the door key in his pocket. I can't see how we'd get it without waking him."

"No." Jayhan's voice sounded disheartened, but he perked up almost straight away. "Maybe tomorrow when we're travelling through the forest."

"Hey, You two! Go to sleep!" came a heavy voice out of the darkness. "We all have a long walk ahead of us. No more noise or I'll come over and clout you."

33

Jon was seated at his desk in the palace, studying a sheaf of reports about damage to the roads from the previous week's heavy rainfall. He sighed. The bundle of reports foreshadowed extensive discussions with Crabtree, the civil engineer in charge of road maintenance, who would bemoan the costs, the insufficient staff and the unfortunate need to prioritize. His hand was just on the bellpull to have Crabtree sent to him when he heard the unusual sound of running footsteps in the corridor; adult footsteps.

Jon frowned and was already half-risen from his desk when a knock sounded on his door.

"Come in."

A liveried page walked in quickly, trying to hide the fact that he was panting from his long run and stood before Jon. Despite his best efforts at maintaining decorum, every muscle was stiff with the urgency of his message.

"Sir, the two children, Lady Natasha and Lord Jayhan, have disappeared," he blurted out. "It looks like they've been abducted."

For a moment, Jon stood stock still, his face pale and rigid. Then an anguished cry broke from him. "Ah no! No, no, no, no." He grabbed his coat from the back of his chair thrusting his arms into it as he headed for the door. "They're not just hiding?" he asked without much hope, knowing that abduction would be the last possibility considered.

"Mistress Josie believes not, sir. She is waiting for you at the rear gate, sir."

"Right. Thanks." Jon sped off, his long loping strides soon leaving the young page behind.

He arrived at the back gate to find Josie and Lady Teresa waiting with stoic calm while one guard after another reported back on their search to the Sergeant standing beside them. Once Jon had been apprised of the facts, all he wanted to do was saddle a horse and join the search.

"No, Jon," said Josie firmly. "Many men are already searching. You must remain here to decide on further courses of action. I'll have your horse saddled. Better to be ready for any eventuality, but for now, stay." She beckoned to the page who had fetched Jon and sent him off to the stables.

Jon ran a hand across his forehead and started to pace in agitation. After a few turns he stopped in front of Josie. "How can you be so calm?"

In an unexpected gesture, the fearsome woman reached out and grasped Jon's arm, giving him a slight smile. "It is worse for you; she is your sister. But we all care about her... and Jayhan." She took a breath. "Jon, what you see before you is controlled panic. And to help her, you must control yours."

"Oh." In response to her kindness, tears sprang to his eyes. He nodded until he could regain control of his voice. "I will." With a supreme effort, he pulled himself together and gave her a crooked smile. "I have. Sorry. Emotional family."

It was then that the news of the abandoned cart arrived.

Luckily for Jon's continued sanity, his saddled horse arrived a few minutes later and, with a quick look at Josie for approval, he set out with a squad of soldiers and a tracker to investigate.

The cart was neatly parked on the side of a residential street, looking for all the world like the cart of a tradesman visiting one of the terraced houses. A small group of children had gathered to gawk at the two soldiers who had been left to guard it. Other than them, everyone was keeping behind closed doors.

Jon dismounted and beckoned to the children. These weren't street ruffians, but they weren't rich either. They approached nervously, their eyes wide with interest.

Jon squatted in front of them and gestured to the cart. "Did you see this cart arrive? And where the people went to?"

The children consulted each other with looks, then a little girl piped up, "We were playing ball in the alley down there. Carts come past all the time, but soldiers don't. Jim saw the red and gold of the uniform. So we all came out to watch."

Jon gestured to three houses closest to the cart. "Do you know who lives in these houses? Might they have seen anything?"

A boy shook his head. "No one there, at the moment. They's all gone off to some big market. They's all traders, you see."

"How convenient," muttered Jon. "And the houses on the other side of the road?"

"The middle one's my Aunt Marcie but she's not well. Her bedroom's at the back of the house, so she won't have seen anything. Cassie's mum lives next door. She might have seen something but the parlour's at the front and I reckon she'll be in the kitchen getting dinner ready."

"Old Joe might have seen something. He sits in the front

room all day long smoking his pipe," said the little girl, eager to be helpful.

Jon felt in his pocket and pulled out a silver coin that he held up. "Who will I give this to, to buy sweets for all of you?"

Several grubby little hands thrust forward but Jon held the coin up, eyebrows raised, until they all looked to the first girl who had spoken.

"Give it to Cassie. She'll be fair," said a boy with a smudge on one knee and a gap in his smile. "Thanks."

By the time Jon had disengaged himself from the children, a soldier was already returning from questioning the old man in the front room across the road.

"He's a sharp one, sir," the soldier reported. "Saw the cart draw up. Saw the driver pull up and get down from the cart. Two men came out of one of those apparently empty houses to join him. Two of the men stood on the street side of the cart, which blocked the old man's view. Then he reckoned they walked around the kerbside of the cart, bent down and disappeared. He hasn't seen any of them since."

Jon frowned. "They could be shimmerers like me," he said, thinking out loud. When the soldier looked confused, Jon shimmered before his eyes, disappeared then returned into view, a wry smile on his face at the astonished stares. "I doubt it though, even though they are probably Kimorans. We're a pretty rare breed."

"Perhaps we should consider more prosaic solutions," suggested the tracker, who was dressed differently in a dark brown, loose-fitting uniform with discrete insignia on his shoulders and lapels. He was a taciturn, serious man who did not suffer fools gladly and clearly did not appreciate Jon's little display. "There's a scattering of compost around the back and kerbside of the cart, so I think the children were definitely taken from the cart here."

Jon glanced up and down the street then nodded grimly. "I agree and I know where they've gone. I lived on these streets for years. Look under the cart, Trevor." As the tracker ducked his head under the cart, he said, "There's a manhole there, isn't there?"

"Yes sir." His voice held a note of surprise. "And there are recent scrape marks on the cobblestones." Trevor straightened. "There is a huge network of tunnels under the city, sir. They could be anywhere. We'll try to track them but if they walk for a while in the water, it could be tricky."

Jon held up a hand to forestall him. "Just a minute. Let me think." He shut his eyes and let his mind wander through the vast network below them and as he did, memories of being frightened, hungry and alone, running for his life, nearly overwhelmed him. He opened his eyes and shook his head to clear it.

"I know these tunnels," he said quietly and couldn't overcome the need to share just a bit of what he had endured. "They are not warm, but they are a lot warmer than being on the streets during a blizzard. And if you know them, you can escape from gangs and marauders. You just have to know the tunnels better than they do." He gave a whimsical smile at the soldiers' stares. "I wasn't always a lord, you know. Well, I was, but I didn't always live a lord's life."

He took a breath to bring himself firmly back into the present. "Anyway, I think I know where they have gone. They will be taking the children to Kimora. There are three outlets that come out close to the edge of the Great Forest. One outlet to the east on the main road, Park Lane, which I think they will avoid, one outlet in the northeast which opens close to the dense northern part of the forest and one beyond the southeast of the city which opens into the southern part of the forest. The route through the southern part of the forest is narrow and overgrown in places but leads more directly to the capital of Kimora, so I think they will go that way. Trevor, you and I and a squad of soldiers will travel to the south eastern outlet, but I think we should send people to the other two outlets just to check those possibilities." He looked around him. "Agreed? Any suggestions or comments?"

"Send back messengers to report our plans to Josie and to organise for provisions to be sent to us at the south eastern city gate, sir," said Trevor, for the first time a note of genuine respect in his voice.

34

An hour later, Jon and Trevor were inspecting the ground around another metal manhole set into a grassy knoll, fifty yards outside the city's wall.

Jon pointed towards the forest. "The tunnel goes for another three hundred yards then opens into the Taramine River. The river is flowing fast after all that rain last week, so I doubt that they will have gone that way, even if they could find a way to open the gating without the key."

Trevor squatted down and ran some earth through his hands. "No. I think you're right. People have definitely come out of the manhole here, quite recently." He looked around himself then his eyes travelled along a line towards the forest edge. He stood up and walked along his line of sight for several yards before reporting, "The footprints are all intermingled and there's a bit of a mess near the manhole, but then the tracks head in a clear line towards the forest. So, it looks like they walked in single file. I've found a few clear prints here and there, enough to say there were three adults and two children."

Jon blew out a breath. "Oh, thank goodness. Sasha and Jayhan must be unharmed enough to walk. That's something."

Trevor frowned and focused on one set of small prints amongst the rest. After a minute, he said, "One of the little ones is limping a bit; not badly, but enough to make the steps uneven." He glanced up, saw the query in Jon's eyes and added, "Can't tell which one. They're both wearing boots, about the same size. Josie might know from the treads, but I don't."

A fresh squad troop of eight men and a sergeant jogged up, barely out of breath after their trip from the palace, packs of provisions on their backs. They too were dressed in the camouflaging dark brown that Trevor was wearing. The sergeant, a neat, well-mannered man in his mid-thirties with a crop of black wavy hair over serious grey eyes, presented himself and saluted. "Afternoon, sir. I'm Sergeant Reece. Seventh squad relieving fourth squad, sir. We have provisions enough for several days if needed, sir."

"Several days?" That flustered look was back on Jon's face.

"Not saying we'll need them, sir, but better to be prepared."

"Seventh squad is one of our elite squads, Jon," said Trevor. "Experienced at... hmm... less straightforward approaches, shall we say, fitter and more used to bivouacking and working in the field."

Jon managed a tight smile. "Indeed? Then welcome."

As they followed the footsteps into the tree line and along a narrow but well-defined path, large raindrops started to spatter on the trees, falling through the canopy to land on their heads.

"Blast!" exclaimed Jon. "Halt, everyone. Get your cloaks out. It looks like this is going to get heavier, but we can't afford to stop."

It only took a couple of minutes for the experienced soldiers to drag their cloaks out of their rucksacks and don them, pulling their hoods up. Then they were on their way again.

The rain gradually gained momentum until the men's cloaks were close to saturated and water dripped from the edge of their hoods into their eyes. Nevertheless, they marched on stoically. Soon bushes began to impinge heavily on the path, and wet branches brushed against them as they passed.

Then they came to Flushing Creek.

Normally it was a trickle, but the recent rains had swollen it, making the water knee-deep in the shallower stretches, opening into deeper pools, its pebbly bottom interspersed with strands of reeds and underwater grasses, waving downstream.

The rain pelted down, making visibility poor. Trevor waited for Jon and Sergeant Reece to join him on the banks. He pointed down to the remains of footprints in the mud along the bank.

"Their prints're nearly gone." He gestured across the stream. "The path continues through the trees just over there and that's probably where they went, but if they've deviated in the water, it's going to be hard to pick up their tracks. The rain is washing them away, even as we speak." He indicated the squad of men who had emerged from the trees behind them and had now gathered along the bank of the fast-flowing creek, hunched against the rain. "Once they get over to the other side, there will be no chance of seeing any last remnants. I propose our men take a rest while I cross over and scout about."

Jon nodded, sending a shower of droplets from the front of his hood.

Reece agreed. "I'll take them back under the cover of that large gumtree we just passed. It wasn't waterproof but I noticed a few dry patches under it. It would be better to take off our boots for the crossing anyway."

The men settled under the tree, taking the opportunity to

light a fire, make tea and bring out rations of dried meat and apple, talking quietly among themselves. Jon was given a share, but he could not sit still, and instead paced back and forth just inside the shelter provided by the tree.

After several minutes of this, Sergeant Reece approached him. "Two things, my lord. Firstly, if you use all your energy now, what will you have to draw on, if or when we find the abductors? Secondly, these men are seasoned campaigners, but they respond better to calm authority."

Jon stopped dead and looked at him. After a moment, he heaved a sigh, pushed back his hood and ran his hand through his hair. "Sorry." Immediately, a swirl of wind sent down a flurry of raindrops out of the leaves. He shuddered as cold water found its way down the back of his neck, but he didn't replace his hood.

"No need to apologize, sir. You are not accountable to me. Just an observation, that's all."

"Thank you." Jon gave a wry smile. "Besides, I would spend the time better, getting to know your men... and vice versa."

Reece gave him a strange look.

"What?"

The sergeant frowned. "Not quite what I meant. Not common for nobles to hobnob with the men. Nobles tend to stay aloof, sir."

"I was staying aloof by pacing... not intentionally, I'll admit. And I would rather not. I find my own company has limited attraction... unless you were planning to stay aloof with me?"

Sergeant Reece looked flustered. "I, uh, no, I usually stay with my men when we are out in the field."

Jon raised his eyebrows. "So you expect me to stand here on my own, with nothing to do and no one to talk to?"

"Of course I will join you, if you'd like," said Reece hastily. "I was not meaning to ostracize you, my lord."

Jon grinned. "As much as I'm sure your company is delightful, I would rather hobnob with your men... and you, of course."

Half an hour later, Trevor returned, his boots in one hand, to find Lord Jon sitting at his ease on the ground, chatting amiably with the troopers. Trevor's boots seemed to be the driest thing about him. Jon sprang to his feet as soon as the tracker appeared and Reece handed the tracker something to eat in exchange for his boots and saturated cloak, which he took to the fire to dry out. "Cup of tea coming up."

"Thanks." He turned his attention to Jon. "I can't be certain, I'm afraid, sir." Trevor took a bit of dried beef and chewed it before continuing. "No sign of footsteps left at all, anywhere on the other side. There are a couple of places where the bank has fallen in a bit, as it might when someone climbed out of the creek there, but equally it could be from the current undermining the bank."

Jon glanced at Reece to gauge his reaction, then asked, "So what...? What does that mean? What do we do about it?"

"We can play the odds and assume they have continued to follow the path we're on, sir," said the sergeant, "but it might be wise to send a few men along any other paths that lead away from the creek on the other side." Reece turned to Trevor. "Did you see any?"

The tracker shrugged. "Nothing as clear as this path and even this path is not obvious. The forest is pretty dense around here. If they did push through into the bush further down the creek, I would have expected signs of their passage; torn fern fronds or recently snapped small branches, but I didn't see anything. I waded through the creek water several hundred metres in each direction – in some places the bush was too dense and close to the creek's edge to walk around."

"You've done a thorough job, by the sound of it," said Jon.

"My thanks. So, we head straight on?"

"I think so, my lord." Trevor glanced at the sky. "The rain's not as heavy as it was but we're starting to lose the light. We'd better cross and get on our way while we can still see our feet."

The rain was easing, and they traversed the creek without incident. More time was lost while the men redonned their boots on the other side of the creek, but after that, they kept up a steady pace, their eyes adjusting to the gathering gloom until it was fully dark. Then Reece called a halt.

"Two choices, my lord. We either set up camp or light torches. If the moon were out, we could keep going, but the cloud cover is still heavy, and we may miss the path or trip over roots or obstacles if we keep going in the pitch dark. If we light torches, we can keep going but it will warn the abductors of our approach... and make us sitting ducks if they plan an ambush."

Jon repressed an exasperated sigh. He knew Reece was right. "Trevor, your opinion?"

"I'm pretty sure we're on the right track. Since we left the creek, I've seen parts of footprints in places where trees have sheltered the path from the bulk of the rain but, if you really want to know, I'm developing a headache from concentrating so hard in such poor light." He gave a grunt. "Even with torches, we might miss a small path running off to the side."

"Sir," another voice piped up.

Jon swung around to find a young trooper tramping through the mud to join them at the front of the line.

"Yes..." Reece peered through the gloom for a moment before adding, "Warren. What is it?" His tone indicated that he knew the trooper would only interrupt if he had useful knowledge.

"I used to come out here hunting with my dad when I was a

boy. There's an old disused woodcutter's cottage not so far from here, off to the right."

"How far?"

"Dunno. Maybe ten minutes?"

"Could be where the abductors are holed up," said Jon, unable to keep the excitement out of his voice.

"At the very least," said Reece more prosaically, "it will give us somewhere to camp for the night. We can't camp on this narrow path. We had better not use torches, though, if it is possible the abductors are there."

Without torches, Warren's estimated ten minutes took them nearly half an hour in the pitch dark, with Warren becoming increasingly unpopular as time passed. Finally, they reached the edge of a small clearing, just as the clouds parted to bathe the area in moonlight. Instinctively they drew back into the cover of the trees.

They could see an old stone cottage on the other edge of the clearing, a straight dirt path leading up to the front door between two small stone-edged gardens.

With calm efficiency, Reece deployed his troops to circle through the vegetation so that they could come at it from all sides. Jon found it hard to stand still as Reece signalled for the troopers to approach the cottage. They ran quickly from one patch of shadow to the next, until most of them were pressed against up the stone walls of the cottage. Silently, they drew their daggers.

One trooper peered cautiously through a window. Inside the cottage, all seemed dark and quiet. He carefully tried the doorknob and pushed gently on the door. It wasn't locked, although no one expected it to be, this far into the woods. As the door swung open, a slight breeze eddied in the doorway.

He glanced at his companions and in a coordinated rush, he and three other troopers threw open the door and ran in, daggers drawn. Another coming behind them lit a lantern. As the lantern lit the room, they gaped in astonishment.

Jon stood before them, hands on hips. "No one here, I'm afraid."

One of the men ducked his head out of the door, then back in again. He grunted. "Just checking there aren't two of you."

"Ah. That's right. You weren't there when I demonstrated earlier." Jon shimmered out of sight then reappeared. "It's called shimmering."

The troopers looked at each other but said nothing. One of them walked outside and signalled the 'All clear' to Sergeant Reece and the other men.

Reece, when he arrived, was not pleased. He tersely ordered his men to bring their packs inside and to get settled for the night.

"We can't go further in the dark, Jon," said Trevor, not unkindly, in response to Jon's ill-concealed concern. "As it is, I think they may have turned off the path and I might have missed it. I'll backtrack at first light and see if I can pick something up."

As Jon nodded reluctant acknowledgement, the sergeant caught his attention. "A word with you outside, my lord, if you please."

Jon grimaced in Trevor's direction before following Reece outside, aware that the sergeant was not happy. Once they were out of earshot, Reece swung around to face Jon, his hands on his hips. "We are not playing games here, my lord. In case you hadn't noticed, my men were careful, stealthy and approached that cottage in a manner least likely to attract the attention of anyone inside."

"I did notice. In fact, I was impressed... but so too did I, in case *you* hadn't noticed."

Reece gave a snort of exasperation. "But you acted impulsively, without my knowledge, without my men's knowledge and without a plan."

"And what exactly was your plan?" Jon's usually cheery voice developed an edge. "What would your men have done if they had broken in, to find a Kimoran with his knife to my sister's throat? Or Jayhan and Sasha tied in the corner and several abductors between them and the door? Pretty risky plan, if you ask me."

"But you placed yourself at risk and reduced everyone's effectiveness by acting alone," protested Reece vehemently. "What if the situation had demanded that you stay shimmered, or invisible, or whatever you call it? Not knowing you were there, one of my men could have inadvertently swung his dagger straight through you, had there been a fight."

"I doubt it," said Jon. "I'm fast on my feet and I'm used to street brawling with knives." He gave a wry smile as his anger evaporated as quickly as it had come. "But I concede your point. We would work better in concert. In fact, I was caught out by the suddenness of our coming upon the cottage and the immediate deployment of your men." He gave a laugh that held no trace of bitterness. "And I am pretty sure you consider me an inconvenient, decorative addition to your force. So, I decided that by the time I could persuade you to take me seriously, the moment would well and truly have passed. So, I just acted."

The two of the had been glaring at each other but at these words, Reece looked past Jon and slowly swept his gaze around the trees on the edge of the clearing then down at his feet as he considered. When he met Jon's gaze again, there was the hint of a smile in the corner of his mouth. "Fair point. In fact, now I think about it, your particular talent could come in very handy... if you were willing to work with me."

Jon smiled. "If that means 'work under your command', the

answer is no. But I am happy to use my skill in consultation with you."

"Fair enough, as long as we don't argue in front of the men. Discuss, yes; argue, no."

Jon gave a small bow. "I am not argumentative by nature, so unless you are, we should rub along well enough."

Reece chuckled. "You're a funny one, for a noble."

"I've had a funny upbringing." The smile on Jon's face slipped a little. "Well, not funny. Not at all funny. But unusual."

"That's what I meant, unusual. And I'm beginning to like you, which is more than I can say for most noblemen I've met."

"Are you? Well, that's nice. Thank you very much."

Reece laughed and shook his head. "Very unusual. Come on, m'lord. Let's go and get some sleep so we can be on the trail of your sister at the crack of dawn."

But all night long, the rain hammered down and by morning, no trace was left of the abductors' footsteps. Even their own footsteps had washed away.

35

S omeone thumped loudly on the door, the sound jerking Jayhan awake. He felt he had only just drifted off to sleep. A surge of adrenalin rushed through him, leaving him feeling jarred and dazed.

It was still pitch dark and rain drummed steadily on the roof. He tried to rub his eyes, but his hands encountered the cloth of the polka dot scarf. After a moment of uncertainty, he worked out that it actually *was* still dark, and it wasn't because he was blindfolded.

"What's going on?" whispered Sasha.

"Come on, you two!" bellowed Shay. "Our squad has arrived. Up and out with you."

Before they could react, the children were hauled to their feet and pushed towards the door. Shay pulled the door open and shoved them outside into the cold of the pre-dawn darkness, where they found themselves surrounded by black-clad figures. The rain was easing, but big drops still fell from the eaves of the hut and from the tree branches overhead.

The children huddled close to each other, pushing against

each other for warmth and comfort. Sasha tried to remind herself that she was supposed to be these people's queen, but this only served to convince her that queens were just people like everybody else. She was scared and cold and tired, just as Jayhan was. Someone flung dark grey, hooded cloaks over them, but by then their clothes were already damp.

"Right. This is Brinta," said Shay, indicating a short, dark-haired, dark-faced woman who was thin but bursting with contained energy and, Sasha suspected, hidden strength. "She and the other three will be coming with us to Kimora from here. Do what we say, and Jayhan will not be hurt."

Beside her, Sasha felt Jayhan shudder inside his cloak.

For several minutes, Shay and Carl bustled back and forth into the hut, collecting provisions for their journey and stuffing them into their backpacks and handing supplies out to the newcomers. Just as the children were being ushered off into the darkness, Ruby came out of the hut and handed each of them a small satchel to throw over their shoulders and a freshly baked herb and cheese scone to hold. "Here," she said gruffly. "Eat that now. There are cookies in the bag to eat over the next few days." She stared hard into Sasha's eyes "They will give you the strength and stamina that you will need."

Sasha gazed back at her, trying but failing to discern her motives, then nodded her thanks. Beside her, Jayhan mumbled something incomprehensible.

They barely had time to eat their scones before they were pushed roughly in the direction of a narrow easterly track. It was still dark, but when Jayhan and Sasha looked up, they could see a pale grey sky in the gaps between the trees and could discern the shapes of nearby bushes.

Jayhan shrugged off the big fist on his shoulder. A small flame of resentment bloomed inside him, blotting out the fear.

These bastards are not going to take us and hurt us and kill us. We are going to get away. Don't know how, but we are.

As they walked, he thought about what weapons he could use to free them. He could shape shift but only to the shape of a person, not an animal as his mother could. And he had his eyes. He now knew he could see through hessian and scarves. What else could he see through? And on that one occasion, his own terror at Jon's impending death had ignited his eyes and sent forth streams of white light that had paralysed their enemies with fear. He gave a little grunt of frustration. But he didn't know how to consciously make them do that.

"*I will work on it,*" he decided, his mouth setting in a determined line that might have given his captors pause, if they could have seen it in the darkness.

Behind him, Sasha, too, was walking with new purpose. She was thinking about the time her amulet had thrown Yarrow across the room and then surrounded Sasha in a black, impenetrable cloud while she recovered from an overload of images. If her mother had lived to see her grow up, she would have taught Sasha the secrets of her amulet, but that knowledge had died with her mother. She frowned. Hadn't Sheldrake said that she was gradually gaining knowledge as she grew up, just by wearing the amulet?

"*Hmph,*" she thought, "*Maybe I know more than I realise. I will focus on my amulet as we walk and see what I can learn.*"

After two long, dark hours they stopped for a break. It was full daylight now and the clouds were beginning to clear. Jayhan and Sasha were both dragging their feet and tripping from fatigue.

"It must have still been the middle of the night when we left," whispered Sasha. "Dawn's very early this time of year."

"No wonder I felt like I'd just gone to sleep... I had."

Shay tied them to a tree and wandered off to chat with the

other troops and to eat the freshly baked bread provided by Ruby. It smelt wonderful, but it was not offered to the children.

"You've got your own," growled Brinta, as she left to join the others.

Sasha and Jayhan turned their attention to their little satchels and, manoeuvring awkwardly with their tied hands, each pushed a cookie out of the other's satchel so they could eat it.

As their lips touched the cookies, a zing of energy jolted through them. They jerked their heads back, then they looked surreptitiously around before meeting each other's eyes.

"Try that again?" murmured Jayhan.

Sasha nodded.

Steeling themselves, they each took a careful bite of their biscuit and chewed, actually enjoying the initial zing. Strength flooded through them... and something more. A sense of hope.

"Huh." After a moment, Sasha whispered, "Hey, have you been planning what to do instead of just being paralysed with fear? Since we left the cottage, I mean."

"Yep. You?"

Suddenly Sasha's face lit with a smile. "Yep. I think she put something in those scones she gave us and now something even stronger in these cookies."

"What're you grinning at?" demanded Jayhan.

"That means the amulet worked on Ruby after all, just as it did on Lady Electra. I thought, when she was working with the kidnappers, that maybe my amulet hadn't overpowered hers, but she's actually helping us, so it must have."

Jayhan thought about it. "Huh. Maybe this is the best she could do without getting herself killed."

"In which case we'd better hide how much better we're feeling."

"And anyhow, if we still look scared, they won't think we're up to something."

"True."

However, this plan was destined for failure. As soon as Jayhan tried to look doleful, Sasha glanced at him and got the giggles, which set him off too. When Brinta broke away from the others to find out why they were laughing, Sasha improvised wildly and said it was because Jayhan's spotty scarf made him look silly. Brinta frowned furiously but in the end, let it go.

As soon as she was out of earshot, Jayhan murmured dryly, "Hmm. So that could have gone better," which nearly set them off again.

With an effort, they pulled themselves together so that they could tell each other what they had been thinking about as they walked.

Sasha said urgently, "I think the key to controlling our powers is imagination. I have to imagine a situation is so bad that my amulet springs to life to defend me. You know, putting me in that black cloud thing and shoving my enemies away, like it did with Yarrow."

"Yeah, but the trouble with your amulet is that it only protects *you*, which," he gave a lop-sided smile, "makes it next to useless if you care about me."

Sasha frowned. "True. That's why they could kidnap me, us. I'll have to think about that."

"And also, remember that somehow, touching me might increase whatever magic you have."

They had no more time for plotting. Brinta called them all to order and the children quickly stuffed down the rest of the cookies they were holding. Begrudgingly, the Kimorans stood up and fell into line in single file; Shay in front, then three more in front of Jayhan and Sasha, with Brinta and Bart bringing up the rear.

"You two looked pretty tired by the time we stopped. We won't go so long without a break this time," Shay reassured them, as they set off once more. "Otherwise we might end up carrying you, which would slow us down even more."

It soon became apparent that while Sasha and Jayhan had gained strength and vitality, Brinta and her troops were feeling grumpy and lethargic. Sasha caught up to Jayhan long enough to jab him in his back with her fist. When he glanced around, frowning at her, she nodded towards their kidnappers and mouthed, "Tired."

"What are you two up to?" growled Brinta from behind them.

"Nothing," they chorused.

Not surprisingly, this did nothing to allay Brinta's suspicions.

Sasha improvised again, trying to sound aggrieved. "Jayhan tried to trip me up as we got back into line, so I just got him back by giving him a jab."

Brinta rolled her eyes. "Just shut up and keep walking."

"Any more of that bread left?" asked Sasha.

"Yes, we've got enough for a few days. But I told you, it's not for you. Now, be quiet."

Sasha hoped that Jayhan would understand the implication; that Ruby's bread was making the captors tired and grumpy, maybe less alert.

He understood all right, although he didn't know what he could do about it. But he would work on it.

All that day and over the next two days, they slogged their way through dense forest, trudged along miles of boring, uneventful straight stretches, stepping from tussock to tussock through sodden ground, and skirting along rocky sections that wound up and over sparsely wooded hills. Occasionally they would jump from rock to rock or be carried across one of the burbling streams that cut through the path.

All the while, as Sasha and Jayhan ate their cookies, they resisted the dragging urge to become disheartened and instead, maintained their energy and sense of hope.

Jayhan worked hard on trying to remember how he had felt, how his eyes had felt, when the Kimoran trooper had grabbed Jon by the neck and threatened to cut his throat. As tiny droplets had appeared in a line across Jon's throat, Jayhan's horror had engulfed him and his eyes had shone forth. But how? Then he remembered that Yarrow had said he couldn't just summon the power. But maybe it would ignite in response to his imagination, as Sasha had suggested.

He tried thinking of himself being threatened. He tried to imagine someone bringing down a knife to slice his arm, but his mind baulked at the image. At first, he couldn't even follow the image through to its conclusion, but after several attempts and a lot of determination, he brought it to the point where the knife touched the skin of his arm. But, try as he might, he couldn't imagine the pain at all. He had no concept of how it would feel. And through all these images, his eyes seemed completely unchanged.

Sometimes he was so busy concentrating that he would trip over a rock or raised root in the path, but it didn't worry him. In fact, as he recovered his balance, he would be glad he had tripped, because he knew that he kept forgetting to act as though he couldn't see.

Then he'd go back to his ruminations.

36

J on slept restlessly, waking often to see whether it was yet dawn. At the first greying of the sky, he was up and out of the cottage. He splashed his face with water from the tank that abutted the cottage and after a slight hesitation, drank from his cupped hands. The water had an earthy taste that was quite pleasant, and he suspected leaves had fallen into the tank over time. He stood up, shaking his hands to dry them, and turned to find the other men emerging from the cottage.

As Sergeant Reece strode over to him, Jon gave him a friendly nod and said, "Good morning. I'm glad to see you're all up. I was just wondering whether I should risk your wrath to wake you all."

Reece gave a grunt of laughter. "We are used to rising with the dawn. Trevor has just headed off to look for tracks but after the night's rain, I don't hold out much hope. I think we will just have to continue on the track we were following yesterday. We just have time to light a fire and make ourselves some tea before he gets back." As Reece saw a wave of impatience cross the young lord's face, he added, "It won't slow our departure, I promise you."

True to Reece's word, half an hour later, everyone was packed and ready to leave. Trevor was handed a cup of tea as soon as he returned and gulped it down as he reported his findings – or rather, lack of them.

Jon reached out and put a hand on his shoulder. "Don't scald your mouth on my account. I can stand another minute or two of inaction." While Trevor gave a quirky smile and took a slower sip, he said, "So we follow the main path from the Flushing Creek again today, do we?"

"Yes. I think it is a reasonably safe bet. I saw no other paths leading off from it and it will only take a few minutes to return to it in daylight."

Once they were back on the main trail, they settled into a fast but relaxed pace and, a little over an hour and a half later, came upon the dilapidated old bark hut, huddled under the trees, where Sasha and Jayhan had slept only a few hours before.

This time Jon glanced at Reece who nodded his agreement. Jon shimmered and approached the hut soundlessly, the only sign of his passing, the appearance of muddy footprints in the wet, scattered leaf mould of the clearing. The soldiers spread out slowly on either side, out of line of sight with the door. As everyone waited with bated breath, the door swung slowly inwards, apparently by itself.

A minute later, Jon's voice sounded cheerily from inside. "No one here. Safe to come in."

Outside, Trevor raised his hand. "Not so fast. Let me go in first and see what I can see before you lot destroy it all."

Reece nodded. "Agreed."

As Trevor entered, Jon pointed to marks on the floor that

hadn't been made by him. "Not here now, but they were, I think. So, we're on the right track."

It did not take Trevor long to find the footprints of three adults and two children in the dust and mud on the hut's floor. "You're right. They were here, all right. But they must have met a third person either here or somewhere after Flushing Creek." He looked around. "Here, I'm guessing. Looks like someone used that fireplace for cooking. A new set of prints, only one, near the fireplace." He pottered around the hut and then moved outside to inspect the ground all around the clearing, gradually working his way east, while Jon wandered back out to join Reece and his men.

When he had finished, Trevor reported, "Three more people arrived here from the east. They milled around for a bit, then all six headed eastward, taking the children with them."

"How long ago?" asked Reece. "Any idea?"

"Not sure. Depends when the rain stopped here. My guess is that we're four hours behind them, maybe more. They may have left earlier than us. They have the advantage of knowing where they're going while we had to wait for the light to see tracks." He pointed eastward. "Still on the same path so far."

"Right. Ten-minute break, then we move on." Reece sent a perceptive glance at Jon. "You holding up all right?"

Jon gave a wry smile. "Physically or emotionally, do you mean?"

Reece shrugged. "Either. Both. You haven't had the rigorous training than this lot have had."

"Physically, fine. I do a lot more than you'd imagine. I have projects outside my work at the palace that keep me moving around." Just as Reece was thinking that he had overstepped the mark and was just going to get a defensive answer, Jon gave a little grin. "But emotionally, I'm a bit up and down. I was on tenterhooks going into that hut, and full of hope. Then, no one there. Grim... But..." he shrugged, "at least we know they've been here and we're still on the right track."

"You're good at pulling yourself together when you need to, aren't you? Even if you get wound up in the first place. Your voice sounded quite cheery coming from that hut." Reece pulled out two hard biscuits and offered one to Jon. "Here. Let's sit down while we eat."

They sat down on a damp log on the side of the clearing, somehow not wanting to go into the hut.

"Thanks," said Jon, accepting the biscuit. He bit into it, having to clench his jaw muscles to get through it. After a few chews, he added, "... for the biscuit and the comment. I think I'm just a naturally cheerful person, so I bounce back to cheery as my default position, even if I sink at times." He glanced sideways at the sergeant. "Sometimes, it has taken quite a bit of effort."

"At least, being a lord, you've never had to worry about where your next meal's coming from," said Reece, with a faint touch of bitterness.

Jon decided to sidestep the possible one-upmanship about who had had the harder past and instead, chose to seek the source of the sergeant's bitterness. "And you have?"

"Often. My father was a lawyer, so to start with, we were comfortably off. But when I was eleven, he was killed by a runaway cart. From then on, my mother had to find work, as a seamstress or a scribe. She was well-educated... her father was a well-to-do merchant... but few people would turn to a woman for their letters." Reece took a rather savage bite of his hard biscuit. "She had trouble getting regular clients and she was proud. She had fallen out with her family and wouldn't turn to them for help. And she never got over the death of my father, either. She took to drinking. Sometimes she spent all the money she earnt on drink... and she lost clients because she didn't deliver on time. Daisy, that's my little sister, and I tried to find odd jobs, but we weren't brought up for it."

"Neither was I," said Jon, then kicked himself for interrupting. "Sorry. Go on."

Reece stared at him for a few seconds then shrugged. "Not much more to tell. As soon as I was sixteen, I enlisted in the army so I could support Daisy and myself, and Mum, if she needed it."

"Huh. I thought you seemed more educated than the average enlisted man."

"I suppose I am. Despite it all, Mum found time, mostly, to teach us our letters, numbers and a bit of history."

"And etiquette, I think."

Reece smiled. "We were just brought up that way. Not strict court etiquette, of course but hmm, I suppose you'd call it genteel manners." He chuckled. "It doesn't always go down well with the men, but they're a great bunch and put up with me."

"You're perceptive and care about the people around you. I'd say you're worth putting up with," said Jon, standing up and holding out his hand to pull Reece up.

"Thanks... for the hand and the comment," Reece said, echoing Jon's previous words. "Sorry I dumped all that on you. I don't usually talk about it. No point really. The past is the past." He called his men to order and they set off down the path that Sasha and Jayhan had been taken down in the pre-dawn.

Once they were settled on their path, Jon continued the conversation. "Sounds like your mum had a hard time of it. But you have a good, interesting job now, don't you? Why are you bitter still?"

Reece hitched his pack more comfortably on his back and blew out a huff of air. "I shouldn't be, I suppose. It's just that... ah, you know. If my father had lived, I'd probably have been a lawyer too, or if I'd joined the army, it would have been as a commissioned officer. Now, I never will be. You're either enlisted or commissioned. You have to buy a commission and pay for the training, all of which costs far more than I'll ever earn." He gave a self-deprecating smile. "I do my men a disservice complaining like this. Enough. I am proud of them and we have a job to do. Let's focus on that."

Jon gazed around at the tall trees above them, the wet leaves shining in the mid-morning sun and the patches of blue sky appearing amongst the clouds. He smiled. "It may not be just what you want, but you seem to have earned yourself a place in a skilful, elite squad who have interesting assignments out in the countryside. Seems pretty good to me. Much better than being a footman."

Reece exploded with laughter. "That's a random comment, if ever I heard one. What made you say that?" He waved his hand. "Never mind. You're right, of course. It is a pretty good job. And I actually love it, most of the time anyway."

Suddenly one of the men came jogging up bedside them. "Sir, someone is travelling parallel to us through the bushes to our left."

Before Sergeant Reece could react, Trevor signalled from up ahead. "Someone off to the right up ahead," he interpreted for Jon.

Then they saw a figure waving frantically from high in a tree further up ahead.

"Weapons ready, men," ordered Reece. "Whoever that is could be trying to catch our attention to distract us, or warn us of an ambush. Be ready for an attack from any side."

Without further instruction, the eight men moved into formation; two facing forward in front of Jon and Reece, two backwards and two facing each side, all with swords and daggers drawn. Then as one, they moved swiftly into the cover of the bushes on the right of the road and kept moving forward along the track. Up ahead, Trevor ran from tree to tree along the side of the track trying to get closer to the gesticulating man. But despite all their precautions, he or any of them would have been sitting ducks if their opponents had archers among them.

Soon, Trevor could hear what the frantic white-haired man was shouting as he waved his scrawny arm. Trevor signalled to the sergeant who turned to Jon. "He wants you, whoever he is. He is specifically calling your name. We'll move up as a group until we're close enough for you to see whether you know him. Then we'll decide what to do next."

As they drew nearer, Jon recognised the scrawny old man. "It's all right. He's safe. He's a Kimoran refugee. He is loyal to me."

Reece gave Jon a strange look, knowing him only as a noblemen in charge of the Transport Ministry. Then he listened to what the man was saying.

"Jonboy. Jon. We have to talk to you. It's urgent."

Jon straightened and moved away from the squad to stand in the middle of the road close enough to shout up at the man. "Beetlebrow. I didn't know you could climb trees. Come down. These men won't hurt you." He glanced at Reece for confirmation before adding, "You have my word."

"Right. Give me a minute. Argus is close by, too. I'll signal to him to join us too. All right?"

Jon looked at Reece. "I can vouch for him too." When Reece nodded, he replied to Beetlebrow, "Yes. Better to have him out in the open with us. No misunderstandings then."

Reece raised his eyebrows. "They're *loyal* to you too? What going on? You're not some bandit lord, I hope."

"What?" Jon frowned in surprise then laughed. "No. Nothing like that."

Beetlebrow had made it down the tree by now. He gave

Trevor a friendly nod as he passed him and shambled over to stand before Jon, gasping from the effort. Then he surveyed the armed squad of men arrayed behind Jon and brought himself up short. He gave an awkward little bow before saying stiffly, "Good morning, Your Highness. Sorry for calling you Jonboy."

Jon placed a hand on his shoulder. "Stop it, Beetlebrow. You can call me Jon or Jonboy just as you always have. Save all that stuff for if we ever get back to the Kimoran court. Now, tell me why you need me."

"Oh yes. Right. We saw Sasharia and her little friend with the pale eyes being marched off, further down this track. Their hands were bound and they had Kimoran special forces troops behind and ahead of them. We ran back this way looking for help. We were planning to go all the way into Highkington to report it until we saw you. Lucky we saw you. I'm puffed out already."

"How many?"

"Four in front and two behind," replied Beetlebrow promptly. "Draya and Rhoda are keeping track of them, but we didn't want to attack in case the kids got hurt. We're farmers and tradesmen, not fighters."

Argus stepped out from the bushes on the left-hand side of the path and raised his hands disarmingly when he saw a swathe of swords swing his way.

"This is Argus," said Jon. "Let him through."

"Ah, Jon. Thank goodness you've come. We've been shadowing your group for a little while now, trying to work out whose side they were on. Then we saw you. So Beetlebrow raced up ahead and climbed a tree to get your attention from a safe place." Argus ran a hand through his mane of greying hair. "We've been worried sick. We just find our true queen is alive and now we're losing her. Those bastards will kill her as soon as she hands over the power of that amulet." He gave an apologetic shrug. "We're no heroes. There's only the four of us. We couldn't do it on our own."

"Don't worry," said Reece, entering the conversation. "We'll get her back and the little fellow too. How long since you saw them?"

"We saw them about two hours ago, but we've been walking this way ever since and they'll have been getting further away all this time."

The sergeant turned to his men. "Hear that, men? We're only four hours behind. Let's step up the pace. We'll jog four hundred yards, then walk for four hundred yards on the east stretches. Can you people keep up or should we keep to your pace?"

Angus and Beetlebrow glanced at each other, then shook their heads. "We can't do that, but you go on. We'll bring up the rear."

Jon nodded. "Thanks, you two. I'll go on with the squad," he gave a wry smile, "although it may kill me trying to keep up."

"Keep an eye out for Rhoda and Draya. They might have more news further along the track," said Beetlebrow. Then he grinned. "See you later, Your Highness. You'll have to get used to using your title sooner or later."

Jon rolled his eyes. "I was trying to keep that quiet, but never mind. See you later."

For the first four hundred yards of jogging, no one spoke but when they slowed to a walk, Reece turned to Jon. "Would you care to explain? I understood that two children, one of them related to the king, had been kidnapped, presumably for the ransom. I wasn't sure why you were coming along, even if the girl's your sister. These jobs are better left to professionals." He shrugged. "But noblemen don't usually have to explain themselves to me, so I just accepted it..."

Jon's eye twinkled at him. "With barely concealed ill-grace, I might mention."

Reece gave a grunt of laughter. "Sorry." He waited.

"It's a long story," said Jon finally. "If I tell you the short version, you'll just ask me lots of questions. So, I'll start at the beginning."

So he told Reece and the listening troopers who he was, of the attack on his family by his aunt, and of his flight from Kimora as a twelve-year-old, with baby Sasha in his arms. He glossed over his years of living on the streets of Highkington and finally, gave a light-hearted sketch of his time as a footman in the Kimoran embassy.

Overcoming his laughter, Reece shouted, "Jog!" and the squad set off for another four hundred yards. Once they were walking and breathing evenly again, Reece considered Jon out of the corner of his eye for a few minutes. Finally, he asked, "So how do things stand now?"

"I am in disguise, or was, as Lord Jonathan instead of Prince Jondarian, and I work as Minister of Transport while I try to organise the Kimoran refugees into a force to be reckoned with. We only recently revealed to the refugees that my sister Sasharia, the true queen, had survived my family's slaughter. With their approval, Sasha appointed me as regent until she comes of age."

Reece stopped dead, open-mouthed, nearly causing a pile-up. "So you're telling me that rightfully, you should be the current ruler of Kimora?"

"Only until Sasha turns sixteen."

Reece shook his head and turned to keep walking. "You are far too self-deprecating. You have all the authority of a fluffy kitten."

Hearing murmurs of agreement from the men behind them, Jon smiled his sunny smile and shrugged. "Haven't you noticed how fluffy kittens usually get what they want?" Suddenly he looked worried. "That's not to say that I'm friendly just to get what I want. I just find people are usually happy to cooperate with me and I'm happy to work with them." He glanced sideways at Reece. "You can't live on the streets for years without realising that everyone has worth in their own way; sometimes well-hidden, I must say." He chuckled. "Perhaps I've never pulled rank because, until recently, I didn't have any recognised rank to pull."

"Perhaps." Reece didn't sound convinced. He gave a wry smile. "Maybe your parents, while they had the chance, brought you up well, or maybe they, too, had sunny dispositions."

"They did."

Jon's words sounded strangled and when Reece looked at him, he realised the young man was holding back tears. He wasn't sure what he should do, especially in front of his men, and finally settled on placing his hand on Jon's back as they walked.

After a couple of minutes, Jon drew a deep breath and as he let it out, gave Reece a grateful smile. "The sadness wells up from time to time. I suppose it will never really go away. And I don't want it to. My mother and my father and my brother and my sister deserve me to remember them. That's the price I have to pay for being cheerful most of the time."

Reece gave him a couple of firm pats on the back and withdrew his hand. "I like you even more, the more I get to know you."

And like the sun from behind a cloud, out came Jon's cheery grin. "Thanks."

Reece grinned back. "Jog!" he shouted.

PART VI

Instantly, all the woodfolk disappeared... except Stefan. He had been aware of the urgent, collective mind message to hide, but he had no idea how to flick into hiding. Besides, his loyalties lay with his parents and his employers. Still, it left him feeling a little bereft. The woodfolk had said they would include him and introduce him to people who might be his kin. Instead, they had left him behind as they disappeared.

Despite himself, Stefan smiled when he saw his parents, Sheldrake and Maud, staring around themselves in shock as hundreds of woodfolk disappeared instantaneously.

"My word," exclaimed his father, wide-eyed and taking a gulp of his wine. "They are most magical, aren't they?"

"And can you do that too, dear?" asked his mother.

Stefan grimaced. "I don't know. I haven't tried and don't know how." Even to his own ears, he sounded petulant.

"Now, dear, I'm sure they're not deliberately leaving you out. They do have a lot on their minds at the minute."

Stefan felt his cheeks growing warm with embarrassment. His mother knew him too well.

Vera leaned forward and whispered, "I can't believe how many people have been living in these forests around us and we never knew."

"It's amazing, sure enough." Ivan looked at Stefan. "Look at all these people who must be your kin." He gave a wry smile. "Pity they don't frequent taverns. We'd make a fortune."

Just then, Stefan became aware of Waterstone sending an image to Tarkyn requesting him to shield himself. Concerned that imminent danger threatened, Stefan whirled around ready for action, only to find Tarkyn clucking his tongue in amused irritation.

"Such a mother hen," mouthed Tarkyn.

Remembering that Tarkyn was, in fact, a visiting dignitary who would normally be given protection, Stefan offered to intercept the new arrival and check their credentials.

Tarkyn gave a wry smile, "You don't have to do that."

"I am a member of the King's guard and as such, it would be my honour." Stefan gave a small bow, and set off down the dark track towards the Creeping Vine.

"Just a minute," called Tarkyn softly. "Sheldrake, are you able to create an enduring orb of light for Stefan to take with him? I could take over the light for our firesite, but I am only able to create light where I am."

Sheldrake beamed, delighted that he had finally found a skill he possessed that the powerful sorcerer did not. "I would be charmed," he said, pushing his glowing orb towards Stefan, as Tarkyn ignited a new one over the firesite.

STEFAN CAUGHT Sheldrake's orb a little apprehensively but found that it was quite cool to the touch. He nodded his thanks.

"I'll go with him," offered Jackson.

"Good. Then he'll have your shield, if he needs it."

"For goodness' sake," growled Ivan, "it's just a stranger approaching. Happens to me a hundred times a day in the inn. I don't go rushing around taking precautions every time. I wouldn't have time to do my job, if I did."

Tarkyn grinned. "Ah, but you don't have an anxious blood brother badgering you about your safety. In times past, I was outlawed by my sorcerer brothers, with a price on my head. Old fears die hard, I suppose. Besides, as you can see, it's in the nature of woodfolk to be wary of strangers." He surveyed the group sitting around the fire. "Please remember not to mention the woodfolk. The secrecy of their existence underpins their whole way of life."

"We won't," rumbled Ivan. "You'd be surprised how many secrets an innkeeper overhears and keeps to him or herself." He shrugged. "And threats aside, I wouldn't want to betray their trust."

Minutes later, Stefan and Jackson re-entered the firelight, escorting a tired, dusty King's Messenger.

"This is Lerrin. We both know her," said Jackson. "I, because I am, or was, in the equivalent messenger service for the Eskuzorian Embassy and Stefan, because he has seen her around the King's castle."

"I know her too. She has often been to the inn on her way past. I'll get you a drink, Lerrin," announced Ivan. "You look parched."

The messenger ignored them. She was focused solely on her task of delivering her message. The tension of her movements telegraphed that it was urgent. Without a word, she approached Sheldrake, who stood as she approached. Lerrin produced an envelope from her satchel and with a bow, handed it to Sheldrake who nodded his thanks. Tarkyn redirected his sphere of light for the mage to read by.

As Sheldrake read the single sheet from the envelope, his

face paled. But with years of experience in subterfuge, he did not exclaim. He glanced quickly around the firesite, evaluating Ivan, Vera, Tarkyn, Jackson and Stefan. Maud watched his reaction but said nothing. Then he considered the possible loyalties of the woodfolk who might be out of sight, but not necessarily out of earshot. Rather abruptly, he asked Tarkyn, "Do your friends read?"

"Not in general, no. They communicate mentally, so do not need messengers." Tarkyn hesitated. "Some of my closer associates have chosen to learn to read, but no one else that I am aware of."

Sheldrake grunted and handed the letter to Maud, indicating that she should pass it on when she had finished reading it. Effusive though she might be, Maud, too, had years of training behind her. She breathed out, "Oh no," and passed the letter to the others without another word.

They sat in stricken silence, not knowing what they could and couldn't say in front of the hidden woodfolk and the messenger, who was unaware of woodfolk.

Having had time to think it through, Jackson let out a breath. "Well, this is awkward." He turned to the messenger. "Lerrin, let me take you back to the inn and get you settled for the night. Is that all right with you, Ivan?"

"Of course. Thank you. We'll be along shortly, I think."

"Thank you indeed, Jackson," said Tarkyn. "You are a prince among aides-de-camp. Don't forget to take Sheldrake's light orb with you."

Sheldrake held up a hand. "Lerrin, just before you go. How soon will you be rested enough to take a return message to Highkington, should I require it?'

"Sir, with a fresh horse, I could leave in half an hour, given the urgency of the situation." Lerrin glanced up at the sky. "The moon is at three quarters, although there are some passing clouds, but generally, visibility will be adequate." She hesitated. "But might I suggest that you wait for further bulletins? When I left, the news was new," she gave a self-deprecating smile at her choice of words and added, "so to speak. I would expect another messenger within the hour with further information."

"You are right, of course. Thank you." He blew out a breath. "Nothing is to be gained from acting precipitously, much as I would like to," he said tightly and nodded to her in dismissal.

As soon as Jackson and Lerrin were out of sight, Autumn Leaves, Rainstorm, Sparrow and Midnight reappeared. Everyone but Tarkyn jumped, still not used to the woodfolk's coming and going. Midnight went straight to Tarkyn and climbed up on his knee.

Rainstorm, who had reappeared next to Stefan, grinned at their reaction but then put an arm around Stefan's shoulder, "Sorry, my friend. We were so preoccupied with all of these new woodfolk, we didn't even send you a message. That was wrong of us. And we must teach you to disappear. I expect you wanted to stay anyway, but in future, we must give you the choice."

Stefan's resentment melted. He gave a wry smile and said, "True on all counts."

While they were speaking, Autumn Leaves was surveying the rest of them seated around the fire. After a moment, he crossed to Maud, squatted down next to her and took her hands in his. "Your hands are shaking. What has happened?"

He glanced at Sparrow, who looked around the whole shocked group and responded promptly with, "Cups of tea, coming up."

In response to his kindness, Maud's professionalism broke down and tears coursed down her cheeks. He took away one of his hands to rummage in his pocket and produce a rather crumpled piece of cloth. "Here," he said, removing his other hand from hers and, instead, putting his arm around her shoulders, leaving her free to wipe her eyes.

Between sobs, she managed to get out, keeping her voice low, "J... J... Jayhan and Sasha have been abducted. It is our worst fear come true."

For several minutes, she couldn't speak as she sobbed into the handkerchief. Sheldrake watched her from the other side of the fire, a frown on his face, but he made no attempt to go to her. Stefan suspected he was working at keeping himself together so he could act.

Autumn Leaves took the opportunity to send a query to Tarkyn, who murmured, "Jayhan is their son and Sasha... hmm... Sasha is their stable boy." He glanced at the darkened trees around them. "Perhaps Stefan can give you more information? Stefan, can you direct your thoughts directly to only one or a selected few people?"

Stefan nodded. "I think so. Let me try it out to check first." After a pause, he asked, "Autumn Leaves, did you get that?" When Autumn Leaves nodded, he glanced at Rainstorm. "Did you?" Rainstorm shook his head.

Ever curious, Rainstorm asked, "What did you say?"

Stefan gave a slight smile. "I said, 'I am sending this to you but not to anyone else.'"

"Oh."

Tarkyn turned to Sheldrake and Maud and said quietly. "I would trust my own group of woodfolk – my home guard, as I call them – with my life and with all my knowledge. As yet, however, I have little knowledge of the woodfolk of these forests."

Sheldrake pre-empted the permission request and nodded. "Go ahead, Stefan. Explain the reasons to Autumn

Leaves and he can relay it to the others of Tarkyn's home guard."

A few minutes later, Waterstone appeared at Sheldrake's elbow, shaking his head, as though he had been there all the time. "This couldn't have come at a worse time, could it? With you two, miles from your home and us, in the middle of getting to know the local woodfolk. How can we help? What do you want us to do?"

Stefan saw Sheldrake stand a little straighter in reaction to Waterstone's practical energy. He even managed a smile. "Thank you, Waterstone. Above all, we need to know where they are. We know they will be taking the children to..." He glanced at Stefan who mindspoke the word, *Kimora*. "The only question is, by which route?"

Maud gave a final sniff and said, "Jon is... was, at the palace. He will have heard sooner than us and be hot on their heels, as best he can be."

"I need to study my maps," said Sheldrake, his voice firmer now. "They are in my room at the inn." He spoke more quietly, "We need to be able to discuss the possibilities away from people whose allegiance we are unsure of."

"I understand," said Waterstone.

Sheldrake's eyes widened. "No. I didn't mean you."

Waterstone smiled reassuringly. "No. I realise that. When you go back to the inn, we will keep in touch with you through Stefan, while we get to know the local woodfolk. Is that all right with you, Stefan? You can join us later if you like." He glanced around. "Tarkyn, where are the local woodfolk at the moment?"

Tarkyn let his senses rove. "They have moved further away now. Lapping Water is talking to three of them about two hundred yards that way," he said, pointing to the south. "They have a lookout posted thirty yards closer, presumably to keep an eye on us. The rest have retreated further from the wiles of man." He gave a little grin at his phrasing.

Sheldrake watched Tarkyn's ability to scan the surrounding woodlands enviously. What an asset his skills would be to the King's Spiders. No use dreaming about that. At least Tarkyn was available to them for the time being. He returned his attention to Waterstone, whose firm kindness had given him direction when his feelings had threatened to railroad his thought processes.

"Thanks, Tarkyn," Waterstone was saying. "So, while no one else is currently within earshot, we can speak plainly. I presume you would like us to find out, if we can, whether any of them have had dealings with the current Kimoran monarch. That would be the only basis for mistrust I could think of." He raised his eyebrows in query at Sheldrake and waited for his confirmation before continuing, "I think it unlikely that they have, given our natural reticence, but we will check. Then, when we are clear about their intentions, we will ask for their assistance in finding your kidnapped children."

"Judging by their attitude to us," said Maud dryly, sipping her tea, "I can't imagine that they have had any interaction with outsiders before."

"No. Neither can I." Autumn Leaves smiled at her as he stood up. "You people head back to the inn as soon as you've finished your tea. We will pack up your things and you can collect them in the morning. You have more important concerns on your mind tonight."

The tables in the private parlour were covered in maps. After some debate between themselves, Maud and Sheldrake had decided to include the Vines in their knowledge of Sasha's heritage and its implications. The Vines' actions and attitudes, reflected in those of Stefan, deemed them to be people of integrity. Besides, several of them had known about Maud's shapeshifting for years and had never breathed a word. Their local knowledge of both the area and the people who passed through the inn was too valuable to exclude.

Sheldrake began by studying a map that showed the whole of Carrador running to its eastern borders and beyond. It was less detailed than some of the more specific maps but gave a better overview. Jackson, as a messenger, and Stefan as a soldier, had a passing knowledge of most areas of Carrador, while Maud brought to bear her knowledge of the people at court, their connections and the location of their holdings. Ivan and Vera had sent Marjorie in to join them, to provide titbits gleaned from the locals. Apparently, customers talked more freely when she was serving them than when Ivan or one of her brothers was nearby.

So, five people clustered around the map as Sheldrake expounded on the possible routes from Highkington into Kimora. Tarkyn took not the slightest interest. He sat at his ease in a chair against the wall, sipping a glass of very fine port. He was a man of many talents, but navigation was not one of them. Leave that to those who had an aptitude for such things.

Stefan glanced over at him and unintentionally caught his eye. Tarkyn smiled and raised his glass, sending a little wave of friendship across the space between them. Stefan couldn't help but grin back. Having seen Tarkyn at work this evening, waving shields and orbs of light in and out of existence, Stefan felt deeply honoured that this powerful sorcerer, the highest power of Eskuzor, had thought it worth his while to delve into his heritage.

Discovering that he was not Ivan and Vera's biological son had hurt Stefan. Deeply. But now a whole new view of his beloved forest had opened up to him. It still amazed him that it was full of people, that their isolated inn was in fact in the middle of a different community.

His distraction must have conveyed itself to Tarkyn, perhaps by the simple medium of his facial expression. Tarkyn rose, holding his glass in one hand and the nearly full bottle in the other.

"Come with me," he said quietly.

Stefan glanced around the people at the table and realised they would barely notice his absence at this stage. After all, Sheldrake was the head of Carrador's intelligence network and knew far more than he about the castle's security and the layout of the kingdom. They would need him more, if the discussion homed into possible paths through the forest. Besides, he thought wryly, his mind was too overwhelmed at the moment to concentrate properly. He nodded and followed the High Lord out of the room.

As they passed the end of the bar, Tarkyn said, "You can bring your own glass or share mine. Up to you."

Stefan gave a little grin, pleased that Tarkyn had thought to include him in the bottle of port and rather liking the idea of casually sharing a glass with someone so exalted. "I'll share yours."

The front bar had only a few patrons left at this time of night and no one paid particular attention to the tall man with the long black hair followed by the familiar sight of Stefan, whose head barely reached the taller man's shoulder. They walked outside into the forecourt of the inn, bathed in a warm light by torches mounted in sconces on either side of the door.

"Let's walk down Park Lane a little, to get away from the light," suggested Tarkyn.

"We're not off to meet up with the woodfolk again, are we?"

Tarkyn looked down at him, his strange amber eyes glinting in the light from the torches. "You don't like them?" He didn't seem to take offence at the possibility, merely holding out his glass of port for Stefan to take.

"Actually, I do. I'm really coming to like your people." He took a sip of the port. "Hmm. That's a good one. Dad doesn't usually let us near that one. No, I like them. It's just that I've had enough woodfolk for the moment. I need time to think."

"Hmm. I thought so. Too much too fast."

Stefan handed the glass back to Tarkyn as they walked away from the glare of the inn's light and into the dimmer light provided by the three-quarter moon. Ahead of them they could see the orange brown of the track spearing off into the darkness between the tall shadows of the trees. Above them, thousands of silver stars shone, their light unhindered by the glow of civilization.

Tarkyn pointed upward. "Beautiful, isn't it? I love being out in the open these days."

Stefan took a deep breath and let it out slowly, letting the tension leech out of him. "Yes, I have always loved it. I spent my childhood disappearing into the forest and watching the stars at night." He cocked his head at Tarkyn. "Do you think that is the woodfolk blood in me?"

"Possibly. Do your siblings feel the same way?"

"Not to the same extent. In some cases, not at all. Anton and Javier would rather be in beside the fire or behind the bar."

Tarkyn sipped the port and walked on for several paces before asking, "Have you forgiven me yet?"

He handed the glass to Stefan again, almost as a gesture of reconciliation.

Stefan didn't hesitate. "Yes. I didn't realize it at first, but you have given me a great gift. Now, when I stand short beside my brothers... and my sister, I will know that I have talents and another heritage that they can never possess."

"Have they been unkind to you?"

Stefan shrugged. "No. No more than to each other. But I have always had a feeling of difference. I look different, I move differently. It is not just my height. It's my whole appearance and demeanour... even my voice, now I come to think of it."

"And I suppose you've had a constant stream of customers coming through your inn commenting on it."

"Yep," said Stefan tightly. He took another sip of port and handed the glass back to Tarkyn. "And all my life I tried so hard to fit in, to be just like my family." He smiled, a flash of white in the darkness. "But now? Now, I don't have to keep trying to be something I'm not. And they all still love me anyway, just as I am. In fact, just as I always was. They don't mind the difference. Only I did."

Tarkyn chuckled. "And how does it feel to be on the cusp

of two civilizations? To be the product of two complex cultures? You are unique, as far as I know. The only woodman living among outsiders."

"Hmm, that's something, isn't it?" He walked several paces in silence before saying slowly, "I don't know. I haven't even got to know the local woodfolk yet and I don't even know who my true family is." He glanced at Tarkyn. "I like being able to mindtalk but I can only mindtalk with woodfolk, and exchange images with you. When you and your woodfolk leave, the local woodfolk may just fade back into the forest and I'll have no one to use it with. Not so 'on the cusp of two civilizations' then."

Tarkyn refilled the glass and took a sip before replying. "No. I don't think they'll do that. Woodfolk have a very strong sense of family. All woodfolk must belong to a family. If all of a person's blood relatives die, then that person is officially adopted into a new family. That's how I became a woodman; by being adopted into Waterstone's family." He shook his head. "No. They won't leave you behind, now they know you exist. They'll find your family or adopt you into a new one." He took a sip and handed the glass back to Stefan.

"I don't want to live with them, you know. I don't even know them or their way of life. I have my own life, my own responsibilities." He frowned as he took another sip. "Speaking of which, I suppose we should be getting back shortly. Protecting those two children is partly my responsibility and I want to do everything I can to retrieve them."

Tarkyn smiled rather smugly. "I thought of that. That is why we are on the road to Highkington. When the next messenger arrives, then we will know it is time to go back inside." Stefan raised his eyebrows in surprised appreciation, making Tarkyn chuckle. "It just shows how preoccupied you are at the moment. I'm sure that would normally have occurred to you."

No sooner had he spoken than they heard the distant sound of hoofbeats that drew slowly closer until a figure on horseback rounded a bend and came into sight, head bent down over the horse's neck.

Stefan swivelled on his heels and headed back to the inn at a dead run. Tarkyn, smiling to himself, wandered back at his own pace.

W hen Tarkyn arrived back at the inn, Sheldrake rushed
outside to meet him, his black coat tails flapping
behind him, and blurted out, all protocol forgotten, "They are
travelling through the dense, southern part of the forest. Jon
worked out they had been taken through the sewers out of the
city. He found their tracks near the south eastern outlet leading
into the forest and followed their trail with a tracker and a
squad of specialist troopers. He sent a message back to Josie,
who is coordinating from the palace, and she sent the news on
to us." Sheldrake had to draw breath at this stage.

"We will find them," said Tarkyn, with quiet certainty.

He gently but firmly steered Sheldrake back inside. "Let's
go and see what the Vines know of that part of the forest."

They passed the two messengers who were seated at a table
in the front bar, drinking tankards of ale and eating a late
supper. Clearly the first messenger, Lerrin, had been so sure
that second messenger was on the way that she had waited for
him before eating.

Sheldrake and Tarkyn entered the private parlour to find

four heads bent over a map that gave greater detail of the forest. Stefan looked up, his green eyes shining with excitement, as they entered.

"Lord Sheldrake, I can see where they must have taken Sasha and Jayhan. Look, sir." He traced his finger along a faint, dotted, winding line that traversed the southern part of the forest. "This is a narrow track that winds through the forest here from the outskirts of Highkington right through to Charville River. It is ironically referred to as The Way Through, because, for most people, it's not. It is very hard to navigate, and few people know about it or use it beyond the first fifteen or so miles. There are a few woodcutters' shacks and hunters' cottages dotted through the trees, close to Highkington but nothing further in, as far as I know." He shrugged. "Many of these places are deserted now."

"I remember," said Sheldrake, nodding slowly. "There was a period a few years ago when bandits were hiding in the woods in that area, in close striking distance to the capital. They preyed on local inhabitants as well as on the city dwellers. Many people had been killed or driven from their homes by the bandits before we finally tracked them down and cleared them out. A big operation, as I remember it." He looked at Stefan. "You said the forest is too large for anyone to know it well, but you have explored more of it than most people, I gather. Have you been along this 'Way Through', the one they appear to be following?"

"Yes, at least I think I have. It took me five days from end to end. It is very convoluted and almost disappears in places. It winds around a marshland and through some of the tallest timber and thickest brush in the forest. I followed what I thought was the trail, but I may have missed a turning that had become overgrown. It is so obscure and so rarely used that sometimes I wasn't sure that I wasn't just bashing my way through."

"So they won't be making very good time," said Maud, straightening from the table. "That is mildly encouraging."

"They will have covered several miles tonight." Stefan carefully didn't meet her eyes so that she could stay focused, but it wasn't necessary; Maud had herself well in hand, now. "But you couldn't travel that path in the dark. So they will have to stay somewhere, probably in one of the abandoned buildings, and leave early tomorrow morning." He grimaced. "Unfortunately, the same applies to Jon and his company. In fact, even more so, I'm afraid, because they will need enough light to follow the abductors' tracks."

Maud heaved a sigh of frustration. "If we travel back to Highkington tonight, we won't arrive until the early hours of the morning. Even if we set out at dawn, just as they will be doing, we will be tired while they are fresh, and we will be at least five or six hours behind."

"And you can't take horses, ma'am. It is far too overgrown for them to be able to force their way through."

Maud looked down at herself and gave a wry smile, "I may appear unfit; solid is how Sasha describes me, but I could easily keep up with you and Sheldrake or whoever accompanied us, on foot. I travel with much less effort as a four-legged animal, perhaps a wolf or large cat... "

Stefan grinned, unaware that he had already been visited by her in the form of a grey cat. "I would be entranced to see it, ma'am."

Marjorie straightened from where she had been studying the map and stood for a moment, a frown between her straight black brows. Obviously too preoccupied to appreciate the moment of light-heartedness, she announced, "I think we need a different approach. Going back to Highkington is completely counterproductive." Before anyone could object, she raised her hand to stop them. "Think about it. You are already twenty miles east of Highkington. I'm guessing they are only ten miles east at the most. It's just they're further south..."

"And cutting the diagonal. So they'll have less distance to travel to Manissa, the Kimoran capital," Stefan pointed to the path on the map "They'll have a longer distance to reach the border than a direct route, maybe one hundred miles, with the path's twists and turns, but they'll hit it a lot further south."

"True, but I think we are all agreed that we can't allow them to get across the border." They were all a little taken aback by Marjorie's sudden decisiveness. "Now Stefan, how far south is this track, and do you know of any tracks that intercept it along the way?"

Sheldrake was nodding his head in appreciation. "Good thought, Marjorie. Stefan?"

"The path begins in the south east corner of Highkington. So that's about eighteen miles south of the start of Park Lane. But it drifts further south as it goes east. By the time it is due south of here, I would say it is forty-five miles south and by the time it reaches the Charville River, it would be... hmm, about seventy-five miles south of Park Lane. But it's not straight by any means, so these are very rough calculations." He leant over the map and propped his head on his elbow as he considered the possibilities. "Hmm. I know a few paths that go south from here, but most of them stop within a few miles." He grimaced. "Actually, *all* the paths I know of stop within a few miles of here. I suppose we could trail-blaze our way through, but it would be difficult. There's a reason other people haven't done it before."

Jackson tapped Stefan's elbow. "Hoy. Move your arm."

Stefan sent him a frown of irritation but complied.

Once he could see the whole map again, Jackson pointed to the eastern half of the forest. "What about the river?"

Stefan stood up suddenly, clearly about to point out how impossible that idea was. Then he paused. "Huh. Let me think about it. It is way longer than the route they will be taking. We would be doing two sides of a triangle while they cut the corner; thirty miles to Bridgetown then, as the crows flies, about seventy-five miles south along the river." He pulled his mouth down at the corners, "But as the river flows, probably more like one hundred and twenty miles, at least, but it would be an easier trip. Not sure whether we'd get to the other end of The Way Through in time though."

A small frown flitted across Marjorie's brow at this last piece of information. "So Stefan, where along the river did you come out when you reached the end of that path, The Way Through?"

Stefan glanced at his sister, so much taller and darker-haired than he. Then he scrunched his face in embarrassment and confessed. "I don't know."

There was an incredulous silence.

A low chuckle came from the armchair in the corner where Tarkyn was sipping his way through the rest of the bottle of port. "*Stefan!*" he exclaimed in mock severity. "How could you? And you were doing so well." Stefan frowned, but Tarkyn smiled sunnily back at him.

"I'm sorry, but no," Maud interrupted them firmly. "That river is the Kimoran border. It is too risky to let them get so close to Kimora before intercepting them. We must find a way through the forest."

Tarkyn nodded his agreement. "Don't worry. We will. You can fly reconnaissance as can Bird, my eagle. We also have the possible resource of the local woodfolk and we definitely have my home guard. I can contact many creatures of the woodlands if need be... forest guardian, remember?... I am sure between us, we will find a way through to your little ones."

"Are you coming with us?" asked Maud, surprised. "I thought you had other priorities."

Tarkyn raised his eyebrows. "I did, until this one came along. I still do, but there is no way in the world that I will leave your dear little son and your dear little stable hand to the machinations of an immoral monarch." Anyone who knew Tarkyn would realise that he had possibly drunk too much, but his sentiments were genuine. He waved his arm, encompassing everyone in the room. "I presume all of you will be coming on the search for Sasha and Jayhan? How could you not?"

Marjorie looked flustered. "I would love to come, but I..."

"You will come with us," said Tarkyn firmly. "Your parents have plenty of help to manage without you for the next week or two. It was your idea after all to cut them off."

Stefan grinned at her. "Well done, sis. Come on. Here's your chance to get out of the pub and see some of the places you hear people talking about."

And Marjorie, her eyes shining with excitement, nodded her head.

Tarkyn unfolded his long frame from the armchair and stood for a moment, checking his balance. The port was strong and he had perhaps imbibed too much. He gave a little smile as he realized his balance was unaffected. Then he transferred his attention to the others in the room. "I will bid you goodnight. I am, of course, off into the forest, to spend the night with Lapping Water... and Midnight... and Gurgling Brook."

From the other people's point of view, there was no 'of course' about it and they all looked surprised.

Tarkyn grinned at their expressions. "You assumed a prince would prefer to stay in this comfortable inn? No. I love my family and my woodfolk friends and they have walked more than a hundred miles to join me. I can neglect them no longer. Jackson and Stefan, could you walk with me some of the way, please? We have arrangements to make for tomorrow."

As they approached the woodfolk's firesite, Rainstorm suddenly appeared next to them and proceeded to walk beside them. "So, tell us. Have they found the little ones yet? Do they know where they are? Can we help?"

"Hello, Rainstorm. No. Yes. Yes," replied Tarkyn as they walked into the firelight. "They have a rough idea of the children's location. They are being taken along a trail in the forest some forty-five miles south of here. We will cut further to the east to intercept them."

The woodfolk were relaxing around the fire, glasses of wine bedside them. The fire cast huge shadows of them against the surrounding trees. Gurgling Brook was asleep, curled up on Lapping Water's lap, while Midnight and Sparrow were snuggled up on either side of Waterstone.

Waterstone breathed out a long sigh. "South east, eh? Even further from Eskuzor."

"I'm sorry, Waterstone, I know you're all tired but..." Tarkyn paused, searching his friend's eyes, knowing that behind the rigid adherence to woodfolk principles was a kind, strong man who had befriended him when all other woodfolk shunned him, exactly because his woodfolk principles insisted that he treat all people as equal. "These two little children need our help... and their kidnappers intend to torture one of them to force compliance from the other." He shook his head. "We can't let that happen, not while there is something we can do to stop it."

Waterstone snorted. "No, of course we can't."

"Tea or wine?" queried Autumn Leaves of the three newcomers, preparing to rise.

"Stay there. I'll get it." said Stefan, heading over to the cache of leftover wine.

"We've been talking to some of the local woodfolk, you know," said Autumn Leaves. "We don't think they are involved with this unpleasant Kimoran queen, but predictably, they could not understand what business it was of theirs that one set of outsiders was abducting another set."

Stefan poured out three glasses of wine, kept one for himself and handed the other two to Jackson and Tarkyn. "Anyone else?" When he had topped up glasses, he sat himself down and took a sip. Then, as his eyes travelled around the group, a big grin slowly spread across his face, completely out of keeping with the spirit of their discussion about abducted children. He tried, unsuccessfully, to hide it by burying his face in his glass.

Lapping Water smiled back at him from across the fire and in response to her mindmessage, Autumn Leaves, Waterstone and Rainstorm focused on him and smiled, too.

Jackson and Tarkyn, watching them, also smiled but they were the audience while the others were the participants.

"I believe," murmured Tarkyn, "that our arms master is enjoying being surrounded by people who look like him. It has been a lifelong bone of contention for him that he looks so different from his family."

Jackson suddenly realised that he was the only non-wood-folk among them and immediately felt that he was intruding. Some of this must have shown on his face because Autumn Leaves looked across at him to say, "You're fine, Jackson. Consider yourself an honorary member of Tarkyn's home guard. After all, you *are* working with him. "

Jackson noticed that he didn't say 'working for' and remembered their views about ranks. He smiled to himself as he realised that in their eyes, he held equal status with his country's ultimate authority. "Thanks," he said, meaning it in more ways than one.

Stefan and he only stayed long enough to finish their drinks, by which time they had sketched out plans for the morrow. They took their leave, knowing they had a lot to do and a short time to do it in before their departure.

40

Well before dawn the next morning, Sheldrake and Maud were seated in the public bar, eating a quick breakfast. Anton was waiting on them while Marjorie dashed in and out asking last minute questions about what to take. Ten minutes later, Stefan and Jackson returned from the rear of the inn to join them.

"Everything is packed and ready to go," reported Stefan.

"But where is Lord Tarkyn?' asked Maud impatiently. "We are ready to leave."

Jackson gave an apologetic smile. "His woodfolk are exhausted after yesterday. They walked all morning, had to flee through the forest in the afternoon, followed by stressful confrontations and negotiations with the locals in the evening."

Maud was unimpressed. "Lord Tarkyn didn't walk miles in the morning. He was here with us."

"Oh." Jackson looked startled. "Didn't you realise? Lord Tarkyn's woodfolk are coming with us, to help retrieve your son... and Sasha, of course."

"Good Lord! That's most decent of them," exclaimed Sheldrake. "I thought they were just going to tell us how to get to The Way Through."

Maud's face screwed up with worry. "But we have to leave as soon as possible. Time is of the essence. I can't possibly just sit around, waiting for them to get up. I'll go mad."

Jackson gave a little bow with his head and said, "Lord Tarkyn said to tell you, that is, to *suggest* to you, that Stefan and I guide you for the first part of the morning and meet them further down the track."

Maud's eyes flashed. "There is a certain high-handedness in that young man's approach."

"Yes, ma'am. I believe the woodfolk berate him frequently for being arrogant and he is, after all, used to his word being law in Eskuzor, although obviously it is not, here in Carrador."

"I may perhaps have to remind him that he has no authority over me," said Maud, prepared to battle it out with him when she next saw him.

Jackson's eyes shone with poorly suppressed mirth, "As to that, ma'am, he authorized me to apologize in advance for his presumption and to explain that he, too, has family responsibilities and, perhaps more importantly, that his little daughter would not be an asset if she were too tired." He couldn't help adding with a grin, "And I think he prefers to sleep in, if possible."

The frown disappeared from Maud's face and she grinned back. "The man is incorrigible. Very well. Sheldrake and I will leave in ten minutes."

"By the way, Stefan," said Sheldrake, "I have sent the King's messengers back to Highkington to inform Josie of our plans, and the King, of course, if he has returned. I have also sent a message to Leon to take charge of the network while I am gone. He's my second-in-command." He shot Jackson and Stefan a glance. "No one else knows, of course. It would never occur to anyone that my coachman-henchman would have any real authority."

"He's always struck me as pretty clever," said Stefan. He chuckled. "No wonder you couldn't trick him into fighting me."

Sheldrake gave a slight smile. "His big, bovine, ignorant look is just his disguise. We both do everything we can to perpetuate it." He rose from the table. "Shall we go, my dear?"

They emerged into a cold, grey morning, misty rain drifting through the trees. The light had come up just enough to see by, but it was not yet full daylight.

Rather self-consciously, both Maud and Marjorie were wearing leggings, not their usual billowing skirts. Sheldrake, Stefan and Jackson pretended not to notice.

Maud frowned when she saw only four backpacks waiting for them. She looked around at her companions. "Which of us is not coming?"

Jackson grinned. "We are all coming. It is just another of Lord Tarkyn's suggestions that it would be better if your belongings were distributed amongst our packs."

Maud raised her eyebrows, once again displeased with Tarkyn's high-handedness. "And why is that? I am perfectly capable of carrying my own pack."

The colour heightened in Jackson's cheeks. "I believe it is so that you can shapeshift if need be, without then leaving a pack that someone else would have to carry."

Her eyes narrowed while she thought this over. "I would have preferred him to discuss it with me but..." She let out a breath. "I can see the merit in it. In that case, I will take turns with Marjorie for the time being."

An hour and a half later, the track they were following petered out at a pleasant little picnic spot near a burbling stream. Stefan swung his pack off his shoulders. "This is as far as I can guide you. Now it is up to the woodfolk."

Moments later, Tarkyn's woodfolk melted out of the seeming impenetrable stand of bush and brambles that barred their track. Tarkyn himself walked up from the stream in muddy boots, holding Gurgling Brook's hand.

"Good morning," he said cheerily, holding up an old cup triumphantly. "Look what we have caught. You show them, Gurgling Brook."

Smiling proudly, the little girl brought the cup over to the new arrivals. Inside it was a large spray of gum leaves and some soap. When Maud looked puzzled, Tarkyn said, "Look under the gum leaves."

Maud gingerly pushed the gum leaves aside and found herself looking at a dozen little freshwater crayfish.

"Yabbies," announced Gurgling Brook.

Maud smiled. "Very good. How exciting."

The little girl nodded, beaming.

Seeing Maud's uncertainty, Tarkyn said, "These ones are a bit small for eating but very good for bait. Rainstorm and I may do a bit of fishing later to see if we can catch something for dinner." He intercepted her gathering frown by adding, "... if we have a break near a stream."

"I might join you in that, if I may," said Sheldrake, as he dropped his pack on the ground and unstoppered his water flask.

"Of course."

"And me," chorused Jackson, Marjorie and Stefan, with varying degrees of assertion.

Midnight, seeming to understand what they were saying, looked up at Tarkyn and smiled while Maud became very busy putting her pack down and not looking at anyone. Without even thinking about it, Tarkyn sent her a wave of warm strength. "We'll have to make sure we do some fishing with Jayhan and Sasha on the way back, won't we?"

She raised glistening eyes and nodded.

Rainstorm walked over and put his hand on her back. "We can't promise to bring them back safely, Maud, but we can promise you that we will give you all the help we can. And remember; within the forests, the skills and knowledge of outsiders are no match for ours." There was no hint of bragging in his voice. His calm assurance steadied her more than any empty promise could have. Then he smiled cheekily. "I like your leggings by the way. Yours too, Marjorie. Much more practical."

Maud's returning equanimity was once more overset, but this time by embarrassment.

Rainstorm chortled. "Don't worry, Maud. None of the people at your court need ever know. And here in the forest, you can merely think of it as fitting in with the mode of dress worn by one of the highest-ranking women in Eskuzor."

"Rainstorm! Stop it," snapped Lapping Water, scowling furiously at him. "You know I don't think of myself like that,"

Rainstorm turned an unrepentant grin on her. "Of course I know. You and I don't give a fig about rank, but I bet Maud does."

Maud was saved from replying to this by the appearance of Sphagnum Moss, Tree Fern and Spinifex, accompanied by two woodfolk, previously unknown to them. A woodwoman of late middle age, statuesque and graceful with long silver hair shimmering down her back stood next to a ruggedly handsome woodman of similar age. The woodwoman held such an aura about her that everyone stopped what they were doing or saying to stare at her. She showed no sign of nervousness even though she had almost certainly never met outsiders before. The man beside her, however, was taut with wariness.

She bestowed a smile on them. "Good morning. Welcome

to our forests. I am Silverwood, healer and keeper of the lore." Her voice flowed over them, rich and deep.

Stefan frowned. "Like a bailiff?"

She gave a slight shake of her head. "No. A storyteller. I tell and listen to the stories and legends of the woodfolk and make sure they are told truly. You, Tarkyn, and you, Midnight, spring from our legends and will become part of our future legends." She turned to Stefan. "As will you. Already the woods are ringing with the story of your loss in the great flood, your extraordinary upbringing among outsiders and your reappearance among us. It is truly a wondrous tale."

Stefan's face reddened and he crossed his arms, looking acutely uncomfortable.

Silverwood smiled and the whole area seemed to light up. "Unlike the forest guardian, you are not used to such attention." She paused for a moment, giving him time. "Stefan, in the days since it became known that you are a woodman, have you not wondered who your actual birth family is?"

Stefan glanced uncomfortably at Marjorie, before looking back at Silverwood and muttering, "Constantly."

"So too have we," she said, rather to the surprise of her listeners. "Many people were lost in that flood. Not just you. Two newborn male babies were among those lost, along with their mothers. Their fathers, who happened to be rostered on to guard duty high in the trees at the time, both survived. An hour earlier and it would have been the mothers safe in the trees and the fathers swept away. Thus are the vagaries of fate." She gestured at the unknown man. "This is Ironbark. Ironbark and Spinifex are my brothers. Spinifex was married to Flowering Gum and Ironbark was married to Wattle Bird. They are the fathers of those two lost babies. Sphagnum Moss is your grandfather and Tree Fern is Spinifex's daughter." She waved an arm that took in all four of the people with her. "We do not know which of them is your father and which your uncle. We could think of no way that we could work it out. But all of us are your family," she moved her gaze to Marjorie, "and yours."

Ironbark hesitated, then walked over to Stefan, even though he stood close to outsiders, and placed his hand self-consciously on his shoulder. "I welcome you back into our family. I am sorry I was not present last night, but I was on lookout duty," he said in a deep, mellow voice. He turned to look up at Marjorie and took a quick breath. "I also welcome you." He gave a lopsided smile. "That wasn't as warm as I meant it to be, but I'm a bit nervous meeting you for the first time. I will thaw over time."

Marjorie smiled and flung her arm around his neck in a hug. He nearly jerked back but stopped himself. "There. That will progress things faster," she said with the cheery warmth of the Vines. "I welcome you to our family, too."

Ironbark gradually returned her embrace and included Stefan in it.

Silverwood approached them more slowly and hovered a little beyond their reach. Suddenly Stefan realised that despite her apparent poise, she was more unsure than Ironbark. He disengaged himself and walked over to her. "So, you are my aunt then and Tree Fern is my cousin...or sister?"

She nodded but made no move. As he stood there wondering what to do next, Marjorie sailed past him and put her arms around both of them. Ignoring Silverwood's lack of effusion, she said, "So look at you, little brother. Two uncle/fathers and an aunty. Plus a grandfather and a cousin-sister."

Stiffly, Silverwood put her arms around them, completing the triangle, while Ironbark stood grinning at them. "Silverwood, they won't bite."

"Be quiet, Ironbark," she threw at him. "I am doing my best. It is not my usual practice to hug complete strangers."

It was now some time since they had reached the end of the track and Maud, although pleased for Stefan, was restraining herself from dancing from one foot to the other in her impatience to be gone.

Seeing this, Jackson spoke up for the first time. "How do you do, Stefan's family? I am Jackson. Do you intend to accompany us because I'm afraid we cannot linger here much longer?"

Spinifex replied, his voice thinner and scratchier than his sister's. "Maud and Sheldrake, I believe your children have been taken. We understand such loss, but we have never involved ourselves in the affairs of outsiders."

"You're bound to take more of an interest now," said Jackson tartly. "Your son or nephew is an outsider as much as he is a woodman." He shrugged. "Besides, your forests are now rife with Kimoran refugees and special forces because of this false Kimoran queen, Toriana. Surely this must be inconvenient for you."

"It is," said Silverwood. "Until Autumn Leaves explained the situation to us last night, we had not realised why so many people were in our forests."

Spinifex looked at Stefan. "What is your connection to these abducted children, Stefan?" he asked.

"I live at the house of Sheldrake and Maud, working as an arms master to train them and their staff to protect these two children. I am also developing the children's fighting skills. Sasha and Jayhan matter a great deal to me. They are almost family."

A brief mental conference concluded with Ironbark saying to Stefan. "Then, if these children matter to you, we will help you find them. Consider it a gesture of..." he shrugged, "friendship, kinship, solidarity... welcome." Then he gave a self-conscious laugh. "I sound silly. I simply mean that woodfolk work together. As a woodman and particularly as a member of our family, you merit our assistance, if it matters to you. That is all."

"Besides," said Spinifex with a flash of humour, "these Eskuzorian woodfolk have no hope of finding their way quickly through our forests."

"He's right, of course," said Waterstone. "We could get you there, but we don't know the fastest routes. I'm glad you're coming with us."

41

Once they had woven their way through a mile of dense thickets, the first day of the journey took them south east through light woodlands where the travelling was easy.

Halfway through the morning, Ironbark noticed an eagle circling high above them in the clear morning sky. He pointed up and said. "Unusual for a mountain eagle to be this far from the Darkstone Mountains. They are usually further south on the eastern side of the Charville River."

Autumn Leaves watched to make sure, then smiled at the woodman. "No. She is a long way *south* of her territory, not north. That is Bird, Tarkyn's eagle. Make sure your woodfolk know not to shoot at her when she comes in to land."

"We never shoot raptors," said Ironbark, with a hint of censure. "Do you?"

Autumn Leaves glanced at him. "No, but I wasn't sure how similar our creeds were."

Even as he spoke, they could see that the eagle was gradually losing height and as they crossed a clearing where an old tree had fallen, the huge black and gold eagle glided in at speed to land neatly but with great force on Tarkyn's shoulder. Tarkyn staggered backwards but managed to keep his feet under him. Then, as she turned to face forward, her tail brushed across his face.

"Ah phtewy," grumbled Tarkyn, his face full of feathers. "Can't you turn the other way, you annoying bird?"

Bird just ignored him and ran her beak down a strand of his long black hair as though grooming him. Autumn Leaves laughed while Ironbark boggled.

"She does it and he does it, every time," chuckled Autumn Leaves. "It's almost a ritual for them."

"Great, isn't it?" Stefan was grinning. "I've only seen it a couple of times. It's wonderful, and the funny thing is Tarkyn just thinks it's a pest having to carry her. See? He has pads sewn on his shirt so that her talons don't destroy his shoulder."

Tarkyn, inevitably, heard them. "It's a pest to have to carry her but I don't think *she's* a pest. I love her dearly. But she weighs more each year. She was just a baby when I first got to know her. Well, not a baby exactly, but quite young. She was heavy then but now she must weigh close to ten pounds."

"And is this part of being a forest guardian, having a familiar animal?" asked Ironbark.

"Not that I'm aware of." Tarkyn flexed his shoulder under her weight while she bobbed contentedly up and down as he walked. "Though I suppose it is a consequence of it. I asked her to track some people for me when she was younger, but she flew too close to them and was speared by an arrow. I rescued her and brought her back to health, which was the least I could do, since she had been helping me at the time. But since then, she has never wanted to leave. I hope one day she'll find a mate, an eagle mate, not me, and raise a family." He smiled and raised his hand to stroke her. "But I would not want to lose contact with her."

Tree Fern kept a covert eye on Stefan as they walked. He noticed but didn't say anything, giving her time to get used to being around outsiders. Besides, he was feeling awkward and couldn't think of anything to talk about. He was just about to comment on the lovely sunny morning when she said abruptly, "You're leaving tracks, you know."

He looked at her in mild surprise. "Does it matter? No one is after us, are they?"

"We *never* leave tracks. Never."

"Oh."

From the other side of him, but in a friendlier tone of voice, Ironbark joined the conversation. "If we did, sooner or later, someone would see them and wonder who had been here."

"It is not just luck that no one has learnt of our existence," added Spinifex. "We work hard at it."

"Oh dear," said Stefan, looking flustered. "I'm a failed woodman before I even start."

Tree Fern sidestepped a dusty patch of path, stepping lightly from stone to stone. "Of course you are. You haven't had our years of training."

"Actually, he has," said Rainstorm, coming to his new friend's rescue. "It's just been different from ours. He is a master arms man, you know. He can hold his own against us in archery. He is so good at weaponry that he teaches other people."

"But we haven't had time to teach him any specialist wood-craft skills yet," said Autumn Leaves. "He only met woodfolk for the first time yesterday. So give him a break. And Tarkyn showed him mindtalking only a few days ago, mostly to check out whether he was truly a woodman. He hasn't even had time to learn the full extent of image and memory sharing."

Up ahead, Silverwood stopped and looked back at Stefan. "Don't let Tree Fern wind you up, Stefan. We will teach you.

In fact, you will have to learn if you wish to spend any time with us. But it is our fault, not yours, that you have gaps in your training." She turned a stern glare on her niece. "And just you remember that, young lady, and be kind."

Tree Fern's eyes narrowed and she looked anything but repentant.

Gradually, the land began to rise and soon, people were saving their breath for walking. Silverwood and Spinifex led them unerringly between the tumbled boulders that lay along the crest of a line of hills, following a narrow, convoluted trail that led to a viewing point where they could look out across the wooded hills to the south. Below them, white water gushed over cataracts into a river below.

"That's not the Charville River, is it?" asked Maud in some alarm.

"No." Silverwood's voice was soothing. "That is much further east. This is the Wandigo River. A lot smaller than the Charville. It has even been known to dry up completely."

"Not often though," said Sphagnum Moss, who was leaning heavily on his walking stave after the long walk uphill. "It springs from the caves that riddle these hills. So it has to be a bad drought indeed, for it to dry up."

Ironbark pointed to the distant horizon. "The Way Through is still far to the south. From what you have said, we need to keep heading southeast. So, we can follow this river for a while, but eventually it turns due east to flow into the Charville."

Bird, whose grip on Tarkyn's shoulder had been taxed by the constant change of direction among the boulders, chose that moment to launch herself off into the space above the falls. Warned by the tighter grip on his shoulder and the tensing of her leg muscles, Tarkyn thrust his right leg backwards to counteract her push from his left shoulder. Bird spread her wings and soared out to circle over the falls, her black and gold wings shining in the sunlight.

"Oh! She is beautiful," breathed Silverwood.

They watched her in awed silence, taking the opportunity to catch their breaths after the long upward incline. When they could drag themselves away, Spinifex led them back from the lookout for a hundred yards before turning hard left, to take them down a steep, narrow path that paralleled the course of the falls. The trees were denser and greener on the steep slope, kept moist by the spray from the falls. The ground underfoot was muddy and slippery, forcing them to hang on to fern fronds or mossy branches as they passed, to keep from sliding.

Three quarters of the way down, Sphagnum Moss lost his footing. He fell heavily and skittered for several yards before he could grab a passing plant to stop himself. Unfortunately, the plant he grabbed was the leaf of a stinging tree. The old man sat hunched in the middle of the path, cradling his stung hand and resisting the impulse to rub it. His face was drawn with pain.

Maud, who had been preceding him, turned back and bent over him. "Are you all right? Have you broken anything? Can you stand?"

"Stinging tree," he managed to gasp.

"Oh no," breathed Silverwood as she glided down the path to reach him. "Oh dear. We'll need something for the pain and some resin."

Maud looked confused. "What has happened? What stinging plant?"

Silverwood looked up and down the path at the party strung out in either direction. "Oh dear. We should have told you. Please listen, everyone. Within these damper forests, a stinging plant grows. It is much more vicious than a normal stinging nettle." She pointed to an innocuous looking plant with slightly furry, spade-shaped leaves, that was growing beside the path next to Sphagnum Moss. "Look. It produces a severe sting, not just when you touch it but for months afterwards. Every time you wash your hand the pain will return. Sphagnum Moss has just grasped one." Her voice became directive. "Spinifex, Tree Fern, Ironbark, we need some resin. See if you can find a black wattle tree or a gum tree that is exuding some. If we can warm the resin and put it on his hand, the tiny barbs may stick to it and we should be able to pull most of them out."

She reached into a pouch she had strapped around her waist and pulled out a small bundle. "Pa, we have to get you down the hill. Can someone go ahead and boil up some water to steep willow bark for the pain, please?" She leant over and tried to get her hand under his elbow without touching the hand that was stinging.

"Wait!" said Tarkyn firmly, coming up behind the old man. "You go ahead and get things ready, Silverwood. I will take Sphagnum Moss down the hill."

She looked dubiously at him. "Don't touch his hand or that plant," she warned him.

"I won't." Tarkyn leant over Sphagnum Moss. "Take a deep breath. I am going to lift you off the ground and down the path. Are you ready?" When he nodded, Tarkyn intoned, "*Ka liefka,*" and lifted Sphagnum Moss into the air on the end of a shaft of bronze magic.

Sphagnum Moss let out an undignified squawk. "Aah! Oh! That sort of lift!"

Grinning slightly but maintaining his concentration, Tarkyn carefully sidled past those ahead of him on the path, intoned, "*Kaya Reeza Mureva,*" and glided Sphagnum Moss through the air in front of him, to deposit him gently on his feet at the point where the ground levelled out. Autumn Leaves was waiting to hold him steady as he landed, while

Waterstone and Sparrow were already gathering wood for a fire.

Silverwood led them to a clearing where they could set up a firesite and solicitously settled Sphagnum Moss against a log.

"It's damp here," he grumbled. "I'm going to get wet trousers."

"Good," she said, obviously used to his grumpiness. "It'll keep your mind off the pain."

"Huh," and, after a moment, "it'll take more than that."

Tarkyn walked into the clearing with a small bundle of sticks that he dropped where Lapping Water was setting the fire. He ruffled the top of her head affectionately and she smiled up at him briefly before he turned to Silverwood. "Tell me about this stinging plant. Can my healing powers help?"

"I don't know. The problem is that the little barbs break off inside the skin and stay there for months until the body gradually expels them. If we can drop liquid resin onto Pa's hand and let it harden, then hopefully the barbs will stick to it and be pulled out." She screwed up her face. "Trouble is, we may burn Pa's hand in the process."

"Oh, don't worry about that," said Tarkyn airily. "I can fix that."

"And," continued Silverwood, "it probably won't get them all out, but it is the best we can do. That and painkillers."

Tarkyn squatted down in front of the old man. "Show me your hand." When the old man's eyes narrowed, he added, "Please. I promise I won't lift you up again."

"Just make sure you tell me what you're doing next time." Sphagnum Moss held out his hand, palm up. It was a little pink but nothing to indicate that apparent degree of pain.

"I did. You just misunderstood."

Sphagnum Moss growled. "Of course I did. We've never seen anything like that before."

Completely unfazed by the old man's irritation, Tarkyn grinned. "I promise I'll be clearer next time." He inspected Sphagnum Moss's hand but couldn't really see anything, then sat back on his haunches. "Let me think about it while you prepare the bark and resin. And I'll be standing by to heal your hand if it gets burnt."

Just then Stefan entered the clearing at a dead run and rushed over. He held out his hand to Silverwood, showing her several knobs of amber coloured, hardened resin. One of them was hard on the outside and still contained liquid resin on the inside. "Look. I found some."

The healer raised her eyebrows. "Well done, nephew. I didn't think you would know what to look for."

Stefan smiled with a hint of pride. "I use wax and resins for my bow strings and I teach the use and care of weaponry. Not quite the same but I know what to look out for."

Silverwood's smile dawned. "A mixture of wax and resin is just what we need, but we need a higher concentration of resin than you would use for your weapons."

"Just a minute. I'll get you some of the stuff I use for my bowstring and you can add this resin to it," Stefan offered.

Ironbark and Spinifex returned, also bearing resin, just as the wax and the resin Stefan had collected were being placed in a small pot on the fire to heat until they liquified. They seemed unconcerned about their efforts being unneeded and gave the resin they had collected into Silverwood's safekeeping.

Once the mixture was ready, Silverwood applied it to Sphagnum Moss's hand. The old man, for all his grumbling, bit down and barely made a noise as the hot liquid made contact with his palm. He endured in silence as the mixture of resin and wax hardened.

When Silverwood peeled the wax and resin away, the skin of his palm was red but not burnt. "Any better?"

Sphagnum Moss frowned as he thought about it. "Hard to tell. My poor hand has been battered by poison and now by heat. I think the stinging has eased but not completely. Can't tell yet if it's the poison that's still stinging, or whether there are barbs left in there. If it's just the poison, it will ease soon, I suppose." He gave a gruff smile. "Thank you, my dear, and thank you, everyone, for trying."

"Would you like me give you *esse*, my healing power?" asked Tarkyn.

The old man waved his hand irritably. "No. Not right now. Don't crowd me. I just need some time to gather my resources."

Sparrow, who was on her way over to him with a carefully prepared cup of steeped willow bark, hesitated, unsure what to do.

Sphagnum Moss waved her over to him. "It's all right, girlie. What's your name?"

"Sparrow."

"It's all right, Sparrow. I need that... and a cup of tea afterwards wouldn't go amiss. Dreadfully bitter is willow bark."

42

They made good progress for the next few hours, although Sphagnum Moss struggled to keep up. He had jarred his right hip when he had fallen, and he could only hold his staff in his right hand because his left hand still stung whenever it brushed anything.

By mid-afternoon, Tarkyn could stand it no more. When they stopped for a tea break, he walked over to Sphagnum Moss and sat down beside him. "Sphagnum Moss, I admire stoicism as much as the next man, but your unnecessary suffering is distressing me. I don't know whether I can fix your hand, but I can definitely fix your hip, if you'll allow me to."

"Don't force him," said Tree Fern, coming to sit on the other side of her grandfather as she handed him a cup of tea.

Perversely, that was enough for Sphagnum Moss to agree. "I don't need protecting, Tree Fern. I am perfectly capable of sticking up for myself," he grouched. He cocked his head at Tarkyn. "Your healing power comes from being a forest guardian, doesn't it?"

Tarkyn just waited and after a moment, the old man gave a

decisive nod. "I'd be mad to pass up an opportunity like this. When it first happened, I was befuddled by the pain and the care from all directions but I'm all right now." He nodded. "Go ahead, young man. What do I need to do?"

"Tree Fern, could you take your grandfather's cup and put it out of the way for a few minutes, please? Then put your hand on his back to keep him steady. We don't want him falling backwards off this log while he's concentrating on the healing."

Sphagnum Moss narrowed his eyes, suspecting, quite rightly, that Tarkyn was including the young woodwoman simply to sidestep her opposition. But he said nothing.

"In a minute, I will ask you to close your eyes. Then I will place my hand on your shoulder and follow my *esse,* my healing power, down into your body. It will feel like a warm stream. Firstly, I will direct the power to your hip, then your hand. If your hand suddenly hurts, don't worry. The feeling will pass."

Waterstone stood close by, cup of tea in hand, watching. "Why might his hand hurt? Healing is not usually painful."

"I don't really know how to counter any barbs or poison that might be left, but it occurred to me that I might treat them as invaders, as I did the virus that attacked Rushwind a few years ago."

Waterstone nodded. "Worth a try."

"Ready, Sphagnum Moss?"

The old man nodded and closed his eyes. Immediately, Tarkyn placed his hand on his shoulder, felt inside himself to his core then sent his *esse* down his arm into Sphagnum Moss. He let it flow down into the damaged hip, soothing and repairing damaged blood vessels and strengthening the tendons. Then he returned briefly to the site of his own hand on Sphagnum Moss's shoulder, to orient himself before coursing his actual consciousness down to the aggravated left hand. Even from within, he could not see the tiny barbs and he could certainly not see the residual poison. But he knew how to counter invasions. Tarkyn drew on his outrage at the concept of the woodman being assailed by outside forces and sent forth a short, sharp blast of anger that burnt through the area around the damaged palm.

Outside, Sphagnum Moss grunted with pain and a short gasp escaped his lips. Tree Fern went to knock Tarkyn's arm away but was stopped by Waterstone.

"Don't you dare," he growled.

A soft warmth coursed through Sphagnum Moss's hand as the abused flesh was soothed. Then he felt the warmth contract up into his shoulder and dissipate entirely. He opened his eyes and looked down at his hand. He carefully flexed his fingers then, gingerly at first, rubbed his hand against the front of his shirt.

"Huh." He smiled broadly and stood up, giving his injured leg a shake. "Huh. That was amazing, truly amazing. Well done, young man, and thank you for your perseverance in getting me to agree to it."

The party was able to move faster after that and by dusk, they had reached the point where the river curved to flow due east. Close by, a sheltered clearing within tall river gums provided a suitable firesite and once they were unpacked and a fire had been lit, a keen group of anglers headed for the river to use Gurgling Brook's yabbies.

Most of the anglers used hand lines wrapped around short, thick sticks, but Lapping Water rigged up a pole with a long piece of line dangling from its end for Gurgling Brook and Midnight to hold so they didn't get their line tangled.

Stefan was diverted from joining them by Rainstorm, who gestured for him to come into the trees away from the others. As soon as they were alone, Rainstorm pointed up into the trees above them. "Look. Autumn Leaves is on lookout duty on this side. So I... we, thought I could teach you how to flick and merge into your surroundings before you get any more grief from your relatives. There is still a lot more to learn, but at least you would know the basics."

Stefan's eyes gleamed with excitement. "I'd like that. I'm dying to learn how to flick. The older relatives aren't unkind, just a bit incredulous. It's only Tree Fern who's snaky about it. I don't think she likes me being foisted into her family."

"No... Maybe not," admitted Rainstorm cautiously. "She's been Sphagnum Moss's only grandchild until now and she seemed pretty possessive of him even before you came along, let alone now."

Stefan nodded. "I think I'll have to tread carefully."

"And she's either your sister or your cousin, and you don't know which man is your uncle and which is your father. That must feel pretty weird." Rainstorm was busy scouting around the gaps between the trees looking for an easy spot to flick to, but he glanced at Stefan to gauge his reaction.

Stefan shook his head from side to side a few times, filled with confusion. "Very weird. I had envisaged a mum, a dad and one or two siblings. Nothing like this. I'm glad I have Ivan, rock solid in my background, to fall back on. He is my real dad, as far as I'm concerned. Ironbark and Spinifex? Well, they feel like a fiction someone is trying to impose on me."

"Give it time." Rainstorm hesitated then stood to face Stefan. "It must matter hugely to them. Ironbark and Spinifex each lost a son and a nephew. And now here you are, and they don't even know which of them you belong to. They too must be feeling uncertain and confused... and sad, too."

Stefan gave an unhappy shrug. "Hard, isn't it? For all of us."

"Yep. Very. Anyway, I'm here to talk to, if you need me. And Autumn Leaves and Lapping Water and Waterstone. We can help you understand the woodfolk perspective outside the fraught knots of your new family." Without waiting for a response, he clapped Stefan on his back. "Now, come on. Let's do some flicking."

By the time, Stefan was ready to re-join the anglers, Marjorie and Jackson had already headed back with three good-sized fish to begin dinner preparations. Ironbark and Spinifex were still seated on the riverbank, fishing peacefully, when Stefan appeared suddenly between them, his face flushed with pride and a hint of embarrassment. They started, then laughed in pleasure at Stefan's achievement.

"Well done, young one," said Spinifex, with the ease of someone who was already a father.

Ironbark just smiled warmly at him and said nothing.

In the next instant, Stefan appeared beside Midnight, grinning his head off. Even before the little boy had finished reacting, Stefan had disappeared to reappear between Sparrow and Tree Fern.

His antics drew a reluctant smile from Tree Fern, who said, "It's not a game, you know. It's a survival skill."

Stefan just shrugged. "They're not mutually exclusive. A lot of people do archery for relaxation and competition and it's also a survival skill."

Moments later, Rainstorm appeared beside him.

"You must use this so effectively when you're fighting," exclaimed Stefan, full of enthusiasm.

Rainstorm chuckled. "No. We use it to avoid fighting."

"Oh." He gave his head a little shake. "You people have such fearsome fighting skills that I keep forgetting you're not at all warlike."

Sparrow shrugged. "We're not great at hand-to-hand combat, because we never allow ourselves to get up close to people who might be a threat. So, we don't practice it as much."

She smiled impishly at Rainstorm, her soft green eyes shining. "But wresting is fun, and I think we could add in a bit of flicking. Could make it interesting."

Waterstone jumped lightly to his feet and wound up his fishing line around a smooth stick before walking over, without flicking, to join them. "I can see having an arms master amongst us is already leading to new fighting tactics. I think we could stage a few wrestling matches at some stage and try it out," his remarks gently reminding them that Stefan had his own special skills that he brought with him into the forest.

By the time the fishing party returned to the firesite, the nervous energy that had been spurring Maud forward, was long gone. In fact, more than that, it had caused her to overtax herself ever since they left the Creeping Vine and she was now struggling to stay awake long enough to eat dinner before retiring. She slumped next to the fire, leaning against Sheldrake, who had returned early from the fishing expedition and was also looking looked drawn and tired. After all, they were the only two who were not used to lives of constant physical activity and, in addition to that, they were bearing the burden of the fear for their own child.

As Maud and Sheldrake watched, several fish, still fresh from their successful fishing, were wrapped in large leaves and buried in the coals to bake.

Tarkyn moved quietly around the fire and sat down beside them. "How are you bearing up?"

"It helps to be doing something; walking," said Maud, with a sad little smile. "But now that we've stopped, it has all come rushing back again, as it always does... and I am so tired and sore."

Tarkyn took one of her hands in both of his. "Lady Maud..."

"Just Maud, if you please."

"Maud. I can't miraculously restore your son to you, although I will do all I can to help. But, will you allow me to use my *esse* to ease your aches and tiredness?"

Sheldrake leaned forward, full of interest, and gave Maud an eager nod.

"If you think it will help." Maud gave a tired smile. "Besides, I couldn't deprive Sheldrake of another opportunity of seeing you at work."

Tarkyn placed a hand on her shoulder. "Close your eyes," he said, then, closing his own, he sent his *esse* into Maud through her shoulder, lacing it with comfort and reassurance. Since she was suffering from overall tiredness and soreness, he did not bother to direct the flow but let her body disseminate it to where it was needed. Maud felt a soft warmth spreading through her, while Sheldrake saw a faint bronze haze hanging in the air around her.

Tarkyn took his hands away, opened his eyes and waited.

A few moments later, Maud opened her eyes and breathed out. "Oh, that's much better. Thank you." She hesitated for a moment, before saying, "I think Sheldrake could do with some of that, if it would not be too much of an imposition and he is willing to accept it. After all, he hasn't done this much walking for a while and must be aching, too."

Tarkyn looked a query at Sheldrake, who said stiffly, "I would be honoured to experience your magic, whether I need it or not."

"Close your eyes then... and allow me in." Tarkyn repeated the process. He became aware that beneath Sheldrake's austere shell, the man was straining to keep himself together as fear for his son threatened to overwhelm him. Amidst the *esse*, Tarkyn sent in waves of compassion and strength, acknowledging Sheldrake's fears while at the same time shoring up his defences.

When he felt he had done enough, he withdrew and opened his eyes.

A full minute passed before Sheldrake opened his eyes. A shudder passed down his whole body, leaving him looking more relaxed and more focused than he had been. Suddenly, his face broke into a broad grin, much less restrained than the usual Sheldrake. "You are a true genius. It is not just your power, which is remarkable. It is your understanding, your connection with other people." He shook his head. "And you are so young for such wisdom. No wonder you come across as arrogant sometimes. You must know so much more than you show, and so much more than those around you."

The colour in Tarkyn's cheeks heightened. "Hmm. I'm not that wise. I have a temper that gets me into strife from time to time."

Sheldrake chuckled. "If that's what rocked the inn the other day, I'm sure it does."

43

S tefan waited until the next day to try out his new skill on Marjorie. They were walking along a wallaby track that wandered through dense scrub in a south-easterly direction. Unfortunately, wallabies were happy to jump over low bushes, so now and then the track would disappear. Then the local woodfolk would have to lead them around the bushes and either join the original track or find another one for them to follow.

Stefan had been waiting all morning for a chance to get Marjorie on her own. Finally, after passing through a stand of long grass, she sat down on a rock to remove a grass seed that had worked its way into her sock. Stefan took a breath, concentrated and flicked to stand in front of her. She was looking down at the time, so all she saw was a pair of booted feet suddenly appear. She flinched back in surprise, then looked up to see Stefan standing with his hands on his hips, grinning at her.

"Do that again," she demanded.

He obligingly flicked to stand several yards further along

the path, then flicked back to stand in front of her.

She grinned in delight. "Oh, well done, Stefan! That's marvellous. So magical. How do you do it?"

"You just have to envisage yourself at that particular place then concentrate on it really hard and then... there you are!" He waved his hand theatrically before giving a grunt of laughter. "Actually, I don't think the woodfolk have to concentrate very hard. Just I do, at the moment."

Marjorie smiled, the supportive older sister. "I'm sure you'll be able to do it with less effort over time." She nodded at him. "Go on. Show me again. Use it to go up the path and I'll join you by foot. We'd better get going and catch up with the others."

As they hurried along the path, a gentle rain began to fall from the low grey clouds overhead. No one thought of stopping and by midday, the clouds had lifted and they were able to dry off in the sun as they walked. By the time they reached a suitable place for their second firesite, they were tired but dry.

After dinner, Ironbark brought over a flagon of wine and poured drinks for Sheldrake, Maud and himself. Then he sat down, just a little further from them than they were from each other, inadvertently reminding them that he was still uncertain in the company of outsiders. He was making an effort, however.

"I thought you would like to know, Maud and Sheldrake, that some of our kin further south have reported sighting a party of black-clad men and women with two children among them, walking from west to east along The Way Through."

Maud, who was sitting closest to him, reached out impulsively and clutched his arm. His eyes dilated briefly but he stopped himself from pulling back. "Oh, Ironbark. What a relief to know they are still alive!" Her eyes glistened and she swallowed before adding, "And that we know where they are. Up 'til now, it has largely been conjecture. Thank you."

Silverwood spoke from the other side of the fire. "It is hard to gauge exactly where they are, relative to us. We have more ground to cover than they do in order to intercept them, but I think we are travelling faster, even though we are not on a designated path. We need to. It would help to be able to see exactly which direction they are in so that we could adjust our path if we need to. Still, we are doing well so far, I think."

Maud glanced at Sheldrake, who gave a little nod. She drew a breath and said, "I have not mentioned this until now..." She gave an embarrassed shrug. "Not many people know of it and I wanted to get to know you woodfolk first." She had the undivided attention of the whole firesite by now. "I am a shapeshifter. I could become a peregrine falcon and fly over the forest tomorrow and reconnoitre for you. If you give me the general direction, I should be able to go from there."

A hubbub of voices filled the firesite, everyone commenting and asking questions at once.

At last, Rainstorm's voice could be heard clearly above the rest. "But why didn't you just change to something that would have found it easier to travel over the last two days? Then you wouldn't be so tired."

She shrugged. "I can't talk when I am in other shapes, although I can share images with Tarkyn. So I would have missed the chance to get to know you, both for your own sakes and for gauging the advisability of telling you my secret." She smiled. "It is useful and fun to change shape, but also isolating. I can't just socialize with the people around me and that is important to me, especially with a new group."

Silverwood's smile dawned. "It has been important for us, too, but your help will be invaluable."

"Excellent idea, Maud, you reconnoitring for us," said Tarkyn, used to working with animals and therefore the quickest to understand the possibilities. "Bird could do it, if she agreed, but a peregrine falcon is much faster. You can fly over the forests, down to The Way Through and be back by mid-morning. Besides, once you are there, you can make decisions about where you need to go to see what you want, whereas Bird would have to be guided from here. You can send images and I can... No, wait. Midnight can sketch out a map with their position and our position marked on it. Pity Sparrow can't do it. She is the best map drawer."

"Midnight and I can do it together. He can share his images with me," suggested Sparrow.

"I think one of us should join you in that," said Ironbark. "We can add our local knowledge, after all. We may be able to help you understand what you are seeing from above, Maud."

The energy levels around the firesite rose and, in working on a joint venture, the gaps between the two groups of wood-folk and the outsiders narrowed appreciably.

Early the next morning, once they had packed up and were ready to leave, Maud prepared to depart.

"By my calculations," said Stefan, "The Way Through should be about thirty miles directly south of here by now. If we are making the progress we need to, in the right direction, they should be on The Way Through but further west than that point. We started out ten miles further east, didn't we?"

"When they were seen yesterday, they had just traversed the Hidden Swamp, which is about thirty-five miles east of the last of the outsider dwellings." said Spinifex. He grinned. "I wonder how they fared with the sand flies? Nasty little things if you don't have the right herbs to deal with them."

Ironbark explained to Maud the route they would be taking until lunchtime, so she would know where to return to. Although she could search for them from overhead, it would be easier if she knew their general location.

She was just about to retire behind a tree to shapeshift

when Rainstorm exclaimed in disappointment, "Where are you going? Can't we watch? Or do you have to undress?'

The colour heightened in Maud's face. "No. I don't have to undress. I always leave from and come back to my original form in whatever I was wearing," she rolled her eyes and gave an embarrassed laugh, "...luckily." She hesitated. "I just find it a bit, hmm ...awkward. Most people don't know about it, so I keep it private. Only on one occasion have I changed in front of people. Even Sheldrake usually discreetly turns his back."

Rainstorm held up his hand. "Sorry I asked. I didn't mean to embarrass you."

She frowned, letting her gaze travel around the woodfolk; both local and Eskuzorian, the outsiders; Sheldrake, Jackson, and Marjorie and the inbetweeners; Tarkyn and Stefan.

"No. I will show you," she said decisively. "Think of it as a token of thanks for helping me to find Jayhan and Sasha." She gave a wry smile. "It's not very exciting though."

With that, she squinted her eyes as she focused on imagining the form of a peregrine falcon. Then, very quickly, she shrank and coalesced into the shape of a streamlined bird of prey, yellow beak and talons, grey back and wing feathers with a cream chest barred with fine brown stripes. She stood blinking for a minute then stretched her wings experimentally. Her wingspan was surprisingly large, more than a yard across. She drew them into her side momentarily before launching herself up from the forest floor, her beating wings drawing her swiftly up into the air. She flew twice around the onlookers at breakneck speed before spearing off above the trees to the south.

"Wow," breathed Rainstorm, "That was really something."

"Yes, it was," said Sheldrake softly, his eyes shining with pride.

Although they were still some thirty miles north of The

Way Through, only thirty minutes passed before she began to send images of the path. She flew straight and true on her mission to find her son, but she also revelled in the joy of speed, her feathers ruffling in the wind of her passage.

Following the information she had received from Ironbark, she soon located the Kimorans. She swooped low over them and could see Jayhan and Sasha walking stolidly, hands tied, in their midst. In a confused surge of rage and relief, she swept up into the air to glide in a circle high above them, ready to plummet down on the person in the lead, to frighten him if nothing else. Then she remembered that if there were a shaman among them, they would be able to tell that she was a shapeshifter. So, reluctantly, she stopped herself. She saw Jayhan squint up at her, then nudge Sasha who followed his gaze, smiled broadly and murmured something to him. Then he too smiled. Maud glided from side to side above the path then, with great resolve, flew upward and away. No animal she could transform into, no matter how powerful, could take down a column of men on its own.

From there, Maud flew along the path towards Highkington until she spotted Jon walking with the squad of Carradorian militia. They were still more than eight miles behind Sasha and Jayhan. She considered shape-changing back to her normal form to talk to Jon, but on balance decided that she didn't want so many Carradorians knowing of her secret. Besides, no plans had yet been devised by Tarkyn, Sheldrake and the others and, at the moment, her own group was significantly further from Sasha and Jayhan than Jon's group was. She was here purely to gather information and relay it back to Midnight and Sparrow, the map makers. She could come back and talk to Jon later when plans were clearer.

Maud had not held the position of first lady in the land for so many years by making hasty, ungoverned decisions and so, she resolutely flew in a broad arc before heading eastward, past Jayhan and Sasha and on further for more than an hour until she could see all the way to where The Way Through met the Charville River. As Stefan has said, The Way Through twisted its way around denser patches of bush, boggy ground and steep hills. At one point, it curved for several miles to the north, before winding back to the south-east, cutting across the last ridge on a long line of hills that were probably the beginnings of the foothills of the Darkstone Mountains. Maud and Sheldrake's party would have far less ground to cover if they intercepted The Way Through at the apex of this northerly curve.

She estimated that it would take Jayhan and Sasha's group another day and half, maybe two days, to reach that point. She thought that Jon's party would be hot on their heels by then, unencumbered as they were with unwilling children, and with less need to follow footprints so closely, now that they were following the same path.

She took herself up higher so that she and the map makers could gain a wide view of the forest. She had now been flying for nearly two hours, mostly at high speed, and she wasn't used to extended periods of exercise like a true peregrine falcon would be. Time for a break. Then, far below her, she spotted a hapless mudlark flitting about in the morning sunshine, catching insects just above the tops of the trees. Without a second thought, she closed off her images to Midnight, folded her wings and dropped into a dive, grabbing the mudlark between her talons with a satisfying crunch. The mudlark never knew what hit it.

Then she settled on high branch and proceeded to devour her mid-morning snack, inwardly smiling at the distaste Sheldrake would feel if she told him. When she was rested and satiated, she flew back in a leisurely manner, enjoying the sunny morning, to rejoin Sheldrake and the others.

PART VII

4 4

I t was four days since Jayhan and Sasha had left the hut. The last three days had been a continuous slog of long hours of walking, punctuated by short, dismal rest breaks, and surrounded by unfriendly Kimorans. Today didn't look like it would be much better.

But late in the morning, Jayhan had a breakthrough. They were walking through a long valley of tall mountain ash, interlaced with tree ferns. If he had had any interest in his surroundings, he would have realised that it was quite beautiful, but his mind was intent on working out his powers.

He remembered that his eyes hadn't reacted when he'd been in danger, when he'd fallen from the tree on top of Sasha's attacker. Hmm. His eyes had only reacted when Jon was in danger. Ha! Maybe his eyes reacted to protect other people, not himself. Behind his blindfold, Jayhan squinted his eyes in concentration, envisioning Sasha being held by two roughnecks before the Kimoran Queen, her arms twisted painfully behind her back, a thug aiming a kick at her thigh. He knew how that felt. Immediately, he felt power surging through his eyes, moments before he received another jab in his ribs from Sasha.

"Stop, Jayhan!" came her warning hiss from behind him.

The sensation cut off abruptly. *Oops.*

Brinta's suspicious voice came from behind Sasha. "Stop what? What's he doing?'

"He's driving me crazy," said Sasha, improvising frantically. "He keeps tripping, which makes me nearly run into him all the time."

To Jayhan's surprise, Brinta stood up for him. "Give the kid a break. He's wearing a blindfold. What do you expect?"

Sasha gave an artistically disgruntled sigh and subsided.

After another dreary two hours, they stopped for another break. While the other Kimorans settled themselves beneath an array of tree ferns, Brinta herded the children to a young eucalyptus tree whose trunk was narrow enough to tie a cord around it. This she secured to the bonds around the children's wrists. Once she was sure they were firmly tied, she handed Sasha a canteen of water.

"Here, share this with the lad. Drink up and eat the rest of that food Ruby gave you. We'll have a twenty-minute rest here," she said, before re-joining her comrades.

As soon as she was out of earshot, Jayhan moved so that Sasha was between him and their guards, screening him from their view. "Right," he said decisively. "First, I'm getting out of these ropes."

Before Sasha could say anything, Jayhan shrank before her eyes into a younger version of himself. When he spoke, his voice sounded higher and more childish. "Shape shifting. Now my wrists are smaller. See? The ropes come off easily." He grinned, then reshaped himself to his true size.

"What about the blindfold?" hissed Sasha.

He shrugged nonchalantly. "Doesn't matter. I can see straight through it anyway."

"You little bugger! You could have told me." Sasha was partly cross and partly impressed. "It's slipped, you know. So you might as well pull it down completely."

Jayhan grinned unrepentantly. "Easier to pretend I couldn't see, if you didn't know."

"But can your eyes send out that white light through the blindfold?"

Now Jayhan looked uncertain. "I don't know. I don't even know for sure that I can make them do it. What did you see? You must have seen something to jab me before."

Sasha nodded. "Yes. I did see white light ... but it might just have been seeping out round the edges of the blindfold."

While they were talking, Jayhan was busy loosening off Sasha's bonds. Suddenly a thought struck Sasha. "Why are they leaving us to ourselves, if they're so worried about you that they keep your blindfold on? I mean, even with your hands tied, you could slip the blindfold off."

Jayhan frowned and glanced over at Brinta's squad. "Just a minute. Weren't there six of them? Brinta, Shay, Bart and three others?"

Sasha nodded.

His blood froze. "Well, now there are only five. Where's Bart?"

"Oh, well done, my little mate," came a deep rumble from the other side of their small tree. "You are a sharp little fella, aren't you?"

Bart stepped out from the shadows of the undergrowth, towering above them. "Got our ropes off, have we? Not for long."

Sasha jumped away from him, but he reached out with his big, beefy hand and grabbed her arm. As she cried out in pain, white light poured forth from Jayhan's eyes. The huge man drew back, cowering in terror. Jayhan pulled Sasha out of Bart's now unresisting grasp and drew her towards him.

But in the other direction, the other guards saw what was happening, threw down their water canteens and ran towards the children.

Sasha grabbed Jayhan around the waist and glared at the oncoming guards, concentrating fiercely. Her amulet seemed to burn on her chest. Suddenly, a silent detonation pulsed out from her, throwing the Kimorans backwards to lie sprawled in the dust. Jayhan felt the power thrusting him outward too, but Sasha's grip on him held him against her. Then, he could see nothing but a thick, velvety blackness.

Beside him, he heard Sasha say jubilantly, "I did it! I made the amulet realise that it has to protect you too, to protect me."

"I don't think so," muttered Jayhan. "I just got pushed pretty hard by it. If you weren't holding onto me, I'd be halfway across the clearing by now."

"Hmph." Sasha sounded disappointed. "You might be right. I did have to strain to keep hold of you. But," she regained her enthusiasm, "you're inside the protection with me now. So even if I have to hold you, I can protect you."

"Stars above, I hope so. I don't feel very brave about being hurt, you know, just so that horrible queen can get her hands on your amulet."

Sasha's arm tightened around him. "Neither do I."

It was then they became aware of noises outside their cocoon of darkness. They heard the shuffling of feet on the soft ground, then Brinta said harshly, "They're in that dark oval thing. Two of you, grab it. We'll just pick it up and keep going. One of the shamans can work out how to break into it when we get to Manissa."

A woman's voice spoke from closer to them. "You get that side and I'll lift from this die."

They heard Bart's angry voice close by. "Little swine. I'll teach them for making a fool of me." After a minute of foot shuffling and grunts of effort, Bart's voice came again, sounding aggrieved. "I can't get a grip. It's sort of spongey and tingly... Ow. My hands are burning."

"Ow. Mine too."

"Find some gloves then," said Brinta unsympathetically.

Inside the oval blackness, Sasha and Jayhan waited in tense silence, Sasha's arm firmly around Jayhan's waist.

"Why didn't my mother do this when my family was attacked?" whispered Sasha.

Jayhan thought for a moment. "Because you weren't near her. You were on the other side of the tent, from what Jon told us. So it was either you or her."

There was a delay, presumably while gloves were being fetched. Then another voice said, "Why don't we throw a cloak over them and roll them up in it?"

"Good idea," came Shay's voice. "Try it."

Jayhan and Sasha heard the swishing of a cloak flying through the air followed by the sounds of material being wrapped around the outside of their cocoon. They heard grunts of effort, all coming from one side, but only felt a slight pressure until suddenly, they were toppling over. They braced themselves but their landing was cushioned by the black oval of the amulet's shield. Then they felt themselves being rolled over and over.

"There," gasped a voice close to them. "They're wrapped up. I think I need a drink after that."

"Rubbish," said Brinta. "You can drink as we walk. We need to get back on the road and get this lot into Kimora before they think of anything else."

"Get a grip. You make it sound as though Kimora's just around the corner. We have the rest of today and at least half of tomorrow, slogging through this, to get to the river. If we don't pace ourselves, we'll never make it."

An exasperated sigh came from Brinta. "All right. Five minutes. Then we leave."

4 5

I t was dark inside the cocoon of Sasha's shield. Jayhan and Sasha were being carried on their sides within the swathe of cloaks that covered the soft but impenetrable black oval. All around them, they could hear steady, rhythmic breathing punctuated by occasional grunts of exertion as their bearers altered their grips, or had to manoeuvre the cocoon past obstacles in the increasingly narrow path.

"So now what happens, do you think?' murmured Jayhan, then, in a lower whisper, "Do you think they can hear us through all this?"

"Don't know to both, but maybe they can."

"How long's this shield of yours going to last?' whispered Jayhan.

"I don't know. It's only happened once before. It knocked me out while it protected me last time. Remember? Because Yarrow's memories were too much for me. You were watching, so you know as much as me, maybe more."

"Hmm. It lasted about two hours then, but you weren't in danger except at the start. It was just healing you." Jayhan gave a disgruntled sigh. "We don't have a clue, do we? We might be in here for days if this thing still thinks you're in danger. What if I need to go to the toilet?" He groaned. "Oh. I wish I hadn't said that."

Sasha chuckled. "Idiot! You'll just have to hang on." After another few minutes, she asked, "Do you still have some of that food Ruby gave us?"

"Yep. I still have a few of those cookies in my satchel. You might have to move your arm a bit so I can reach them." As he felt her arm slide upward, he said in sudden alarm, "But don't let go! I might get thrown out of here."

"I won't. I promise. Anyway, you'd only end up inside the roll of cloaks at the moment."

"Yeah, but when they unwrapped us, they'd be able to hurt me and make you come out, too."

"True. Good point, except I don't know how to stop it or come out of it."

"But they mightn't believe you and then..." Jayhan's voice trailed off and she could feel his chest heave under her arm.

Sasha gave him a squeeze, and said soothingly, "Come on, Jayhan. We'll find a way through." She gave her head a little shake, wondering where she came up with this nonsense. She had no idea how they were going to get away. But never mind. She was ten and he was only eight, so she had to look after him. "Now, where are those cookies?"

For hours, they were carried within their cloak-wrapped cocoon. From time to time, they could feel jolting as they were passed to a new set of bearers. Now and then, they were dropped onto the ground with a thud as the Kimorans stopped for a rest. Jayhan's bladder became an increasing focus of his attention.

When he whined about it, Sasha said shortly, "I will never

speak to you again if you wee on me," which was enough for him to maintain his self-control for a while longer.

On their fourth stop in their cocoon, which must have been sometime in the late afternoon or early evening, they heard new voices outside.

Brinta greeted the newcomers and explained about the cloak-wrapped lump lying on the ground. "We have seen no sign of pursuit, ma'am," she said. "Which doesn't mean there isn't any, just that they are not close enough for us to see. With any luck, they haven't figured out which way Shay brought them out of Highkington. But even if they have, I am hoping that they are still a few hours behind us."

"Good," came an unknown woman's voice, carrying a note of authority. "But we don't want to take chances. You people have your work cut out for you over the next few days making sure you get them to the border. Leave the pursuers to me. I intend to make life very difficult for them."

Even as she spoke, Sasha and Jayhan heard the rattle of leaves, as a light breeze sprang up.

"Ooh," breathed Sasha. "I think she's a shaman. My amulet feels warm on my chest."

Outside, something light skittered past them, driven by an edgy breeze. The breeze gradually became a wind.

"Is she making a storm, do you think?" asked Jayhan. "Can shamans do that?"

"Think so. Yarrow says they, we, can work with natural elements. She'd have to be a strong one, though."

"Well," came Jayhan's voice in the dark, in that familiar tone that meant he was coming up with a hare-brained idea that might actually work, "No matter how strong she is, your amulet's stronger than hers. So, can you stop her? If someone's trying to rescue us, we don't want her making it hard for them, do we?"

Sasha sounded doubtful. "Maybe. I don't know what I'm doing, you realise. And what about the shield? If I focus the amulet's power on this shaman, maybe there won't be enough power to keep the shield up. What d'you think?"

"That would be a blessing in disguise, if you asked my bladder."

"Jayhan! I'm trying to be serious."

Now they could hear the wind beginning to roar through the treetops.

Sasha felt Jayhan's shoulder move as he shrugged. "Just seems to me that while we're in this cocoon, we have no hope of escaping, have we? So maybe we have to take our chances."

"Hmm." There was a long silence within the cocoon. Outside came the first faint rumbling of thunder. Using every ounce of his will power, Jayhan did not press her further and eventually Sasha heaved a sigh. "All right. I'll try."

Sasha focused on her heartbeat and the warmth of the amulet on her chest. She didn't think about overcoming the other shaman or the forces that were being unleashed. She just focused on her own heartbeat, slowly becoming aware of herself as a small part of the forest around her. It was almost as though her heart was beating with, and for, the forest, in concert with the trees' own ponderous rhythm. Gradually the darkness in the cocoon around Jayhan and Sasha began to pulse in time with her heartbeat, gently at first then growing more insistent.

Outside, everyone was intent on watching the shaman as, head thrown back, she held her arms aloft, muttering incantations up into the sky, drawing air from the east to lift and swirl it into the growing storm. No one noticed when the cloak-wrapped bundle lying on the ground began to throb like a huge, dark grey heart. The pulsing grew stronger and stronger until suddenly, the cloaks ripped apart, strips of material flying outward, strands of grey cloaks swirling upwards into the roiling clouds above.

Then a spear of black light streaked from the remnants of the cloaks across the open ground. It slammed into the shaman's chest and engulfed her in a dusky cloud. The haze around her pulsed once as though drawing in a breath, then sent a blast of white light shooting upwards to hit the clouds above and spread out beneath them in a silver sheet, crackling with veins of lightning.

The Kimorans watched transfixed, as silver light flickered across the underside of the cloud mass, irritating the clouds into rumbles of discontent. Now and again they heard a half-hearted clap of thunder, but the light was slowly but surely dissipating the storm clouds. A few minutes later, a gentle rain began to fall, bringing the Kimorans' gazes back to earth.

Which was when they realised that their shaman and their captives were gone.

46

At lunchtime on the fourth day out of Highkington, Trevor trotted over to Reece to report that they should have a look at strange marks in a clearing before passing it. He led Jon and the sergeant over to a tree where confused footprints overlay each other. The tracker studied the bark of the trees closely and discovered signs of a rope having been tied around a young eucalyptus tree's trunk. The signs were subtle, just small patches of bark rubbed away. Nearby was a patch of singed grass and close to that, an area where the grass had been flattened by something. Further away they found shallow indentations, almost skid marks, on the ground which spread out from the singed grass.

"Almost like marks from an explosion," mused Reece.

They studied the singeing and the patch of flattened grass but couldn't come up with a plausible explanation for them.

"And another thing," said Trevor. "The children's tracks disappear after this clearing. The six adults' tracks still clearly follow the path but... no kids' footprints."

Jon's eye lit up. "Maybe Sasha and Jayhan escaped?"

Trevor shook his head. "I don't think so. Think about it. If they'd escaped, the adults' footprints would head off in several directions looking for them. But they don't. They just keep walking along the path towards Kimora." A thought struck him. He walked along the path a little, bending down and examining the footprints. Then he straightened. "Hmm. Two sets are deeper than the others. I think they are carrying the children. I don't know why or how, but I'm pretty sure that what's happening."

"Well, with any luck, that should slow their pace a little," said Reece.

A crease of worry appeared between Jon's eyebrows. "Oh dear. I hope they're not injured and having to be carried because they can't walk."

"Let's not paralyse ourselves with grim imaginings." Reece gave Jon a clap on the back. "Come on. The best we can do is to work on closing the distance between us and them." He turned to make sure the squad were watching him. "Right. Fall in. Jog!"

By mid-afternoon, Jon was at the end of his strength. The last stretch of the path had been smooth and relatively wide, so they had alternated jogging and walking for the last four hours with only short rest breaks, but Jon had not had the months of rigorous training that the elite troopers had had. As Reece once more yelled, "Walk!" Jon bent over, gasping for breath.

Eyeing him, Reece waved a hand at his troops, "Right. Fifteen minutes' break. Trevor, when you've recovered, could you go ahead and scout the terrain? Just to the top of that next hill will do. I just want some idea of how much longer the terrain will be suitable for keeping up this pace." He smiled wryly at Jon who was still gasping between swigs from his water canteen. "If the terrain becomes more difficult again soon, we might as well persevere and keep up this pace up while we can. If it continues to be easy traveling, we'd better pace ourselves enough for you to keep up."

As Jon went to protest, Reece raised his hand. "No, I won't leave you behind. There is no way I am leaving a prince assigned to my troop, alone in woods that may be swarming with Kimorans,"

Jon bit his lip. "I'm sorry. You were right to be so longsuffering at my addition to your troop, weren't you? I'm holding you all up, and really, all that matters is that we catch up with the abductors." He ran his hand through his wavy, sweat-darkened blond hair. "But I couldn't have stayed behind, you know. I'd have gone mad." He gave a whimsical little smile. "Perhaps my sanity counts for something."

Reece gave a grunt of laughter. "Perhaps it does. We can't have a madman running Kimora."

Jon looked uncomfortable. "No, not ideally. Although I fear my aunt, the current ruler, must be close to mad, to be so cruel to so many people and so power-hungry. I hope I haven't inherited any of the evil that runs in her veins."

"I don't think for a moment that you have."

"Maybe I have a darker side you just haven't encountered yet?"

"Have you?"

Jon thought for a moment, particularly about his time on the streets, then shrugged. "Maybe. But I wonder how I would react if I had my aunt at my mercy... or Sasha's abductors..."

"Jon, we all have a darker side. It's just a matter of degree and what we do with it. Do we allow it to rule us, or do we rule it?"

"Huh. You are wise for your years, Sergeant Reece. I wish I had met you sooner. I would have liked someone like you – well, you – to talk to, over the last few years." He gave a shy smile, then looked away. "Do you think, when this is all over, that you might like to stay in contact with me?"

Reece gave a shout of laughter, and slapped him on the knee, grinning broadly. "You really are one out of the bag, aren't you? I've never met such an illustrious person who is so diffident. Actually, I don't think I've ever met anyone as illustrious as you; not to talk to, at least. Of course I would love to stay in touch. I think some of the boys would, too, if you asked them."

Jon smiled and looked around at some of the closer men. He cocked his head and raised his eyebrows in query, which prompted cheerful acceptances from everyone.

"Of course we would. You may be slow as a tortoise, but you're good company," said Warren. "And very interesting," he added, with a quick grin.

"Oh, you have no idea how interesting I can be," said Jon dryly. "I can tell you all about new road surfaces they're trying out and which streets have potholes, which roads have been washed out by the recent rains. Absolutely riveting." His smile faded as he saw Trevor returning.

"Sergeant, in half a mile or so, the road seems to disappear into a thicker section of the forest. If it's as dense as it looks, we won't be able to run through it. In fact, we'll be lucky to find where the path goes and push through it."

Reece blew out a sigh of exasperation. "Well, we've done the best we can. On these open stretches, we will have been travelling at one and half times their speed, may be more. So I reckon we've made up at least two, may be three hours, which means we're five or six miles closer to them than we were three days ago." He grimaced. "We're getting closer but they're still an hour or two ahead of us." He looked at Jon. "You ready? We'll do one last run while we have the chance." He checked that all his men were up and packed. "Right. Walk for four hundred, so His Highness here can catch his breath. Then we jog."

As they reached the dense tangle of the thicker forest, having jogged the final five hundred yards, Jon gave a gusty sigh of relief. His head was throbbing from over-exertion, his legs felt wobbly and his knees were threatening to buckle. He had to grab hold of a tree to keep himself upright.

"Look," said Trevor, giving him time to rest by pointing to a discernible line of broken or bent branches and fern fronds. "This dense bush is making it hard for them to carry their load. So, even walking at a normal pace we'll be gaining on them. It can't be long now."

Reece gave Jon an encouraging smile. "In fact, we may be getting so close that I should probably send Trevor and one of the lads up ahead to make sure we don't stumble upon them unawares." He passed his water canteen to Jon. "Here. Have a drink. We'll give it another five minutes then get moving again."

The next two hours were slow going, as they pushed their way through long grass and undergrowth that had a nasty tendency to be prickly. The canopy was high above them and blocked out a lot of the sunlight. Gradually, the ground began to rise as they made their way from the valley floor up to the top of a line of granite-strewn hills. It was a hard slog, warm, damp and steamy. Reece keep them going by promising to stop when they reached the top.

Towards sunset, the last branch was pushed aside, and they finally crested a rise that didn't lead to yet another rise. On the plateau at the top, ragged gumtrees and soft grasses grew between rocky outcrops.

Jon was not the only one this time who was tired. The entire troop threw themselves down on the grass amongst the rocks and broke out their water canteens and rations.

Trevor, who seemed indomitable in all circumstances,

walked to the edge of the plateau and looked out across the next valley. The side of the hill they were on was thick with trees, but a grassy section ran along the valley floor before the track once more disappeared into the forest. The tracker squinted into the fading light then turned to Reece. "I think I saw movement over there, just at the bottom of the next incline. We'd better stay away from the edge in case we can be seen against the skyline. Anyone watching the sunset, which I do every chance I get, might see us as silhouettes against the sky."

"Hear that, men?"

Someone gave a tired guffaw. "No chance of me standing up anytime soon."

Trevor studied the wisps of cloud in the eastern sky that seemed to become more substantial as he watched. A cool breeze sprang up and sent him diving into his pack for his cloak. When he looked again, woolly white clouds had formed. As he watched, the clouds expanded, rolling in on themselves as they grew in height and width. They darkened into storm clouds and the wind picked up. Soon it was howling through the treetops up the hillside towards them.

"Storm coming," Trevor said over his shoulder, as the first rumbles of thunder could be heard. A loud crack of thunder and the raging wind nearly drowned him out as he shouted, "I've never seen a storm build up so fast. We need to find shelter or get the tents up. No, wind's too strong. We'll never get tents up in this." Even before anyone started moving, he said, "Just a minute. Something strange is happening. Quick. Get over here and look. But stay low. I felt... I'm not sure what... a detonation of some kind." He pointed. "Look. Over there. Just inside the tree line."

Drawn by the urgency in his voice, the men scrambled to the edge of the plateau and lay on the grass, looking out, just in time to see what appeared to be, from this vantage point, a flash of black light. Then they drew in a collective breath as a pillar of white light streaked upwards and bled across the underside of the clouds. The thunder rumbled a few more times then faded away completely and the wind began to die down. Then, before their eyes, the clouds began to dissipate.

"What on earth was that?" asked Warren.

Trevor shook his head. "I have no idea."

"Whatever it was, it wasn't natural," said Reece, frowning. "That storm came out of nowhere. Then, *poof!* It was gone."

"Poof, eh, sir?" quipped one of the men.

Reece gave an amused smile. "Yes. Definitely, poof!"

Jon was looking thoughtful. "Shamans can raise storms."

"Can they? Hmm."

"Maybe someone tried to raise a storm, probably to cause us some grief, but overcooked it and burnt themselves out," suggested Trevor.

Jon shrugged. "Maybe. It certainly looked something like that." He smiled wryly at them. "Well, at least we know they are up ahead and, at the moment, in sight. We're doing well, aren't we? Now all we have to do is catch up the last couple of miles, approach them unseen and somehow extract the little ones without endangering them."

"So, one last push before dark?" asked Reece.

Jon rolled his eyes. "I asked for that, didn't I? At least it will be downhill."

47

By the time Jon and the Carradorian troopers reached the source of the flash of black light, daylight was almost gone. There were two black, seared patches on the ground and the remnants of one, maybe two, shredded dark grey cloaks. Trevor lit one of their lanterns to study the ground in the fading light. He circled the whole clearing, squatting down from time to time to check particular spots. Then he walked a short way to the east examining the footprints, before reporting to Reece.

"Sir," Trevor glanced at Jon then back to Reece, "two things. The abductors were joined from the east by at least five more people. But more importantly, I think the children are no longer with them." He waited for the exclamations to subside before giving the reasons for his conclusions. "I don't know whether someone took them in another direction, or whether they escaped, or what happened, but no footprints head east. Footprints are chaotically superimposed over each other all around the clearing, then they head in all directions, but mainly in several northerly directions." He gave a slight smile. "Just as I said they would, if the children had managed to escape."

"So, can you see the children's footprints?" asked Jon eagerly.

"Maybe," said Trevor uncertainly "It's been raining, you see. Not enough to completely wash away their prints but enough to obscure them. He walked to the rags of the cloaks that lay strewn on the north-west edge of the clearing and squatted down. "Come over here and have a look." He pointed to four small footprints. "See? They look like they might be heading north, but once they get off the track, the grass and undergrowth, especially after rain, has obscured their trail."

"And look, larger feet have followed them," said Jon, his blood chilling at the thought.

Suddenly Reece was all business. "Right, we'll set up camp here tonight. Be aware that the Kimorans are all around us in the surrounding woods, looking for Sasha and Jayhan. At any time, one or several of them may return to this clearing. So, I want two men on guard at all times. Trevor, is there any point in trying to track the children tonight? We will, if you think there's a chance we may find them."

Trevor looked at Jon, but after a moment's hesitation, shook his head. "No, Sergeant, We're more likely to run into a Kimoran and get ourselves killed. I'm sorry, Jon. So near and yet so far."

Suddenly, one of the men spotted a light off the road to the north, back along the track towards Highkington.

Jon, Reece and Trevor exchanged glances.

"There's the remains of a fire here," said Reece. He kicked it with his boot. "Still some glowing coals in the ash."

"They probably lit oil lamps with brands from the fire before they headed off," suggested Trevor.

"If that's the Kimorans, why is the light down that way?" asked Jon. "The children's footprints head straight off the road, due north."

Trevor came back to look at the point where the small foot-prints had disappeared. He stepped off the road and walked several paces into the scrub before coming up against a barrier of thorny bushes. He shrugged. "Can't get through here. You'd have to go around."

"If they have lights and we don't," said Reece slowly, "we may be able to sneak up on them in the dark and at least eliminate a few Kimorans. It'll give the kids a better chance of getting away, even if we can't track them ourselves in the dark."

Trevor studied the sky. "Not much light left, but the moon's coming up soon. I think we can manage to find our way if we're careful."

There were grunts of assent from the men.

"Good. We'll leave two men here to guard our gear."

"Sir," said Warren, excitedly. "There's another light down there in the trees to the north-east."

"In that case," Reece amended, "we'll split into two groups. Jon with me and three troopers. We'll head towards Highking-ton. Trevor, you lead the other three towards that light to the north-east. Warren and Davis, stay here and guard the camp. Now men, make as little sound as possible; it's better to be slow and silent. We don't want them to know we're following them."

As they crept along the side of the road, Reece whispered in Jon's ear, "Now Jon. No shenanigans. Please. I can't order you but I'm asking you, let the five of us act as a team, watching each others' backs."

Reece felt a pat on his back. "It would be my honour to be part of your team," whispered Jon back.

Reece smiled in the dark.

It was not long before they drew level with the light in the trees. By this stage, they realized that the light was actually two lamps, two or three hundred yards north of the trail, moving in two zig-zagging paths between the trees as the Kimorans searched for the escaped children.

Reece called a halt while they considered their next move. Keeping his voice low, he said, "Including the five newcomers, there were at least eleven Kimorans, weren't there?

"Sir," murmured one of the troopers, "they might have thought it more likely that the children would head back towards Highkington, in which case they would have sent more people down this way."

"Good point," agreed Reece. "I think, however, they would have sent at least a pair in the other direction. But our group of five may be dealing with seven or more Kimorans."

Jon watched the steady movement of the lights. "Our advantage is they don't know we're following them."

"And," added another trooper, "that they will be night blind from their torches and won't be able to see beyond their ring of light, while our eyes have become accustomed to the dark."

"However," said Reece, "should they turn suddenly and flash their light in your face, you will be dazzled while they will be used to the glare. Keep your eyes down as much as possible so their light doesn't catch a reflection in your eye and give you away, and to stop you from getting dazzled."

Since the men had had extensive training in night combat, this last little speech was actually meant for Jon, without Reece explicitly saying so. Jon listened earnestly and only realized much later that he had been its sole target.

"And also remember," said Jon quietly, "if you want to disappear completely, just ask. You must be touching me or touching someone who is touching me. Then I can shimmer you and myself invisible." He smiled cheerily. Although no one saw the smile in the dark, they heard it in his next words. "As long as Reece thinks that's a good idea."

"Would this shimmering affect our perceptions, or our ability to act or hit the enemy?" asked Reece.

"No."

"All right. Thank you. We'll keep it up our sleeves as a possibility. Each of you men may choose independently to avail yourselves of Jon's offer if the situation calls for it." The sergeant waved a hand forward. "All right. Spread out. Let's catch them before they catch us."

As they crept nearer, they could see that all the Kimorans held long, curved swords at the ready and in the other hand, either a lamp or a foot-long dagger. They were working their way methodically through the trees, sweeping their lamps back and forth in front of them.

Jon, whose survival on the streets had depended on being one step ahead of the opposition, considered their apparent single-minded focus on finding the lost children and decided all was not as it seemed. Surely the Kimorans would know that pursuit was not far behind. Even in their panic to regain their prize, they would not forget to guard their backs. Would they?

Then Jon spotted a man fifty yards ahead and to his left, leaning against a tree, on the side away from the lamps. The man's night vision would be as unimpaired as his own. Jon let his gaze wander to the right and found another man in a similar position near the other lamp. Reece and the three troopers were slinking forward, crouched down, heading more towards the righthand lookout, too far away for Jon to gain their attention in the dark without making enough noise to alert the enemy. He had only moments to intercede before the lookouts saw them and ambushed them or raised the alarm.

He shimmered and ran forward lightly. As he ran, he drew his stiletto, a memento from his years on the street that he carried with him always. He circled around behind the man on the left, then closed in and clamped his left hand across the man's mouth. As soon as Jon touched him, the lookout disappeared within the shimmering. Then Jon brought the stiletto up and slid it silently between the man's ribs, straight into his heart. Jon held the man's weight as he slumped to the ground, keeping the death as silent as possible. He pulled out his blade, wiped it on the man's jacket and let him go. Immediately, the man re-appeared, lying motionless on the ground, still on the far side of the tree from the lamplight.

None of the Kimorans had seen a thing.

But Reece had. His eyes widened in alarm as he caught the movement in the shadows, and he signalled to his men. Now they were within twenty feet of the man on their right, but they had still not seen him. Their focus was on the dead man. Jon caught the flash of steel in the lamplight of a knife raised, ready to throw.

Reece was looking Jon's way and there was no time to warn him. Unless Jon acted, one of the troopers would be killed. Jon reversed his knife in his hand and gripped it firmly by the long, narrow blade. He couldn't see the other lookout in the gloom, but he had seen where the knife glinted. He drew back and threw, aiming for a spot two feet lower and a little towards the road.

He saw Reece and the three troopers flinch back as the knife flashed past them, its flight caught in the lamp. A gasp of pain and the dull sound of a weapon hitting the forest floor made them turn and finally they saw the man on their right, now clutching a slim, wicked blade protruding from his chest.

But the Kimorans had heard it too, this time.

"Go, go, go!" yelled Reece, all efforts at subterfuge abandoned. "Keep your eyes down."

The numbers were even but the Carradorians had the element of surprise and their night vision intact. Reece and his troopers surged forward, catching the Kimorans before they could turn properly and prepare themselves. As the Kimorans squinted into the darkness, the troopers kept their eyes trained on the ground, using their peripheral vision to dodge the flailing swords of their opposition and to stab upwards with their own weapons.

It was over in minutes. There was no chance for finesse in the poor lighting and three of the Kimorans lay dead and the fourth badly wounded, when Reece stayed his hand from a killing blow.

"Hold," he shouted to himself and his men. "I'll let this one live. Then we can find out what happened."

A slight rustle in the leaves on the forest floor, left of the Kimorans, had them whipping round, ready to attack, but Jon's voice said, "Don't worry. It's only me." When he was sure they weren't going to rush him, he shimmered into view, his stiletto once more sheathed and out of view.

He bent down and picked up a fallen lantern that had managed to stay alight during the little melee and was now threatening to light the detritus on the ground. He raised it so that he could study the faces of the fallen Kimorans. When he swung it onto the face of the man Reece had spared, he grunted in disgust. "Shay. He betrayed his fellow refugees and nearly killed Lord Sheldrake... and me, of course. He must be one of those who escaped from prison. And here he is, straight back to work, hurting my family and my friends."

Jon took a breath and spat out, "You're a bastard, Shay." He straightened up and produced a small cloth bag from an inner pocket, opened the draw string, extracted two small packets and handed them to Reece. "Here. I presume you have some sort of bandaging with you. Moisten these with a bit of water and smear them on whatever you bind his shoulder with. They will deaden the pain and prevent infection."

Reece looked puzzled. "Why are you helping him?"

Jon glanced at Shay then back at Reece. "Because he will slow us down if we don't look after him and I presume we will be taking him with us. And because... I don't do unto others what they do to me, just for the sake of it." Reece and his men had seen a new side of Jon, confident and deadly, but suddenly he smiled his sunny smile. "Just part of being a fluffy kitten, I suppose."

Reece's eyes narrowed, not buying Jon's disarming charm so easily this time. "And are both of their look-outs dead?"

"Yes," said Jon quietly, his smile gone. His eyes slid away from the sergeant's face, uncomfortable with people seeing this side of him.

Seeing this, Reece reached out and gripped him by the shoulder. "You, Lord Jon, are an enigma. Your skills with a knife are as breathtaking as they are unexpected... and we have you to thank for at least one of our lives."

Jon gave a self-deprecating shrug. "Years of practice. I'm not too skilled with a sword but I can wield a knife." He met Reece's eyes. "And I learned to fight when, every day, my life depended on getting it right. Self-preservation is a great motivator." And beneath his voice, they could hear a faint trace of well-hidden bitterness.

48

J ayhan and Sasha plunged through the long grass and threw themselves into the undergrowth.

"Ow," muttered Jayhan, as he pushed his way under straggly, sharp-twigged bushes. Their thin branches caught at his clothes and he kept having to drag away or unhitch parts of his surcoat that were caught.

Sasha was not faring much better. "Blasted bushes! We would have to find the clingiest, sharpest bushes in the whole forest to crawl through."

"Ow," yelped Jayhan again. "Something bit me."

Sasha curbed a sigh of exasperation. "No, it didn't. It's just the thorns. Some of them are razor-sharp. Come on. We're nearly through."

They wriggled and crawled their way through the dense bank of prickly shrubs, Sasha leaving shreds of her dress behind her on the sharp thorns, until finally, they could drag themselves free and stand up. Sasha's gown, not that she cared, was a tattered wreck. They found themselves inside a tall forest, where little light, especially now that it was dusk, penetrated.

High above them, they could hear rain pattering on leaves. Now and then, a large drop of water would fall from above to land close by, or, if they were unlucky, down their necks or on their faces.

Few bushes grew beneath the distant canopy. The forest floor was damp and much of it was exposed earth or leaf fall. Knobbly tree roots snaked their way across the ground in places, some of them tall and thin like miniature curved walls. Mosses grew on tree trunks and fallen logs. Although it was beautiful, Sasha and Jayhan could barely see it in the fading light and to them, it seemed dark, lonely and threatening.

Jayahn took a deep breath. "Right. Stay here. Back in a minute," he said quietly and stepped off to the side between the trees until he was out of sight of Sasha. He returned a few minutes later. "Phew! That's better. Now I can concentrate on running away."

"Know what you mean," said Sasha, with a grin.

Jayhan looked surprised. "Did you go too?"

Sasha nodded. "Come on. I don't think they can get through the bushes we crawled through, but they'll find a gap somewhere and we have to be as far away as we can be when they do."

They walked away from the bank of bushes and the path as quickly as they could. Even though their eyes adjusted to the gloom, it was too dark to run. Jayhan's pale eyes saw better in the dark than Sasha's and so, after a short protest, Jayhan took Sasha's hand and led her from one tree trunk to the next, murmuring directions as they went. A few times, one or other of them tripped over raised tree roots or rises in the ground. Only having their hand held by the other saved them from falling heavily.

Then they heard voices off to their left.

"Oh no. They've found a way into the forest," whispered Sasha.

"Well, we knew they would," said Jayhan.

"Yes, but I was hoping they'd take longer."

Jayhan gave a little snort in the darkness. "Yeah. So was I." He increased the pressure on Sasha's hand. "Watch out. There's a big tree root to step over here."

Once the root was safely negotiated, they turned to look in the direction of the voices. As they watched, a pinprick of light came into view. It was still distant, flickering in and out of sight as it passed between trees.

"If they have a light, we can't outrun them," said Sasha. She looked around at the smooth towering trunks. "We have to find somewhere to hide."

"And hide our tracks."

"We can't do that in the dark." Sasha sounded close to panic.

"We can a bit. Wait here. I'll walk on damp patches off to our right for a hundred yards, then come back on leafy bits. Then we'll walk on leaves."

"Go on then. Hurry."

Two minutes later, he was back. "Forget it!" he said. "There's a light in that direction as well."

Giving up all thought of covering their trail, they blundered on through the trees, panic making them clumsy in the dark. It wasn't long before they missed seeing an obscured root and fell heavily in tangled heap, both gasping in fright.

Sasha was the first to recover. She worked hard to slow her breathing and when she felt able to speak, said, "Right. Let's think. What did we trip over? If you didn't see it, maybe it was covered in bushes or leaves or something we could hide under."

"I'm sorry, Sasha. I should have seen it. I should have

looked better." The little boy sounded close to tears. He gave a little hiccough of suppressed sobs. "And my leg hurts."

From her wise old age of ten, Sasha ignored this last little gambit and patted his arm. "Don't worry. We're both doing our best. Let's feel around and see if there is anything here to hide under," she gave a forlorn attempt at a giggle, "since we're down on the ground anyway."

Jayhan gave a dutiful grunt of laughter in response, knowing she was trying to cheer them both up, before turning his attention to their surroundings.

Suddenly, a hand clamped over his mouth and an arm grabbed him around the chest. He flailed and writhed, trying to break the grip.

"Shh," came a quiet voice in his ear. "I'm Draya. Remember me? I'm one of the Kimoran refugees. I'm not abducting you. I'm saving you from my countrymen." She paused to let her words sink in. "All right? Can I let go, without you screaming blue murder?"

Jayhan thought about it and realised that if he screamed, the nearby Kimorans hunting them would hear him, which would be counter-productive whoever this person was. He nodded and the hand was removed.

He looked around at Draya and saw an older woman holding Sasha around the shoulder, but not forcibly. He squinted through the gloom. "Rhoda?"

"Hello, Jayhan," she said quietly. "We've been shadowing you for days. Beetlebrow and Argus headed back to Highkington to bring help three days ago when we first saw you, and we two have been following you and your abductors, hoping that something would happen so that we could help you."

"We would have loved to attack them and stage a daring rescue, but we'd just have been captured ourselves. Brave, we are. Silly we are not." Draya stood up and virtually lifted

Jayhan to his feet. "Come on. Up you get. We have boltholes all through the forest but there are none nearby. Those bastards are hot on your trail. We have to go."

"If you show me which way to go, I can help guide us in the dark," piped up Jayhan. "My eyes, you know." Despite his best effort, he still sounded embarrassed saying it.

Sasha brushed herself off. "He's really good at it," Jayhan heard the grin in her voice, "except when he's panicking." She took hold of Rhoda's hand. "It's better to hold hands in the dark... to hold each other up if we trip."

Draya took Jayhan's hand and they led the way deeper into the forest. Concentrating as they were on the way forward, no one looked back. So none of them saw the lights swing wildly, or that the lights returned to the road, now in the hands of Jon and his companions.

PART VIII

49

Once Maud had returned from her flight, Ironbark, Spinifex and Silverwood conferred with the local woodfolk to adjust their path so that they would intercept The Way Through at its most northerly point. Now that Maud had actually seen the children, the whole group felt a renewed sense of urgency.

The revised path began by leading them through a swamp, winding from one piece of dry land to the next. The ground underfoot was spongy peat, which was pleasant to walk on, but the air was full of midges and mosquitoes. It was not long before a halt was called so that Silverwood could dole out an herbal salve to keep the insects at bay. Maud and Sheldrake exchanged dubious glances at the windiness of the path but Ironbark, intercepting one of these, assured them that it was still quicker than detouring around the swamp.

By mid-afternoon, they had left the swamp behind them and were threading their way through scrubby bushland composed mainly of scratchy paperbarks. On the other side of this were a series of low hills, covered in a forest whose dense canopy filtered the light and reduced the amount of undergrowth. Tree ferns filled the gullies, but the ridges were only lightly covered, making them easy to traverse.

The party made such good time that they decided to keep going for a couple of hours after dark, using luminescent orbs provided by Tarkyn and Sheldrake to light their way. They camped in a pretty clearing next to a cold, clear creek that gurgled its way over rounded pebbles, providing a friendly backdrop to their conversation around the firesite. Cold meat and fire-baked damper were prepared and eaten. Tarkyn noticed, but knew not to mention, that Waterstone's and Gurgling Brook's voices blended in with the sound of the creek so much that they had to speak up to be heard.

They set off early the next morning, hoping to reach The Way Through by mid-afternoon. A slight breeze played through the trees and soft white clouds floated in the strong blue sky overhead. A perfect day for travelling.

But as they emerged from the trees on the other side of the hills, Rainstorm stopped dead, his eyes widening in horror. "Oh, my stars! What do we do now?"

Before them stretched a flooded plain, hundreds of yards across.

Stefan turned to Spinifex. "Is this normal? Do you know the way around it?"

"No," replied Spinifex slowly. He scratched his head uncertainly. "The recent rains must have flooded the creek. Usually the path we're on would lead us straight to a series of stepping-stones that would take us across it without a second thought."

Waterstone considered. "If it's not too deep, we could wade through, I suppose."

"How can we tell?" said Ironbark. "It's so wide. Could be anything under there."

"We might have to go around," said Silverwood. "I wonder how far it stretches to the left and right?" She went out of focus for a few minutes but then shook her head. "No woodfolk nearby to tell us."

"Could Bird have a look at it for us from overhead?" asked Rainstorm. "Maybe there's a ford nearby."

Tarkyn shook his head. "Not right now. She's far away, hunting, at the moment. I think she needs to feed before she would be willing to return."

Almost as one, everyone turned to Maud.

She gave a scowl in return that was, fortunately, underpinned with a glimmer of laughter. "You can see why I don't want my gift widely known. I am *far* too useful... and," she added primly, "I don't always want to be useful." She waved her hand and smiled, "Obviously today I do, since I want us to reach my son as soon as possible. Very well. Hmm." She thought carefully for a few minutes, keeping them all waiting. "Right," she said suddenly. "An osprey is what we need. Very good at seeing into the water."

Moments later, a beautiful brown and white bird of prey stood on the ground before them, her head just above the height of their knees. Although her head was white, broad brown streaks ran horizontally through her eyes prompting Rainstorm to say, "Those stripes almost look like heavy eye makeup."

In response, Maud turned her hard eyes on him and, even though she glared up at him from only a bit above knee height, he wished he hadn't spoken. Then she turned towards the water and took off, beating her wings strongly to pull her upward. She circled above them, appearing almost all white from underneath, only dark at the wrists of her wings.

For a time, Maud simply circled a little above tree height over the area in front of her friends, but she soon discovered that, despite her excellent vision, she could not see very far into the muddy water. So she turned her attention to the objects that stuck out from the top of the water at different places, using the tops of trees, bushes and grasses to try to gauge some idea of the water's depth. It looked as though it could be at least five feet deep in places and who knew what potholes, ponds or streams lay beneath it.

She flew slowly off to the east to check the extent of the flood, noticing that her wings felt more powerful but carried her more slowly than her peregrine falcon form had done. The water extended for several miles in this direction, spread out across the plain. It looked like it was a water course that had overflowed its banks. Her heart sank. It would take at least half a day to skirt around it to the east. To cheer herself up, she banked into an unnecessarily tight turn as she headed back to scout out the western extent of the flood.

The land rose in this direction and it did not take long for her to find the stream that fed into the flooded plain. As it flowed down through the hills, the stream was deep, contained by steep rock banks. She flew slowly along its course, looking for somewhere they could cross. With a start of hope, she saw up ahead a huge mountain ash which, at some time in the past, had fallen across the stream. Its trunk was broad and still strong but covered in mosses and possibly slippery. Still, it would do. This time she did not stop to hunt since everyone was waiting on her information to be able to move on.

As she flew back towards the group, she noticed a shadow on the water below her Suddenly, she felt the force of a strong predatory mind challenging her right to approach Tarkyn. She sent out an urgent image to Tarkyn, even as the size of the shadow on the water increased alarmingly.

Maud threw herself sideways and fled into the shelter of

the trees, just as the talons of a great mountain eagle raked along the edge of her wing. Bird was huge, so much bigger than she was, and Bird was angry; protective of Tarkyn and of her unique connection with him. Heart pounding, Maud winged her way carefully through the confines of the trees. This was not her osprey form's normal territory. She preferred the open cliffs, plains and water. She heard Bird's shriek of outrage above her, as the mountain eagle shadowed her, gliding over the trees, waiting for her to re-emerge.

Maud landed under a tree fern and, after giving herself time to catch her breath, transformed back into her own shape. She found she was panting in fright and trembling. She inspected the outside of her right arm and could see beads of blood soaking into her shirt. She took some time to recover before edging out from under the tree fern, scanning the sky above the treetops for Bird. Sure enough, the eagle was still there, circling overhead. Squaring her shoulders, Maud stood straight and walked firmly towards the rear of their group.

Jackson spotted her first and ran over to her. "Are you all right? We saw Bird go for you, but she wouldn't respond to Tarkyn."

She nodded, still shaky. "Yes. I avoided her. Just. But I might need a new shirt."

Jackson put his arm around her shoulders and steered her towards the group, forbearing to ask her what she had discovered.

Since they had been due for a break anyway, a fire had been lit and Autumn Leaves approached her bearing a cup of tea. "Looks like you need this. That bloody Bird has no manners at all."

They led her to the firesite where Sheldrake took over from Jackson. "You gave me the fright of my life, my dear, or rather Bird did. You did very well to dodge her."

Silverwood rolled up Maud's bloodstained sleeve and inspected her wound. "Not too bad. Just a long scratch. A bit deep in places." She frowned in thought. "Hmm. It may get infected, depending on what has recently been on Bird's talons."

"No, it won't," said Tarkyn firmly, walking over to place his hand on her shoulder. Without any preamble, he sent a stream of *esse* into her arm, laced with a quick jab of irritation, which he had no trouble in summoning at the thought of Bird's behaviour, to combat any lurking germs.

"Thank you both," said Maud, feeling a little swamped by the care being shown her by so many people at once.

Tarkyn gave her shoulder a final pat before walking to the other side of the fire, looking thoroughly disgruntled. "Least I can do. I will be speaking to Bird at some length about this."

Maud smiled. "Don't be too cross with her. I don't think she understands shapeshifting."

"No. That is what I will try to explain to her. But also, she needs to desist if I demand it." He gave a lopsided smile. "She won't follow commands automatically. She is far too independent for that. But she has to realize that if I am emphatic, I may know something about the situation she doesn't and to at least give me a chance to explain."

"I can see why you said 'speak to her at length'" said Waterstone. "Pretty difficult to explain all that in images."

Waiting for the briefest pause in the conversation, Sheldrake interrupted, "So, Maud. What did you find out? I don't like to press, but I fear we are running out of time."

Maud swallowed her mouthful of tea, then described what she had seen.

"Hmm. Sounds like a doddle for us woodfolk, but possibly a bit trickier for you outsiders," said Rainstorm.

"My thoughts exactly," said Maud. "If the worst comes to

the worst, and it is too slippery for us to keep our footing, we can bum across, I suppose. I am not shape-changing again until Tarkyn has spoken to Bird."

Tarkyn shook out his cup and walked over to put it in his backpack. "Don't worry. I will stand close to the end of the log, ready to levitate anyone who slips."

Following his lead, everyone prepared to leave. Lapping Water and Autumn Leaves put out the fire and covered the ashes, while others packed away the kettle and tea leaves.

"Pardon me for asking," said Sheldrake, "but why don't you just levitate everyone over the flood?"

"Too far and too many," replied Tarkyn shortly. "Besides, I don't usually do things for people if it is possible for them to do it themselves." This may have sounded selfish if they hadn't already seen him use his power to help Sphagnum Moss, Maud and Sheldrake at various times. "Firstly, I'd end up at everyone's beck and call, and secondly, it would diminish their own independent skills."

Sheldrake smiled broadly. "I can see you've thought this through."

"Always," said Waterstone, his blood brother. "Well, almost always. Many issues have arisen from Tarkyn living among us as a sorcerer and as our liege, that have required ... hmm... guidelines, you might say."

In a very short time, they were on their way again. As they emerged from the trees, a great shriek heralded Bird's arrival. She flew in, landing on poor Tarkyn's shoulder, digging in with her talons before going through the rigmarole of turning herself to the front. As they walked west along the edge of the flooded plain, Tarkyn was clearly preoccupied with trying to explain things to his ferocious, independent pet.

When they reached the huge log, they found a thick rope strung from one side to the other, about five feet above the log.

Spinifex grinned at their surprise. "As we neared this part of the forest, we were able to contact some woodfolk in the area. They offered to help but," he gave an embarrassed grimace, "they don't actually want to meet you."

"Understandable," said Sheldrake. "In that case, thank them for us, would you please?"

Despite the rope, Tarkyn stood by, waiting to catch anyone who slipped, but everyone crossed safely, and they were able to continue on their way. However, skirting the flood had cost them a couple of hours and so, as dusk approached, they were still more than an hour away from The Way Through.

The wind was picking up and dark clouds were beginning to form overhead. It looked as though they were going to get wet if they kept going and didn't find shelter.

Suddenly Tarkyn stopped dead, causing Lapping Water and Rainstorm to canon into him. He raised a hand to silence any protests they may have been going to make and gazed far into the forest. Without a word, he walked to large ghost gum and placed his hand on its trunk.

"Someone or something is connecting with the forest, drawing on its power," he murmured.

The clouds above them were thickening and darkening. A distant clap of thunder heralded the coming of a storm.

Moments later, a concussive force thrummed through the trees, making every person catch their breath. Then silver light streaked across the underside of the clouds. The clouds rumbled and grumbled above, as the silver light seemed to eat into them, breaking them apart.

"What on earth is that?" demanded Rainstorm. "It's not normal lightning. I've never seen anything like it."

Without another word being spoken, the entire company broke into a run, anxious to reach the source of the disturbance. It only took them a couple of hundred yards, however, to realise that a precipitous entry into an uncertain situation was impractical and dangerous. Besides, although everyone was pretty fit, none of them were trained long distance runners and were running out of breath. They slowed and came to a halt, gathering together to confer. Autumn Leaves, who had been carrying Gurgling Brook, breathed a sigh of relief.

By no coincidence at all, Sheldrake ended up next to Tarkyn. "Tell us about this power you sensed."

Catching his breath, Tarkyn glanced at Sheldrake who seemed unperturbed by their run. "You're fitter than I thought you were." Tarkyn, who had run with Bird bobbing unconcernedly on his shoulder, took another breath before answering, "Someone was drawing on the power in the forest, not just from the trees as I do, but from everything around them; trees, rocks, earth, air." He shook his head. "Do you know anything about this?"

"Perhaps," said Sheldrake. "Go on."

"Then another power, similar but far greater and less disciplined, overwhelmed the machinations of the first and..." Tarkyn hesitated, trying to find a way to explain, "and blew it apart."

"Is the wielder of the first lot of power still alive, do you think?"

Tarkyn shook his head. "No idea. I can't imagine that person is very well, after having their power swamped like that, but I have no idea what we're dealing with. Do you?"

Sheldrake nodded briskly. "I think so. From what I have read and from what I have learnt from Yarrow, Sasha's shamanic teacher, and from watching Sasha herself, I would say that Sasha has overwhelmed a lesser shaman."

Tarkyn looked startled. "What? A little girl, using magic aggressively? I thought shamans were all about healing and mysticism, not attack."

"They are, as a general rule. But Sasha is the High Shaman despite her lack of years, and, in the natural course of events, all other shamans are linked in with her. If they have been corrupted by the current Kimoran queen, Sasha can break that compulsion. We, *she*, did it with Lady Electra and, I think, with one of the women who attacked a group of refugees we were with, a few months ago."

"And did it cause that great lightning display?" asked Tarkyn.

Sheldrake shook his head. "No. Something else is at play here that I haven't yet come across. The only pertinent knowledge I can offer is that I believe shamans can affect the weather."

"I hope the Kimorans have not hurt Sasha in retaliation," said Lapping Water, "... or she has not hurt herself. That's a lot of power for a little girl to wield."

"We need more information before we barge into a rescue." Maud held up her hand. "You don't even have to ask this time. I will be our scout and try to find out what is going on."

Sheldrake gave a sigh of relief and smiled gently at her. "Thank you, my dear. But do be careful." He turned to Tarkyn. "I trust your eagle will allow her safe passage?"

"If you transform in front of her, Maud, she will understand that you are one of my friends." Tarkyn, with Bird glaring down from his shoulder, stroked her head. "She doesn't attack my friends."

"No, not quite," put in Rainstorm caustically. "She just intimidates us."

Maud shrugged. "An eagle couldn't catch a peregrine falcon even if it tried." She took a breath to ready herself. "Right. Watching, Bird?"

Without further discussion, Maud transformed herself into her favourite peregrine falcon shape. Bird squawked in surprise and ruffled her feathers. Tarkyn took the opportunity with Bird to pair images of Maud with images of the peregrine falcon to reinforce the point. Maud simply took off and sped through the trees, leaving them all behind, as they turned and kept walking towards The Way Through.

50

W hen Jon, Reece and his men returned to their campsite and their gear, they found two rather bemused troopers making polite conversation with a middle-aged woman, whose upper-class accent and general air of grooming belied her style of dress. Her face lit up when she saw Jon.

"Maud! What are you doing here?" He ran forward and before he had time to think, grabbed her in a bear hug. "It's terrible, isn't it? Your Jayhan and my Sasha. How did you get here? Where's Sheldrake? We've been closing on the abductors for days, but now Sasha and Jayhan have run off into the forest somewhere and it's too dark to look for them. We've just killed a group of Kimorans and taken one prisoner, but there are a few more to the east. With any luck, Trevor and his group will have taken care of them. Then at least, Sasha and Jayhan will be safe from Kimorans and all we'll have to do is find them."

Maud was laughing and crying all at once. Finally, she pulled back and wiped her eyes, but didn't disengage herself from his arms. "Jon. Jon. Calm down. Sheldrake and Lord

Tarkyn and Stefan and... a few others are about an hour north of here. Less by now." She straightened herself up and eying the gathering troops, inclined her head. "How do you do? I am Lady Maud Batian. I would like to thank you all, for coming to the aid of my son and his friend."

Reece gave a stiff bow. "How do you do, ma'am? I am Sergeant Reece. It is surprising to come across you so far from Highkington. We are doing the best we can for your children." He caught sight of Trevor and the other half of their squad approaching. "But if you'll excuse me, we are rather busy at the moment."

"I should hope so," she said acerbically, displeased at being dismissed so quickly. Then she turned and saw the men arriving. As they came withing the corona of the lanterns, she could see that one man was limping and another's sleeve was slashed, the edges of the cloth soaked in blood. A third man was holding a piece of cloth to a gash in his forehead, trying to staunch the flow of blood.

Without instruction, the two men who had been left guarding the camp immediately rummaged through packs to produce bandages and salves. They sat the incoming men down and set to dressing their wounds.

Trevor resisted their ministrations until he had limped over to Reece to report, glancing with some curiosity at Maud. "We killed five, I think, but three more got away. As they ran off, one of them yelled over her shoulder, 'You haven't won yet.'" He shook his head tiredly. "Well, we haven't, until we've found those children..."

"No, you haven't," growled Shay, their Kimoran prisoner, to himself. Seeing they were listening, he glared up at them from where they had dumped him on the ground.

Maud looked curiously at him. "You're the man who betrayed your fellow Kimoran refugees and struck Sheldrake with that tree branch, aren't you? Up to your old tricks again. Do you specialize in hunting down children?" she asked scathingly.

Even as she said the words, she exchanged a glance of dawning understanding with Jon.

"Oh, my word!" exclaimed Jon, turning to Shay "You're the expert shaman hunter that Queen Toriana sent two years ago to find Sasha and her amulet. You're the reason she had to leave the orphanage early."

Shay gave a nod of acknowledgement. "I nearly had her then, and I just missed her at Bryson's. By the time I'd tracked Bryson and his family down, she was no longer with them." He shrugged. "Lucky for her. Unlucky for them." He gave an unpleasant smile. "It took a lot to convince me they no longer had her... and that they didn't know where she had gone."

"Huh." Maud expelled a breath in surprise. "So, for all that he beat her as his wagon lad, he didn't betray her. Strange man."

"Brave, determined man, if he knew and didn't tell me," said Shay, giving Bryson a dispassionate evaluation. He held their gazes, a smug smile playing around his lips. "It's not over yet, you know. Three of my team got away and they're already scouring the forest while you stand here exchanging revelations with me. Three of them. That's enough."

Not surprisingly, this galvanised Maud into action. "Right. Nothing for it, I suppose." She looked around at Jon and the troopers before homing in on Reece. "Sergeant Reece, this man is an encumbrance. Would you be so kind as to have him blindfolded and tied up, well away from us?"

When Reece frowned, Jon said, "Lady Maud knows what she is doing. She is the King's personal advisor, based on her merits."

Reece's eyes narrowed. "So, does this mean you are taking over command, ma'am?"

Maud waved her hand airily. "Oh, not at all, young man. I don't have the authority to do that. I merely made a request. If you accede to it, I will take you into my confidence and work with you. If you don't, I will work alone."

Reece glanced at Jon, clearly feeling beleaguered by the presence of two nobles.

Help came from an unexpected quarter. "Come on, Reece," said Trevor, clapping the young sergeant on his back. "Give them the benefit of the doubt. After all, Jon has proved himself to have hidden depths and he vouches for the lady." His eyes twinkled, rather uncharacteristically for the prosaic tracker. "And speaking for myself, I would like to know what secrets Lady Maud may reveal."

Reece's mouth twisted into a reluctant smile and Maud could see he was trying to find a way to save face in front of his men. He gave a little bow. "Since it is in our own best interests to be as informed as possible, I will accede to your request, ma'am."

Maud smiled broadly and murmured, so quietly that only he could hear it, "Well done, young man."

Once Shay had been hauled away to a distant tree and blindfolded, Reece turned to her.

Maud made sure she was close enough to the injured troopers so that they were included, then looked around at the others. "Now, do I have everyone's attention?" Until this point, she had been the confident *grande dame*, but now she looked a little embarrassed. "I have a particular talent that allowed me to arrive in your midst so suddenly and will help us to track down the children. I do not share knowledge of my talent widely, as I use it to assist Sheldrake and his Spiders. So, I would appre-

JENNIFER EALEY

ciate it if you kept it to yourselves. The more people who know
of it, the less use it is." She took a breath. "I am a shapeshifter."

The troopers, who were very well disciplined, did not
betray any reaction but Jon grinned broadly. "Marvellous, isn't
it? I expect that's how you got here. Is it, Maud?"

Despite themselves, several of the troopers exchanged little
grins at Jon's enthusiasm.

"Yes, it is. I arrived as a peregrine falcon, but it is too dark
and the canopy of the forest too dense for me to have spotted
the children on my way here. I now intend to become a bloodhound to track the children, now that I have a starting point,"
Maud smiled disarmingly, "unless you have any better ideas,
Sergeant Reece? I am happy to consider all options."

Reece blinked. "Uh, no ma'am. To be honest, you have
caught me by surprise and my mind is struggling to catch up."
He gave a little smile. "I'm glad I chose to listen to you,
though." He gave a little bow. "And I am sorry if I was less than
helpful. Things were rather fraught when you arrived."

"Quite all right. Things are still rather fraught, Sergeant,
and I wish to be on my way immediately. Jon, of course, will
wish to accompany me, but who in your squad will come and
who will stay? It seems to me that some must stay here to care
for the wounded and to guard your belongings."

"Yes, ma'am." Reece sent forth a string of orders which left
a disgruntled Trevor and four troopers at the campsite, while
Reece and the other four troopers stood ready to accompany
Jon and Maud. "I'm sorry, Trevor. You, of all of us, other than
Lady Maud apparently, is best qualified to track the children,
but you are injured, as are Morris and Symmons. And you
three need at least two men to protect you and our gear. You
know I would take you otherwise."

Trevor nodded reluctantly and gave a tight smile, little
more than a quirk of his mouth, in acknowledgement. "It's just

as well the only Kimorans left are focused elsewhere. We would have little hope of repelling an attack."

"If you need it, I may be able to provide extra protection, but how, is one secret I will not share." Maud smiled around the group. "By the way, as a dog, I can receive images from Lord Tarkyn and I can understand you. But I cannot speak orally to you in return. Feel free to treat me as you would any dog, assuming you are kind." Maud took a deep breath, glanced around self-consciously, then transformed before their eyes into a droopy-eyed, long-eared, solid bloodhound.

For a moment, she sat still as she conveyed images to Tarkyn, apprising him of the current state of play. She knew no more about the cause of the surge of power they had witnessed from afar, but she could tell him that the children had escaped and were heading northward. She also sent a suggestive image of woodfolk protecting Trevor and his men. She followed this with an image of herself as a bloodhound and left Tarkyn to reach his own conclusions.

With that done, she dropped her head and began to sniff around the campsite. She quickly picked up Jayhan's scent. She needed none of his clothing or belongings to use as a starting point. She knew her own son's scent. Maud followed it off the path to the point where it disappeared into the dense, straggly bushes. She huffed and padded westward until she found a gap large enough for her and the men following her to crawl through. As soon as they left the path and entered the tree cover, the darkness pressed in.

"Just a moment, ma'am," murmured Reece. "We can't see where we're going. We are going to have to light a lamp. I know it's risky, but it's just as risky trying to keep up in pitch black. Um..." He glanced at Jon beside him for direction, but Jon had no idea what he wanted. "Um, ma'am... if you catch the scent of people other than the children, could you alert us? Then we'll dowse the lamp immediately."

Maud wagged her tail a couple of times, which he took as acquiescence. Once the lamp was lit, she doubled back and snuffled around until she picked up the scent, at the place where Sasha and Jayhan had emerged from the bushes. Then she sat and waited for the men to catch up.

Jon couldn't help himself. He stroked her head and crooned, "Good girl," then grimaced in embarrassment, which was luckily lost in the dark.

Maud nudged her head under his hand, indicating that she wanted more stroking. He chuckled and stroked her again. Reece frowned, giving Jon a quizzical half smile. Jon shrugged in return and kept stroking her head until everyone was bunched up around them.

"Right Maud, onward."

51

Sasha and Jayhan stumbled on through the dark with their two companions. Sasha wondered whether meeting up with Draya and Rhoda had been all that helpful. It made them feel safer, she supposed, but it slowed them down. She was sure that just she and Jayhan would have made better progress. For a start, they now had to wait for twice as many people to recover from tripping over tree roots and rocks in the dark. And without Draya and Rhoda, Sasha could have been holding Jayhan's hand and been in direct contact with the person with the best sight, instead of groping along in his wake. Admittedly, Jayhan and she had fallen over a few times too, but... And another thing, Rhoda was wearing a voluminous skirt which kept billowing out in front of Sasha and nearly tripping her up.

Sasha gradually became aware of the sound of wheezing and, looking up, realized that Rhoda was struggling with the pace. Thinking about it, she remembered that Rhoda was a few decades older than Draya. *Oh good. Best of intentions but not really up to the job of running wildly through the night, chased by abductors. And where are we going? Do they really have any idea where we are headed in this darkness?*

Suddenly, a huge shape loomed out of the trees to Sasha's right and grabbed her arm. She let out a shriek of fright then immediately wished she hadn't, knowing it might alert everyone for miles around of their location. She tried to yank herself free, but the big hand held her firmly and dragged her away from Rhoda. Now, the last thing she wanted was to be parted from Rhoda.

"Jayhan!" she yelled desperately, giving up any hope of subterfuge.

But Jayhan was already spinning to face her, his eyes as bright as searchlights, white light streaming from them. He pulled his hand out of Draya's grasp and rushed at the attacker, who stared in horror at the apparition approaching him. The attacker's grasp on Sasha's arm went limp and he stood defenceless as the little boy barrelled into him, sending him a few steps backwards. Then Sasha, too, threw herself at the attacker and got in a hefty kick to his shin, causing him to howl in pain.

Everyone in the forest would have heard that, she thought, *but too late now.*

Her blood was up and she and Jayhan kept flailing at him with their fists, all the pent-up fear and frustration of the last few days powering every blow, while the searing white light from Jayhan's eyes kept the man cowering in fright, unable to react. Then a movement in her peripheral vision caught her attention, as Draya swung a solid branch in an arc to connect with the Kimoran's head. He dropped like a stone.

As they stood there panting, both from fright and effort, Sasha heard a mournful baying somewhere in the trees.

"Listen! That's Maud!" she exclaimed. "Jayhan, your mum's here! Let's go."

Forgetting all about heading further from the road, they ran and stumbled back the way they had come. Minutes later, Maud loped forward to greet them, with Jon and the troopers strung out behind her.

Sasha and Jayhan threw their arms around her neck, sobbing in relief. Then Sasha disentangled herself, threw herself into Jon's arms and cried into his shoulder. Reece and his four troopers looked on in great satisfaction, pleased their chase had had a happy ending.

But they were not out of the woods yet.

Rhoda and Draya caught up and stood uncertainly just outside the ring of people. Alerted by movement in the gloom but unable to see what it was, Reece and the troopers went on the offensive, but relaxed when they saw that the two women weren't clad in black.

Jon peered through the gloom at them, then broke into a smile. "Hello. Reece, men, this is Rhoda and Draya. They are the other half of the little group of Kimoran refugees we intercepted a couple of days ago. So, you kept up with them, did you, Rhoda? And you were there to protect them when they managed to escape? Well done!"

They glanced at each other. "I'm not sure how much help we were," said Rhoda. "I suspect we may have actually slowed them down."

A wave of guilt flowed through Sasha as these words so accurately reflected what she had been thinking, and she hoped that none of her thoughts had conveyed themselves to Rhoda. She slipped down out of Jon's arms and walked to take hold of the older woman's hand. "You helped. You made us feel safer. So thank you." She gave a little smile. "And don't forget, Draya did hit that man with a big branch."

Suddenly, Maud shook her head, her long, soft ears hitting Jayhan in the face and pushing him, laughing, away. As soon as he had let go, she transformed into her true form. The first thing she did was scoop Jayhan into her arms and hug him close. The second was to turn to Jon and Reece, her voice tight with urgency.

"Sheldrake, Tarkyn and the others are another mile or so north of here. Not far. But we have trouble. According to Lord Tarkyn, scores of Kimorans have been spotted moving towards us from the east."

"*Scores?*" Reece's voice came out as a squawk, much to his embarrassment. For a moment, he felt a flicker of panic as he considered his wounded men, his split force and its small size compared to the incoming threat. "Scores of them?" he repeated in a deeper voice. He straightened up, pulling himself together.

Maud was reassuringly calm. "Lord Tarkyn has suggested that we would be safer if we joined forces with them." She omitted to mention that his communication had been considerably stronger than a suggestion, aware that she had to tread carefully with Reece. "Do you agree?"

He nodded firmly. "I agree. We must keep these children safe at all costs. Even four more people will help."

"Oh," said Maud, "there are more than..." She trailed off as she realized that her need to reassure the sergeant had nearly led her into betraying the presence of the woodfolk. "Uh, what I mean is, they are far more in power than just four. Lord Tarkyn is a fearsome sorcerer and Lord Sheldrake is a mage, more learned than fearsome I'll admit, but still with powers greater than your average man."

"That's my dad," put in Jayhan proudly. "He's pretty good."

Reece noticeably brightened. If he hadn't been in front of his men, Maud suspected he might have let out a sigh of relief. "Right. Let's go."

52

"Local woodfolk report that the first Kimoran attackers will arrive within minutes." Silverwood's mellifluous voice held no hint of fear. "They are spread out on a wide front, threading through the trees, searching as they come."

"How many?" asked Tarkyn.

After a brief mental consultation, Silverwood replied, "Not sure, but over eighty and less than two hundred."

Tarkyn felt a wave of consternation emanate from his companions. He quelled his own reaction and sent back a wave of reassurance. "Sheldrake and I have shields. We can keep you safe."

"Not if we want to fight off the invaders," said Waterstone tersely "We can't shoot through your shield and even though you can, you can't attack that many at once on your own, even with your power ray and your *Shturrum* spell, particularly if they are spaced out among trees."

Spinifex looked puzzled. "We don't need your shield. Why would we? We'll just flick into hiding."

"You forget, Spinifex. Sorcerers and outsiders can't do

that," said Lapping Water.

Tarkyn's mouth twisted ruefully. "And *I* forget that wood-folk rarely need my protection and have evaded outsiders in their forests for countless generations."

"Let's walk and talk. We must hurry," urged Sheldrake tensely. "We must reach Maud and the children before this new wave of Kimorans does." As they turned and began to stride south, Sheldrake asked Stefan to walk beside him. "Stefan, when the woodfolk flick into hiding, what will you do? Decide now, so that when the time comes, you don't hesitate."

"I'm not leaving my sister in danger," replied Stefan firmly. "I'm staying with Marjorie."

Marjorie, who was walking just ahead of them, turned and waited for them to catch up with her. "No, Stefan. I will be safely inside a sorcerer's shield if they attack us. You are a master arms man. Get up into those trees with the rest of them and use your expertise. We will need every competent arms man or woman to defeat them, if it comes to a confrontation."

Just then Tarkyn received new images from Maud. He turned, smiling broadly. "Maud has found them."

A quiet cheer went up.

"How did they look?" asked Sheldrake, his narrow face alight with excitement. "Are they all right?"

Tarkyn grinned at him. "Fit and healthy and smiles all over their faces."

"They must be very relieved, poor little things," said Lapping Water. She shifted Gurgling Brook from one hip to the other but kept walking. "How many are with them now? How much protection do they have?"

"They have two women with them. I don't know where they came from... and Jon and five Carradorian men in dark brown uniforms, if that tells you anything, Sheldrake. And Maud, of course."

"Men in brown uniforms are elite Carridorian troops, specialists in survival and undercover work. The women..." Sheldrake shrugged. "I don't know. Maybe some of the Kimoran refugees. Couldn't say without seeing them."

"They're not far away. I have told them of the approaching Kimorans. Maud thinks if they walk towards us, and vice versa, we should meet up in about fifteen minutes."

"Let's go then," urged Sheldrake, as he started walking, half jogging with excitement. A few minutes later, he asked Silverwood, "Can any of your people see them, so we know that we're heading in the right direction?"

Spinifex answered for her. "We're right on track. Keep going. See that hill up ahead? They are coming up the other side of it."

But suddenly, ahead of them, they saw dark figures emerging from the trees on their left and spreading across the narrow path to bar their way.

"Woodfolk, go!" ordered Tarkyn, all thought of handing over control lost in the urgency of the moment. "And you too, Bird." He shrugged his shoulder, getting a squawk for his trouble. But he was determined. "Go Bird. I can't deal with you and all of this at once."

With a disgruntled shriek, she flapped her great wings, giving Tarkyn a thump on the head for good measure as she rose into the air and disappeared above the trees.

"Jackson, Marjorie, mind Gurgling Brook," said Lapping Water, thrusting her child into Jackson's arms. "Please." She gave a brief smile and disappeared.

Tarkyn frowned in surprise at her unilateral decision to allow their woodfolk sorcerer child to be seen by outsiders, but he had no time to worry about it now.

In an instant, only Sheldrake, Marjorie and Jackson stood

with Tarkyn on the path, one holding a little woodchild, encased inside the bronze dome of Tarkyn's shield.

"Keep walking," he said. "We have to get to those children. They only have eight adults with them and some of them aren't fighters."

As they neared the first of the Kimorans, Tarkyn received a query from Waterstone that he relayed to Sheldrake. "Arrows or slingshots? Do you want them dead or unconscious?"

Sheldrake looked startled. "Oh, my word. They are good, aren't they?" He would have preferred more time to think through the political ramifications but with the need for a snap decision, he erred on the side of mercy and political caution. "Slingshots."

Even as the word left his mouth, seven of the dark clad figures blocking their path slumped to the ground.

"Keep walking," said Tarkyn grimly.

Six more fell. Those left standing looked frantically around themselves, torn between fear of the unseen attackers and their need to keep Tarkyn's small group from joining up with the children. But they took heart as more of their comrades emerged from the trees to bolster their numbers.

In the distance now, they could hear the sounds of blades clashing. Both sides redoubled their efforts.

Tarkyn's shield came up against the first line of Kimorans. He sent a shaft of power through his shield that tore into the ground at the feet of their attackers. As they stumbled backwards in shock, Tarkyn pressed forward, gaining several yards before they recovered.

Suddenly, the sound of clashing steel stopped. A sense of dread crept over Tarkyn and Sheldrake.

"They've stopped. Why? They can't have beaten the Kimorans so quickly. There are too many of them," said Marjorie, voicing everyone's fears.

53

R eece, Jon and the four troopers had deployed themselves around Sasha and Jayhan as they set off on the final leg to join Tarkyn, Sheldrake and the others. At her request, Draya had been given someone's spare sword so that she could take her place among them. Maud and Rhoda stayed beside the children.

"We can help too, you know," protested Jayhan, looking up at his mother, who was firmly holding his hand.

"Especially if there are any shamans among them," added Sasha.

"I'm sure you can," replied Maud, her tone placating rather than convinced, even though she had seen both of them in action in the past, "but you are their target. They won't even bother to fight us if they can just grab you and run."

"True," said Sasha in a small voice, but she clasped her amulet and focused hard on her heartbeat, hoping that she might be able to affect any shamans who came in range, even if she couldn't see them. She could only try.

They trudged on up the hill between shadowy bushes and

under dark branches, whose leaves gained colour and lost it as they passed beneath them with their lamp. They were all tired after a long day but were driven by the wish to join up with allies against the incoming Kimorans. It was now full dark, and although the lamp was a risk, they had decided on speed over caution. But every sense was stretched for sight or sound of new interlopers.

"Look!" said Jon, pointing ahead. "I think I can see a glimmer of light reflecting in the trees."

Reece frowned. "Rhoda, could you shield the lantern for a minute, so we can see better, please?" After a few moments, he nodded. "You're right. Jon, I think the source of the light we can see is somewhere over the other side of the hill. Not far now," he said hearteningly. "They must be just over that ridge."

It was just as well they had shrouded their lamp. It meant their adjusted eyes took a split second less time to see the dark shapes swarming towards them out of the shadows.

"We're under attack!" shouted Reece. "Keep the lamp dowsed. Stand firm, men... and women."

Blades came whistling out of the darkness. Jon ducked under a sword and stepped in, driving his dagger into his assailant's chest. A slighter but muscled woman came at him from the side with a roundhouse swing of her blade. As Jon tried desperately to wrench his blade from the first assailant to defend himself, the woman fell to the ground without a word. Jon frowned, unable to see who had saved him.

"Thanks," he muttered, as he turned to face the next assailant.

Beside him, Reece was clashing blades with a tall man whose longer reach was making his defences difficult to breach. His attacker pressed him hard, but Reece refused to step back and let him get any closer to his charges behind him. In a sudden movement, the man dropped the tip of his blade, unbalancing Reece. The Kimoran drew his arm back for a killing blow, and with sickening clarity, Reece knew he wouldn't have time to recover. Then the Kimoran's eyes rolled up in his head and he fell limply to the ground. Reece blinked in surprise. He looked around for his saviour but could see no one in reach.

"D'you see that?" he muttered. "He just dropped where he stood."

"Yep. Happened to me, too," replied Jon, between heavy breaths.

Hearing this, Draya gave her head a slight shake but had to keep her focus, as two assailants rushed her in a pincer movement. She sidestepped one and swung her sword around just in time to block the other, but as soon as she had her eyes on the second, the first one closed in behind her, swinging a backhand cut at her ribs. She braced for the blow, but instead, the sword clattered from the man's nerveless hand. Draya glanced at the falling man without comprehension, but had no time to contemplate the cause, as the second man came at her again.

Dark-clad figures were rushing them on all sides. Reece and his men were hard-pressed. Jon and Draya helped to make the circle stronger, but it was still a pitiful few against scores of well-trained opponents. All around them, Kimoran men and women dropped in their tracks. No one understood why. But heedless of their falling comrades, the black-clad figures came on, stepping over their bodies.

A shout of pain issued from the circle protecting the children, as one of the troopers was sliced across the forearm. Then Jon, stepping sideways, stood on a loose rock and his foot went from under him. As he slid down and sideways, three assailants homed in on him, seeing him as easy prey.

From behind Reece, came an anguished yell as Jayhan twisted his hand out of his mother's and rushed forward, his eyes blazing with white light. Immediately, the three assailants and the attackers on either side of them cowered back, all the fight gone from them. Then, they simply keeled over, and lay unmoving.

Jayhan stopped dead, shocked by the unexpected success of his charge. He had never knocked people out before. But the light from his eyes could not reach all the attackers. Shielded by those in front of them, many kept pushing forward. Jon rolled to his feet and bodily returned Jayhan to his mother, saying, "Thanks, young one, but stay back," before returning to his place beside Reece.

Jayhan frowned in frustration as Maud took a firmer grip on his hand. "Ow, Mum. You're hurting me."

Her grip lessened only slightly.

"Well done, Jayhan," murmured Sasha. "*I* thought that was great... but stay with me. I don't want to lose you," she said. "Your eyes worked really well, but they only affect the first row in a crush like this. Not enough people can see them."

They stood in the darkness, surrounded by larger people, hearing the grunts of effort, yells and screams of pain, and the constant clash of steel. Sasha watched in gathering horror as angry, hate-filled faces loomed out of the darkness, all with the sole purpose of capturing her. She clung close to Rhoda.

At least one Kimoran was on her side... and Draya. *But all these other people... Was Kimora just a land full of vicious killers, now that the refugees had left?*

Unseen in the trees around them, a score of woodfolk took careful aim to send small rocks speeding viciously towards Kimoran attackers, whenever the need was dire or when they could get a clear shot.

Directly above Maud, Stefan lay along a branch with Autumn Leaves on the next branch to his left and Spinifex to his right. He sent a constant barrage of pebbles from the small shanghai wherever he could get a clear shot at a Kimoran's temple. Silverwood, Tree Fern and Iron Bark stood in the next tree along.

Other woodfolk he had not met were strung through the surrounding trees, all firing on the enemy to protect the children in the beleaguered group below.

Suddenly a feeling of kinship, of being part of a powerful, skilful nation of people, welled up inside him. For a few moments, Stefan let his gaze take in the hidden might of the woodfolk around him. He glowed with pride that he was one of them.

"Quick! That one," said Autumn Leaves in his mind, bringing him back to his task. "She's about to chop into Reece. I can't get the angle from here."

Stefan sent a small stone whizzing towards the side of the attacker's head and a moment later the Kimoran fell, knocked out cold.

"Well done," came Autumn Leaves' mindtalk. "Another to your right."

Stefan continued to aim and release, aim and release, with a growing sense of desperation. There were so many of them. He knew that, in the end, the woodfolk would prevail, because the Kimorans couldn't fight off an unseen foe.

But not fast enough.

A constant stream of black figures appeared out of the darkness and despite their best efforts, he and the woodfolk couldn't dispatch them fast enough to save the depleted circle that was fighting with growing desperation to protect the children.

Below him, another trooper cried out and collapsed as a sword was driven into his thigh. Draya moved to stand over him, lashing out savagely at anyone who came within reach until Rhoda and Maud could pull the wounded man back behind the fighting. As Rhoda and Sasha struggled desperately to staunch his bleeding leg, the circle contracted to keep him and them safe within it. Jon, Draya and even Reece and his remaining troopers were breathing in ragged gasps as they blocked and thrust, their arms growing sluggish against men and women who stepped forward, fresh and eager to fight.

Another wave of assailants thrust at them. In answer, the gallant defenders dredged the depths of their strength in what they feared would be a final effort.

Then, at the back of their awareness, they felt a movement within the circle behind them.

Suddenly, Maud bellowed, "Disengage and step back. NOW!"

Her voice was so sure and so vehement that they obeyed without question. Immediately, a dark haze appeared between them and the Kimorans.

In their surprise, several of them stepped back even further, treading on the feet of people behind them. Most managed to stay upright, but Jon fell in a tangled heap. From his position on the ground, he looked up to see the haze extending in a dome over them and a small boy standing close to Maud, looking down at him.

Jon wiped his sweaty forehead and frowned. "Who are you? Where did you come from... ? What's going on?"

Maud calmly re-ignited the lamp, showing them a small boy with dark brown hair and brilliant green eyes, watching them warily. Maud put her arm around his shoulder. "This is Midnight. He is... a sorcerer and, I believe, a guardian of the forest. He is also Lord Tarkyn's ward." She waved her arm at the dome which covered them and which they could now see was dark green. It was holding at bay a bevy of frustrated Kimorans. "This is his shield. He has just saved our lives," her mouth twisted, "... unless you thought you were going to continue to hold out against those hordes out there."

Reece ran a hand through his hair and got out between

gasps, "No ma'am. I did not. We would never have given up, but it looked like we were going to die trying." He glanced out at the faces surrounding them in the darkness. "They seem endless. They just keep on coming." He took a deep breath and let it out, releasing some of the tension from the fighting. Then he squatted down in front of Midnight and smiled. "Thank you, young man."

Midnight glanced at Sasha and Jayhan then around at the men and women towering over him in the close confines of his shield. He brought his gaze back to Reece and nodded solemnly.

"He's deaf," explained Maud quietly, "but I think he understood what you said. He is frightened of strangers, so it has taken great courage for him to come amongst us." She gently stroked his head. "Now I think about it, he is the only one who could have. Tarkyn and Sheldrake can raise shields but neither of them could have flicked to stand among us."

"Flick?" asked Jon.

"Flick, uh, move instantly from one place to another, only within sight and not through objects, only around them. So you couldn't escape from jail by flicking, but you could flick into hiding behind a tree."

Jon raised his eyebrows and smiled. "Very interesting." He reached into his pocket, pulled out a bit of dried apricot and held it out to Midnight, with an encouraging nod.

Midnight took the offering, the side of his mouth quirking slightly in acknowledgement. He didn't eat it but put it in his own pocket for later.

After a bemused moment, Jon turned to Maud, "So, can we keep walking up the hill inside this shield or do we have to stay still? I have had no experience of sorcerers' shields."

"We can move, provided, of course, that Midnight does." She frowned out into the darkness. "But I'm not sure how well we will be able to plough through all those people between us and the others." She tapped Midnight on the shoulder and pointed at him, then everyone in the shield, before making a walking motion with her fingers and pointing up the hill. She tilted her head in query.

Midnight turned to look up the hill and came face to face with a montage of angry faces. He jolted backwards and for a moment, his shield flickered. But he took a deep breath, clearly steadying himself and the haze around them became, if anything, denser.

"Sir," said Warrun, "these Kimorans are still dying all around us. I just saw another one keel over."

For a minute, everyone watched the people outside the shield and sure enough, their attackers were slowly but surely succumbing to some unknown phenomena. Despite their comrades falling all around them, a horde of determined men and women still stood across the upward path, pressing in against the outside of the shield.

"I don't know who's doing it, sir. I can't see anyone. Maybe it's some strange malady. Whatever it is, it saved our lives over and over out there."

"I don't know any more than you, Warrun," replied Reece.

He was distracted from saying anything further by the sight of Midnight, who tilted his head as he tuned in to a distant mind. Midnight gave a little grin before thrusting one hand forward, sending a ray of dark green magic spearing though his shield to blast the dirt at the feet of the Kimorans blocking their path.

The Kimorans stumbled backwards in shock.

Midnight immediately pushed his shield forward into the gap. Then he glanced around his companions to check their reaction. Jon and Reece nodded vigorously and smiled. Jayhan and Sasha patted him on the shoulder, their eyes shining with excitement.

So, he turned once more and tried it again. But this time, his shaft of power didn't have the shock value and although the Kimorans shied out of the way, they quickly regrouped. Midnight tried again but the same thing happened. The Kimorans regrouped before he could move the shield forward.

"Jayhan, he needs more power. You can help him," said Sasha urgently.

Jayhan's eyes widened. "Yeah. So I can."

He grabbed Midnight's hand, which made the boy jump with fright and shy away from him. For a moment, the shield flickered.

"Gently, Jayhan," scolded Sasha.

Jayhan grinned sheepishly at Midnight. "Oops, sorry." He pointed at his hand that was still holding Midnight's and gestured to indicate that Midnight should send another shaft of power. Midnight frowned in confusion but after a moment, took a deep breath and sent forth another shaft. This time, the power hit the ground with a sharp retort, sending dirt flying high into the air and gouging a deep rut in the path. Some of the assailants were thrown off their feet by the strength of the blast. Before they could press back in, Midnight pushed his shield forward and glanced at Jayhan

"Onward!" shouted Jayhan, grinning and waving his other arm.

Midnight almost smiled in return. Almost. Then he turned forward once more and thrust his hand out, sending another blast of power scattering the opposition and tearing up the path. As he pushed forward, he began to grin and suddenly, he and Jayhan were just playing a game and having fun with his power. Over and over, he sent forth Jayhan-enhanced shafts of power and slowly they progressed up the hill.

Now they could see that Sheldrake's light orb had crested the hill and they could see that it came from a bronze-coloured dome containing four people. A tall man with unusually long, black hair stood at the front of the shield, employing the same tactic as Midnight and sending forth bronze power rays that forced back the Kimoran attackers. And all the while, the numbers of attackers thinned as they dropped one by one to the ground.

Within minutes, the two hemispheres of light had forged a path to each other. When they were touching, Tarkyn stood with his hands on his hips looking down at Midnight, his strange amber eyes glowing with pride at his ward's achievement. "Well done, Midnight. You are the cleverest, bravest boy in the whole world," he said, matching images to words.

Midnight beamed.

PART IX

54

With a flick of his wrist, Tarkyn enlarged his shield and lifted it up over Midnight's so the little boy could drop his. Instantly, the dark green dome disappeared, and Midnight sagged a little at the release of effort, then ran forward to jump into Tarkyn's arms. Tarkyn hugged him tightly and swung himself in a full circle, while Jackson and Marjorie patted his back as it flew past. Jayhan dodged past them into his father's waiting arms.

Tarkyn swung Midnight onto one hip and collected himself enough to welcome the new arrivals. "Hello, Maud. Well done to you, too; finding the little ones in time. Close run thing, I gather." He looked at the others in the little group. "Hello, Lord Jon. I believe we met at that excruciating, formal luncheon at the King's palace. Hello, Sasha. I don't know the rest of you, but I am very glad to see you. I am Prince Tarkyn, High Lord of Eskuzor." He smiled disarmingly. "But if you wish, you may call me Tarkyn for now." He raised his eyebrows. "Now, who are you people?"

Reece gave a neat bow and said, "I am Sergeant Reece and

these men are half of my squad, Your Highness. The rest of my men are back on The Way Through."

"So I understand. Don't worry," said Tarkyn. "We're protecting them." He transferred his attention to Reece's men. "And your names?" Long gone was the time when Tarkyn would take anyone for granted.

Warrun and the other three troopers looked faintly surprised but introduced themselves.

"And may I also present Draya and Rhoda, refugee shamans from Kimora," said Jon, "who shadowed the attackers for several days and were ready to intercept the children and look after them when they escaped."

"Pleased to meet you all. The actions of all of you have been heroic in protecting the children." Then Tarkyn frowned and looked closer. "I see two of you, at least, are wounded. What we need is a fire and cups of tea while I repair the injured."

"We can do it," said Rhoda firmly. "We just haven't had the chance 'til now, other than a quick bandage."

"Really? Are you forest guardians, then? Can you communicate with animals?" asked Tarkyn, intrigued. "I thought forest guardians were very rare. They are, in Eskuzor."

Draya gave a short laugh. "No. We're shamans. We can't talk to animals, but we can heal; some of us better than others."

Reece looked puzzled. "But My Lord, we are still surrounded by the enemy."

Tarkyn waved his hand dismissively. "Oh, very few left now. Don't worry about them. The important thing is that you're safe."

"Right." Reece just looked dazed. He felt his command had well and truly been wrested from him but didn't have the energy to resist, or even the wish to, at the moment.

Marjorie glanced at him to see if he was going to say more,

before offering, "Jackson and I will make the tea. We didn't have to fight like you did, so we're not tired."

"Thanks. Thank you very much." Reece pulled himself together enough to ask, "And might I ask, Sire, who your companions are?"

"Oh, I beg your pardon," said Tarkyn. "I should have said. This is Lord Sheldrake. He's the one hugging Maud and Jayhan, and this is Stefan's sister, Marjorie."

"You already know Stefan, Reece," put in Jon. "The arms master."

As Reece nodded, Tarkyn continued, "And this is the estimable Jackson, my aide-de-camp, who is holding my daughter, Gurgling Brook. Jackson, could you please take over shielding us? I am growing weary. I would ask Sheldrake, but he is providing us with light which, I must say, he is managing to maintain while reuniting with his wife and child. You never know, Sheldrake, I might be able to teach you to do two spells simultaneously."

Sheldrake held his little family close to him. "Not right now." Maud and Jayhan exchanged a glance of surprise. That Sheldrake so easily dismissed a discussion of magic showed them, even more than his embrace and his beaming smile, how much they meant to him.

Tarkyn gave a grunt of laughter. "No. I didn't mean right now." He stared around into the gloom, completely ignoring the remaining Kimorans. "Any trees nearby? I'm feeling a bit light-headed."

Sasha watched the bemused looks on her companions' faces as Tarkyn bounced from one topic to another. He was so energetic and enthusiastic and... commanding. She wondered whether she would have to be like that to be a queen. She didn't think she had it in her. She wondered whether the people in Eskuzor were nicer than the Kimorans.

"Midnight might find it helpful, too," he was saying. "He used an enormous amount of power for a little one... and doing two spells at once. That takes a lot of concentration."

"Impressive little fellow," said Sheldrake, his arm still around Jayhan.

"Jayhan helped Midnight, you know," said Sasha, loyally giving him credit while at the same time envying him the attention that Sheldrake was giving him. "Jayhan increased Midnight's power so that he could make bigger blasts."

Something in her voice or her stance must have given her away. Sheldrake looked over at her, where she stood holding Jon's hand. He smiled at her and tweaked a finger. "Sasha, my little stable hand. Come and give your employer a hug. I missed you, too, you know."

Sasha took two nonchalant steps towards him, then, giving up all pretence, rushed over to him. Sheldrake disengaged himself from his family to pick her up and hug her to his chest. Maud and Jayhan had never seen Sheldrake so demonstrative.

Tarkyn watched Jayhan stand to one side, quite happy, in fact pleased, for Sasha to share his family. "You're an impressive young man," he said to the little boy, meaning it in more ways than one. "What an interesting skill you have. Well done."

Jayhan gave a little shrug. "Thanks, but Sasha thought of it." He turned and grinned at Midnight, "and it was really fun, wasn't it, Midnight?"

Midnight grinned back and sent Tarkyn images of them blasting their way up the hill, showing him the difference Jayhan's power had made, and at the same time, without consciously meaning to, showing him the friendship they had struck up.

Tarkyn smiled down at his little Midnight and stroked his

hair, beginning to slow down. "Thank you, Jayhan. He loved it."

Maud waited a moment before saying, "Tarkyn, there is a good-sized gum tree a few yards to your left. It may involve stepping over a few Kimorans, though."

He peered in the direction she had pointed. "Only a couple. We'll push them out of the way and deal with them later." Once he had sat down with his hand on the tree, he exhaled and let his shoulders drop. He looked around at everyone watching him and gave a slow smile. Then he said, speaking more slowly, "Sorry. I've been babbling, haven't I? I'm a bit wired up. I suppose all of you are too, aren't you? I am so pleased that we have Sasha and Jayhan safe. Congratulations to all of you." He took another deep breath. "Right. Bring forth our wounded, Pieter and Ramon, isn't it? Then I can watch Rhoda and Draya strut their stuff while Sasha and Jayhan can tell us what caused that amazing lightning in the sky and how they got away."

"... and you can tell us how Midnight found us," added Jon.

"Oh, that's easy to answer. He felt Jayhan's strong reaction to something, probably one or all of you under threat, and followed it to its source by flicking several times until he reached you. I didn't ask him to. He was up in the trees at the time and just realized your need was dire." Tarkyn smiled down at Midnight, who was sitting within the crook of his arm, munching the apricot Jon had given him earlier.

Sometime later, when everyone was installed with cups of tea and the wounded troopers had been healed by the two shamans, Tarkyn drew a long breath and said, "Once all the Kimorans are knocked out, we'll have some work to do, disarming them all and trussing them up before they come round again."

"Only knocked out, are they?" Jon gazed around at the

bodies strewn around them; large, small, wiry, solid, many dark-skinned like Sasha, many as light-skinned as he was. "I'm glad." He gave a slight, self-conscious smile. "After all, these *are* my people."

That smile spoke volumes. Jon and Tarkyn both came from a royal family and both were, according to birthright, brother to a queen. They were both tall, but Jon was fair and willowy, while Taryn was strongly built and dark-haired. Jon was friendly, gentle and whimsical while Tarkyn was sure and strong, but also kind. Tarkyn had always lived with the sure knowledge that it was an honour for people to meet him, whereas Jon had lived for the last ten years in obscurity, alone and unsupported.

Tarkyn gave him a gentle smile. "So I understand. Sheldrake and Maud have honoured us with your story; yours and Sasha's. So I have some idea how you must feel. When I was trying to prevent my brothers from beginning a civil war, I always tried to avoid killing their soldiers. I wanted to protect Eskuzor, but not by destroying its citizens."

"Huh." Jon looked thoughtful. "I'm pleased to hear that..." A frown gradually gathered on his face. "But how exactly have you managed to disable so many without killing them and without any visible armed force?"

55

Jon expected Tarkyn to explain proudly how he or they had managed it but instead, he looked uneasy and embarrassed. After some hesitation, he replied, "I'm afraid I can't tell you that right now."

Jon and the troopers and the shamans looked intrigued and Tarkyn could see they were conjecturing wildly.

"Interesting," said Jon. "So, it's secret sorcerer's business, is it? Some kind of spell that will wear off over time?"

Tarkyn was almost tempted to let him think that it was. It was a good explanation that would cover up the existence of woodfolk. He let out a sigh and gave a wry smile, aware that his integrity often landed him in difficult situations that dissemblance could avoid.

"Not exactly," was all he said. He diverted the conversation by becoming business-like. "Now, time to get to work. Reece, I think we need to look after the wounded men you left at The Way Through. Jackson, would you take Draya and Rhoda down there, please? Can you hold a shield for that long?"

"How far is it?" asked Jackson. "How long will it take us to get there?"

"About an hour, maybe less," said Reece. "Maybe one of my men should accompany them to show them the way."

"No need," said Draya. "We know where we're going. Are all the Kimorans unconscious now?"

Tarkyn looked distracted for a moment before saying, "Yes, I believe so."

Draya nodded briskly. "Then we have no need of a shield. You have a lot of Kimorans to disarm and tie up and a short time to do it in. So, you get cracking and so will we."

Ah, thought Tarkyn, *matriarchal society. Like the independent woodwomen but more so.* He didn't like her tone of voice but didn't argue. "Very well. We'll meet you there as soon as we can."

As they watched the lantern carried by Rhoda bob its way down the hill and into the trees, Jackson said, "Does that mean I can drop my shield now?"

Tarkyn considered the options. "I think so, but until tomorrow morning when we can see what we are doing and are sure the threat has passed, I want Jon, Jayhan and Sasha to remain within a shield. I don't mind whether it is yours or Sheldrake's."

"I would like to stay with Jayhan... and Sasha," said Sheldrake. "Midnight might like to join us, too, if they have become friends. Then I can bed them down and they can get some sleep. We won't need a light. We can just settle down somewhere and wait."

"If you can manage it, Lord Sheldrake, and if you children aren't too tired," said Reece, "I suggest that you walk down to The Way Through before bedding down. The site down there is better for a large group to camp the night and it is close to a stream, whereas here, we are on top of a ridge with no water supply close by. Then, we can work our way down the hill to join you and we can all bed down in the same place."

Jon, who was actually the most tired of this little group, having walked all day like the others and then fought a pitched battle, nodded. "We can do that, can't we, little ones?" He smiled at Midnight. "Are you coming too? Then we can use your shield while Sheldrake provides us with light for the walk. What do you think?"

Tarkyn relayed Jon's words into images, knowing Midnight was much more likely to feel brave enough to go with relative strangers, if he had a role to play. Midnight glanced up at Tarkyn, who assured him that he would join him in a while.

Soon after they had departed, Stefan appeared beside Tarkyn. "Well, that was a close call, despite our best efforts. Midnight came just in time." He swung his rucksack off his shoulders and proceeded to bring out several large rolls of thin leather strips, which he laid on the ground. He grinned. "You might need these if you're going to truss up scores of Kimorans."

Tarkyn's face cleared. "Oh, good. That's one problem solved."

"And I think you'll find that many of them have already had their weapons removed and their hands tied. Some of them still have wounds that need to be bound."

"Hello, Stefan," interrupted Reece. "Haven't seen you since I finished my training. Where did you spring from?"

In answer, Stefan flicked twenty yards to appear right next to Reece, making him rear back in surprise. "I can flick like Midnight does; a recently discovered talent I didn't know I had."

Reece raised his eyebrows. "That's bloody handy. I wish I

could do that. So why weren't you with Lord Tarkyn and the others?" he asked, a hint of censure in his voice.

"We decided that I could use my archery skills better by positioning myself in a tree. So I was above you, but not within the shield, helping to stave off the hordes that were attacking you."

"So that why some of those Kimorans just dropped where they stood. Good work. You saved Jon and me more than once." Reece smiled in apology for doubting him. "You should have come down sooner. You missed out on a cup of tea." Then a frown developed on his face as he thought about it. "I know you're good, but you couldn't possibly have felled all of those Kimorans on your own... could you?"

"No, of course not."

Reece was clearly waiting for further clarification, but Stefan dodged the unasked question by addressing himself to Tarkyn. "Sire, do you think someone other than you could direct the operation of securing the Kimorans? I need to speak privately with you."

Tarkyn nodded, glad to have a way to escape, in order to confer with his woodfolk. "Reece? Could you organise your troopers, please? Work your way from here down towards The Way Through. Maud, Marjorie and Jackson, are you happy to work with the troopers? Stefan and I will meet you at the other end, if not before." He reached out to Marjorie, who was now holding Gurgling Brook. "I'll take her off your hands now. Thank you for looking after her."

"It's a pleasure." Marjorie smiled and tapped her on the nose. "She is such a sweetie and she stayed so calm amongst all that noise and turmoil. No trouble at all."

Gurgling Brook smiled sunnily and waved at her over her father's shoulder, as she was borne away. "Bye-bye, Marjee. Bye, Jasson."

Stefan followed Tarkyn off the track into the trees on the right. As soon as they were out of sight and earshot, Stefan's family and Tarkyn's woodfolk appeared around them.

Tarkyn beamed at them. "Well done, my friends. What a marvellous job you've done. And I presume, Silverwood, that your kin also assisted us. So, thank them too, if you would."

Rainstorm bounced up to him. "I liked your power blasts through your shield. Very spectacular. And what about Midnight? One minute, he's next to me in a tall gum down the path a bit; the next minute, I see his shield appear way down the track, right in the thick of the fighting." He shook his head admiringly. "Brave little fella, especially after all he's been through."

"But now," said Waterstone, cutting to the chase, "we are in a right pickle. How are you going to explain all these unconscious bodies strewn about the place?"

Autumn Leaves huffed, "Jon came up with a perfectly good explanation, but did you accept it, Tarkyn? No."

Tarkyn, who knew his extreme integrity sometimes drove Autumn Leaves to distraction, smiled sympathetically. "It did cross my mind that it would be convenient to let him think that it was some sort of magic spell. But," he shrugged, "you know I don't like deceiving people. It's so disrespectful to them. But also... well, you know me. I couldn't have pulled it off. He'd have asked how it was done, or something else that would have had me floundering in prevarication in no time."

Autumn Leaves gave a grunt of laughter. "True."

"I'm afraid none of us thought this far ahead," said Ironbark. "After all, we thought we would only be dealing with the original abductors. It was only at the last minute that we realised the numbers involved. By then, we were committed to assisting you."

"Knocking out a few here and there could have passed unnoticed." Sphagnum Moss sighed. "But now... "

"Now, if we leave it unexplained..." Lapping Water reached out for Gurgling Brook, "I'll take her. Hello. Did you have fun?" Once the little girl had nodded, her mother continued, "If we leave it unexplained, these troopers and Jon and those children will make up all sorts of stories, and rumours will fly all over Highkington. Fairly counterproductive, I would have thought. It would direct too much attention to the forest."

"And by the time those troopers tie up the last of the Kimorans and remove their weapons, they are bound to notice bruises on some of them from the rocks we shot at them, even if they can't identify the ammunition," said Tree Fern.

Lapping Water noticed that Tree Fern sounded more mature and less defensive than usual. Maybe the action had given her a sense of purpose.

A gloomy silence fell.

After a minute, Lapping Water said, "We might as well sit down. I don't know about you people, but I'm tired from all that climbing through the trees looking for good positions to aim from. We haven't stopped since those Kimorans appeared."

"I'll make tea," said Rainstorm brightly.

"Good idea. I'll get a fire going," said Tree Fern, causing some raised eyebrows amongst her family, who were used to her being abrasive.

Sphagnum Moss settled himself against a fallen log and watched as a small fire sprang to life in the midst of a neat pyramid of small twigs. As Tree Fern fed large twigs then small branches onto it, he asked, "How many of these outsiders are there altogether? Not counting the Kimoran intruders, of course."

"Sheldrake, Maud, Marjorie and Jackson, you have already met, "said Tarkyn, ticking them off on his fingers as he brought them to mind. "Then there are Jayhan and Sasha, the two children we rescued, and Jon, who is Sasha's older brother. There are also the two shamans, Draya and Rhoda, and couple of Kimoran refugees, Argus and Beetlebrow, who are likely to join us later, I understand. Besides that, there are ten troopers. That is all."

Spinifex boggled. "That's *all*? That is at least seventeen new outsiders who are probably working out, as we speak, that a hidden force of people has come to their aid."

"Oh well, don't worry," said Stefan, with a touch of acid in his voice. "There are hundreds, possibly thousands of outsiders who have seen me over the years. So it's not as though they haven't seen a woodman before. I've met Jon, Reece and all the troopers before and even trained some of them."

Spinifex spluttered. "Yes, but..."

"Yes but what?" pressed Stefan. "What are you going to do? Kill them off because they might work out the existence of woodfolk? Why don't we just go for wholesale murder of everyone I've ever met?"

Waterstone moved quietly over and put his hand on Stefan's arm.

"Stefan," he said in a low, calming voice, "I think some of your resentment at being abandoned, however unintentionally, by your woodfolk kin, is currently getting in the way of rationale argument. No one has suggested killing them all off..." he gave a cheeky smile, "although it is, of course, an option."

"Not a good one though," said Ironbark repressively, worried that Stefan would fire up again. "After all, what's the point of saving them all, if we just turn around and kill them? Not sensible."

"Stefan, my son-nephew," said Spinifex patiently, "give us a chance to adjust. Four days ago, I had never met an outsider in my life. But more than that, our whole creed forbids it. You think nothing of it, but for us, these last few days have been a constant strain, interacting with outsiders. It's not that I don't like them. I do, actually... and I am becoming easier with them. But..." he waved his hand. "... never mind."

Stefan stared at him. "So does that mean you're uneasy with me?"

Spinifex stared back at him. Then his mouth quirked. "Oh, totally." This rather took the wind out of Stefan's sails. "Be honest. Don't you feel a little awkward with us? You're an unknown quantity to us, just as we are to you. I'm sure we'll get over it in time, but at the moment, we're all unsure and self-conscious."

Suddenly Stefan chuckled. "True. Now at least we can all be self-conscious together." He grinned around at the other members of his woodfolk family and they all laughed or smiled in return, relieved to have it out in the open.

Tree Fern walked over and slipped her arm through his. "So what they're saying, cousin-brother, is that they're nervous about meeting so many outsiders. We can't meet them when the Kimoran invaders are around to see, obviously. Now that *would* be too many. But I think we've decided to let them know who we are." She looked around. "Yes?"

Silverwood glanced at her brothers before saying firmly, "Yes."

"But they have to be sworn to secrecy, of course," said Tarkyn. "Normally, they would make their oath to me, but I'm not their liege lord. Sheldrake or Maud are the King's representatives and since the troopers are the King's men, maybe one of them can take their oaths."

"They can make their oaths to us," said Silverwood firmly, cutting through what was, to her, the irrelevance of hierarchy. "It will, after all, be a pact between them and us; that they keep our existence secret, in return for their lives."

"Right," said Tarkyn, looking a little embarrassed. "Good idea. I should have thought of that." He frowned repressively at Rainstorm who was chortling into his cup of tea, just as an unexpected communication came through from some of the woodfolk stationed further down the path.

The two shamans strode off down the path, stepping between the unconscious forms of their compatriots. As they reached the spot where they, Jon and the troopers had made their desperate stand, Rhoda heard someone groaning.

She put her hand on Draya's arm. "Wait. Listen." She swung the lantern over the sea of bodies, looking for the source of the sound. "Ah. Here, Draya."

Rhoda held the lantern up while Draya leant over to inspect a young woman who had a shallow sword-cut along the side of her head. Draya squatted down to inspect it carefully. After a few moments, she straightened and said, "I can't see why she was knocked out. That cut wouldn't do it. It looks a bit messy with blood seeping through her hair, but it's not deep. I think we can repair it quickly before we move on."

"But why isn't she staying unconscious like the others? She wasn't knocked out by our friends in the trees. They made sure their victims wouldn't rouse too soon, so we and they could have a chance to immobilise them."

Above them, watching from nearby tree branches, four

woodfolk froze in shock. *They know about us.* Frenzied messages shot to the woodfolk stationed above Marjorie and Jackson. They checked with the woodfolk who had been near Maud and then to those with Tarkyn. None of them had told the shamans about woodfolk.

Oblivious to the consternation raging overhead, Draya looked closer then put her hand inside the woman's collar to pull out a moonstone amulet on the end of a silver chain. Without a word, she brought out her own amulet and watched as soft light from the two amulets beat in unison. She looked up at Rhoda. "I think Sasha's proximity must have freed this shaman from Toriana's hold."

Rhoda nodded. "That would explain why she is recovering at a different rate from the others. Her blackout was from a different cause."

"I think we'd better rouse her and take her with us."

Just then, they heard a twig snap under someone's foot, then the crunch of forest floor detritus as someone walked heavily towards them from the south. Rhoda held up the lantern, peering into the darkness, her heart hammering in her chest. "I'm beginning to regret our refusal of a shield. Too independent by half you are, sometimes."

"Rubbish. Whoever it is, isn't a threat. They're making no effort to conceal their approach, are they?" She raised her voice. "Hello? Who are you? Come and join us." As they heard the sound of stumbling, she added, "Are you all right?"

The footsteps righted themselves and a minute later, a disoriented woman in dark clothing came into view. As she came closer, they could see that she was middle-aged with her grey hair dishevelled, fuzzy strands sticking out in all directions. Her uniform was actually dark blue with pale orange trim. Her eyes were unfocused, and she seemed close to collapse.

"Hello?" said Draya again. "Can you hear us?" Then she frowned and looked closer. "Hang on. You're Arquin, Lady Arquin, aren't you?"

"Major."

"Major Arquin?" When the woman nodded, Draya exchanged worried glances with Rhoda and her hand went down to the pommel of the sword she was still wearing. "She's a powerful shaman, this one," she muttered to Rhoda.

The woman gave an out-of-focus smile. "Hello. I'm looking for... I am looking for the true Queen. She's out here somewhere."

Draya narrowed her eyes. "Just a minute. Are you the shaman who instigated that huge storm?"

"Yes. Have you seen her?"

"Who? Queen Toriana? So far from court?" asked Draya, testing.

The woman leant closer and nearly lost her balance in the process. She managed to coordinate enough to get her finger up to her mouth. "Shh. No. No, I don't think so. No. It's my amulet, you see. It's changed rhythm. It's beating faster. Not a lot, just a bit. But it's different. I notice these things, you see." She gave a sluggish frown. "And a little while ago, it was beating very fast indeed, several times, in fact."

"Really?" said Draya. Then her voice became hard, "You've come to take Sasharia back to your Queen Toriana, haven't you?"

Arquin reared back at Draya's tone. "No, I came to take an *impostor* into custody, but ..."

Rhoda and Draya looked at each other. Then Rhoda said, more gently than Draya had been speaking, "Could you show us your amulet, please?"

Arquin squinted suspiciously at them. "What for?" she asked drunkenly. In answer, Rhoda held out her own amulet.

Arquin peered at it for a time, studying its gentle pulsing. "Hmm... hmm." She pulled out her own and held it beside Draya's. "Hmm. Same. You looking for her too?" She let her amulet fall to the end of its chain then passed the back of her hand across her forehead. "I'm so confused. A huge power swamped me, nearly tore me apart. I don't remember much after that. Might have passed out. I've managed to pull my mind together now... mostly. But now... now..." She gave a gusty sigh. "It's like a huge weight has gone from my mind but I haven't adjusted to the lighter load."

"A huge weight *has* gone from your mind, I think," said Rhoda, "The compulsion placed on it by Toriana. Without that, a shaman would never have set out to hunt down the true High Shaman."

Abruptly, Arquin sat down on the ground. "Oh. That wicked woman. She made us believe that the bandits who had killed her sister were now parading a young girl wearing a false amulet as the true heir. She said she wanted her brought back alive so she could question her about her fellow conspirators and quell any possibility of a rebellion." She smiled mistily up at them. "So I'm right. That young girl really *is* Princess Sasharia." She shook her head in wonder. "Oh my word, she's powerful."

Rhoda and Draya glanced at each other. Then Draya bent down and put a hand under the older woman's arm.

"Come on," she said briskly, helping her up. "We have work to do and if you recover enough, you can help us. Rhoda, see if you can rouse that other shaman enough to get her on her feet. We have to go."

They made their way down to The Way Through, guiding the two dazed shamans. When they emerged onto the track, the two troopers on guard confronted them, challenging their business. When Rhoda and Draya explained their part in the actions over the last few hours, Trevor and the four troopers clustered around them, eager to hear what had happened, and delighted that the children were safe.

The troopers led them over to their fire where Beetlebrow and Argus, dusty and exhausted, were seated. The two refugees had finally caught up with the troopers and were now watching the arrival of the shamans with interest. The second shaman, Berundi, was still looking dazed but Arquin was starting to recover. They sat down quietly amongst the Carradorian troopers without a word. The men offered them cups of tea.

"Hello, you two. Glad you made it," said Draya briefly, before responding to the offer for tea. "Thank you, that would be lovely, but we can repair the wounded while we sip."

"We've already cleaned and bandaged the wounds," said Weston, a trooper whose upturned nose made him look deceptively boyish. He was on the defensive. "I don't think they'll fester."

"Well done. I am casting no aspersions on your first aid. But I'm talking about healing." Draya indicated Rhoda and herself. "We are shamans. We can heal. That's why we came on ahead; to put you boys out of your misery."

The three wounded men glanced at each other, looking anything but convinced.

"Sergeant Reece sent us," said Draya inaccurately, deciding he had tacitly sanctioned it by not objecting.

"Well then," said Trevor, still sounding dubious, "I suppose we had better let you have a look."

Darya began work on Morris, while Rhoda moved over to sit on the ground beside Trevor's bandaged leg. She smiled reassuringly up at him. "Let's take this off and see what we have, shall we?"

She gently unwound the bandage, taking even more care as she reached the point where it was stuck to the seeping wound.

She peered closely at it, struggling to see well enough by the light of the fire.

"Would you like more light?" offered a trooper, brandishing a lit stick.

"Thank you," said Rhoda. When she had finished her examination, she looked up at Trevor. "It's deep, isn't it? Sword thrust?"

Trevor nodded, clenching his teeth as she placed a fresh piece of cloth over the wound and placed her hands on it. But she was so gentle that he gradually realised he had no need to brace for more pain and, rather sheepishly, relaxed his jaw.

"And how did you fare, here on your own, Trevor?" asked Rhoda, as much as anything to distract him. "Did any more Kimorans come through here?" She kept her hands carefully in place on Trevor's calf as the wound slowly pulled together under the influence of the healing power seeping into it.

Trevor shook his head. "A few times we thought we heard someone approaching," he jerked a thumb at Shay, "and that one would go on alert. But each time, it went quiet again. After a while, we decided it must have been animals wandering around in the undergrowth that we'd heard."

"Maybe," said Draya noncommittally. She patted Morris's arm. "There. That should be better."

The young man moved his arm gingerly, then through a greater range. Slowly, a relieved smile dawned on his face. "Thank you." He turned to the other wounded trooper, ready to bring him to Draya, but saw that he was already receiving attention from Arquin.

"She is also a shaman," said Draya. "So is Berundi, but she is in no fit state to heal at the moment."

Rhoda gave Trevor's leg a final pat and a couple of troopers helped him to his feet. He tried a couple of experimental, successful steps and his face lit up. "Who'd have thought? It's much better. Thank you."

Arquin was still working on the sword-cut on Symmon's arm, when Jon, Sheldrake and the three children arrived, walking within the green haze of Midnight's shield. It wasn't until they came into the firelight that the green dome could be seen clearly.

Trevor's eyes widened. "Well! Will you look at that? Is that really a magic shield? I've heard of them but never seen one before." He frowned into the green dome. "Now, I know Jon, but who are these little people? Let me see. This must be Sasha, you're the only one in a skirt," he gave a rueful grin, "what's left of it."

At Sasha's name, Arquin's head whipped around and she was torn between rising to greet Sasha and continuing with her healing. After a moment, she resolutely returned her attention and energy to the young trooper's arm, holding to her duty as a shaman.

"And you, with the pale eyes that the king so admires, must be Jayhan," continued Trevor.

The other troopers looked on in surprise as the usually taciturn tracker greeted the children. Unaware or uninterested in the stir he was causing among his comrades, Trevor turned to Midnight. "And you must be Midnight, the hero of the day. Draya and Rhoda told us all about you. Oh yes, that's right. You can't hear, can you?" Trevor gave him an enthusiastic thumbs-up and smiled broadly at him.

Midnight gave a half-hearted wave back and hid behind Sheldrake. Sheldrake raised his eyebrows at being overlooked by Trevor. "And I am Lord Sheldrake, Jayhan's father."

"Don't mind Trevor, my lord," said Morris smoothly. "It's just we've been dying to meet the children we've spent so long chasing down... and I think he must be a bit euphoric because his leg has stopped hurting."

"This is a night of wonders, to be sure," said Symmons, gawking at them. "First, miracle healing and now, a sorcerer's shield."

Arquin had now finished her healing and, motioning for Berundi to join her, walked over to stand before Jon and Sasha. As Berundi and she knelt, their right hands on their hearts, everyone stopped to watch.

"Sasharia," said Arquin, softly but formally. "I acknowledge you as our true queen and High Shaman." She turned her eyes to Jon, "and you as Kimora's regent. And I give you my faith and my duty. All my resources are at your disposal."

Berundi has recovered enough to say, "I too give you my faith and my duty." Her face threatened to crumple but with an effort, she controlled herself. "And I am so sorry we attacked you."

Then they pulled out their moonstone amulets and held them in front of them. Sasha glanced at Jon before pulling out her own obsidian amulet. For a full minute, they knelt before Sasha, watching their amulets pulse in time with hers.

Then Arquin raised her head and smiled mistily at Sasha.

Sasha hitched a breath and whispered, "Thank you."

"Please rise," said Jon, aware, as Sasha was not, that they would not rise without permission.

Arquin rose to her feet. "And, Prince Jondarian, I give you my word of honour, as an officer and a peer of the realm, I will not run and will not try to harm your comrades." Her voice hardened as she glanced over at Shay. "But don't let that snake go. He's the one who sent the carrier pigeon to the Queen requesting a full company to ensure the safe delivery of Sasharia, the true queen, to her, and no doubt giving her all the information he could. Unlike me, he has never been under a misapprehension about the identity of the child we were seeking." Her voice gathered anger. "He has no soul. He is a mercenary who works purely for money, not honour, and he won't stop until he fulfils his contract. A failed contract would damage his reputation and mean less work for him in the future. That's all he cares about."

As she stepped back, she seemed to calm herself. "However, he too has been injured and I think I should put him out of his misery."

This was just ambiguous enough to delay people's reactions. Unopposed, Arquin walked up to Shay, who watched her warily as she approached. Before anyone thought to stop her, she thrust a sharp little dagger deep into his chest. With a grunt, he slumped forward against his ropes. Without a backward glance, she turned and walked away.

She raised her eyebrows at the shocked silence and addressed Lord Sheldrake, who was the most senior Carradorian present. "He is, *was*, a known traitor to the true queen... and he betrayed his fellow Kimorans. Your jail did not hold him. I do not want to chance having him abroad again in Carrador, threatening Sasharia and her brother." Arquin gave a little satisfied smile. "So, as my first act of fealty, I have just made the world a little safer."

After a moment, Trevor said quietly, "Warrun, Symmons, move him out of sight. Not nice for the children."

Sasha crossed her arms and said in a sharp little voice, "I'm glad he's dead. He hurt Jayhan and was going to keep hurting him." But her face was tight with shock and she looked close to tears.

In the trees above them, woodfolk were waiting for Tarkyn, Reece and the rest of them to arrive before introducing themselves but, at the sight of her distress, Rainstorm couldn't contain himself. He flicked down to appear in front of them and smiled at her. "Hello, Sasha. I am Rainstorm."

Autumn Leaves appeared next to him, giving Rainstorm a harassed glance. "Rainstorm. You were supposed to wait. Hello, all. I am Autumn Leaves."

Rainstorm just grinned cheekily at him before turning to the troopers and shamans. "Hello, all. We woodfolk have been your back-up team. Those animals you thought you heard out there in the undergrowth? They were Kimoran soldiers that we knocked off before they got to you."

Lapping Water, deciding it would be better if she, too, came down to keep Rainstorm in check, appeared on the other side of him holding Gurgling Water, who promptly leaned dangerously far out of her arms towards Midnight. "Minnight. Minnight."

Rainstorm grabbed the little girl before she fell and placed her gently on the ground beside him, keeping her hand in his.

"And I am Lapping Water."

The troopers and shamans were still staring speechlessly at them when Tarkyn, Maud, Reece and the others walked up. Not having seen them flick into existence, Reece frowned at the woodfolk in suspicion. "And who exactly are you?" he demanded. He scowled at Rainstorm. "Hang on. You look like Stefan. Are you his brother?"

Silverwood, not liking his tone, decided to shock him into civility. She flicked from a tree further down the road to stand in front of him, her long, silvery hair shining in the light from the fire.

"Good evening," she said formally, "my name is Silver-wood. I believe you know my nephew, Stefan, the arms master." Ironbark and Spinifex appeared behind her and she waved vaguely to indicate them. "And these are his...father and uncle. Stefan is not related to Rainstorm."

Sphagnum Moss and Tree Fern appeared and were introduced to an increasingly stunned audience.

Waterstone and Sparrow stayed up in the trees above, watching with unholy mirth. They decided they would stay put, since the troopers and shamans had more than enough to cope with at the moment and besides, father and daughter were having far too much fun watching from the sidelines.

For several minutes, pandemonium reigned as those who had only just met the woodfolk asked question after question of those who already knew of them, or of the woodfolk themselves.

When the noise level subsided enough for him to make himself heard, Tarkyn raised his hand, then his voice. "We still have much to sort out, but, thanks to the concerted efforts of everyone here and of those watching from the surrounding trees, Sasha and Jayhan are now safely among us." He paused briefly, but not long enough to allow the chatter to start up again. "There is, however, a consequence for receiving this help from the woodfolk. Silverwood will explain."

Silverwood came to stand beside Tarkyn. "We woodfolk, as you may have gathered, live deep in the forest, apart from outsiders. Before today, no woodfolk in Carrador have ever interacted with outsiders." Seeing puzzled glances at Stefan, she faltered.

Iron Bark took over. "Stefan was lost to us during the great floods and was brought up by the outsiders who own the Creeping Vine Inn. He is one of us and yet he is also one of you. Because he cares for Jayhan and Sasha, we made his cause our own and fought by your side to rescue them."

Silverwood gave a small smile of thanks, before continuing, "Despite the anomaly of Stefan, keeping our existence secret from outsiders is still central to our whole way of life." She turned to Draya and Rhoda, her green eyes hard. "So we were shocked to hear you two casually revealing your awareness that we were in the trees above you. For how long, and how, have you known about us?"

Rhoda and Draya looked at each other for direction. Then Rhoda shrugged and turned back to Silverwood. "Not sure how long. Maybe always. We knew you didn't want anything to do with us, so we didn't try to make contact." She gave a little smile. "Your business is your own, after all. You allowed us to live as refugees, unmolested, in your forests. So, that was enough."

"We have people like you in Kimora," Draya explained, "but we call them treewrights. They, like you, keep to themselves. People outside the forests know of them but accept that they wish to be left alone."

"I see," said Silverwood slowly, again unsure how to proceed.

Lapping Water came to her rescue. "That is not the case here, or in Eskuzor. In Carrador and in Eskuzor, the secret of woodfolk's existence is sacrosanct."

"Any woodman or woman who betrays our existence is exiled," continued Autumn Leaves, "and only under very special circumstances have we ever allowed outsiders who have seen us to leave the forests."

Sheldrake turned to Stefan. "Perhaps in the years to come, your unique position may bridge the gap between our two peoples, so that woodfolk will feel less need to isolate themselves from us outsiders."

Stefan's gaze wandered from Silverwood and his family to the group of Eskuzorian woodfolk, from whom Rainstorm stood grinning at him, and then onto the more familiar figures of Marjorie, Reece, Sheldrake, Maud, the children and the troopers.

Lastly, he glanced at Tarkyn, who had engineered the

whole discovery of his dual heritage and gave him a wry smile. "I hope so. For better or worse, some outsiders in Carrador now know about woodfolk and know what they are looking at, when they see me. It is a beginning."

"Perhaps it is," conceded Silverwood. She took a breath. "But as things stand now, all woodfolk are sworn to keep our existence secret and now we ask, *require*, of you that you also make this oath..." her mouth quirked as she added, knowing this would be unpopular, "... on pain of death."

Reece scowled. "On pain of death? That seems extreme."

"Not as extreme as killing all the outsiders who saw us today," said Spinifex phlegmatically, "which was the other option."

There was a fraught silence...

"In that case," said Jon, smiling cheerily, "this oath sounds like a great idea."

Dear reader,

We hope you enjoyed reading *The Green-Eyed Man*. Please take a moment to leave a review, even if it's a short one. Your opinion is important to us.

Discover more books by Jennifer Ealey at https://www.nextchapter.pub/authors/jennifer-ealey

Want to know when one of our books is free or discounted? Join the newsletter at http://eepurl.com/bqqB3H

Best regards,

Jennifer Ealey and the Next Chapter Team

ABOUT THE AUTHOR

Jennifer Jane Ealey was born in outback Western Australia where her father was studying kangaroos on a research station, one hundred miles from the nearest town. Her arrival into the world was watched, unexpectedly, by their pet kangaroo who had hopped into the hospital. Having survived the excitement of her birth, she moved firstly to Perth and then Melbourne where she spent most of her formative years. She took a year off to ride a motorbike around Australia before working as a mathematics teacher and school psychologist in England and Australia, a bicycle courier in London and a publican in outback New South Wales.

She now lives in a country town just outside Melbourne with her two spoodles, working by day as a psychologist and beavering away by night as a novelist. Her first fantasy series, *The Sorcerer's Oath,* has been published by Next Chapter and comprises four novels; *Bronze Magic, Wizard's Curse, The Lost Forest* and *The Wizardess. The Green-Eyed Man* is second in the Dark Amulet Series, which is set in the same world as *The Sorcerer's Oath,* but in a different country.

BOOKS BY JENNIFER EALEY

The Sorcerer's Oath Series

Bronze Magic

Wizard's Curse

The Lost Forest

The Wizardess

The Dark Amulet Series

The Pale-Eyed Mage

The Green-Eyed Man

The Dark-Eyed Shaman (coming soon)

Printed in Great Britain
by Amazon